The Disa

GW00792287

A Polish D(

Rufus Garlic is an author of novels and short stories. He writes about the thin, troublesome line between good and evil, about the capacity of good people to do awful things when survival is at stake and of forgiveness, and of forgiveness withheld. Sometimes he hightails it in quite the opposite direction and writes comedy – just for humour's sake.

Also by Rufus Garlic

Of Fat Cats and Small Fry

Betting

Sacked

Sari Sari Burning Bright

The Skeleton in the Closet

The Legacy

Rufus Garlic

The Disappearance Club
Or
A Polish Detective in London

Thinking Plainly

Published by Thinking Plainly 2015

Original cover artwork by
Susan Angharad Williams with cover design by
The Captured Picture Company.

The author would like to acknowledge *Cat on a Hot Tin Roof* by Tennessee Williams referenced in Chapter 3. Also, *Gypsy Folk Tales* by Francis Hindes Groome for the two lines, 'a woman smoking a big black pipe' and a boy, 'with eyes as darkly mischievous as any fox cub's – and when he was given a bowl of soup he lapped it up as a fox cub would too' in Chapter 4.

ISBN: 978-0-9932378-2-9

Dedication

LOLJTOLOLA

For Granny Paula because grannies aren't just for
Christmas – they're for birthdays as well.

The Rufus Code

There are **codes and mystery trails** incorporated within this novel. Those hoping to solve them will have to identify particular landmarks and pubs – and work out linkages between them. The codes are variously letter, number and geometry based. I have detailed below a number of clues and clarifications:

The nature reserves to which Janek refers in Chapter 3 are actually one nature reserve in Chislehurst, Kent - known as *Scadbury Park*. It is best accessed via its entrance in Old Perry Street, near *The Sydney Arms* pub.

The church in Ch. 3 is an amalgam of St John's the Evangelist Church and St Lawrence's Catholic Church, both in Sidcup.

The pub described on pg. 72 is actually *The Windsor Castle* on Campden Hill Road, London.

On pg. 206, the pub and its tree-lined meadow approach where Janek and Sarah drink together are actually *The Rambler's Rest* pub and its environs. They can be found in Chislehurst, just off the A222, tucked a little way back from the road.

The dog reference in the dedication, as well as those throughout the novel, are not just incidental. They are an integral part of the cipher. Indeed, in Chapter 14, the drunk fisherman and his dog, are in essence my paternal grandmother's father and his faithful hound.

She would stand guard, teeth bared over him whenever he was less-than-sober-horizontal.

Almost all my other works, particularly the short stories, have at least one pub within them. Dogs also abound. This is not by chance. Although my code can be solved with information contained in *The Disappearance Club* alone, the other stories all provide additional clues/sites.

The code itself is at the end of this novel. He/she who solves the code…or believes he/she is detective enough to have done so, please visit the website:

www.thinkingplainly.com

Happy hunting, think out of the box, and garlicly good luck.

Contents

The Disappearance Club
Or
A Polish Detective in London

Chapter 1

South-east Poland 1943

…'He's dead, I tell you.'

'No. Look, there – his chest – it moved. I'm sure it did…He's breathing,' sobbed the old man.

'Thank God. Thank the Blessed Mother.'

'See…And a pulse there at his neck too.'

'Oh the Blessed, Blessed Mother…'

'Stop that and help me. Help me, woman. The lad could die yet and then Roman Zaleski will be back for us. He'll make us cut our own throats, he'll burn us alive; you know what he is capable of.'

The woman felt her sweat cool and fear raced a sprint down her spine. 'What should I do?'

'The lad's head…lift up his head. See if there is any way to slow the bleeding. Christ, he's in a bad way.' The man bent right down to the boy, but his own legs, pained in some dreadful, searing way would barely support him.

'Leave him to me, you can do no more,' mouthed the woman. 'You must do something about your legs.' She hunched to cradle the boy. Her hands steamed with his blood; the flagstones of the floor were slippery with it. The teenage boy lay as still as water on a clement day. His head was cracked…right open. The wound was jagged, irregular, awful – like a claw hammer-shattered coconut.

'I can't save him, dad!' the woman wailed.

'What?'

'I can't. Look at the blood.'

'You'll have to. You've got to. If the little bastard doesn't survive, our lives aren't worth a hog's turd. If Zaleski comes back and the lad's dead, then that's it. We might as well die with him.'

The woman looked up through tear-magnified eyes. They were rodent-grey and she showed her teeth like a rat too. 'But can he ever really return, though? Zaleski? You know, to hold us to account?'

'What?'

'Well can he?' she snapped.

The man screamed as he accidentally touched one of his own injured legs. The sickly smell of spreading infection wafted from his limbs and it was some time before he could speak again. As the pain eased, damaged cell by damaged cell, he set his grimacing mouth to speak: 'Oh he'll return. He's a survivor, that devil. One day he'll be back…and God knows who he might bring with him. Now just save the boy. You must.'

****

South-east London 1976

For a corner plot house, 33 Orchard Road had fence panels remarkably clear of graffiti. This wasn't because the local midnight yobs hadn't happened upon them, rather it was because ivy is not a good matrix for spray paint. The panels were festooned with rolling yards of the stuff. It grew over the top of the boundary and right down to the pavement where aggressive tendrils disturbed the footfalls of passers-by. There was a winter flowering cherry in the garden too, hard by one of the fence posts, so that its beautiful crown was as much the walkway's as it was no. 33's. There was also an alder tree and farther down the garden, an ancient willow. All overshadowed the pavement.

The willow was as broad as an oil drum, but no taller than a second floor cornice. All its photosynthetic energy had been turned into girth. It writhed fantastically, such that the trunk was actually horizontal for half its length. And beneath this broad limb a stream giggled over black flint and green frogs and fleeting silver fish, quick as children at play.

That was the limit of the garden, but for a pair of wooden doors where the fence ended. On one was a letter 'D', on the other, a letter 'C'; both very prominent, whitewashed in, looking out onto the road. Each was a foot high and set at an eleven year old's height from the ground. When the doors were shut, the two letters were just inches apart, either side of the latched divide. No ivy obscured them, but such was

3

the arresting nature of the 'D' and the 'C', positioned where one might expect a more traditional DO NOT OBSTRUCT or IN 24 HR USE, that this brace of doors had not been graffitied over either.

It was 7 am, a bright Monday morning, and the bolt was being drawn. The wood quivered a little: the last winter had been a hard one and the grain had warped in the unrelenting damp.

A man appeared in the gap between the two doors. He secured each side with a brick and stepped out of his garden to the pavement beyond. There he set down a small dustbin and a bundle of newspapers, rudely tied. Then he turned, retraced his steps, kicked away the bricks and snapped the 'D' and 'C' back together again. A sharp ear would have picked up that the bolt was not slotted back; the doors were only latched shut. And a very sharp eye would have noticed, in those few seconds that the doors had been left open, what lay behind them. There was a garage, near the back of the garden, about three metres from the stream and as is usual with corner plots, it was set at a right angle to the road. The 'D.C' doors served the driveway to it.

That was where any similarities ended, for the garage had no car in it, no up and over door, no hard concrete floor: beneath its pitched roof was actually a well-appointed office. There was a strong mortice-lock door, windows and a chimney for its little wood-burning stove. Within were chairs, either side of a mahogany desk – unwarped – the 'garage' was carpeted and damp-proofed.

Shelves and cabinets lined the walls. There was a tiger skull for a paper-weight and a basket full of discarded correspondence. On the back wall was a framed photograph of a teenage boy, about a metre square. It was black and white. The lips had been rouged in though, which dated the image to the 1930s or 40s, when such effects were fashionable. The boy was about thirteen years of age. His chin was midway between childhood's softness and manhood's testosterone surge; the bridge of the nose the same. But his eyes were still unmistakably young: sweet, trusting, laughing, full of merriment's light. The silly dash of red for a mouth was incongruous, but it didn't matter because the eyes did all the smiling necessary.

Outside, a dustcart was coming up Orchard Road. It wheezed its way, travelling only as fast as the slowest man on the team. He was an old boy with a limp and a stoop. The other guys looked out for him: no one said anything, but every cart-follower of the 10-strong crew knew that the single bin and tied roll of newspapers outside no.33 had his name on them. The heavy old carpets and fox-torn offerings of farther up the road, and the big communal bins at the council houses, were the remit of the younger men.

The old boy slung his share into the back of the cart and rested a while. Blood was pounding at his right temple, keeping perfect time with the deep throbbing he felt at his varicose veins. It was a strange effect - the two complaints were a metre and a half apart. He rubbed at his head, then at his calves.

There was no doubt that he ought to hang up his dustman's gloves, but the local authority seemed to have overlooked the fact that he was past retirement age and he liked the lads he worked with. Since his wife's death, in 1972, the social contact meant more to him than his health, so he always limped his way through the round, whatever the weather. The other dusties knew that they would probably have to pick him up one day, dead weight, like they knew that he was the only one of them not doing the job for the wage packet. Once the driver had asked him whether he would rather ride up in the cabin…'None of us'll tell…' but the old man had shot him such a look that it had never been suggested again.

The dustcart stopped for him.

He was catching his breath after the dustbin and newspapers, but also looking at the 'D' and the 'C' of no.33's double doors. The two letters had puzzled him for years. What did they mean? They certainly weren't the remnants of a longer word or phrase: nowhere was there evidence of any other letters having been screwed down or nailed in. Someone's initials perhaps?

If he had been a younger man, if he had not been wheezing so brokenly, he might have knocked on the door of no.33 and asked. Indeed, he might have done it any of a hundred times; the little conundrum had always intrigued him. But an old fellow had to be careful. There was no point doing anything which might get him noticed - like knocking at doors. The council might hear of it and thereby remember that he existed, still walking the beat, still doing a job which a younger man could do far better.

The cart driver shouted out, 'Come on Cyril!' and the old lad stumped off after the call like an aged dog whistled for its walk. It was ten past seven.

As the dustcart rounded the corner, the man who had put out the bin and newspapers was walking down no.33's front path. The old timer, still pondering the two strange letters, wished that he could say something, but kept in mind his unusual position vis-à-vis his employers and remained silent.

The householder was four-fifths the way down his path, almost level with the white roses at its head. He was checking his pockets for change – probably setting out for the morning paper. He was about sixty with both laughter lines and sorrow's wrinkles. He had an intelligent face: sharp chin, expressive lips, lively eyes. Mole black brows contrasted with blue irises. He was of average size, trim in the belly for a man of his age, light on his feet too. His nose had been extravagantly broken at some point in the past and curved crazily to the left. He smiled at the warmth of the new day.

'Hey mate!' called Baz, one of the youngest and most tattooed members of the garbage crew, 'What's with the 'D.C.' out back. What does it mean?'

'Disappearance Club,' replied the man beneath the crooked nose and the bright eyes; 'The Disappearance Club.' He smiled broadly. He had good teeth – a full set.

Cyril quickened his pace. 'What did he say, Baz?' he gasped. 'What did he say?'

'Didn't catch it…What did you say?' asked the human tattoo.

'Disappearance Club. That's what the 'D' and the 'C' stand for. The Disappearance Club,' repeated the man from no.33, still rooting in his pocket for coins.

'What does that mean though, 'The Disappearance Club?' asked Cyril, limping up and dangerously out of breath. He drew level with the other two. The old boy felt that he could ask now, seeing as someone else had raised the subject. His face was all a-quiver with excitement, like a squirrel's before a hazelnut.

'Come along some time. Down to my garage. Find out for yourself. I'm open seven days a week, nine-till-six. No need to knock, so long as you come through the doors at the bottom of the garden.' The voice was genuine and warm as summer sunshine.

'You sure? You wouldn't mind?' checked the old man, emboldened by the stranger's easy manner.

'Nine-till-six,' came the reply. And the man from no.33 was off on his way, a neat little head of hair receding down the road…but not at his forehead. Cyril had noticed that.

'Funny bloke. Foreign accent. Nice mind,' he thought. 'Good head of hair on him too – for a man of his age.' Cyril scratched his own bald, sweaty head and nodded. He would go. One day he would take the fellow up on his offer. He would find out what this 'Disappearance Club' business was all about.

'Come on Cyril,' cried the man who had asked the first question.

Cyril trotted dutifully after, past nos. 35 and 37 and 39, until he was level with the cart once more. Then he started coughing.

The young lads from down the street, who drilled footballs against the ivy-clad fence, had more of an idea than most what went on at the arse-end of no.33's garden. The ad hoc team – about seven strong – met most days and whenever their ball sailed over the fence, past the alder and the willow and the winter cherry, they would knock at the double 'D.C.' doors and ask for it back. These unintentional shots were actually the best goals they ever scored, for the tree limbs and branches and leaves were the finest goalkeepers in the district. But when the trees did let one in, the man who sat all day in his garage-office ('the man with the crazy eyes and crazy nose' as they called him) would always let them have it back, always and without any of the usual adult grumbles.

Unless he had company.

Every once in a while - one time in twenty-five maybe - he would not stir an inch for them. Their game would be at an end; until later, or even the next day, when the ball would be discovered by the earliest bird among them, stuck gently into a forked branch of the cherry, where it bowed low over the pavement. This only happened when the man had company though, in that little room of his, down by the willow and the stream and the whitewashed 'D.C'. And try as the footballers might, they could never rouse him until his visitor had left.

The lads even saw these visitors sometimes. They were an easy breed to spot, heading down Orchard Road. They were always men, generally in mid-life. Some had tired, drawn faces, burned by life's acid, others glowed beneath skins of contentment, as if good living had massaged out their wrinkles and recharged the eyes through which they viewed the honeyed world. In short, they were extremes. Never came a man who ambled averagely – not to the 'D.C.' doors. Plenty like that walked past, or turned their everyday keys in the everyday locks of the neighbouring houses or in the doors of the cars parked outside them, but these were not the cast of men who called at the garden of no.33.

And when the visitors came out, by the same enigmatic doors, they were never turned average-looking by their experiences within – whatever they were. Again, the footballing boys would note their extremes of emotion. Sometimes it happened that the ones who went in cheerful came out looking newly saddened, or the previously dejected emerged full of yeasty zest for life. Such reversals were not unknown. Whatever, no Orchard Road footballer ever discerned a blankness about these faces. Theirs were not the expressions of average men.

It was ten o' clock and eleven-year-old Tommy Macey sliced his first kick of the day. It found a gap between cherry and alder and dropped with a soft thud into the garden. It sounded like a flower bed landing. The boys were not concerned. The guy at no. 33 was not precious about his garden and besides, it was only the first day of the summer holiday: they had not even begun to try Old Crooked Nose's patience with repeated requests.

'You spaz,' said a ginger-haired boy from the flats at the end of the road.

'Homo,' returned Tommy.

'Wanker…'

Childhood's lexicon always stands firm against tolerance and liberality.

'I'll knock,' said a lad considerably smaller than the others, 'I know 'is name. Me mum told us yesterdee.'

'What is it then, Phil?'

'Mr Lipsz. It's got a 'z' at the end. It's foreign, like. We got a letter for him at our house. Mr Lipsz.'

The ginger-haired boy made farting noises. Phil

continued over them, 'Lazy bastard postman gave us letters for no.25 as well, and a birthday card for a little girl in Orchard Court, wherever the hell that is.'

'Go and get the ball then,' snapped Tommy, showing no concern for birthdays in Orchard Court.

Phil crossed to the double doors. Being short for his age, the 'D' and the 'C' stood out clear inches above him. He looked up at them. He had asked his mother what they stood for, but she hadn't known. He knocked – quite loudly: two generations of kids had come to these doors and not one of them had ever been shouted at. Ten seconds elapsed. Phil could hear footsteps, then a thumb on the latch.

'Yes. Yes. You will be wanting your ball…The great striker kicks high again.'

The man already had it under his arm. He smiled, just out of one side of his mouth. As a result, his nose flared out even more crooked than usual. It really was a fantastic hooter.

'Thanks, Mr Lipsz.'

The man nearly dropped the ball. He looked at the boy, down the full, curving length of his magnificent nose. No one down Orchard Road had called him by name in years. It amused him that such a little lad should be the first in so long.

'It's pronounced 'Leep-sh,' he replied.

Phil stared at the nose. And stared some more.

'I got it in the war,' said Mr Lipsz, following the boy's gaze. He wiggled the end of his nose provocatively, exaggerating its sickle shape.

Phil maintained his gaze. His mother would have ticked him off for rudeness, but he could tell that the man didn't mind.

'Did it get shot by our side?'

The old man roared with laughter. He dropped the ball, contorting with mirth. The other boys, ten metres off, sniggered, a little uneasily; unsure what to do in the face of such naked emotion – from an adult.

Mr Lipsz tried to repeat Phil's line back to him, but he just hooted and spluttered and guffawed over the words, sounding like a drunk trying to blow a duck whistle.

In time he subsided.

The ball lay at rest in the gutter.

'Can I quote you on that my little soldier? When I have my friends over? May I?'

The boy shrugged. 'Well how did you get a beezer like that, then?'

'I fell out the back of a lorry. It was carrying blankets to the Eastern Front and I was trying to steal them. I lost my footing and ended up bouncing along the road, with this nose and no blankets. The driver did shoot at me actually, but he missed. I was lucky – the Germans did not usually miss.'

'You was shot at by Germans?'

The man nodded, 'After falling out the back of a German lorry.'

The boy stood pondering. Mr Lipsz smiled, waiting.

'You was shot at by Germans?' Phil repeated.

'That's right.'

'So...'

'So...?' echoed Mr Lipsz.

'So...if you was shot at by Germans...'

Mr Lipsz nodded.

'You're...?'

'I'm...'

'You're...?'

Mr Lipsz smiled tolerantly. 'Let me help, my little historian. You are wondering: if I am not a German and I am also not an Englishman, then what in the hell am I?'

'Yes,' replied Philip with all the directness of youth.

'I am a Pole. That is, I am Polish. And your grandfathers and I...' Here the man waved expansively to include the whole street when he said this, '...Your grandfathers and I, we all fought on the same side in the war.'

Phil could hear the ball thudding behind him and Mr Lipsz could see that he was being summoned by its beat. He knew that he had only a few more seconds of the boy's attention. 'Do you know what the Eastern Front was?' Mr Lipsz asked quickly.

Phil shook his head.

'Or where Poland is?'

The boy looked uncertain.

'Well you know my name and that's a start. Any time you want to know the rest, you just let me know.'

'Thanks,' replied Phil, turning for the game.

'But you have not told me who you are,' called Mr Lipsz, summoning him back.

'I'm Phil Whitehead. I live at number twenty-eight. We got a letter for you the other day. It was full of money and we was gonna keep it, but in the end my mum said that we couldn't, so I was sent round to put it in through your letter box. An' I did, all of it, 'cept for the fiver she'd already spent on fags.'

Mr Lipsz stifled a guffaw at this beautiful honesty.

Then Phil was gone, on his little terrier legs, and Mr Lipsz was left wondering which of his clients was £5 short.

After his dust round, Cyril bathed. Usually he took his time in the water, but not this afternoon. He was in and out like a three minute egg - just long enough to scrub up clean.

It had really got in among him, what that chap had said about the Disappearance Club. For a couple of hours he had not been able to stop thinking about it, nor the invitation which had been extended to him. Then, all of a whimsy, he decided that he would take the man up on his offer – that very day. So he had rushed home, had shown himself to the soap, and now he stood, dripping before the bathroom mirror. He examined the ravages of time. Everything seemed to have slipped down to the mezzanine level and he had veins in his legs like blueberry clots. Cyril took a step closer to the unforgiving glass. He was just concluding that men do not really lose hair, it just passes down through the tops of their heads and out of their ears and noses in unseemly great tufts, when the phone rang. He flapped soggily to the landing.

'Hello?'

'Alright Cyril? It's Norman here. Wondering whether you're up for a game of whist at *The Frog and Tongue* pub tonight? There'll be near enough ten of us.'

'Yes, mate. Thanks for letting me know. I'll be there.'

'But you don't know when it is.'

'When is it?'

'Eight o'clock. And drinks are…'

'Right. See you at eight then.'

Cyril put the receiver down. He hoped that he hadn't pissed Norman off. It was two buses back to Orchard Road. He had to get cracking, not fanny around gassing about whist. He dressed quickly, ignoring the mirror. There wasn't time to waste staring at his beef jerky body either.

He stepped outside. There were a lot of other old people about. Most likely, they hadn't yet worked out that it was the summer holidays, so were still in a rush to get things done before school kicking out time. Cyril had never felt unduly bothered by kids, but he knew some folks of his generation thought that they should all be shot and reconstituted as liquid manure.

A 21 wheezed into the bus stop. Cyril stepped on. His own breathing became a little laboured too, and until the vehicle pulled away, he and the engine sat there rasping at one another. He really hoped that the foreign fellow had meant what he'd said about nine till six and coming round, because it was a long way to go for nothing.

The bus spluttered off.

Cyril tried to work it out: The Disappearance Club? What on Earth? Maybe the members all met up once a month to discuss famous disappearances: Lord Lucan, The Marie Celeste, those planes over the Bermuda Triangle?

Cyril had come up with half a dozen possibilities by the time he boarded the second bus. But none of them sat well with his image of the broken-nosed guy at no. 33, so he decided to admire the view out of the window instead.

This was a classier neighbourhood than his own:

there were splashes of green parkland, big houses with expensive cars outside them, and delicious, trim mothers in place of the doughy, fag-raddled women who pushed prams down the streets at his end of town. Through the glass, he took in their lovely forms: the shapely buttocks, the high breasts, and the elegant now-you-see-me-now-you-don't curve of their necks, lashed by provocative little pony tails.

Cyril felt a stirring down below, looked, and wheezed. 'You silly old sod,' he said.

His stop was coming up and he didn't want his dick to be erect when he stood. It wasn't seemly in a man of his age. He fixated on Roy Hattersley addressing The Labour Party Conference. That usually cooled his fires, and at speed.

Roy did the job and Cyril disembarked without embarrassment.

Orchard Road was a ten minute walk, past a school, a playing field and a little parade of shops. The delicious mothers were still much in evidence, so it was a pleasant stroll. The greenery was a joy too. In this district, the council allowed the trees their branches; downtown everything over three metres was aggressively pollarded. Here the cherries and crab apples displayed their majesty: amputation by postcode.

He turned right at one with limbs thicker than his waist and left at another with municipal benches arranged thoughtfully and hexagonally around its trunk. A last left and a further long right and he arrived at Orchard Road. Here the area became a little more down-market again – not as far down as where he lived, but there were poky houses and council terraces mixed in with the big old Victorian and Edwardian piles. He nosed into some of the gardens – peered over their fences.

No.33 was 100 yards away.

Cyril started to feel self conscious. Noting national tree scandals and peering into gardens was one thing, actually walking into one of them and asking what went on inside was quite another. Even with an invitation it seemed intrusive, rude even.

A gang of boys was playing football up ahead. The ball kept thwack-thwacking against a fence and Cyril calculated that they were playing right where he needed to be. He walked slowly, as if labouring with dustbins once again. The ivy and the arching boughs of no.33 loomed. Their leaves seemed to Cyril to be waving him away. He proceeded even more slowly then he stood heron-still. The double doors were straight ahead, the letters 'D' and 'C' clearly visible.

The boys stopped playing football.

'There's one,' he heard a little lad say.

That was it. Cyril spun away, defeated. He might possibly have pulled it off without an audience, but with such a knowing crowd identifying him and nudging and winking at one another it was quite impossible. In his embarrassment he collided with someone coming the other way. Cyril apologised, not looking up.

'Not at all dear fellow. Both not looking where we were going,' soothed a familiar voice. It was rich with the vowels of Eastern Europe.

Cyril blinked upward. There was the broken nose of his morning acquaintance.

'Have you come to see about my Disappearance

Club?'

Cyril nodded shyly.

'I hope you haven't been waiting long. Sometimes I get a little peckish and the baker down the road does unusually good pastries. I have enough for the pair of us.'

He noticed the doubt in Cyril's face, 'Really I have, and there will be tea as well.' All the time the man had been leading the way back to the mysterious double doors. He nodded to the boys. They smiled back.

'Hi Mr Lipsz,' said one.

'That's my name: Janek Lipsz,' he explained to Cyril, simultaneously waving at the boy and ushering the old man in through the unlocked doors. 'Nice lads. Can't kick for toffee though. I field their shots ten times a day.'

Janek Lipsz led the way into his garage-office, indicated a chair and cleared a couple of paper-free spaces at the table.

'I'm Cyril,' Cyril volunteered timidly. 'You said I might pop by, like. You said so this morning.'

'Yes of course, I remember. I never forget a face. It comes with the job.'

'The job?' pondered Cyril, interest trumping embarrassment. Mr Lipsz sensed the change in him.

'I'm always glad of company. If I get one customer every four days I'm doing well, so most of the time I'm stuck down here all alone.'

'What do you do here?' asked Cyril getting right to the nub of the matter.

Janek Lipsz smiled. 'Not before cakes and a cuppa,' he said. 'Even mysteries must wait for English tea, huh?'

Cyril nodded agreement, but inwardly disagreed. His curiosity was now cat-killing in scale, so Danish pastries were little more than an irritation, no matter how gorgeous. He munched dutifully through them, peering about for clues. They were inside a garage-cum-office. There were neat piles of paper, sorted left and right, also a large skull to hold the trickiest down. Underneath them all was a map of the world with every capital city detailed. Cyril noticed a heavy stick leaning against Janek's chair. It was made of ebony; he could tell that. His grandfather had been a carpenter and had educated him to the look and feel of all the great woods: oak for furniture, crab-apple for tool handles, ebony for dark, solid beauty. The stick was inches thick. It wouldn't weigh much less than its same length in granite.

'It's for protection, case someone tries to rob me, or any of my clients try it on,' explained Janek, following his gaze.

Cyril put down his tea, determined to use this morsel as a way in past the cakes. 'Why would they want to try it on? Your clients?'

Janek Lipsz took the bait, 'They're not always stable people you know, the people I help. Occasionally, just very occasionally, there's one or two of 'em need a little crack on the coco to help 'em behave.'

Cyril scratched his head. Janek laughed at the stereotypical little movement. 'Mostly they're as good as gold though. Just want my little bit of help and then off they go.'

Janek stuffed the last of the pastries in his mouth. Cyril waited while he chomped them down.

'You'll be wanting to know where they go,' he said at last, tongue still working the last of the syrup from his molars. 'They go everywhere and anywhere. You see this is The Disappearance Club. There's actually no mystery; it does exactly what you'd expect from the name. People come here and I facilitate their escape from lives they consider unbearable - off to new ones elsewhere.'

Cyril really sat up now, like a school boy trying to impress a no-nonsense dinner-lady. 'Where do they go?' he asked breathlessly.

'Abroad often, but also to other parts of this country - had a fellow escape to Sidcup once. I didn't see the point in that really. Do you know that they built the bypass before the town?' Mr Lipsz howled at his own joke. 'Seriously though, I do get people running away to all sorts of places. Generally I don't pass comment on whether they should leave; it is not my place to tell a man whether he has reached the end of his tether or not. And I prefer that my clients choose their own destinations, although that does not happen as often as I should like. My main jobs are: easing the process of their leaving, supporting them once they have gone, and if necessary, providing a helping hand should they ever choose to return.'

'You help people to vanish then?'

'That's right. Without trace, if need be. I provide a service which allows them to start over, afresh – anywhere in the world.'

'The Disappearance Club,' Cyril said to himself, banishing all thoughts of The Marie Celeste and The Bermuda Triangle.

'That's what the 'D.C.' stands for, you see? Say a

man has been grinding away at the same old job he's hated since he started it at seventeen, and now he's fifty-two. He's just found out that his wife is having an affair, also no one in the house ever listens to a word he says, except the dog, which has just died. That's when he comes to see me and I ease his passage from all the pain and hurt...'

'You set him up abroad?' interrupted Cyril.

'Yes and no.'

'Uhh?' said Cyril confused.

'He either comes with a definite choice of destination or I help him to one, here or abroad, but he chooses his own new path once there. What I do is sort out the problems and glitches en route. Also I provide a little security, so that he has the chance to return should he ever want to. In many ways, I'm really disappearance insurance.'

Cyril's brow started to knot and furrow again. His hand reached for the corrugations. Janek Lipsz jumped in, 'Ever had money in a bank account you forgot all about?'

Cyril shook his head, 'Never had enough cash money to do that.'

'Sure? Could be as little as one pound.'

A dim memory came percolating through to Cyril, from about seven years back. 'Yes, actually. I got some money when my bank became a PLC: about thirty pounds. Soon as I could I ran round and took it out, but I left one quid in there to keep the account open.'

'It won't be.'

'Won't be what?'

'Open....any more. Not if it's been more than three years and you've done nothing else with the account.'

'Course it will. That's why I left a pound in it.'

'No it won't. The banks give you about thirty-six months. And then if there's been no activity on the account they shut it down. It becomes what is known as a dormant account. They do store the money, in case you ever come in and claim it, but reissue the account number to someone else.'

'Get away!'

'Absolutely true, I'm afraid. If you went back to the same bank now you'd have to prove your identity all over again and even then, there'd be no way of getting your old account back. They'd just open you up another – assuming that they still wanted your business.'

'So where does my dormant quid fit into what you do?' asked Cyril.

'It's an illustration. Look…say you run away from this country, for whatever reason. And say you are gone for ten years. Now, if you want to return, there will be no bank account for you. And ten years living incognito isn't exactly a reference for a new bank account is it?'

'No,' agreed Cyril.

'Well that's where I step in. I keep the account going. You send me money from wherever it is you've run off to and I pay it in for you – religiously. For a small fee of course. If it suits, I'll even arrange appointments with your bank manager and turn up as you. I can even get my clients loans and overdrafts, so that they are able to set up in business wherever they are. Usually the bank account is readdressed here. That way no one becomes suspicious. See?'

'So you're a middle man?'

'Exactly. And the financial end of it is just one facet.'

'What?' frowned Cyril, whose vocabulary was not top notch.

'Just one side of the business….also I maintain contacts and relationships for people. I'm a safe house where an escapee husband or an absentee father can keep in touch with his family without ever actually revealing where he resides. Each party sends their letters, cards, presents, whatever, via me. I'm very discreet.'

Cyril nodded at the simplicity of it all.

'I also maintain relationships with doctors and dentists, so that my clients do not disappear off the system. I got myself two free fillings last year, pretending to be someone who actually lives in The Dominican Republic. You see, most of these people wish to remain on the National Health Service books – just in case.'

Cyril wondered why there wasn't a Disappearance Club down every suburban street. It all sounded so perfect.

'Why aren't there disappearance clubs everywhere?'

'I've always wondered about that. I suppose other people have thought of the idea, but not on the same scale: one friend relays letters to another, a trusted buddy here runs an account for an absent chum there. I just guess no one but me has ever thought of broadening the service out to strangers - and charging for it.'

'How do these people found out about you?'

'Ads in Private Eye and by word of mouth.'

Cyril was loving this. It was so cloak and dagger. He ran through all the information he'd been told, weighing it. It was the best bit of mental exercise he had had in years. 'But what about the wives and children?' he said at last. 'Don't they come down here hammerin' on your door, demanding to know where their husbands and dads and grandads have gone?...I mean, if you're taking letters off of them too, they must know that you live here.'

'Course they do,' replied Janek, 'although they usually call at the front door. Generally it's just business comes to the back...or people I invite directly, like you. And I have advance warning when the bell goes – the sound is wired down to here. It's either Avon calling, the gas man, or pissed off relatives.'

'What do you say, when it's pissed off relatives?'

'Lie...if I answer at all. My duty is to my client. I just tell family members that he collects and delivers his post in person and that he does so whenever the fancy takes him. I say that I have no control over the process. I tell 'em that I am as non-plussed about their loved one's whereabouts as they are. They have no idea that I actually post their letters on.'

'Do they believe you?'

'Usually people do – believe what you tell them - but not always.'

'But you do manage to get rid of them?'

'More often than not...' Janek paused. 'Did you see a blue Renault outside, on your way up the street?'

'I wasn't really clocking cars; too self-conscious about coming here, actually,' said Cyril.

'It's parked just up there, level with my kitchen,' added Janek, pointing. 'The lady in it cases out the joint every day and gets her kids to do the same, weekends. There's always a few like that, hoping against hope to catch a glimpse of their loved ones arriving to collect or to deliver something. I feel sorry for them, but I can't divulge the truth - I can't divulge them anything – not and keep in business.'

Cyril sat perfectly still, reflecting on the morality of this.

'With a few families, I even go out and hand 'em letters from their missing persons,' continued Janek, 'Straight into their hands, through the car windows. I tell them that their husband, or lover, or father, or whomever it may be, called when they had driven off for the night.'

Janek Lipsz saw Cyril's look, recognising it at once. 'Hey,' he said, raising both hands, 'It's not just that I have a living to make, mine is a constructive business, not a destructive one. A good twenty-five percent of my guys return – one day. And when they do, it's thanks to me that they are able to slot right back into society and, occasionally, start back up with their families again. Without my services, there'd be bugger all chance of that – no bank account, no contact over the years, no bridge forged between here and wherever they ran off to. That's the whole point of the Disappearance Club: a man can leave, but he never entirely leaves. Not while I'm alive and still in business.'

'What happens if you pop off?'

'Then the contacts and the service pop off too, but that's no reason not to offer the service in the first place. It's like the damp proof course on your house: the guarantees are only worth anything so long as the business remains afloat and the director above ground. That's true of any service; mine or the fellow's in the High Street office.'

Cyril rubbed his cheek. 'How long you been doing this?'

'I've been helping people disappear for thirty years…twenty of them from here, and the rest from a windowless booth above an optician's in Beckton. That was where I first set up.'

'Does it pay well? If you don't mind me asking?!' asked Cyril, colouring up.

'Well enough to buy this place, but not well enough to reroof it,' answered Janek, pointing up at the main house through his garden-office window.

Cyril looked up at the four-bedroom house, also at the mould-grey tiles and crooked chimney.

Janek continued, 'I take five percent on all cash transfers, ten percent on moneys hidden or buried, £50 a year flat rate to forward post and sort correspondence, £50 to keep an account current, and that includes the £25 I need to pay in to stop the dormancy bells from ringing at the banks' admin divisions. In addition, I am gifted money sometimes. It occasionally happens that a man dies wherever he is hiding out and wants his relatives to receive the assets and money he has amassed. It tends not to be much: disappearing may be the stuff of romantic dreams, but generally it is not a route to riches. These guys often ask me to arrange everything, regardless of whether there is an official will or not. Mindful that they have left me a great dollop of difficult work - while they are lying peaceful in a foreign church yard - most leave me a little sweetener; not just to cover my expenses, but also because they fear that without it, I might just ignore their wishes and run off with all the money myself.'

Not quite sure where his temerity came from, Cyril asked, 'Have you ever just pocketed it all?'

Immediately the air seemed sucked out of the office. Cups no longer chinked, chairs no longer scraped, shoes no longer shuffled. As if in stereo sound, Cyril could hear the cries of the boys playing outside and the thud of their football, high above Janek's silence.

A greyness came over Mr Lipsz. His cheeks pruned inward above a trembling jaw and he snapped shut his eyes, as if to blink away a painful memory. The change in him was extraordinary. Cyril felt sure that he would be asked to leave.

'No, never,' he replied at last, holding up a restraining hand. 'I always endeavour to get money and valuables to their rightful owners.' Janek looked like a charcoal drawing of himself, ruined by rain. Cyril was unsure whether he should stay. The old dustman averted his eyes, stared at the back wall with its huge framed photograph. He noted the handsome lad of early teenage. The picture, although black and white, seemed to possess more colour than the living face seated before him.

'So you would never consider disappearing yourself?' asked Janek.

Cyril could see how hard it had been for the man just to compose himself enough to ask the question. Cyril looked back at him from the photograph, saw that Mr Lipsz's cheeks were filling out again and the colour returning along the outer lines of his face. He felt sorry for what he had asked, but determined not to say so. Instinctively, he knew that any reference to the subject would once again leach the colour from the face opposite. He knew too, that Mr Lipsz's question was just mere words, picked to chase away the silence and embarrassment which had been precipitated.

'Who me?' he replied. 'I'm far too long in the tooth for that game. The place I'll be disappearing to - and it won't be long now - even you couldn't help me back from.'

Strangely this allusion to death seemed to lift the atmosphere in the room.

'Oh you're not that old,' flattered Janek, still a little reedy in voice.

Cyril felt that he needed to reveal a little weakness of his own, in order that the balance between them be restored: 'I forget to pull up my flies when I've been for a pee... sometimes I even forget to pop my little fella back in an' all.' He laughed a little. So did Janek Lipsz. The mirth between them grew and replaced the chill in the room. 'It can be embarrassing in public,' added Cyril.

Their combined laughter sounded far beyond the garage-office. The cat hunting yellow-bellied newts by the stream heard it, and flattened its ears. The boys playing their football heard it and the woman sitting in her blue Renault, waiting to catch sight of a husband long-gone, heard it. Her face had been chiselled sour by the hard years of waiting and she scowled at the floating laughter.

'That's not old age,' chortled Janek, 'Old age is

when you forget to take your cock out at all!'

This time birds rocketed at the guffaws, the boys actually paused in their game to listen, and in the blue Renault, the lonely wife mopped dripping tears off her chin. She sniffed; soon her daughter would arrive for the evening shift, and then she'd be spared this awful masculine joy.

Janek Lipsz brewed a couple of fresh teas. Cyril was asking him whether he was ever bothered by the police.

'They come about once every four months. Used to be more often, but not any more. They have a pretty shrewd idea what I do here, but I'm not breaking any laws, least not ones that matter, and they're far too busy with stabbings and muggings and hit-and-runs to case out the joint and prove that my missing persons don't really turn up here to collect their post.'

'So you tell the police the same as the relatives – that you're a drop-in centre for runaways?'

'Yes,' nodded Janek, liking Cyril's phrase. 'That's rather good. I'll use it next time the flatties are round.'

'Don't they ever pressure you?'

'Now and then. See, some of my escapees go on the run because the law is after them. And even the hitherto blameless ones are not above taking out loans they have no intention of paying back, or running up credit card debts. The police sometimes come and visit me then.'

'What do you do?'

'Nothing.'

'Nothing?'

'Finance companies won't pursue people abroad anyway, so the information I hold on overseas escapees is worthless. And back in the early days, when I did help out once - provided information - on a fellow who had run off only as far as Yorkshire, it transpired that it was the remaining family members who were taking out loans in his name and spending the money themselves. I swore then that I would never again reveal anything. And I haven't. Over time, the police have learned that I'm a stubborn old sod and I've never been arrested or subpoenaed, not once.'

'What would happen if you was superpeaned?' asked Cyril with the grammar of the dustcart. There was not a flicker of derision from Janek.

'Then I might be in trouble... Maybe have to disappear,' he laughed.

'There's no one 'ud know better 'n you how to,' replied Cyril.

'I'd be just like Lord Lucan,' came the reply, the vowels rolled in rich Polish fashion.

'That's funny, Janek, I was thinking of just that same guy on the way over here. I was on my bus and passing the time trying to guess what it was you might be up to down in your garage. And I had this idea that you had a club all set up to find people like him,' said Cyril, a little self-consciously, both at the admission and at actually using Mr Lipsz's Christian name for the first time.

'Now that is a good idea for a club,' Janek grinned. 'It would be twenty quid to join and for that, you'd get a giant picture of Lucan and a yellow whistle. Anyone who thought they'd found him would have to blast away on their whistle until all the others came running and scooped the fellow up in a whacking great net.'

'Yeah,' replied Cyril, enjoying the image. 'Think

how many big blokes with taches they'd catch.'

Things went quiet for a moment as each man savoured the genial spirit in the room, particularly Cyril. It was unusual to be so welcomed by a stranger. Then he asked suddenly, 'Up on the back wall, who's that a photograph of? That boy?'

The warm silence flashed away. What replaced it was just as noiseless, but sharp and hard and painful, like hunger looking in at a feast. Janek Lipsz looked down for long seconds and then up again. The eyes he levelled at Cyril were soft and calm, but twitching blood vessels at his neck and temple belied them.

'Someone I lost. Many years ago.'

'What happened to him?' asked Cyril, curiosity trumping tact.

'It is a terrible story and I am in no mood to tell it.'

'Did he disappear?' whispered Cyril, pushing his luck.

'I am in no mood to tell it,' repeated Janek, more sharply this time. 'I have enjoyed your company and your jokes, Cyril. We have had a good time, you and I, but the boy's story is no fellow to fun and laughter. It would not be right.' Janek stood up from his chair. 'It is nearly seven. I will drive you back.'

Once in the car, Janek brightened considerably. The journey was full of jams and red lights and jaywalking pedestrians, but he talked good naturedly through them all. So much so, that by the time they neared Cyril's home, Cyril felt comfortable asking Janek whether he would drive him the extra mile to *The Frog and Tongue* pub. He did not want to be late for Norman, not after being so clipped with him on the phone earlier.

'We are playing whist – a quid a round. We're not much good. You're welcome to join us.'

Janek did not answer. He had stopped the car at a green light. After ten seconds he noticed his error and accelerated forward.

'I'd like to buy you a pint anyways,' added Cyril.

'I have to get back I'm afraid, but thank you.'

Janek pulled up outside the pub. Cyril climbed out, but did not shut the car door. 'We'll be playing here all night, if you finish what you've got to do. You'd probably win the game of whist; I'm the youngest bloke in the hand.'

Even in the half light of the vehicle, Cyril could see Janek's face become stricken with the same ashen pallor as before. Once again his cheeks were lost to some awful inner demon. Janek closed his eyes and shook. 'I never play cards,' he replied, 'Never.' And then without one backward glance he turned his car away from Cyril and drove off with the passenger-side door still hanging open.

CHAPTER 2

Two days later the boys were hard at their football once more. Four times they had asked Mr Lipsz for their ball back and four times he had obliged then suddenly Phil shouted to the others, 'Keep it low, lads. We won't be getting it back again today…'

Down the road, nose practically against the 'D' and 'C', was a well dressed, portly man of early middle age. He reached a hand out for the door latch then snatched it back and knocked instead. He had the kind of face one sees on men who are not used to knocking before entering. He looked like a money-bod: well-heeled and fat on profits which should have been shared out more equitably. There was a redness about him which suggested a choleric nature. In his left hand was a neat document wallet, in his right, a Malacca cane. Mr Lipsz answered the summons and read all these things, particularly the cane.

'Is this The Disappearance Club?' asked the man.

'It is. I am Mr Lipsz. Come in.'

'I heard about you from a friend,' said the money-bod, following.

'Oh yes?'

'Yes, he said you'd be able to help me.'

Janek turned to face the man once more. He had shut the double doors behind them and they were now on the threshold of his garage-office. 'Two things before you enter,' he said. 'First I must know your name and…'

'Francis Teak,' the man interrupted.

'And second, you must leave your stick here.' Janek indicated a large plant pot. 'Garden rules, I'm afraid.'

'Why?' shot the man hotly.

'Because this is my patch and because you do not have a limp.'

Francis Teak sniffed. 'Can you shut those bloody boys up? I can't think with that ball thudding all the time.'

'Yes I can.'

Teak dropped his stick in the pot. The ball thudded against the fence twice more.

'Aren't you going to then?'

'No.'

Janek had seen the type scores of times before: chisellers and swindlers. Francis Teak required his services for very pressing reasons. Somewhere out there in the business world would be a pension fund, criminally plundered, and it was now time for those whose noses had been longest and deepest in the trough to vanish. It would be something like that behind this corpulent fellow's knocking at his door. Probably, Janek would read the details of what he'd actually done in the business pages of the next week's *Times*. Yes…this man needed to disappear before his collar was felt - Janek knew the type very well.

'Sit down,' he said.

The man already had.

'How can I help?' Janek enquired, fingers pressed

together, head on one side like a parrot's.

'I need to get to South Africa without leaving a trail. I need to go before next Monday. I need a lot of money wired there, but I want to keep a brace of accounts open here. They're not in my name, not my real name. I also want you to bury some money here in Britain for me, when I'm gone, at a spot I know.'

'Why can't you do it yourself?'

'Too risky.'

'How much will I be burying?'

'Two hundred thousand.'

'And is that just a small proportion of the total amount involved?'

'Correct. And your end of it is sixty grand. I know your rates and that's much more than you charge.'

'Why so generous?'

The football thudded loudly and Francis Teak winced. 'Because I want top-notch service,' he said through his grimace.

'I accept,' nodded Janek.

The man sat back and smiled. He spread his legs wide. His body language proclaimed that he had always known that Mr Janek Lipsz would jump at the offer.

Mr Lipsz wanted to crack him one in his ridiculously exposed crotch. '...On one condition.'

The smile vanished and the legs snapped back to.

'Doesn't sixty grand get rid of conditions?'

'Rather it makes them,' replied Janek coolly. 'You must not tell anyone that I have hoarded away cash for you. That is essential.'

'Yes, yes, alright.'

'No, Mr Teak. This condition cannot be passed off with an airy 'yes, yes, alright', for if it ever becomes common knowledge that I am a walking treasure map, it will only be a matter of time before the police find me dead in the woods minus my fingernails. So if word gets to me that you have blabbed, I will dig up your money and I will spend it.'

Now the man really sat up. 'You have my solemn word that I will be as silent as the grave.'

Janek nodded. 'Then the rest should be easy to arrange. I assume that you have the necessary paper work with you there?' asked Janek, indicating Teak's document wallet, 'May I see?'

Janek spent ten minutes looking over it, his forehead furrowed with concentration. There were over forty pages, but he was so practised that he could take in every word in that time. 'Thank you,' he said. 'That is very clear. I anticipate no problems.'

'There'd better not be,' retorted the man, still trying to be top dog.

Janek ignored the swagger in his voice… 'There's one other thing.'

'Another condition?'

'No, a favour.'

Francis Teak was shocked. He hadn't expected this. He wobbled his head. His silly fat chins flapped about. His little fish eyes stared.

Janek stood up and pointed to the huge photograph behind him. The teenager in black and white stared down. 'See this boy?' he began.

'Can't miss 'im. I've never seen a bigger photo.'

'I lost him in 1943. That's thirty-three years ago.'

Money-mover Teak looked bored.

'I lost him in 1943,' hissed Janek. 'And I need to find him. I want you to keep an eye out for him - as a favour to me - on your travels, wherever you go. He will have changed considerably. Look.'

Francis Teak looked at a piece of paper which Janek had pulled from inside a cabinet.

'This is an artist's impression of what the boy would look like today - as a mature man. I want you to take the impression here and a small copy of the big photograph. And then just keep an eye out. If you see anyone you think might be him, contact me here. All my details are on the reverse side of the little photograph.'

'I've got your contact details already, got them from the guy who told me about you.'

'Well now you've got them twice. See, they're on the back here.' Janek indicated exactly where and handed the man the two wallet-sized impressions.

'You think he's in South Africa then?' asked Teak taking them.

'No. I have no idea where he is. I ask the same of every person who uses my services, regardless of where they are headed. That way I cover the whole world. One day I will find him.'

'Makes no sense. You haven't even told me his name.'

'Joseph.'

'Joseph who?'

'Just Joseph.'

'That's it? Joseph? This guy means so much to you, and you don't even have a surname!'

'Never knew it,' Janek replied sharply.

'Ok,' answered Teak, deciding already that it was a ridiculous business.

'But will you do it? Really do it? Will you keep your

eyes open?'

'Alright, alright, I'll see what I can do,' Teak lied.

Janek knew that this piece of shit would not bother - he just wanted rid of him now, wanted the nasty, bloated thief out of his office. 'I'll take my cut out of the money you want burying. Just give me £100 now for immediate expenses,' he said dully.

Teak peeled five notes off a dirty great wad and tossed them onto the desk between them. 'You keep the information in the document wallet; everything you need is in there. I'm going to bag a flight for later this week. I'll be in South Africa by midday Sunday at the latest. I've got your number and address; I'll call you early next week,' he said.

Janek didn't answer at once. He had turned to look at the black-and-white face behind him. His own profile stood out against the glass and a more perceptive and a more empathetic man than Francis Teak would have noted in it, a deep, deep sadness and a heavy, oppressive guilt.

'I'll await your call,' replied Janek turning.

Teak yawned. He extended a hand. Janek shook it – a mere business formality. Then the man rose to leave. He left the office-cum-garage, picked up his cane from its flower-pot stand and flicked the latch on the double doors. All the time Janek sat still, watching him leave. Not one more word did he add, nor one inch did he move. Then he noticed the photo he had handed Francis Teak, left, face up on the desk in front of him. The artist's impression was next to it, similarly discarded. That the swindling porker had just dumped them, acted upon Janek as a fox does a hound dog. With a guttural snort he took after Teak, the five twenty pound notes he'd just been given still in his hand. It took mere seconds to catch up with his man, who was walking past the footballing boys. Teak turned at the noise of Janek's rapidity.

The boys stopped their game. An adult in a rage is as arresting a sight as anything in Nature.

They saw Mr Lipsz take the stunned fellow by the short hairs at his temple, ball up a twenty pound note and shove it clean up the man's nose. A line of blood trailed down Teak's shocked face and his right nostril ballooned out grotesquely where the foreign body had been shoved up it. The boys stood open-mouthed.

Then Janek hit him, full in the mouth, Teak's fleshy lower lip splitting against his teeth. There was an even greater rush of blood and the boys broke their silence and whooped. They cheered for Mr Lipsz and egged him on to plug the fat guy again. To their disappointment he did not, merely shouted: 'Take your dirty business and fuck off. Go on. I wouldn't help a rat like you for all the filthy money you've stolen.' And then Janek stormed back through his garden doors and secured them with a curse.

Francis Teak stood there stunned, paralysed at the sight of his own blood and paralysed at the collapse of his plans.

'Dirty little Polack,' he hissed.

He was jolted into action when Janek hurled his documents over the garden fence. As if responding to the crack of a starting pistol, Teak whirled about, snatching the papers up and cursing the wind as it carried them in a hundred different directions. The boys goggled at this bloodied pinstripe suit, dancing for sheets of A4. They did not lift a finger to help him, for their loyalties lay firmly with the man who always returned them their ball.

Back in his office, Janek gathered up the photo and artist's impression that the leaping man outside had abandoned and stared at them. There was an awful shame in his eyes. Then he opened a draw and placed them carefully within. The drawer was full of these pictures, all the same. Many hundreds of them.

Then, just like the woman outside in her blue Renault, Janek let fall a tear. Quickly, lest a salty drop damage its precious contents, he slammed shut the drawer.

For an hour afterwards there was no football; the boys were too busy re-enacting what they'd seen. A couple of them had witnessed a drunken brawl before, with lots of swearing and rolling around in the dirt, but this had been an entirely different affair: nice Mr Lipsz in a daylight punch-up! Phil slow-motioned the lip-splitting right-hander for the others to appreciate.

Francis Teak had scuttled off with his papers. He had managed to catch about seventy percent of them. The rest were stuck up trees or were flapping comically around television aerials. He had sworn at the boys for not helping him gather them up.

Phil, who had a strong sense of territory, had answered back, 'You can't fight and you've got a lip like Donald Duck, you fat wanker.'

Now the boys had the street to themselves once more. One of the papers had floated down from on high and they were poring over it. 'United Holdings Ordinary Shares, 25p each. Execution only,' a tall, bony lad read. 'What the hell does that mean?'

'Dunno. But they can't be worth much. Not at

twenty-five pence. Chuck it away, let's play again,' said Phil. And they did, all afternoon, but were careful to keep the ball low, for a man who can fight is respected, and a little feared, by boys, and none of them were keen to disturb Mr Lipsz again that day.

Thus it was, at nearly six o'clock, that they feared also for a little, slight man who walked timidly up to Mr Lipsz's double doors and knocked. They had not seen him wander up, so unobtrusive had been his tread. But now they stopped all play to watch what would happen next - not just because the man was another stranger, arrived on what was already a strange day - but because Mr Lipsz might think that the knocking was one of them. They wanted to see how the angry old Pole would have received a boy after his ball.

'Kevin Keegan is it?' smiled Mr Lipsz, drawing open one of the double doors. As he could no longer hear the boys' volleys he had assumed that the knocking was one of their summonses.

'I'm sorry, it isn't,' stammered the slight, diffident man.

Janek looked from him to the watching boys. He saw that Phil had the football under his arm. 'No, it is I who am sorry. These boys,' he said indicating, a broad grin illuminating his face, 'They give me my daily exercise fetching their rotten shots. I thought you were one of them.' The stranger looked a fraction more at ease. 'Come in,' he soothed. 'I am Janek Lipsz.'

The man followed him to the garden office. Once inside, he hadn't fully set down the attache case he was carrying before he started to weep - huge, wracking sobs. 'I want to disappear,' the man wailed brokenly.

'That is what I am here for,' answered Janek, passing the man a handful of tissues. 'May I ask your name?'

'Charlie Moore,' the man quavered.

Janek nodded.

'I wish just to vanish. Vamoose.'

Janek nodded again. 'Vamoosing we can do.'

'I was thinking of Finland,' the man said.

'As good a place as any,' returned Janek.

Charlie Moore looked as if he had expected the professional to scoff at his choice of destination.

'Not too cold?' asked Charlie, sniffing out a few more sobs.

'A man may disappear for many reasons. Climate is not one of them - not in my experience.' Janek paused... 'Why do you want to go away, Mr Moore?'

Charlie's eyes, still wet from his recent tears, flickered with embarrassment. 'I have fallen in love,' he confessed, blushing.

Janek waited.

'My wife is not happy. It is not with her I am in love.'

'And you wish to start over with a new woman?'

The redness in Charlie Moore's cheeks deepened and spread down his chin, an inch a second.

After ten seconds Janek spoke, 'One thing a man acquires in my line of work is tolerance...'

'I am leaving my wife for another man,' Charlie blurted.

There was a joke in there, but not a hint of a smile did Janek betray. He carried right on, just as if he heard the same motive every day...'Disappearing is the easy part. It is maintaining links with the old country which is difficult. You will want a bank account and a pension fund maintained, also you should remain registered at a doctor's practice here. People are happy to flee abroad, but when they become infirm, often they wish to return home to die. I have seen this many times.'

Janek looked up to see the whites of Charlie Moore's eyes.

'I am sorry to be morbid, but I cannot do a thorough job without detailing you the facts. There is nothing for you to worry about and not much for you to do either. That is my job. Even with the GP we select, if need be, I can pretend to be you and go to see him at his clinic…maybe once a year. I do a good line in shamming back complaints.'

Charlie smiled weakly.

'What about contacts? Who do you wish to keep in touch with?'

'I've thought about that. My daughter, definitely,' replied Moore.

'Address?' asked Janek.

'That's the problem.'

'Why?'

'She still lives at home with her mother - my wife.'

'No problem.'

'No?'

'No,' repeated Janek. Send your post here to me and I will see to everything else. Is your daughter still at school?'

'University.'

'Don't they have pigeon holes at universities?'

'I don't know, I'm afraid. It's her first year.'

'There will be pigeon holes,' Janek assured Charlie.

If you give me a photograph of her, I'll hang around the first couple of times, actually check with my own eyes that she collects her mail from them.'

'Thank you,' said Charlie breathlessly, really believing for the first time that he might actually escape, might actually carry out what had been for so long just a pipe dream. The thought gave him confidence enough to talk terms. 'How much do you charge?'

'A hundred a year, but give me one-fifty today and we'll call it quits for the first two years,' replied Janek. He could tell a timid wee beastie when he saw one and had decided to ease Charlie's way as much as running costs would allow.

'Oh thank you. Thank you so very much.'

Janek stared at the mild-mannered man before him and wondered what job it was that he would fail to turn up for soon. Maybe he was an accountant or a teacher - one with bad discipline.

'I won't miss my work,' smiled Charlie, as if reading Janek's look. I was in the planning department at the local council: crushingly dull work. There are only so many extensions a man can turn down before he begins to see his alarm clock as a personal enemy.' He paused for a few seconds, and in that time all cheer drained from his face. He twisted round to look out of the office window and squinted up at the main house. 'I didn't ever turn you down for an extension did I?' he asked with a tremble.

'Never even applied,' laughed Janek. 'There are rooms in the house I don't go into from one year to the next as it is.'

Charlie Moore looked relieved.

'Does your new partner want to see me too?' asked Janek quietly. The question seemed more tactful at low volume.

'Oh no. I'm afraid he doesn't trust anyone. He tried to talk me out of coming here today, actually.'

Janek smiled. He had made a conscious decision to do lots of this - smiling - in order to set the man before him at his ease.

'I am very discreet. Even when the police stick their noses in, I keep schtum.' Immediately, Janek knew that he had said the wrong thing. Charlie writhed and grimaced in the seat before him. 'Will they? Will they get involved? I couldn't cope with being hounded by the police.'

'Oh no, no, no, no, no!' Janek soothed. 'Not in your case. Only happens in very rare cases. I was just illustrating what I wouldn't ever do, even in the case of one offs. You're situation is a totally different kettle of fish, totally different,' he continued, doing a fairly good job of digging himself out of trouble.

Charlie wanted to believe him. 'What about my work?' he asked, 'Won't they sniff around?'

Janek snorted. 'Employers don't give a damn about their employees. They will ring your home, maybe five times, and then write you off. Unless you abscond with something of theirs, they will lose interest in you as soon as you are off the pay roll. To the boss, you will cease to exist before he has even learned your replacement's name.'

'My wife might be rather different,' replied Charlie Moore. 'Are you prepared for that? Say, if she finds out that you helped me? I don't see how she could, but just in case she ever did?'

Janek liked the man before him - he had evidently decided that it would be wrong to just up and flee without warning the person helping him of the consequences he might face as a result. Janek spread his arms expansively, so that the tips of his fingers touched his filing cabinets. Then he leaned across to speak to Charlie, 'Please don't be offended by what I say now: a husband often has a central role in fashioning his wife's authority. The unyielding cement of her temper gets laid down over their years together, and hardened during that time too. Often with new people and those she has not been able to act upon so repeatedly, her teeth are pulled and her claws drawn. I have seen this many times. Be assured, I am more than a match for anyone who comes a-knocking at my door demanding information - even your wife.'

Charlie Moore looked sceptical.

Suddenly Janek could see the years of domestic dominance in the Moore household and he wished that he had a view of the back of Charlie's head, to see whether the myriad hen-pecks had left scars. 'You will like Finland,' he said, 'The Finns are a laconic people - they do not speak a lot - and when they do, it is generally not at volume.'

Both men smiled at what had been left unsaid.

'Do you need anything more from me?'

'Yes,' Janek replied. 'Quite a quantity of documents I'm afraid.'

Charlie took out a notepad and a pencil with a rubber on top.

'That won't be necessary; I've got a printed list - details everything from passport to NHS number to those little photographs you take of yourself in

Woolworths.'

Charlie put away his pencil.

'Here,' said Janek handing him the list.

Charlie read down it. There were eighteen items for him to get.

'Do you think you'll have a problem with any of them?'

'One or two will take a bit of finding. No more than an afternoon's work though, at the most,' replied the soon-to-be ex-town planner.

'Excellent,' beamed Janek.

'Excellent,' repeated Charlie Moore back to him.

'I'll give you two days, just to be on the safe side. Afterwards, return with the full complement off that list and then you'll be free to depart whenever you choose.'

'Excellent,' said Charlie once more. He stood up to leave, extending a very grateful hand. Janek shook it, but maintained his grip longer than was conventional. The man destined for Finland grinned a little uneasily. His fingers went limp in Janek's grasp.

'Please do not go yet. I have a favour to ask you, Mr Moore. Sit down.'

Charlie sat and smiled broadly once more. He was keen to be of any possible assistance. At the beginning of the day he had feared that the Disappearance Club might prove a ridiculous scam, now that he knew it was on the level, he was keen to show his gratitude to its founder. 'Anything. Ask away,' he replied.

Janek shifted self-consciously. He introduced the giant photograph behind him from his chair. 'This is a picture of a thirteen-year-old boy named Joseph. I have no fuller name for him than that. I lost him over thirty years ago, in the war, and I want to find him again. That desire is the most pressing thing in my life. And I ask every person who uses my services to keep an eye out for him on their travels, wherever they may go. No country is more likely than any other to be his home. No leads have ever led me in the direction of Finland, but then again they have not led me away from that country either. I do not want you thinking that you are starting out any warmer or colder than any of my other members who are out there keeping their eyes open. For that is what you are now - a member of a club. And all club members are bound by two things: your desire to escape your old lives and your commitment to looking out for my Joseph. That is, if you will agree to do me this favour.'

'Absolutely. Not a problem….' Then Charlie Moore paused, seemingly unsure whether he should say what was on his lips.

'Go on,' nodded Janek.

'But won't he have changed? I mean, a thirty year old photograph of me would show a very different person from the one in front of you now. I was good-looking for starters.'

Janek nodded and stood up, turning to the cabinet with the hundreds of smaller photos in. The door slid on well-oiled hinges. 'Here,' he said, passing the two impressions that Francis Teak had dumped. 'One is a miniature of the photograph on this wall, the other is an artist's impression of what the boy would look like today, as a forty-five year old man. I would like you to take both and to contact me here if you ever think that you see the person in them. And then I will come to you, wherever in the world you are.'

'My God, what if I am mistaken? What if the man I see is not your Joseph?'

'That will not matter, beyond the fact that my search will not have come to an end. I will be glad to see you. I will buy you a drink and I will take a few days out of my life here, to catch my breath before returning home. Never will I blame you for calling me to a man who proves not to be Joseph - rather I will thank you for taking my search seriously and contacting me.'

'Is he a relative? Have you something for him?' asked Charlie, forgetting his usual reticence in matters personal, so stimulated was his interest by the strange request.

The question was barely out in the air between them when a gauntness came over Janek's face: the skin under his eyes sagged and the brokenness of his nose seemed to become even more exaggerated. Against the whey of his face, his freckles stood out darkly. It was not quite as strong a physical response as Cyril's questions had elicited, but the sensitive Charlie Moore picked up on the changes very quickly: 'Oh I am sorry; I did not mean to pry. I quite forgot myself. Be assured, I will look out for your Joseph with great care and diligence. You can rest assured on that point,' he blurted, stumbling over some of the words.

Janek tried to master himself. Very rarely could he keep his composure and field questions about the boy - even when he knew that he had to raise the topic with those who would be off searching for him. No amount of inner preparation ever made it easy. It had been worse with Cyril, the old dustman, because on that occasion, Janek had not psyched himself up at all.

He had been taken entirely by surprise. But it wasn't much better with Charlie either. He kicked himself for letting the same nausea afflict him again. Right from the beginning of the interview with Charlie Moore he had known that the Joseph discussion would come. Why couldn't he maintain a professional front, at least until these men left the office?

Janek answered at last. 'It is not your fault. Your questions were quite innocent. I carry a great sorrow within me. There are things I have done which I wish could be undone. But that cannot be; the war was a terrible time and brought out the worst in many of us. Do not mind me…I would be most grateful if you would be observant in your new life and be my eyes in Finland. Keep a look out for Joseph. I am sorry that I have dampened the atmosphere. You are not the first I have made uncomfortable in this way and you will not be the last.' Janek paused, 'Perhaps it would be best if you left now. When you come back in two days' time I will be much recovered. You have my word on that.'

Charlie left as quickly as good manners allowed. He did not want to appear to be scarpering from Mr Lipsz's company.

When he was alone in the dark of his garage office, Janek shook his head at himself. He remembered his spasms before Cyril, the fist-fight of earlier in the day, and the nausea he had just felt.

'Next time,' he said to himself, 'Next time you must show more self-control; such displays will not help you to find Joseph. A hundred-to-one this frightened little Charlie Moore will be far too scared to tell you of any sighting, just for fear of your reaction. You must get a hold of yourself, Janek. Next time…next time, you cannot be the same.'

CHAPTER 3

Charlie Moore was far too wary of the Joseph-issue for Janek's 'next time' to be when he returned with his documents. Twice Janek tried to turn the conversation round to the boy on the wall and twice his client displayed a look of utter panic. He would only sit there and repeat, 'I will keep a good look out, I promise. I will keep a good look out, I promise.'

In the end, Moore spent only fifteen minutes in the office, wrapping up details, before leaving, Finland-bound. Janek didn't doubt that Charlie would keep his eyes open, but at no point had he managed to engage the fellow in meaningful discussion about the old photograph and the person in it. Janek cursed inwardly, for he had really prepared himself mentally to discuss Joseph - had even swigged down an early G&T to that end.

'Scared him off, you fool,' Janek hissed at himself as the door closed behind his rapidly retreating client. 'You were too intense the other day.' He sighed, 'You can't look like death at the mention of Joseph and then expect these runaways to feel comfortable contacting you when they think they've found him. They just won't bother.'

Janek started to count the total number of Joseph sightings his escapees had informed him of. Forty-one?...Forty-two?...Not very many really: considering that he had been searching for over three decades. And every single one of them had come to nothing.

'It's because you can't control yourself when the subject is raised,' he fumed…'You need practice.'

Just then the first ball of the day pounded against his fence. It might just as well have been his head - the sound had given him an immediate idea. 'Phil!' he shouted, 'Phil!' without even drawing open the double doors first.

The football game guttered to a halt. 'Yeah, Mr Lipsz, what is it?' came Phil's voice from the pavement.

'I want you to pop over here when you're done with your game. It's not right a boy of your age not knowing what the Eastern Front was – too many people died there for you not to know….I'm going to tell you.'

Phil had other things planned for his post-football time: watching TV, duffing over his little brother - but Mr Lipsz did return the ball every time he was asked, so it seemed wise to agree to his request. Therefore he muttered to himself, 'Eastern bloody Front,' but called out loud, 'Sure Mr Lipsz, when we're finished.' He turned to his friends and pulled one of those faces that only children can do well, where one side is all crunched up in dismay and the other maintains its youthful softness.

The others laughed at him. 'History lesson! History Lesson,' one called and another lisped, 'Pleathe Mr Lipthz, pleathe Mr Lipthz, what was the Eathtern Fwont, thir?' But they were careful not to be overheard, for a man who returns footballs must be kept on side…especially one who throws punches in public; for an adult who fights in the street flies in the face of all convention and can never be taken entirely for granted.

It was Janek's plan that he would provide the boy with a little detail on the Second World War and then bring up the subject of his Joseph. Phil would be a perfect audience: captive, non-judgemental, and not expected to do anything with the information. Janek could practise his delivery on him, thereby polishing it up for his customers and so become more comfortable with the whole procedure. Seated in his office he wondered why he hadn't ever tried something similar. In truth, he had never before been on anything but purely ball-retrieving terms with previous generations of children.

All afternoon the ball thudded and all afternoon Janek honed what he would say to Phil - as if gearing up for a public recitation. No clients called to disturb these careful preparations.

At ten to five Phil rapped on the garage doors. 'Hi there,' he called, not much looking forward to his history lesson. Janek had him seated in moments.

'Cup of tea?'

'Alright.'

'Biscuit?'

'Alright.'

'Cake?'

'You bet.'

Phil beamed. Already, History didn't seem quite so bad.

'Now then,' began Janek pouring them both a cuppa, 'the Eastern Front was where most of the fighting went on in the Second World War. Germany and the Soviets… you know what the Soviets are?'

Phil nodded.

'Well they hated each other worse than hell. They fought without pause and without mercy. What they did to each other was a hundred times worse than anything that happened between you Brits and the Germans. Neither side thought anything of stripping their captured enemy naked and setting a hose pipe on him in the middle of the Russian winter. And there the guy would be left in a block of ice, frozen solid - deader than roadkill. And any man who tried to retreat, even one step back, was shot by his own side…

…Stalin, that's the guy who led the Soviets, he ordered eighty year old men to fight German tanks with sticks, just so that the tanks had to stop for a few seconds to shoot them. And he had any man who refused killed, so desperately did he want those few extra seconds to hold off the German advance. And all those seconds added up, you know, until his men and the Russian winter sapped the lifeblood out of the Nazis, one by one, and left them with their dead eyes glittering washed-out blue in the snow.'

Phil grinned in his chair. Like every young boy he enjoyed hearing about blood and guts and believed in the romance of killing.

'You like that?' asked Janek.

Phil grinned some more.

'That is good. It is a good sign. In this great country of yours, this England, there are even men three times your age who grin in the same way. It shows that you have all been lucky enough to live in a time of peace. Those of us unlucky enough to be touched by war, never again believe in its glamour.'

Phil thought he understood what had just been said and snapped the grin away: he was getting told off for sitting down and listening! If only Mr Lipsz knew that he got told off for the exact the opposite, every day at school.

'No lad, I'm not having a go at you,' chuckled Janek, reading the boy's body language, 'just making an observation…And this conflict,' he said, continuing, 'was much bigger than anything you Brits or the Americans were involved in.'

Phil looked sceptical.

'Oh yes. In one battle alone, The Battle of Kursk, there were more men killed on the Eastern Front, than the total British dead in the whole six year war.'

Phil stuffed his face with cake to make sure that he did not grin.

'When Hitler allocated his Panzer divisions…' Janek looked hard at the youth to assess his probable vocabulary. '…When Hitler decided where to send his tanks, he dispatched nine to the Eastern Front for every one sent against the Brits and Americans. If it had been the other way round there would have been no storming up the Normandy beaches at all.'

Phil had done the Normandy Landings at school so nodded at this as he scoffed cake. 'What did you do? Was you on the Eastern Front?' he asked through the icing.

'No. I was a lieutenant in the Polish army and when we were defeated by invading forces I could no longer be a lieutenant, because there was no army left for me to be one in. But I stayed in my country and fought on quietly and secretly. That is the only way a people can fight, when their army has ceased to exist. They dynamite bridges and railway tracks and stab enemy soldiers who have had too much to drink and booby-trap vehicles and steal supplies - and get tortured too, when they are discovered and captured. It is called being a resistance fighter...'

'Is that what you was? A resistance fighter? Like when you fell off the back of that lorry and got your nose splashed across your face?'

'Yes. That was one of my less successful ventures.'

'And did you ever kill anyone?' asked Phil excitedly, his teeth all gummed with jam.

'Yes, I'm afraid I did,' admitted Janek, shaking his head at what he had known all along - that boys can only really be weaned off the thrill of war by direct personal experience.

'How? How?' trilled Phil.

Janek paused a moment, wondering whether he should answer...

'...Once I was sniping in the woods with a hunting rifle. An eight strong German patrol came by. I picked off a young man from two hundred metres away. He was no more than twenty years old. I chose him because he had a red ribbon tied to his rucksack - for no other reason than that, and I shot him clean through the throat. A minute later he was begging his commanding officer to kill him because he couldn't breathe through the blood and so his oberstfuhrer - that's his captain - did. Then I shot the captain too.'

Janek waited to note the effect of this story.

'Really?' asked Phil.

'Really,' nodded Janek.

'Wow. Brilliant,' Phil cried. 'What about other

times?'

'There were lots of other times and lots of other ways,' Janek replied flatly.

Phil had the uneasy feeling that he had said something wrong, so he changed the subject the best way he knew how. 'Can I have some more cake? The biscuits are good, but the cake is to die for.'

Janek might have smiled at the choice of words if he hadn't caught Joseph's eye in the photograph as he turned for cake. He carved Phil a monster slice and then swallowed down a little phlegm of nervousness: 'Aren't you going to ask me about that picture?' he said, a little reedily. He pointed at the photograph and the cake knife shook in his hand.

'It's big enough,' was Phil's reply.

'It was taken many years ago.'

'Not you, is it?'

'Oh no, no, no,' Janek replied quickly.

'Who is it then?' asked Phil between bites.

'His name's Joseph. He was not much older than you when that was taken. And I was supposed to look after him, but I didn't. Not properly. And I lost him in that war we've just been talking about. He survived though and I've been looking for him ever since, to try to make up for what I did.'

Janek's voice took on the honeyed quality of sadness and honesty combined. It was a sound that Phil had not heard from him before and his jaws left their cake for a moment. In a twinkling of insight, the perspicacity of which stunned Janek, he asked, 'Is that why those people come here? To your door? To help you look?'

The sadness was shocked out of the old Pole.

'Yes,' he said simply. 'They help me. They look for Joseph, but still I don't find him. And I am fast becoming an old man and I don't want to die without finding him and seeing him again, and without setting things right between us.'

Still Phil's jaws were cake-free.

'Do you want to see an artist's impression of what he would look like today?'

Phil nodded.

'Here,' said Janek, handing him one that he had set aside for the purpose.

Phil looked hard at it, taking a keen interest, 'Looks like my maths teacher, 'cept my maths teacher's got ears right slap up 'gainst the side of his 'ead - looks like an otter he does…This Joseph guy, though,' Phil continued, 'Do you know for sure he's still alive?'

'I don't know anything for sure,' whispered Janek, his voice coming from somewhere small and frightened. And he sat before Phil and Phil saw, not the fist-fighter of two days before, but a tired old man who reminded him of his own grandfather, just before he'd gone into hospital for the last time.

A perfect tear rolled down Janek's face. Phil heard his internal mother telling him that it was time to leave. 'I've got to go now, Mr Lipsz. Thank you ever so much for the tea and the cake. And thank you for telling me about the Eastern Front. I didn't think I'd be interested, I just came because you always give us our ball back, but I was interested in the end. Really I was. And the cake was great.'

Janek pulled himself back from dark places; such honesty had to be acknowledged. 'Thank you for coming,' he said, smiling.

Then Phil was gone, like a snake through a crack: his internal mother was growing most insistent and also, there was wrestling on ITV.

Janek went up the garden and inside his house. If anyone called on business, it would take a moment's thought just to try the front door bell.

Inside number 33 there was a lot of good dark furniture - old wood. And paintings on the wall too - mostly of the natural world. They were his own work. He liked landscapes, but not just any old vistas; his preference was for patches of scrub, even old brownfield sites, which were in the process of being reclaimed by woodland. The spread of thin wispy birches and ash trees, as they recolonised the land, spoke to him of the permanence of Nature and its God-like resilience. He saw plots like that all the time: at the back of the Co-op where he shopped, in the grounds of a derelict factory which could not be touched because it was a listed building, beside railway tracks, and within rundown old building sites - where the freeholder had run out of money. He painted them from memory, when he had the time, and business was slow: occasionally clients found him in his office, palette in hand, addressing his easel.

These oils were hung in most of the rooms. They were the only things up off the floor. Newspapers were strewn everywhere, all showing evidence of hard reading. Letters lay in little piles: bills and offers and financial correspondence. There was no Disappearance Club material among them, though. Such communication was never demoted to the household mounds.

In addition to all these things were many curios: a stuffed hyena which guarded his hall, an Edwardian cash register on the landing, a number of swords, an eighteenth century boar spear, two statues of armour, a witchdoctor's throne from West Africa, fossils of all sorts and sizes, and a human skeleton. The last was mounted on a bend in the staircase and it had become a habit with Janek to say goodnight to it on his way up to bed. Also, in one of the living rooms was a talking manikin which had been rescued from a bonfire outside the local drama college. It was done up as a pirate and if one pressed a button on its back, it would inform all listeners where they might find a king's ransom in Spanish doubloons.

The house itself was functional, except for various parts of the plumbing which had been crying out for attention since the Early Jurassic. Janek was deaf to their belchings and clankings.

He sat opposite Long John, the pirate manikin.

'Well…?' he said.

Long John's button had not been pressed, so the pirate did not respond.

It seemed to Janek that the conversation with Phil had been a success - after a fashion. The lad had been a good listener and he, for his own part, had faced down and out-stared his demons…at least for a while. So why did he feel like the gristly underside of a cheap beef joint – all stringy and grey? Maybe the tears? Maybe the details about shooting people? But there was something else as well…some dim inkling that was not to do with his past. Something quite different. Something he had to do – and he was not at all sure that he was in the mood to have to do anything.

'What the hell is it?' he enquired of the living-room pirate.

Beside the manikin was the day's newspaper. Janek scanned the front page, took in the date…

'… Shit. It's Friday… Of course.'

To his right, on the seat of an old oak chair lay a play script, dirty with thumbs and ink and cat hair.

'Am I going to go then?' Janek held the script in his hand as he asked the question out loud – to himself, to the air, to the pirate model.

Long John stared blankly ahead.

'I'm expected. And I've got a big part,' he grumbled.

An old grandfather clock chimed. Not a very valuable one, but a sturdy chunk of old wood with a clean motion. It was 5:45.

'Oh come on.'

Janek crammed the script into a bag. He had grown accustomed to talking to himself, particularly when deliberating things. Rather than being a badge of insanity, he considered it very sensible and natural in a person living alone, although he couldn't ever remember doing it before the war. Maybe in those happy days there had just been too many other happy people around to talk to.

At two minutes past six he swept out of the house at speed, lest he talk himself out of the decision he had made: he was going to go to the amateur dramatics group at the local church hall. For a month they had been working on Tennessee Williams's *Cat on a Hot Tin Roof* and everyone thought Janek's Big Daddy impressive.

About six weeks before, Janek had noticed a

ghostly pallor to his skin. It was summer, but he seemed enveloped in something which might have been a waste product of yoghurt manufacture. So, when time and the Disappearance Club allowed, he started going out in the sun - just walking along the streets and in some of the local nature reserves which straddled the border between his town and the next.

It was on a board by the wayside that he first noticed a wanted ad, for actors to form a local group. He had stopped to read it. Then down another little track-way he had seen the same poster again. This second time he had taken down the contact number. From that point on, this constitutional of his changed from being a mere stroll to take in the sun, to a tough process of yomping-cum-decision-making. Socialising was not something Janek did much of, and almost never outside his home. If he were to sign up for this acting lark, then people would expect him to attend a communal venue with dependable regularity. He mulled the matter over.

Of course this involved much talking to himself - mothers gathered up their children as he passed, and dogs, noticing their owners' anxieties, barked and snarled at him. But by the time he returned home, Janek had made up his mind…After a few minutes on the phone he had agreed to attend the first meeting. Since that day, he had turned up to four out of the last five sessions. Often he shilly-shallied before going, but these wobbles were the mere delay before plunging into a cold pool. Only on one occasion had his work with the disappeared kept him home. Every other time he had been the first up at the church hall.

So it was this evening, after his chat with Phil, that

he started to relish the prospect of being Big Daddy once more, even before he was at the end of Orchard Road.

He was going over lines when his eye caught the red glint of the Renault woman's. Hers were crimson with hostility and tears. She had been waiting all day, like every day, for the merest sign of her missing husband. Janek coloured up with guilt. Her eyes followed him and watched his cheeks match their colour. He turned the corner at double-pace. 'That woman,' he hissed. And Janek was glad that he was out of no.33 and his office and all the secrets that they held.

The drama group was made up of an eclectic bunch, as all such groups are. In addition to Janek, there was a retired history teacher, a young chap who sold spare parts for motorcycles, a gay tailor who wouldn't let anyone else play Brick, the woman from behind the information desk at the library, two youngsters from the local sixth form who were deeply in love but dared not tell one another, three chunky blokes who obviously lugged heavy things about for a living, and a large, smiley woman in her forties who came with her ridiculously beautiful daughter, Clara. Everyone had learned her name at the first telling. Also there was the vicar, The Reverend Tony Collier, who involved himself in every club that practised at his church, except kung fu. He attended Bridge on Mondays which he loved, Badminton on Tuesdays which he thought good for him, Chess on Thursdays which he tolerated, and Rhythmic Rascals at the weekends which he loathed: for an hour and a quarter, the under-fives made a terrific amount of noise attacking one another with maracas and glockenspiels. He had tried the kung fu class on its inaugural Wednesday but a young parishioner had kicked him in the testicles and he had decided that that was beyond the call of even God's work. Rhythmic Rascals wasn't much safer - the smile he wore throughout seemed stitched on, but he kept attending so that the Church might be in pole position to snatch up and save the town's youngest generation of souls. Friday evening *Cat on a Hot Tin Roof* was manna from heaven in comparison.

So when Janek arrived, the Reverend's smile of greeting was as genuine as the one he wore on Bridge evenings. Rather fittingly he was playing The Reverend Tooker in the play and was raring to get his teeth into Act Two. 'Hello, Janek,' he said. 'Nice evening for a brisk stroll.'

Janek's cheeks were flushed. 'Yes. I must have covered the mile here in just over ten minutes. Not bad for a sixty-five year old.' He looked at the church noticeboard and saw a kung-fu leaflet pinned up. 'Maybe I should try that,' he added.

'No. I shouldn't bother,' said the clergyman, losing his smile immediately. 'They're savage that lot. You'd be lucky to do a mile in a day after a session with them.' A little vein was quivering just below the vicar's nose. Janek thought he'd better change the subject.

'Am I the first here?'

'Yes. If you don't count the rectory fox. It's been hard at the fried chicken remains under the churchyard yew all afternoon. I think the tramps are back sleeping underneath it, now that it's summer once more and the nights have turned warmer.'

'You don't mind them there?' asked Janek.

'If God's holy acre can't accommodate the destitute, then where in this world is there left for them to go?'

'I'll bet you have to clear away half a dozen cider cans the morning after their little visits.'

The Reverend Collier nodded his head. 'There are many things we must stoop for in this life. I have always found cider cans rather easy.'

'And the tramps, they cause no more trouble than that?'

'They used to light fires, but I asked them not to and they stopped at once. I explained that I feared for the big old trees. Not another have they lit since; maybe because they value the trees too - as umbrellas. And besides, kids won't come in the graveyard of a night when there are tramps in residence. They just won't. That means there is less casual damage and vandalism. So really, the down-and-outs are guard dogs for the church - free of charge.'

All the time the reverend spoke through a smile, so that Janek knew that he was being informed, not censured.

They only stopped talking about the local derelicts when the beautiful Clara and her mother arrived. The older woman lowered herself into a chair which sat very tightly about her hips. Petite little Clara stood sweetly by, looking like her mother's dinner. She was really very lovely. Her eyes were like summer sunshine: the irises broad whorls of caramel. Her hair seemed made out of the same stuff. Every facial bone was small but firm, like a beautiful gadget put together by a watch maker's sedulous hand. She was twenty-two.

Her figure was perfect, going in and out in all the right places. No doubt she thought her buttocks a shade too large in the way that women generally do, but Janek and the Reverend thought that they were just right, in the way that men generally do. And she had a little pearldrop necklace which dangled to just the right depth. There it nestled in bosomy softness.

Janek looked away and engaged the mother in conversation. She was called Dorothy. He did a lot of this, especially when the other men were around - particularly the spare parts guy and the three strapping fellows who filled their shirts so well. Then Clara couldn't walk two paces without them all offering her something, telling her a joke, helping her with her lines, or plain ogling her. At the same time her mother just became invisible. Janek had noticed this; and there was a lot of the woman to render invisible. So he took it upon himself to include her and draw her out from the sidelines, which of course made him rather a favourite with the pair of them not that he didn't ogle the daughter too when a quick opportunity presented itself.

He was asking the mother about tips for learning lines when the rest of the cast arrived.

'There's a load of bloody winos swigging cider down by the gravestones,' said Bill, the most strapping of the strapping lads. 'You want us to move 'em along for you vicar?' He indicated himself and his two friends.

'No that won't be necessary, thank you.'

'Well if you're sure. Personally, I think if you don't knock a few 'eads together early, like, you store up problems for yourself later on.'…Bill noticed that his two friends were already moving towards Clara. Immediately he stopped worrying about stored-up vagabond problems. 'Hello Clara,' he beamed.

Janek watched. These three guys had lighted on amateur dramatics as a way of meeting girls, he was sure of it.

Clara smiled coyly back and tossed her hair like a foal at a stile.

She had a job at the council sorting urgent letters from the two-weekers. 'Those to be filed and forgotten about for two weeks,' she explained.

Clara had opened her mouth, so a further surge of testosterone gathered around her – the retired history teacher, the motorcycle chappie, even Michael, the gay tailor, who although very happy with Gary, his handsome guy at home, still appreciated the beauty of the female form.

'Sometimes we don't even get round to answering them for three weeks,' she tittered.

Janek turned to speak to the vicar, but the man of God was moving Clara-ward too. Funny, he thought: if that girl was an ordinary, plain, little miss, she could giggle out the council's entire correspondence policy and no one would take even one step closer to her to listen. He couldn't see Clara anymore, for the press of men.

The two six formers had come in last. They had eyes only for one another and were talking quietly in a corner. The woman from the library couldn't make it - she had family problems: the reverend had received a message. Clara's mother sat solidly alone, still wearing the church hall chair tight around the hips. Janek turned to her. 'Like bees to honey,' he laughed, indicating the Clara-throng.

She nodded, 'It's the same everywhere, Janek. Even at the old folks' home when we visit her grandmother. There's some of the old boys there still got some life in them, I can tell you.'

'She's a lovely looking girl.'

Dorothy looked warmly at Janek. 'You're a gentleman though.'

'Maybe I just think the competition is too strong,' he joked.

'Would you believe I used to attract the same sort of attention?' simpered Dorothy from beneath a batted eyelid.

'Who could doubt it?' lied Janek.

Dorothy arched her neck flirtatiously. It was the only part of her which had not grown fat over the years. She touched Janek's hand with her left forefinger and clucked, 'Oh you.' She left her finger there a shade longer than necessary…Janek was saved when the vicar called the group to attention. He had not been doing so well in his attempts to gain the delicious Clara's attention. The three chunky chappies were scaffolders and they had been telling all sorts of stirring stories of steel poles crashing down on people and on cars and of hair's breadth escapes from roof tops. In comparison, God just did not register.

Between them they actually performed Act Two rather well. Tennessee Williams slips a lot of emotion into it and the group desire for Clara seemed to have whipped everyone up to the right kind of mood.

Janek's Big Daddy was better then ever. He had the lines off pat now, so his acting was not constrained in any way…

'CRAP,' he boomed… "When you are gone from here, boy, you are long gone and nowhere. The human machine is not no different from the animal machine or the fish machine or the bird machine or the reptile machine or the insect machine!..."

When they finished Janek was actually sweating; great big beads of the stuff. 'I must look an absolute state,' he said, wiping away sleevefuls.

'Good, honest sweat,' volunteered Bill. 'Nothing quite like it.' He clapped Janek on the back. It was a friendly swat, but Janek's flesh stung beneath the younger man's power. The scaffolder had those knobby muscles between neck and shoulder which are the real indicators of physical strength. 'Trapeziums', Janek thought they were called, or something like that. Big biceps had nothing on them for genuine brute force.

'Careful Bill,' said Dorothy, showing female care for Janek. 'You'll break him.'

Bill seemed to see Dorothy for the first time then replied, 'Naah. He's a tough old sausage aint cha, Jan?'

'I try my best,' Janek replied, 'and then when I turn up my pacemaker I try again!'

They all laughed at this, including Clara who was now leaning her shapely figure against her mother's acreage.

'Hey,' said Bill, wishing that she was leaning against him, 'Why don't we all go to the pub? Make a night of it like?'

His friends nodded vigorously.

'How about it preach?' he said, borrowing some of

the diction of their play. 'Does God allow you a drink on Fridays?'

The reverend snatched a sly peek at Clara...also his mind turned to the two sessions of Rhythmic Rascals he had in store over the weekend: surely a couple more hours drinking her in - as well as a little booze - was deserved, seeing as his penance was already so set in stone.

'Well I have been picking up cider cans from His hallowed ground all week, so I think that He might allow me a touch of the stuff myself.'

'Now ya talkin', grinned Bill. 'What about youse two?' he said, nodding at the pair of seventeen year olds who so desperately wanted to hold hands but were too shy to move the requisite inch closer. 'A bit of drink in ya, and you'll really admit what fings you wanna do to each uver.'

The two youngsters scuttled away quickly, shaking their heads and blushing, warming the evening air with their cheeks.

'That was a shitty thing to say,' said Janek, 'Even if it is true.'

'Oh dry up, Jan. I probably done 'em a world of good. They'll be snogging now, before they're even out of the church grounds.'

Janek shrugged. Dorothy nudged him along a little and he found himself outside the church hall, at the centre of a body of amateur Thespians heading for *The Seven Stars* in the high street. On their way they passed the young couple in a tight embrace and Bill's raucous mastiff of a laugh proclaimed to all that he had been right all along. 'Told ya,' he said, winking at Janek.

The pub was a lovely relic. There had not been a thing modernised in it since the 1860s, save the old gas lamps. There were snugs galore with little dividing screens between them. The doors serving each were barely four feet of the ground and the floor sloped off at haphazard angles. There were nicotine stains and cobwebs of admirable thickness. Two brothers had owned the place for years and both had lived well into their nineties. During that time they had loved the place as much as they had hated one another. So when the big breweries had arrived with enticing offers, one would agree terms only to be contradicted by the other. This went on for years while all the other drinking holes were bought up, knocked about and ripped apart in the name of modernity. So when the two old boys did finally die, within days of one another, the locals suddenly woke up to what a museum piece they had on their doorstep and persuaded the new freeholder to preserve it, as if in aspic.

Janek was first to open the door. Dorothy was right behind him - very close behind. All the others were four yards off pace, clustered around Clara. She was escorted inside via cavalcade.

It was Alex, the little motorcycle spares man, who seemed to be doing best with her. Certainly she was listening most attentively to what he had to say. He didn't have half the sinews of the scaffolders, but he did have one of those pretty little-boy faces. But little-boy faces do not decide where to sit, so the group ended up standing: Bill and his mates were men who stood at the bar and they expected everyone else to do the same. They did not ask if this was the general preference, just assumed that it would be. Also they bought the first round of drinks, which lent them an authority in addition to the breadth of their shoulders.

It was a good evening: Stewart, the retired history teacher was dry and witty, Dorothy was warm and friendly, The Reverend Tony Collier drank whisky and grew irreverent. Janek enjoyed their company, particularly Tony's: he had always preferred his religion through whisky fumes. Clara basked in the attention of the boys: she still seemed to rate Alex's company most highly, but did giggle at Bill's rough humour too. The lads were close about her.

The drinks flowed and time skipped past, so that when last orders were rung, all of them were shocked at how rapidly time had beaten its silent wings. Janek got in quickly with the group's order. He had bought a round already, at about nine-thirty, but was happy to dip into his wallet again.

When everyone had a drink, he turned to his own pint. It was a beautiful real ale, with a strong, frolicsome smell. And one could just about see through it. He held the glass up against the light, to appreciate the thick loveliness…

Janek slapped it down. Through the dark amber he had seen something disconcerting. He couldn't be sure - but he thought he'd seen Bill run a hand over Clara's arse. Stewart, the history teacher, was busy talking to him. Janek didn't hear a word. He was taking in the scene: the girl looked a little flushed, but Alex was jabbering on as if nothing had happened. Bill was talking to his friends, also as if nothing had happened.

He must have been mistaken – a distortion of light through the glass. He turned back to Stewart, leaving just one eye on the young set.

Then two minutes later it happened again. Unmistakably this time. And Alex noticed too - Bill reached down with his pint-free hand and caressed Clara's buttocks, clearly, expansively. She shook his hand free and shifted position, telling him timidly, embarrassedly, but definitely, to stop. He didn't.

Alex made a rush forward, but Bill's two friends blocked his way and manhandled him to one side. Dorothy shouted. Then the whole pub was watching: the three pushing and shoving, the beautiful but protesting girl, the huge man and his hands - both left and right fondling now, fingers tight on his little catch.

No one had their eyes on Janek. So although they heard a glass break they did not know whose it was or that it had been smashed deliberately. Bill was too drunk and too lustful to notice anything....until the point of a long shard was stuck just above his Adam's apple.

'Let her go,' bellowed Janek, easing the glass in a fraction. A little rill of blood trickled down the shard and collected in Janek's shirt cuff.

Bill let her go, eyes on his two friends. They returned the stare, trying to guess what he wanted done.

Janek read all this, 'Move, and I'll cut 'is throat out,' he spat. They froze.

Bill turned his eyes on the older man. They were cold and hard - little chips of gravel trying to weigh up whether the foreign bastard would ram the glass home or not.

'Not,' he determined...His fist caught Janek plumb in the right eye. It was a solid blow, but because

Bill had been twisting free of the glass at the same time, the punch lacked full force. Janek reeled back; the shard of glass spun out of his hand, cutting it. No one in the pub moved a muscle, except Bill who was coiling all of his for a full-blooded assault. He bulled forward.

Janek clutched at the counter, righting himself. He snatched up a bar stool which had been vacated by a frightened drinker. He turned and swung it - too late - a huge haymaker from Bill clubbed down upon his ear. Janek's nerves, along the line where jaw meets neck, sprang into a polka of searing pain. An inch higher and the night would have been all over.

The momentum of the blow and his own drunkenness staggered Bill. His friends dashed forward. 'No,' he shouted. 'The cunt's mine. I'm gonna splash 'is ugly nose the uver side of 'is face.'

Next to the pub's unimproved fireplace was a heavy iron poker, notched with age. Janek snatched it up with his right hand. With his left he jabbed the bar stool, trying to ward off the advancing Bill; he held it before him like a lion tamer, his knuckles white against the strain. He raised the sooty poker above his head and his shoulder trembled with determination.

Bill made a grab for the stool, 'You gonna brain me, Polack?'

The first poker blow hit his wrist. And gorilla though he was, Bill roared with pain at it. Janek followed with another and another, until the stronger, younger man was backing up…But only as far as the next bar stool, which he snatched up with his good arm. Quickly, massively, he swung it in great arcs, one handed - and beat down Janek's into a rubble of legs and shattered wood. All the time the older man slashed with the poker, but his blows were becoming weak with fatigue.

In the end, age and weight prevailed: a huge blow bore Janek to the floor and he landed with his makeshift sword beneath him. Bill loomed over his head, raised the stool high, and steadied himself to bring it seat-edge crashing down.

Just then a police siren blared.

Bill's corded muscles tensed.

Then there came an answering siren.

Suddenly the silent crowd became loud: they jeered the younger man, jostled his friends, closed about Bill a little, snatched up their own stools. And from behind the bar, the landlord stepped, with a rottweiler on a short chain and a rounders bat in his fat hand.

'See Jan,' sneered Bill, 'They're brave now. But where was they when it was just you and me, huh?' He set the stool down, ugly in his adrenaline. 'You're a tough old bastard. I'll give ya that.'

Janek raised himself groggily up. And Bill sleeved the blood from his cut neck. He stared at it, then turned to Clara: 'Sorry love, you shouldn't be so bloody gorgeous. Couldn't help me self.' The next second he and his two friends were gone, split second, out of the saloon bar door.

The pub exploded into noise. Everyone was animated, although Janek could see this out of only one eye. He felt his blood run a slightly more common pace. The drama group gathered about him. One of them thrust a drink at him. But it was a wet nose his palm closed against. Then a growl. He snatched his fingers away. It was the pub rottweiler.

'You're fuckin' barred,' snarled the landlord. If I see you 'ere again, I'll have the dog take yer fuckin' leg off.'

The Reverend Collier drew himself up, cocked his chin to one side in order that clear inches of dog collar be exposed, 'Now look here, my man,' he said…

'I ain't no one's man. I 'appen to own this place. And you're barred too.'

The police forced their way through the crowd. They had seen the dog and had seen the rounders bat and had seen Janek's thick ear and a thick eye.

'Everyone back away from each other, now,' said a chunky sergeant. 'Drop the bat, John.' The policeman looked at the dog. 'Drop him too,' insisted the police sergeant.

John, the landlord, thrust the Rottie behind the bar. 'The guy who done all this is gone,' John snapped.

'That true?' two of the other policemen asked Janek.

Janek nodded.

'Do you know his name?'

Janek shook his head.

'What does he look like?'

Janek shrugged, 'Pretty average.'

'I'll tell you what he looks like: like a great, fucking ugly ape, that's what, and I know his name,' shrilled Dorothy.

Janek took Dorothy's hand in his and drew her a half-step to him, silencing her. 'We've sorted the matter out. We won't be needing you, officer. Thank you,' he said.

'You sure? We could get a couple of cars after him.'

'There is no need.'

'Madam?' one of the policemen persisted with Dorothy.

Janek stared hard at her through his one good eye.

'There is no need,' she trotted out.

'Come on boys,' snapped the sergeant. 'Pub brawls is always a waste of time. Always the same - no one knows nothing, no one's seen nothing.' And as they left they cleared everyone out, regardless of drinks half drunk.

After a fair deal of twittering and cooing around Janek, the drama set split up. Alex and the history teacher took Dorothy and Clara to secure a taxi home. The vicar, Tony, stayed with Janek who refused to do anything but walk back home.

'But what if Bill and his mates are heading the same way?'

'It won't matter.'

'Of course it will. They might kill you.'

'Bill's not the type. Once a fight's over, it's over. I saw that in his eyes when he last spoke. Believe me, I know the type.'

'Then what about the other two? They were sly hangers-on...would stick you between the ribs as soon as say hello.'

'They're nothing without Bill. I know that type too...I'm not doing anything but walking and that's that,' replied Janek. 'Thanks for the evening,' he added, striding out.

Tony stood still for a moment, looking pained. He ran a nervous finger round the slack of his dog collar.

Janek was fast disappearing into the gloom. He slipped one last, envious look back at the taxi rank then called out, 'Hey! You! Janek! Wait up a minute. I'm coming with you.'

Janek turned and waited.

'I never do anything but walk, if the distance is less than three miles. Never,' he explained to Tony.

'I still think you might have made an exception tonight. Have you thought that they might follow you home? Find out where you live?'

'I told you, the whole thing is over.'

With every step taken, Tony's idea of a taxi ride withered, until it ceased to be even a remote persuadable possibility. Then he gave himself up totally to starting at shadows, jumping at noises, and rereading in his mind's eye, newspaper accounts of hospitalised innocents, set upon at midnight. He looked at his watch - it was midnight.

CHAPTER 4

'Do you do that sort of thing often?' Tony, the vicar, asked, his fear making him more direct than usual.

'Fight, you mean?' replied Janek, walking at an easy pace. 'It's funny...I've actually fought twice this week. But before Wednesday, I hadn't fought in years – decades in fact. Maybe it's something in the air.'

Tony nodded. 'Did you see what that Bill fellow was up to straight away?'

'Actually, I wasn't sure at first. And Clara's such a sweet little thing I couldn't tell from her reaction. When I was sure, and when he wouldn't stop, I saw red.'

'That business with the glass though, where did that come from?'

'I don't know. It certainly wasn't planned. I guess it came from the fact that he was so much bigger and younger and stronger than me.'

'And it was why you didn't tell the police anything?'

'I cut him didn't I?'

'You did,' Tony nodded.

'Mmm, I think the police would have been more interested in that than anything else. Naturally Dorothy couldn't see beyond the fact that I had protected her daughter, which was why she was up for gabbing all to that police officer. But the odds are she would have got me on a charge, not Bill.'

'It was a brave thing you did.'

'It was just the moment. A different time I might have done nothing.'

'I don't believe that. Not you.'

Janek didn't reply. He was lost for a minute in the events of the night - or some other time.

When they turned up Orchard Road it was nearly half past twelve. Years ago, when Janek had first moved in to number 33, there would have been bats flying about at this hour, and owls too, very occasionally. He started talking once more, telling Tony how different the night sky had been back in those days: 'I came from a tiny little box in Beckton and it was like moving to the countryside coming here. The bats reminded me of back home in Poland – we used to have them in our barn. The cat would bring them in sometimes and my mother would tear after them with a broom. The cat too. But it never learned; still brought the bats in.' Janek was trying the key in his front door. 'It died in the end, falling off the barn roof trying to catch them. So much for cats always landing on their feet.' Janek stepped inside the hall and immediately a large Abyssinian tomcat leapt for his chest, certain of being caught and embraced. 'That's why I keep a cat now. Reminds me of the old times, when my parents were still alive. I had four once, but it's just me and Oskar now.'

Tony stood on the doorstep, smiling, his dog collar reflecting the porch light. Any casual observer would have thought him collecting for the church bazaar.

'I know it's late, but would you like a coffee, before you head off home?' invited Janek.

'No, no, thank you. It's a bit of a walk.'

'Then I'll give you a lift. Which way do you go?' asked Janek.

'Back up by the church.'

'What!' gasped Janek, easing down the purring Oskar, 'We passed the church twenty minutes ago!'

Tony smiled weakly and shrugged.

'Did you come all this way to see me safely home - you - in your dog collar, to protect me from being attacked by Bill and his mates?'

Tony nodded. 'Not that I would have been much use. More of a hindrance probably. You'd most likely have ended up protecting me,' blushed Tony.

Janek smiled - a beam of genuine respect. 'About that coffee,' he said, 'I won't take no for an answer. Or the lift.'

'Are you sure?'

'The fight sobered me up. So did the night air. I'll fix us up some coffee and cake, and afterwards, drive you back.'

'If you're sure...I was all set to walk you know.'

'I know you were. That's why I'm about to break out my best coffee and the last of my cake in honour of you,' Janek replied. He clapped the clergyman on the shoulder and switched on a light. From the corner of the hall the mangy hyaena stared malevolently at Tony. The artificial light flashed off its glass eyes. Tony edged behind his host, laying a timid hand on his arm.

'Spotted hyena. Careful, he doesn't like strangers,' laughed Janek. Then added, 'He's stuffed.'

'I thought he was real for a moment,' replied

Tony, embarrassed. 'One doesn't see them, not even in zoos.'

'There was a big private school I was caretaker of when I first arrived in this country…and back way before my time, in the last century, when their bright young things graduated, they were often sent abroad to carve out their fortunes from the far-flung Empire. And some of them sent back what they shot on hunting expeditions. The school took to stuffing and mounting them. Then times changed, or they needed the space - something like that - and the animals were just hauled into a skip. The lot of them. This fella,' said Janek, stroking the hyena's broad head, 'was one of the last chucked out, so I nabbed him.'

Tony ran a hand over the creature's pelt too. 'It's coarse like wire,' he exclaimed.

'Well you wouldn't expect one of these fellows to be velvety soft, would you?'

'I suppose not.'

'People think they're just scavengers, but actually they're very active predators of livestock. They attack people too, given the chance. In Africa they are hated. In rural areas the tribesmen believe that witches ride them at night. Really believe that,' stressed Janek, 'And they won't shoot them or spear them, for fear that the witches will seek vengeance for the deaths of their steeds. Crazy, huh?'

Tony nodded and Janek led him into the kitchen where he set the kettle going. Toast too.

'But in my old country, Poland, we used to have some pretty strange beliefs ourselves…Once at my great grandparents' house - so I was told - a curious sort of wagon pulled up. It was drawn by two skeletal horses, thinner than hunger itself, with their forelegs shackled together. On the top of the wagon sat a woman smoking a big black pipe; and around it four children were playing, all grubby, but full of the joys of life. My great-grandfather, being a sociable man, and generous too, hailed them and offered them a meal, much to his wife's annoyance, who thought them dirty, suspicious folk. It was always said in the village that my great-grandfather would have anyone for dinner, but it was his wife who had to do the extra cooking and cleaning. Anyway, there was one child among them he took a shine to - a fellow of nine or ten with eyes as darkly mischievous as any fox cub's - and when he was given a bowl of soup he lapped it up as a fox cub would too! Well my great-grandfather hooted with laughter at this and showed this lad round the farm, after the meal, so I was told. And the boy would not leave our plough-horses alone; stroking them and patting them and plaiting their manes and cooing their names at them.'

Tony took his tea, toast and cake, but remained listening, rapt.

'Well, so good had this lad been with the horses that my great-grandfather offered the family to stay. He felt sorry for the woman with no man to help her bring up her children and there was easily enough space for them in the farm's back fields. And more than that, he needed a good stable boy to tend his horses. Everyone seemed happy with the set up, apart from my great-grandmother, who disagreed with it from the start.'

Tony laughed, trying to figure out where this story was heading.

'But strange things started to happen as soon as that little lad set to work in the stables - my great-grandfather could not fault him on his care of the horses...certainly he tended them like brothers, but there was also no doubt that they were sickening for something. Every day the beasts got weaker, so much so that soon they were no good for ploughing, no good for riding; no good for anything, but looking weak and jaded. For weeks this went on. And the woman and her children did all the odd jobs around the place, so the farm bumbled along even though the horses were off colour. Then one of the animals died, and my great-grandfather was as upset as he was perplexed, and he determined to get to the bottom of the business. From that day on he watched over those horses unstintingly, but not once did he see anything but that dark-eyed little lad caring for them and caring for them and caring for them.

Then looking out of his bedroom window late one night, because the mystery of it all would not let him sleep, he heard a strange growling and snuffling coming from the stables. It was first light of the early hours, so he snatched up his hunting rifle and ran down the stairs. Outside he was stealthy though, so as not to give warning to whatever was in his barn.'

Tony was as wide-eyed as a child.

'And when he threw those barn doors open, a sight was revealed to him which set him to emptying that old rifle, bullet by bullet. For attached to the neck of each horse was a wolf: two dirty great big ones and four gangly pups. And they all had blood oozing thickly down their muzzles and necks. They were milking the horses' jugulars. Well, two of the wolves my great-grandfather shot dead right away, another he hit in the foreleg, so that it snarled awfully and led the escape away, still vermin-fast, even on three legs. It and the three others streaked out of the barn window like they were ablaze and my great-grandfather ducked after them. With his last bullet he brought down the other adult and then watched the rest of the family disappear in the long grass of his fallow fields. Well, without reloading he gave chase, scared for the family camped in their wagon at the bottom of his fields. It was hard, rutted land to cover in the half-light, but he was a good man and knew that he must warn his workers.'

Janek drained his cup before continuing.

A story-teller's skill, thought Tony - to increase the suspense.

'Imagine his surprise then, when that old wagon came clattering towards him at top speed, pulled by the same two horses which had first brought it to a stop outside his house - except my great-grandfather noticed that they were now much fatter and fitter than before. And driving them, straight at him, was a grown man he had never seen before, but who had - definitely had - those same feral eyes as the boy he had taken on to look after his horses. And as they galloped closer he could see for sure, even by the weak morning light, that the man had to be the boy's father. Had to be, by the set of him. And what was more, his left arm lay crazily on his lap, broken and bloodied.

It was only by jumping at the last moment that my great-grandfather saved himself - and then the wagon was gone.

But it was the next morning the mystery really

deepened, because in the dew of his west field lay the mother who had dined with them on that first night, the one who had arrived smoking her pipe. She was quite dead, shot through the heart. And two of her little ones were found dead in the barn too - one of them the boy who had shown such an interest in the horses and had worked so tirelessly with them.

My great-grandmother showed my great-grandfather no sympathy. She told him he should have listened to her from the start and never taken vagabonds in. She set him to burying the corpses under the barn floor and then to keeping his mouth shut.'

Tony clapped appreciatively. He loved yarns and folk tales. 'The old man told someone though. He told you, or he told his own kids.'

'No. He didn't ever tell a living soul. That was my great-grandmother. Why else do you think she comes across whiter than white and so bloody right about everything?'

'She told the story?'

'Oh yes. And the whole village believed it. I was told it by my mother the day I broke into the forbidden barn.'

Tony lost his smile.

'Oh yes,' nodded Janek, 'it was all boarded up and its window was bricked up too. But I found a way in under the eaves. And when I started to dig with my spade – I had it in my little boy's head that there was Russian treasure buried under the floor - I found a bone. A long one and took it in to show my mother. Didn't tell her where I found it. But she knew.'

Tony sat back, arms folded. 'A human bone?'

'That's right. A femur.'

'You don't honestly expect me to believe that.'

'What? About the werewolves or the bone?'

'Well, both.'

'Oh the bone bit's true. I can remember levering it out of the soil. As for the werewolves, all I'm saying is that the village believed it.'

Tony coughed on his cake - didn't stop for a whole minute. Then just as Janek was about to fix him a drink of water and a slap on the back, he stopped, and set his watering eyes on the story-teller. 'What was the point of that story?'

Janek gave a little shrug, 'To show that it's not just Africans who believe wacky things, I suppose.'

Tony was red in the face, and not just with coughing.

'Come, I am sorry,' said Janek softly. 'I have angered you - at least disturbed you - and that is not what I intended, certainly not after you saw me home so selflessly.'

But Tony was not to be put off: 'So what do you believe? Actually believe happened?'

Janek prodded at his bad eye which was beginning to purple up. 'Believe to be the truth?' you mean.

'Yes,' the clergyman demanded.

Janek sat down opposite his man and Oskar, the old tomcat, seized the opportunity to settle himself onto a comfortable lap. 'You see,' he said, massaging the cat's ear, 'Poland was a country riven with lots of ethnic tensions and jealousies. It's calmed down rather now, but in my great-grandparents' time those divisions were as old and as rigid as the ones between - well - between cats and dogs.' Janek tried Oskar's other ear. 'And the gypsies - for that's what the wandering family were - were not well liked; hated by many, actually. But my great-grandfather always had time for them. As a young man he used to visit them when they came to the area - sometimes even enjoyed a roast hedgehog with them at their camp sites. The gypsies would plaster the animal with clay and then roast it in the embers of a fire. After an hour they'd take out the ball, break open the clay, and the spines would peel away with the clay, leaving only the succulent roast within. He thought it delicious. Sometimes he bothered my great-grandmother to make it for him - actually fetched her hedgehogs from under the bramble patch - but always she refused. I was alive in the last few years of their lives and I actually remember him asking her. But as for visiting the gypsies, that I only heard about. He stopped doing that long before my time, so I was told.'

'But what about all the incredible stuff? Werewolves and all that?'

'How long have you been a clergyman, Tony?'

'Eleven years.'

'And always here, in this country?'

'Yes.'

'It's a good place, this country. And these are good times. Ninety-nine per cent of the people who ever lived on this planet have not been so lucky as us. You can be an individual here. There's barely anyone I've met on this lucky little island knows how important that is. That's because it has been a thousand years since anyone arrived on your shores and took your individuality away - by force. Poland's never been so lucky. It is a nation of would-be individuals, because there has always been someone or some creed ready to assert a more aggressive individuality over the country.'

Tony nodded.

'My great-grandfather demonstrated his individuality by befriending the gypsies everyone else in the village hated, including his own wife.'

Tony nodded again and Janek exhaled hard before continuing. 'Now if you are asking me whether I believe that there was ever a family of werewolves on my family farm back home, I would say, categorically, no: men do not change into wolves and nor do their children. But if you put me on the spot and ask me what I really think happened back in 1847, or whenever it was, then I think something did happen, and that it was far worse than any blood-sucking shape-changers.'

It was one-thirty, but The Reverend Collier had no regard for the time. His eyes were hard on Janek, eager for more.

'It was the understanding in my great-grandparents' day - I wouldn't go as far as to call it a law - that the travelling people were allowed to stay only three days in any one place before they had to move on. During that time they could not be troubled or harassed in any way. Then if no one in the area offered them permanent refuge in those seventy-two hours they had to move on - or else - their little window of protection expired, as it were.

Now little rural villages can be intolerant places and I think my great-grandfather stretched the tolerance of his village by extending an invitation to his gypsies way in excess of the usual seventy-two hours. And I suspect, too, that some of his warmth towards the gypsies stemmed from the fact that he had a little of their blood in him. I don't know that for sure, but I think it probable, particularly after the beating my mother dealt me when I once suggested it to her. I don't think she would have struck me so hard or quite so many times if there had been no truth in my innocent words. So, adding two and two, I can imagine that my great-grandfather might have been given an ultimatum by the village community to decide which he was: honest, decent citizen of the hamlet, or dirty gyppo. And the ultimatum was backed by a threat. Now whether he then took the law into his own hands and forced those travellers along to protect his family and property and standing in the village, or whether a band of men from the village came and did the job for him, I don't know, but I think that people died before the matter was resolved, and that they were buried in my family's barn. And afterwards it suited everyone to remember the victims as supernatural demons who got what they deserved, rather than people, which would have meant facing uncomfortable truths and guilts…' Janek looked at the dog-collared vicar, '…So you see, the Devil was at work on my great-grandparents' farm whichever way you look at it.'

'Are you sure that those bones you pulled out of the barn were human?'

'It was just one bone. And I'm quite sure. Human bones are not that rare in Poland's troubled soil. And anyway, I saw hundreds in the war against which to compare my barn relic. It was human alright.'

Tony was silent for a moment. He looked up at the old man before him with his damaged eye and swollen ear. And he stared at his hands, now wrapped around cake, but which were capable of wielding shards of glass or cradling the cold bones of barn-murdered undesirables.

'Did you see a lot of killing in the war, Janek?'

'Oh yes. It became routine in the end. Fighting in the Resistance was not clean work, often not very moral either, truth be told.'

'But you were fighting for freedom - that individuality you spoke of.'

'Mmm. But what we got was the Soviets.'

'But you weren't to know that, when you were resisting the Nazis.'

'True. But resistance work is not clean. Sometimes I even tell people that I fought on the Western Front, in uniform, for you Brits, rather than admitting the truth. In fact, it's only because I'm still a bit drunk that I am telling you now. I told a young lad today too, but he doesn't count - he's too young to condemn me. See?'

'No I don't bloody well see. Fighting in the resistance was heroic.'

'Wasn't it just!' spat Janek with a passion which scared Tony. 'Shooting men who have turned collaborator just because they want a few extra chickens to feed their starving families, or a guarantee from the local peaked cap that their daughters will not be molested. Or garrotting German teenagers, not yet old enough to shave, just for the army-issue lugers hung on their flab-free waists. There were hundreds of dirty murders like that for every Nazi officer we ever picked off. It's only liars - those who were really fighting on the other side - say with pride that they were in The Resistance. The real ones, like me, just cry for the poor bastards they killed, as well as the friends they lost.'

The Reverend Tony Collier was silent as the shallow graves he was imagining. Outside, a mating fox screamed.

'Foxes,' Janek said, turning to his guest. He noticed the pallid face of the clergyman and his dry lips. Janek stepped closer to him, 'I'm sorry. I have ruined the mood of our evening. After the glow of drink - when it starts to recede from my system - then I get rather too emotional and too truthful than is proper. You must forgive me.'

'It is forgiveness I was thinking on,' replied Tony. 'But not mine…it was yours actually, for yourself. And God's forgiveness too, perhaps. Tell me Janek, have you ever considered coming to church on Sundays?'

'Yes. I've considered it.'

'But you have not ended up attending?'

'No.'

'May I ask why? I think it would do you good, if I may say so.'

'At your church?'

'Any church. But mine is always open to you. I think you need God more than you realise.'

'You may well be right, but perhaps I am not yet so old as to fear Him enough to turn up.'

'That is quite a thing to say before a priest.'

'As you must have gathered by now, I am only dealing in truth tonight.'

'Truth then, Janek - why so irreligious? Help me to understand.'

'Ok, Father, seeing as you bring it up. Answer me this. A priest once told me that the worst sin of all is to know the love of God and then to turn away from it. He assured me, that a clergyman who lost his faith and believed no more, was the only sinner absolutely guaranteed to burn in hell. Was he right?'

'Well...'

'No 'well'...and don't umm-de-arr me either. True or not, Tony?'

'Depends on whether he returns to God or not, Janek'

'Before his death, you mean?'

'That's right Janek,' replied Tony.

'But a man who lived a really evil life but who died repentant would be welcomed into the kingdom of heaven? Even if his deeds were heinous and ninety-nine per cent of his life defined by them?'

'He might be.'

'Might?'

'That's right, might. It depends.'

'Depends, eh? Alright then, Tony. Let's be specific. Say that tonight Bill and his chums were all alone with our lovely little Clara and things got out of hand. And fight and protest though she valiantly did, they ended up raping her, then murdering her to hide the fact of what they'd done. You follow?'

Tony nodded.

'Now imagine that you, a priest loses his faith. Say you become so pissed off with the famine in the world and all the brutalities and all the murders and all the rapes of this sorry little planet and can no longer bring yourself to believe in your benign God anymore. But you still work for good in your community, because you are a good man. And like tonight you walk home silly old sods who fight in pubs even though you're shitting yourself with fear. And you still turn up to Rhythmic bloody Rascals every weekend because you wish to support the young of your town - don't tell me that you enjoy it, because I see in your face you don't whenever I pass by of a Saturday.'

'Janek, I hate it. With a passion.'

'There you are then - you are a selfless man with an eye for the greater good, no matter how much your concern for others may pain you, or even endanger you. Essentially you are a good man. And let us just say that you lost your faith as I have described, but still carried on doing those things…Then you would remain a good man nonetheless. Agreed?'

'Yes, I would remain a good man.'

'Now just say for the sake of argument that Bill and his mates live selfishly all their lives: that the rape-murder of Clara was neither the first nor the last awful crime they commit. But they are lucky and the law never catches up with them. Then, all of a sudden, on their deathbeds they repent their sins and request God's forgiveness. Now according to Christian belief, they will be admitted to heaven, but you will not, for all your goodness is nullified by your rejection of God's grace, whereas their evil is expunged by a last minute prayer which benefits no one but themselves. And they may or may not meet Clara again at God's right hand, depending on what state her spotted soul was in when they murdered her. Now, have I got my Christian teachings right?'

'It is indeed a heinous sin to know the love of God and then willingly renounce it.'

'Please! Was I right, in essence?'

'It would have to be a very sincere repentance for

Bill and his friends to enter the kingdom of heaven.'

'But it could happen, the way I described it? A good man could be denied heaven in those circumstances and the murderers could be admitted?'

'Yes.'

'You are sure?'

'Quite sure, Janek.'

'Thank you. Then you need never again ask why I do not grace your congregation. I carry very great guilts within me, it is true, but it is not lunacy will help me come to terms with them.'

'But listen my friend…'

'Please, that is enough,' interrupted Janek. 'I have been far too serious for far too long…Please.' He searched about for a change of subject…'Here, look at this cat. He is upside down in my arms. I have his two hind feet and tail in one hand and I am stroking his banana-ish stomach with the other. And he is purring like an old tractor engine. Look and listen: I think that a good cat is more a musical instrument than a pet. A man must learn to play it with skill and love and sensitivity. Every cat I have ever had has trusted me like this. Here, have a go.'

Janek placed the throbbing ball in the vicar's arms and the clergyman tried his fingers along the cat's stomach.

'See,' Janek exclaimed triumphantly. 'None of this stupid scratchy business you get with cats which are kept merely as pets, not as musical instruments.'

Tony was impressed, but not enough to give up on his lone sheep in the wilderness…'Are you sure Janek? Sure that you have nothing you wish to unload? To get off your chest?'

'Confess, you mean?'

'If you like.'

'Only my love of cats.'

And the two men laughed as the old grandfather clock in the hall chimed two o' clock and they were laughing at something else when it did the same at three.

But when Janek returned after dropping Tony off home he was not laughing. When he came back through his door there were tears on his face. The events of the night, and the conversations of the night, had repeated on him, and now they were weighing heavily. Also Renault woman was still outside, for she had fallen asleep in her car. And Janek had seen in her face, lines beyond the usual ones of tiredness and age; lines that only measureless sorrow can etch, and seeing them had prompted him to trawl the darkest recesses of his own sorrows and past and conscience.

And so Janek went to his little secret place.

Only very rarely did he dare.

In the hall-cupboard under the stairs, hidden within a fake utilities meter, was a small safe of his own construction. There was even a miniature dial set in its face, which actually spun, powered by battery. It had been a breeze for him to make - a man who had constructed precision bombs in the 1940s to lay under lorries and bridges and railway lines.

Now he eased the twin lock system open and the front half of the meter pivoted free. A tiny light clicked on. Inside was a drawstring bag, made of silk and also a chamois-leather envelope. He reached for the latter, upsetting the little bag as he did so. Out of it tumbled half a dozen diamonds, each a few carats in size and brilliant in lustre. Janek ignored them and with a quivering hand, took up the chamois-leather envelope. By the time he had lifted it to face-level, both his hands were shaking as if afflicted by degenerative disease. He struggled against his physical distress to lift the soft leather lid. Trembling fingers fumbled the contents which slipped to the floor.

A single photograph lay on the hall carpet, identical in style to the one hanging in his garden office, but much smaller. The image had the same deep eyes too. They stared back at Janek as he looked down at the picture. Through tears he saw the same haunting beauty he always did when courageous enough to open the little envelope. The picture was of a girl in middle or late teenage, strikingly lovely in her first bloom of womanhood. Her face was a perfect oval, wonderfully defined in the black-and-white of the photograph. One of Janek's tears splashed heavily on to it and he snatched the picture up as if it were under threat from acid. Hands still shaking, he slid the precious object back inside its chamois cover and laid it back within the safe tray. The diamonds were still half in their bag, half out of it.

'I will,' said Janek, 'One last time…I must.' And he reached in for the gemstones. Six had spilled out, but the bag was lumpy with more. His hand traced their sharp outlines, then he snatched up one of the free ones: big, cut into hundreds of perfect facets, and aggressively ablaze with its own radiance.

'This one,' he said to himself, 'One last time.'

Then Janek locked the little 'meter' once again and quickly turned the key on its strange contents. He slammed the understairs door to and slid down, back against it, sobbing.

CHAPTER 5

Janek didn't bother with the tube. It was a clement day and he felt that the stroll from Charing Cross to Hatton Garden would steel him for the bargaining ahead. The diamond was inside a tobacco tin, wrapped in cotton wool. He had kept his hand clamped around the little container all the way from No.33 and the sweat was beginning to ooze between his fingers. The heel of his palm was cramping a little too.

He knew the name of the jeweller's he wanted: *Oschner's*. Last time, old man Oschner had given him £8000 for a single diamond - after haggling. That was some years back, though, and Janek had not followed diamond prices in the intervening years. His amateur calculations thought twenty grand would be about right now. Whatever, the old man had told him to return if ever he had any more to sell.

He found the establishment after only one wrong turn.

Janek stood in the doorway, waiting for the man within to do his sizing up-security thing. He could almost hear the fellow sorting him: sixty-something, white, member of the hat-wearing classes, grotty coat which had been expensive once, one educated looking eye…one blackened eye!

It was the black eye which caused the pause. Janek

knew that. It was a beauty: puffily purple.

The door buzzed and a single index finger beckoned him to enter.

'Good afternoon,' said the young man, immaculate in a cravat and bespoke suit.

'Good morning,' replied Janek, starting badly: it was ten past one.

The man smirked at his eye. 'What can I do for you, sir?'

'I'd like to see Mr Herzog Oschner please.'

'I'm sorry, sir, but that won't be possible. Mr Oschner died five years ago.'

Janek had not expected this.

'Oh. I'm sorry. It is many years since I was here last. He purchased a diamond from me once and now I wish to sell another.'

The young man smiled. 'You could show me, sir.'

Janek was reticent. In his mind he was so set to do business with the beetling-browed old proprietor, it seemed wrong to be starting in with someone else. And someone so young. Slowly he eased the lid off the 'Old Virginia' tin. The man opposite him raised a Jeeves-like eyebrow at the unconventional packaging…The brow was deflated as soon as the eye beneath it beheld the diamond-proper. It illuminated the counter between them as midday sun does the clear mountain torrent.

'Mr Oschner, sir! You'd better come out and see this, sir,' quavered the young fellow, who was fumbling his cravat in an unconscious little imitation of Oliver Hardy. A ruddy-faced man of early middle age appeared almost immediately. Janek saw in his face the lines of the dead Oschner: strong chin, little hammocks beneath the eyes, just beginning to bag-up.

The new arrival took in Janek's damaged eye - and thought for one second that that was what his employee had called him to see. Anticipating trouble he judged the distance between himself and the emergency buzzer. Then he saw the diamond on the counter. Its effulgence trumped completely the lividity of Janek's bruise. At once Janek became a most valued patron. Oschner Junior's face twitched visibly, as a pointing hound's might at its first partridge of the season.

'Herzog Oschner used to buy diamonds from me - quite a few years ago. I was wondering whether my stones were still of sufficient quality to interest you?' said Janek, sensing his advantage.

'I am his son, Albert Oschner.'

'And I am Janek Lipsz.'

'May I?' asked Albert, tilting his head respectfully at the stone.

'Of course.'

Albert took the diamond up in one gentle hand and pored over it. Then, carefully, he set a jeweller's glass to his right eye. For three silent minutes he examined the stone's every facet. Its radiance leapt ferociously off the eyepiece.

He set down both glass and diamond.

'It is a splendid stone.'

Internally Janek heaved a sigh of relief. Albert appeared to have inherited his father's honesty as well as his face.

'I will give twenty-five thousand for it…Thirty if you can come here with more stones of the same quality.'

Janek tried not to let his excited surprise show in his good eye; he fixed Albert Oschner with the technicolour one instead. 'I do have others; but I will not be bound. The diamond is worth thirty thousand whatever I choose to do with the rest.'

Albert let his tongue run a full circle round his gums. It was an ugly little effect. Janek felt sure that he had not picked up the trick from his father.

'I can get you a banker's draft by five o' clock - for thirty thousand pounds. Call back then.'

'I will,' replied Janek and tucked the diamond back into its little carrying case. He resettled his hand around the tin. The door buzzed him out and he was back walking the London streets once more.

Inside *Oschner's*, Albert was lecturing his young employee: 'That was a diamond! Only once before have I seen one to match it. It will make a magnificent ring. But Peter, if anyone ever comes to the door with an eye like that again, do not let him in - that man excepted.'

'Yes Mr Oschner.'

'And now I must go to *Coutts* at once and get that banker's draft. You will watch the shop.'

'Yes Mr Oschner.'

The proprietor turned for his coat.

'Mr Oschner, are we going to check the stone's provenance? Might it have a bad history?'

'Peter, stones like that always have a bad history; usually from the day they are pulled out of the ground. It is best not to ask questions. Ask them only of little old ladies with little old diamonds, otherwise, pay a fair price and keep your mouth shut.'

'Yes sir.'

A minute later Mr Oschner was buzzed out too and the place was left to Peter and his cravat. For a while he swanked up and down the counter pretending that the shop was his then he sat himself down with an unimproving magazine.

Janek decided to walk up to The British Museum. He had a few hours to kill and the place had always filled him with awe. There was an Aztecs exhibition on. Janek took his time, lingered over the glass cases. He marvelled at the obsidian daggers and the jewellery of a turquoise which seemed too rich to have been fashioned by mortal hands. In another gallery, The Native American clothes were as intricately perfect as he remembered them. And the golden oldie, The Egyptian Room, still had in it the wonderfully preserved man with his russet hair, the mummified cats, and the model boats pulling their funereal cargoes to the next world.

Janek loved his history old. There were no fewer atrocities back there, but they were softened by the distance of time, so he could not see his fellow man reflected in them quite so clearly - or himself.

The museum corridors were wide and airy. The summer light muscled its way into the big spaces. Down corridors there were little brown doors with 'private' etched on them. Janek wondered what would happen if he barged through one of them and set his diamond down on the table before some old beak with white hair. Would the man call for security to bundle him out? Would he direct Janek to the Hatton Garden jewellers? Or would he offer Janek more than thirty thousand pounds for the stone? Probably he would offer him less.

He came to a door which was not marked 'Private'. It was the museum café. Along with the Egyptian Rooms and the Native American artefacts, The Lemon Cheesecake was another of the perennial wonders of the place. Janek snuggled down with a right-angled wedge and a dark coffee. In the chair beside him someone had left the day's *Times* newspaper: *Monday 30th July 1976*.

Between mouthfuls of cheesecake he skim-read the headlines: it was the advertisements he was after. There on page 13 was the issue's first whole page ad. It was a charitable appeal, for famine relief in Africa. There was a picture of a pitiful little lad with a grotesquely extended stomach and pipe cleaner legs, along with an address to send donations to.

Janek took in the size of the thing - it was like a poster - and nodded. Earlier in the day he had rung *The Times* and enquired about rates for an even bigger, double spread ad. He had explained that he was an old customer: back in the sixties he had commissioned the same. It had cost six thousand pounds then. He was told that such coverage now cost twenty.

Twenty thousand; that was the same price as a house.

Janek had decided to try the newspaper method once more. He would get a quality reproduction done of the photograph in his garden office - Joseph as a boy - and one of the artist's impressions of what Joseph, the man, would look like now. Then he would have the newspaper run a double page print of them both: a huge missing person appeal. There would be his phone number to ring if anyone had sighted him, there would be his address in Orchard Road to contact too. And the wonderful thing about *The Times* was that it was an international publication with a cross-continental readership. He knew that there were hazards. For starters there would be the huge volume of responses, most of them crappy, some of them from nutters who simply craved attention. Then there would be the hoaxers just after a bit of money. Other responses would be genuine and he would have to travel to check them out; probably to many different countries.

This had happened the last time and it had all come to nothing. But that fight in *The Seven Stars* had shaken up more than just Janek's right eye and he wanted to try again. Relying on escapee derelicts to keep an eagle-eye out was such a long shot: a million to one they would be far too busy watching their own backs, dodging the glare of private dicks and creditors, to notice much, even if Joseph passed within an inch of them.

The diamond was going to pay for the appeal. When the old Mr. Oschner had been alive, he had done exactly the same – cashed in one of the gemstones to pay for a double page spread. The attempt was worth the money. The cause was worth every penny.

Janek Lipsz was wonderfully happy, for the first time in a long while, because in his mind he imagined success. He imagined travelling to Caracas, or Arizona, or Singapore, or Cordoba, or New York, and actually finding the boy for whom he had been searching so long. Not a boy any more, but a man, and actually seeing him again - with his own eyes…

…Janek was smiling. It did not mean that he would be at rest, for that would not be the end, nor even the beginning of the end, but maybe it would be the end of the beginning. Janek stopped quoting Churchill to himself and then grew scared for he knew that Fate does not like the plans of desperate men, and there in the museum café he tried to pretend to Fate that he did not care whether the newspaper appeal was successful or not…

…But Fate would know because no man spends the price of a new house on something he does not care about, so Janek stopped feeling happy, and began to fret instead. He bit seven of his nails down, nibbled furiously at the skin of his cheeks.

The newspaper man had said that he could have a preview copy by the following Saturday, with the real print run scheduled for the Saturday after. That was in less than two weeks' time. Janek had to wire them the payment by the coming Thursday before anything could be officially sanctioned. He tore at another nail, hoping against hope that this new Oschner fellow would be as good as his word.

He was. Janek arrived at 5:02 and left with the banker's draft at 5:05. Albert Oschner shut up shop behind him, delighted with his day's business. Janek, though, strode off at speed; he had one other thing to do before his day was done. The sale of the diamond had raised him more than he needed, a great deal more. When he paid in the draft and settled with *The Times* newspaper there would still be ten thousand pounds in his account, sitting there in full bloom of five figure health. It had no business there – he had to convert it back: into diamond form.

Janek did not want to buy diamonds at the same place he had just sold one. He felt that Oschner would be rather hard-nosed in trying to recoup some of the thousands he had just paid out. He would have to try elsewhere.

Jewellers' shops in Hatton Garden are like newsagents elsewhere: there is one every other step. But none of them would let Janek in. It was the combination of the black eye and being past five o' clock. No one wants trouble at any time, but at such proximity to closing time it would be particularly insupportable.

At last a grey little place down a side street allowed him entry. Within was an equally grey little man who regarded Janek with suspicion. The fellow was short-sighted and had not seen Janek's blackened and blood-shot eye when he was standing without, only his age and gender. Now that he saw the eye, he read it as a badge of disrepute and expected its wearer to ask for money or drink.

Janek spoke quickly, 'It is an honourable bruise. I got it defending a lady.' The man behind the counter heard the Polish lilt in his voice and softened. He had lived with Poles after the war and they had been good people, very kind to him. He nodded. 'My apologies. A black eye is like a scar down the cheek: it creates a bad impression. It is really very unfair. First a fellow suffers the injury then he suffers the prejudice afterwards. What can I do for you?'

Janek had rehearsed his response: 'I want to buy a diamond. A quality stone. Cut or uncut, it makes no difference to me, but it must be top quality.'

'I have some that you could look at. Do you have your own eyepiece?'

Janek shook his head.

'If I may say so, that is rather a giveaway that you do not know diamonds from crystal turds.'

Janek laughed at the image. 'Then you will have to help me, my plain speaking friend.'

'Right. What exactly are you looking for and why?'

'I've told you what, or as close as my expertise can manage to articulate it. As for why…a friend entrusted some diamonds to me and it has become necessary for me to replace one of them. Colour and cut are immaterial, but quality is everything.'

'Dipped into the fund have we, sir?' winked the man.

'Something like that.'

The man laughed at his own comment which brought a deep wheezing out on him. He was still huffing and puffing when he reappeared with a felt tray and half a dozen diamonds. They were beautiful stones, but not as large as the one Janek had just sold.

With the borrowed lens Janek looked over each of them.

'Shall I tell you what you are looking for?' laboured the jeweller.

'Yes please.'

'There should be no fractures in the stone; external or internal…at least, very few. The cut should be balanced and suit the shape and colour of the gem - remember that the diamond is made smaller in the cutting so the process must really improve lustre for it to have been worth the loss in carat weight. Most importantly, look for clarity. There should be no milkiness in the stone: you want to see brilliance, but you also want to be able to see your own hand through the diamond too.'

'Thank you. No one has ever told me that before,' Janek replied.

'That is because you probably talk only to the owners of these shops,' said the man, indicating the wider area with a wave of his hand.

'You are not the owner of this establishment, then?'

'If I were the owner, I would not have told you what I just have. To a proprietor, a man either comes armed with this knowledge or he does not. Owners see themselves as businessmen, not educators.'

'But do you have the authority to sell me these?' asked Janek a little brusquely.

'Of course. What would be the point of me standing here all day if I could not sell the merchandise? Tell me, which one are you interested in?'

'Ten thousand pounds' worth.'

The man's wheezing intensified.

'What would that get me?' continued Janek.

'All of them - and some more,' replied the man, trying hard to control the reediness in his voice. He reached beneath the counter, sliding a lock as he did so. Quickly, he produced another tray. His hands were fluent with experience and immediately he separated off three more gemstones; one of them yellow, the other two the traditional colourless variety. His dextrous fingers worked in contrast to his fitful breathing.

'I think my boss could just about stand the loss of

these nine in exchange for ten thousand pounds. That's a good deal. If he paid a penny less than seven grand for them way out in the boondocks of Sierra Leone I'd be very surprised. You won't get better anywhere along the length of Hatton Garden,' he said.

Janek believed the wheezing fellow.

'It must be cash, mind.'

'Right. You have a deal. I will return on Thursday. Can you hold them that long?'

'Certainly.'

'And I will bring ten thousand pounds in cash.'

'And I will throw in a magnifying eyepiece,' smiled the man, so that you are properly equipped next time.'

'You will make a diamond dealer of me yet,' laughed Janek. 'Thank you for your time and for your honesty.'

After this exchange Janek left the shop, turned a couple of corners, slipped down a tiny alley and came out at *The Old Mitre Tavern*, just off Ely Place. There he enjoyed a celebratory pint. Earlier, he had just wanted to get home to hear his messages and read his post, and catch up generally, but the twin successes of the day had mellowed him, and he felt happy in his little corner of hidden London.

CHAPTER 6

Two weeks later the response to *The Times* appeal was staggering - Janek's phone did not stop ringing and the postal service had to send a special van round to no.33 in order to deliver his mail.

Every hour of the day Janek sorted the replies. There were people who had sent in addresses, people who had sent in Polaroid snaps of likely individuals photographed in the street, even people who thought one of their relatives was the man in the newspaper. In his office were three enormous piles: Good, So-so and Bollocks. Each piece of correspondence, and every lead, was assigned to its respective pile. And at the end of each day Janek made a bonfire of the 'Bollocks' tower as well as three quarters of the 'So-so' one - after he had picked through it once more.

Then came the real work. He had to make hundreds of follow-up phone calls, send countless letters by return of post - and still keep the usual Disappearance Club business running. Luckily only a handful of new customers turned up at his garage doors, so his attention was not heavily divided.

After a few days it became clear that there were half a dozen genuinely hot leads. Four were in Britain and two, overseas. They would all need travelling to. The UK ones could probably be done in one week - all four of them. The two abroad, would require a week each. One was in Portugal, the other in Mexico. The Mexican sighting was particularly promising. It was one of the replies sent in with an accompanying photograph; the man in it could have posed for Janek's artist's impression of a mature Joseph. And the man's eyes could have been lifted from the black-and-white original itself. When Janek had first seen the photograph he had bitten his own tongue. The valves of his heart had surged open and shut, half with excitement, half with fear. The likeness was extraordinary and he was transported, on the instant, to both his dark past in Poland and to a bright future in Mexico. He had trouble breathing and his face flushed.

This had to be the one to start with.

Janek clutched at his office desk and stumped for the door.

'Phil,' he shouted, 'Phil, you out there?'

The football had been thudding all day, although no one had yet sliced a shot into his garden.

'Yeah, Mr Lipsz, by the lampost.'

'Well come over here. I've got something to ask you.'

Phil ran: Mr Lipsz's standing had soared yet higher since he'd come home with such a magnificent shiner, and one of the boys' dads had actually witnessed him fighting in the pub - 'and with an absolute monster of a geezer'!

'Hi Mr Lipsz,' said the lad coming into the garden.

'Hello Philip. How would you like to earn some money?' asked Janek, getting straight down to business.

'You bet, Mr Lipsz.' He paused a moment. 'I ain't got to clean nothin' up 'ave I?'

Janek's face flushed once more, this time with mirth. 'No. I'm going away and I want you to pop over here while I'm gone and look after the cat. If you'll scoop out a tin of food a day and give Oskar fresh water every day too, I'll give you a fiver. I'll only be gone a couple of weeks.'

Phil nodded vigorously, already spending the money in the toy shops of his mind. 'When you off?' he asked.

'In the next few days, if I can get the flights.'

'Where you goin'?'

'Mexico, Phil. That's in Central America.'

'Ar know where Mexico is – we done it in Geography. You goin' on 'olidee?'

'Not a holiday. Business.'

'You found that boy of yours? I saw all them letters come.'

Again, Janek was shocked at the perspicacity of the lad. Immediately his easy requests and calm offer of money turned into shy awkwardness: Phil seemed to see right through him, to the very cog-turnings of his life.

'Maybe,' he stammered, 'maybe.' Then timidly, self-consciously, he took out the precious polaroid which had been sent to him. 'See here,' he said, quieter than snow on glass.

'What?' asked Phil.

'Here,' repeated Janek, handing him the new photograph. 'Compare it with the artist's impression you've already seen.' Janek got a copy from inside his office. Phil looked at them both for half a minute.

'They could be twins, Mr Lipsz.'

'So it's not just me then, Phil? You see the likeness too?'

'Oh come on. Sure I do. A fellow would 'ave to be blind not to...So when did you say you was goin'?'

'In the next few days. I'll come and call when I'm going - to give you the front door keys. Make sure you double lock it every time you leave. I'll show you how.'

Phil paused a moment, suddenly looking diffident himself. He handed back the photo and artist's impression, but the look did not fade.

'What is it, Phil? I can tell there's something. Come on, out with it.'

Phil looked at his feet, then spoke in a rush, 'It's me mum, she thinks you're a bit weird, see, and I don't reckon she'd be too keen on me doin' jobs for you. Not for money, like. So how about you don't call round at all, just give me the keys when you see me in the street? I mean I'm 'ere wallopin' me ball against your fence every day ain't I? You could do it then...'

For a second Janek considered being offended...

'...And 'ow about we call it a tenner and I'll tickle the cat behind the ear, right regular like?' added Phil.

Then Janek couldn't be offended, not after a little gem like that. 'Phil, you're an absolute card.'

'Mr Lipsz, I du know what that means, but if it's somefin good, then that's me,' the boy laughed.

'You bet it's something good,' smiled Janek.

'And I hope you find your Joseph, Mr Lipsz, really I do.'

'Thank you Phil. I hope so too...You remembered his name.'

'Course I did. Like I said, I was interested in

everything you told me the other day. Didn't think I would be, but I was. Even took a couple of books out of the library, I did, about The Eastern Front and Stalingrad. They're hard goin' mind - first books I've read since Christ knows when.'

'Well keep going with them. We'll talk about what you've read when I return.'

'Sure Mr Lipsz,' fluted Phil as he slipped back to his friends on the other side of the fence.

Problems with flights and another mountain of correspondence meant that it was five days before Janek could leave. He packed extremely lightly and pushed his front door keys into Phil's hand when he heard the first ball of the fifth day ricochet.

'No one else but you in the house, got it?' whispered Janek.

'No one else but me,' replied Phil, conspiratorially.

'And there's twelve pounds,' said Janek, counting the money into the boy's hand, 'You'll have to tickle behind both Oskar's ears for that.'

Janek's flight was at three in the afternoon. He had plenty of time, but there was one last thing left to do. Leaving Phil to his football, he went back inside and straight to his understairs cupboard. There he eased open the eccentric little safe. Quickly, lest he be tempted to open the chamois envelope once more, he scooped up the silk bag of diamonds. Within were the old ones that had lain there for years and the nine new stones he had bought from the straight-talking man in Hatton Garden. He slipped the whole bagful into his inner jacket pocket, made sure that its button was fastened down, and then waited by the front door for the toot of the taxi he had ordered. In one hand he held a small travelling case, in the other, his stout stick, cocked in readiness against potential muggers.

The roads to Heathrow were very clear, Janek's excitement building. But his was a very personal excitement and he resented the constant jabber of the cabbie: 'It's the coloureds I blame…Ted Heath's a poof…gotta be Shilton in goal every time…steal our jobs, steal our 'ouses…Where do you come from then?…But where do you really come from?…you Poles is alright…had a Frog in the here the other day…it's the coloureds I blame…'

At the end of the journey Janek was an expensive fare poorer and he absolutely knew that the driver blamed 'the coloureds' - for everything. It had been a nasty little trip and Janek did not tip the man. Once on the airport concourse, though, excitement really began to thrill his blood. He could feel it hammer at the little bones in his ears and surge at his lips and fingertips   he was off to find Joseph.

He was off to find Joseph!

It was two years since his last trip abroad. That had been occasioned by a good solid lead too, provided by one of his Disappearance Club people - a fellow who had fled a crappy job, a crappy marriage, and mortgage arrears the size of Kent to start again under an assumed name in Texas. The man had stayed in frequent contact with Janek and one day he had phoned to say that there was a guy who looked like his missing person working in one of the government offices in Houston. Also he had seen the name plate on the guy's desk: Joseph something. Janek had caught a plane the very next day.

In the end, though, it had all come to nothing. The fellow was a Joseph, but a quite different one - albeit one with uncannily similar features to Janek's lost boy. The man who had escaped England for Texas, the one who had made the sighting and provided the information, was mortified, so he spent the next four days treating Janek and showing him the sights.

This helped soothe Janek's disappointment, not on account of the special treatment he received, but because he was able to appreciate first-hand the fruits of his Disappearance Club: his client had set himself up in the Sacramento Mountains on a big horse and cattle ranch. Eagles soared on the thermals and coyotes howled at night, also the man had a grandchild visiting him which showed that contact with his daughter had been maintained. The escapee considered Janek responsible for this and was immensely grateful. So although the Joseph sighting had come to nothing, Janek had been brought face-to-face with his part in someone else's happiness. This had really mattered to him, had given him that little extra push which all men need from time to time, just in order to keep buggering on.

And now, all these years on, he was off to the Yucatan peninsula...

The travel books said that it was a paradise of sandy coves and lemon groves and tumbling waterfalls - not that he was going there to take in the tourist sights. He would see this Mexican 'Joseph' and if he didn't turn out to be his Joseph, then he would leave straight away for Portugal and check out the other sighting. There was no photograph with the Lisbon fellow, just a description and an assurance that the man was the right age and hailed from Poland originally. What made this lead almost as exciting as the South American one was that the old places referred to in the letter sent to him, matched almost exactly the stamping grounds of Janek's Polish youth. But within these positives lurked the seeds of doubt, for they couldn't both be describing the right man, and therefore it logically followed that they might both be detailing the wrong man.

Janek tried not to dwell on this. He kept himself upbeat. In fact he was so upbeat that he spilled his airport coffee in excitement and then smiled genially at everyone through the resultant brown mess. Afterwards he decided that it was necessary for him to get a few G&Ts inside him, in order that his nerves might be kept under control. Janek reckoned that such fumbles might arouse suspicion if they occurred at check in and he did not want to get searched. His precious cargo of diamonds was not illegal, but he didn't much fancy accounting for it either.

In the end, boarding was a doddle. No one frisked him, no scanners were offended by him; all the security people took him for a Johnny-average old geezer. The diamonds itched a little in the darkness of his breast pocket, but when he was actually seated in the aircraft, they eased up their tip-tapping at his pectorals.

The flight itself was first-rate: bright ocean, even brighter skies and yet more gin. He rarely took the stuff at home – probably because he knew that he liked it too much. Next to Janek was a man who did nothing but sleep, which was a wonderful boon - after his cab driver experience.

Janek read and reread the letter which had been sent to him and poured over the photograph to which it alluded. A slight snoring purred from the sleeper beside him: still there was no pain-in-the-arse neighbour to nose into his business. The photograph was a compelling piece of evidence. Janek called to mind the young Joseph of 1943. He saw a teenage face, but one which might well have grown into the visage on the Polaroid snap. He smiled happily.

Hope is wonderful thing. The brain produces it and then it spreads, until the whole body is plump with it. So it was with Janek and it rendered the tea the stewardess spilled on him less scalding than it otherwise would have been and the earache which flared up in him over the North Atlantic, less insistently painful than it would otherwise have been. Janek drank in the picture on his lap and the address of its sender: Postal 114V Merida, Yucatan, Mexico. He had telephoned ahead and was expected the next morning, by an Alberto Hernandez – the man who had actually taken the photograph.

For the night, he had booked himself a room at a little place near the airport. It was cheap and clean, so Alberto had told him, but in Janek's state of excited anticipation, it would not matter if cockroaches cascaded out of the taps and the chamber maids did nothing but chew tobacco.

As the plane touched down, Janek felt a jolt of nerves. Hope tussled with them a while, so that by the time his bags were being checked in at Mexico City, he was feeling tired. But no one bothered with his pockets at this airport either, so it did not really matter that he was not alert.

Alberto Hernandez was right - the hotel was a little peach.

Janek took out the letter and the photograph and the diamonds and placed them all on the bed.

Could this really be the time? The time he finally handed these gems to their rightful owner? When he made up for his sins? Janek felt his hair stand on end and his stomach churn at the prospect. He sat down amidst the diamonds, to save his wobbling legs. Would Joseph know him, recognise him after all these years? And would that bitch who had tended Joseph have told him the truth about what happened? Probably not.

Janek buried his face in his hands, pressed his eyes, until the darkness swam purple then fixed the wall behind the bed with his mottled stare.

The morning came after a sleepless night. Only once did he nod off, but his dreams were so full of booted men and screaming women and shootings and the harsh grate of shovel blades on cold earth that he had woken sweating and moaning. After that he had not dared close his eyes again, so he was up and ready hours before the car for Merida was due.

Janek sat on the edge of his bath and revolved a diamond between finger and thumb. He spent two hours like that, lost in the occupied Poland of his memory, locking horns with his inner self. It was asking him some particularly tough questions.

A car horn saved him. His transport.

Senor Alberto Hernandez was a big noise in avocados – he had thousands of hectares of the things.

He was sending one of his men on the half-day journey to fetch the man from London, England – maybe the trees needed to be watched as they grew, so it was impossible for the boss-man to come himself! That was what the driver was muttering to himself anyway, after a bumpy and sweaty trip down the coast road.

He greeted Janek with all the enthusiasm of a camel and nodded and grunted him into the passenger seat. It was exactly what Janek needed: a cold, silent driver, unlike the one who had taken him to Heathrow. The guy was poor – Janek could tell from the threadbare quality of his clothes and the coarseness of his skin, which proclaimed hard years spent hacking and hoeing in the fields, out under the punishing sun. Instinctively Janek patted his parcel of diamonds and wondered what the outcome would be, if this surly driver were ever to discover the contents of his pocket.

The ride was hot, slow and seemingly on roads constructed out of a corrugated material. Very quickly, Janek's spine and buttocks understood why the man had not been very welcoming.

After about five hours they finally turned into an impressively green estate. There were show-case plants and imported trees everywhere and the lawns were immaculately green. That took money in Mexico. Even Janek, an outsider, knew that: the natural state of grass in Mexico was shrivelled and brown. Ostentatious wealth was a good sign – Senor Hernandez would be on the level, not cooking up stories for a payout.

The man himself came out of a huge and dazzlingly whitewashed house. He was of average height and with a full head of side-parted hair. His moustache was as fulsome as his fringe. He looked every part the stereotype of a well-to-do Mexican. When Janek stepped out of the car, the welcome he received was genuine. It could not have contrasted more with the driver's. That silent man was already turning the car round. The estate dog was not taking its lead from Hernandez, however. On a short chain, just ten metres away, a large Fila Brasileiro, the great guard mastiff of Central America, was turning somersaults of fury. Janek had met these animals a few times in his travels. They are hard-wired to hate everyone and everything they have not met before the age of six months. This one looked about five years old. In the Americas people in the know simply avoid them whenever possible; it is uninformed strangers they make their meals out of.

Janek didn't like how the chain tether was beginning to give in the ground and tried to lead the hand-shaking inside. His host took the hint, bellowed at the dog, and ushered his guest within.

It was a sumptuous place. In hot countries, a man displays his wealth by having large, airy, cool rooms, lots of water and greenery and hunks of ice in expensive drinks. Janek sipped the latter while he was shown the former. There were fountains gushing careless gallons and delicate little plants which obviously required sedulous care, and at the centre of the house was a huge indoor garden. By most ingenious design, all the main ground-floor rooms of the dwelling opened onto this massive area. There was a waterfall within it and lush plants and wonderful butterflies dancing kaleidoscopically about. They supped on sugared water from little dishes.

There was a glass ceiling too, cunningly disguised, so that the myriad butterflies could fly about without ever escaping. Beautiful little finches were similarly constrained within this indoor garden. Guinea fowl rushed about at Janek's feet as well and air conditioning kept the temperature at an ever-comfortable seventy degrees. The tiny finches were of surpassing loveliness: two thirds the size of sparrows, but as colourful as kingfishers. They gabbled their little songs as Alberto Hernandez spoke:

He had taken *The Times* for years because he liked the Business section. The articles helped him to follow his European investments. So it had become a habit with him to sit down with the paper every morning. That was how he had come to see Janek's missing person double spread.

Senor Hernandez explained that he had dealings with most of the other big producers in Mexico and that one of them, an even bigger grower than he, employed whole ranks of managers to oversee his estates. And it was one of these managers who had reminded him so strikingly of the artist's impression in *The Times*.

He had not been able to find out the man's name though, because the big plantation owner had started to become suspicious of the uncommon attention being paid to his employee. The head honcho had thought that he, Hernandez, was trying to poach the fellow for his own estates. It was all that he had been able to do, just to take a quick photograph – the one Janek had been sent.

Hernandez explained that Janek would have to go on his own to the ranch - pose as a buyer from

England - and see the manager for himself, so that he could make his own judgements. The ranch was not far away; maybe fifteen miles and whatever the outcome, food, drink and a bed for the night were guaranteed upon his return.

To Janek's relief, the same driver as before was summoned to take him; Janek would need silent time to compose himself for the meeting. Hernandez had briefed him on the avocado pear business and what a European buyer would be looking for in a Central American producer. Nerves were wracking him though; five minutes into the ride he had forgotten most of what he'd been taught. In his mind's eye there flashed only Joseph, the boy, and the last time they had been together, in war-torn Poland. Could the things he had done ever be forgiven? Weren't they simply unforgivable?

The driver knew exactly which part of the estate to approach in order to catch their man. After forty minutes they arrived.

'You ready?' asked the driver in faltering English.

'No,' Janek squeaked in undisguised fear.

'You have to be. Boss want me back by four.'

Janek stepped out and the red dust of a proper Mexican field billowed and swirled about his brogues. Approaching them down a long ochre and orange path was a burly man with another Fila Brasileiro on a short lead. They took an eternity to arrive, then the big fellow peered over the cattle gate that separated them. While the dog howled insults, Janek's driver addressed him. He explained that Janek had come from London, England, to see avocadoes, that he represented a big grocery chain and that he had the authority to sign contracts. Janek understood nothing but the proper nouns, and nodded sagely at them in spite of his nervousness.

After quite a while, the man, if not his dog, seemed convinced and allowed the two visitors entry. They were being taken to await the estate manger - the fellow Janek was trembling to meet…

…At the end of the long path, he and his driver stepped into a long, low, white-walled compound and were shown to a couple of chairs beneath a fan. Its blades spun rhythmically. Shadows danced in perfect time. Heat boiled and shimmered the distance.

The hypnotic effect coaxed out Janek's past. The blades and the shadows became the clattering jackboots and the screaming girl and the gunshots of his dreams. The hot images leered bloodily at him, just as they had the night before. Then for a moment Janek's inner self became entirely uncontrollable and it turned into The Reverend Tony Collier: a huge and angry Tony Collier:

'So who the fuck do you think you're kidding?' the giant reverend sneered. 'No one's gonna forgive a vicious bastard like you. Not after what you did. And what about his sister, huh? Have you forgotten about her? You're wasting your time, my little black sheep…like you've wasted every minute of the last thirty years. Ten-to-one Joseph'll just have that big fella set his dog on you.' The reverend gargled a triple whisky at him, 'Take your fucking face off it will, and you'll deserve it.'

Janek shook away the vision. Sweat snapped off his head with the force of the movement. Swallowing hard, he fastened an internal shackle upon his inner self. Somewhere within the compound rich Mexican voices were debating. Janek strained to hear what they were saying. Try as he might, he could not square any one of them with the voice he remembered: Joseph's 1943 tones. But that had been a boy's voice, speaking in Polish and thick with desperation.

Janek bit his lip and his hand found the diamonds in his pocket: they would show the quality of his remorse. How many other men would have left such wealth untouched for so long?

He heard the slam of a door and footsteps approaching.

No part of Janek failed to pound. His neck ached and his hair stuck sweatily to his crown. He closed his eyes and exhaled deeply in an attempt to control his heart-rate.

A figure strode up. Janek forced his eyes open. He walked with an extravagant flick of the knee - a confident gait. Janek stared at each stride as it snapped out. The man arrived in a scuff of leather on soil. Janek dared not look up.

He missed all the opening pleasantries, although he was dimly aware that he had been addressed. Then the manager tried to engage him on avocadoes. Still Janek stared at the man's knees. He was wearing corduroy: expensive, supple corduroy…At last the man took him by the elbow. Janek was terrified. His inner self had not prepared him for physical contact, even though his Reverend-Collier-of-the-mind had slipped in the bit about the dog.

Janek flashed a quick, frightened upward glance. The man was clean cut, with a classic face. He was no older than thirty-five. Immediately Janek blurted out, 'You are too young, far too young.'

The manager drew away his hand. He spoke good English: 'Sir, I assure you, it is quite usual for a man of my age to be managing such an estate as this.'

'But you are not my Joseph, not at all, although your general cast is much the same,' returned Janek, quite forgetting the role of foreign buyer he was supposed to be playing.

Manager and burly fellow and red-eyed dog looked at one another.

'I think there has been a mistake,' Janek said rising. His inner self was hooting derision.

The two men narrowed their eyes, swelled their necks. The fila brasileiro smelled their suspicion and bared its teeth.

'I must leave,' Janek croaked.

Garbled Spanish followed. Janek crouched behind his own incomprehension. His driver was trying valiantly to explain the unexplainable. Janek thought that he might have been struck at one point. The dog surged malevolently about. Suddenly, Janek felt himself impelled back along the orange and ochre path, together with his driver. They had lost every particle of their welcomed status. And through all the growling and shouting and embarrassment, Janek felt his disappointment keenly.

Back at the field gate, the emergency of the situation lent Janek and his driver the legs of athletes: they both vaulted it. The Joseph-like manager swore after them. So too did the burly sentry...Janek and his driver were in their car and screeching away almost as soon as the expletives were uttered. Janek caught sight of the Joseph lookalike in the rear-view mirror - angry and red faced in the dusty wake of the car.

Another false hope. Another failure.

The man faded from view.

There in the back seat, Janek gazed upon the growing liver spots of his hands and wondered in sorrow whether he had time enough left to ever find the real Joseph. Maybe his Joseph was dead. Maybe he was just chasing a wraith around the world, with the Grim Reaper leading him on…

Janek crumpled.

Two bumpy miles further on, the hitherto reticent driver nudged him. He offered Janek a bottle of mescal. 'For your pain,' he nodded.

Janek tossed back a stinging mouthful. And another. And another. And another. It was a strong stuff, but his pain was too deep and too fresh to be much dulled. There on that Mexican road back to Alberto Hernandez's, Janek howled and howled like a baby.

CHAPTER 7

Lisbon was even worse. There was no 'Joseph' there at all. An unscrupulous bastard had simply noticed the newspaper double-spread and had tried to make a fast buck out of Janek. The man, an Arnold Sampson, lived in Sheffield, but did a lot of his confidence-tricking and sharking out of Portugal, because the fraud laws there were so lax and the sentences, so wonderfully derisory.

His plan was a simple one: over the years of conning and blood-sucking, he had learned that those looking for lost people were often easily led by their emotions, ruled by them, even. So it was his practice to arrange nebulous meetings, turn up forged documentation and other plausible seeming evidence - for a price - and then to disappear with the money, while his unfortunate dupes waited for their long-lost whomsoevers to turn up. It was a nasty little trick which had kept Arnold Sampson safely out of real work for well over ten years.

Before responding to Janek's *Times* appeal he had done a little homework on his man – a real detective job. He knew for example, how long Janek had been in the UK, he knew also the name of his home town in Poland. He knew of his Resistance past and where the majority of his operations had taken place and that he had been a captain in the Polish Armed Forces - until Hitler and Stalin had rolled their armies over it. All these facts were held on file as part of Britain's immigration record and Sampson had a friend well placed in the civil service to sniff these juicy titbits out.

Many war-time East Europeans were investigated for potential war crimes involvement, because the British were keen not to be seen to be harbouring those with blood on their hands, particularly by the Soviets who were liable to make unlimited capital out of any Western oversight. So Janek had been scrutinized, on arrival at these shores, and the information on him kept. And thus, Sampson, years later, was able to cobble together a passably accurate picture of his past. He even found out that Janek Lipsz had been tortured by the Nazis at a minor camp near Cracow: Janek had seen a British Army doctor for treatment on both his kidneys after the war and the medical notes taken had been stapled to the other details on him. Arnold Sampson got hold of all this and some recent stuff too: income tax records, information off the electoral roll, a few bank details.

Armed with these facts he had written to Janek to inform him that he knew of a Joseph living in Lisbon who had lived rough in Cracow during the war, who had survived capture twice, and had then got out fast to Portugal before the Soviet stranglehold tightened fully on the old country. Sampson swore that he was a dead ringer for the images published in *The Times*.

There was no photograph provided, but it was a hopeful Janek who had rung Mr Sampson.

Mexico had dented this hope a little, so when Janek

landed in Lisbon he was not quite as brimful with blind optimism as Arnold liked his victims to be, but the man was a professional and wasted no time in working his parasitic magic. He dropped Polish names, he spoke of the national dishes, he stressed how little some people's appearances changed over time, he interspersed his narrative with a few Nazi torturers, but then had the dexterity to draw back when he saw the agony revisited on Janek's face. And the name 'Joseph' rolled so mellifluously off his tongue, that it didn't seem to matter that he had no surname to back it up, nor photograph, nor address, nor definite place of work for his man. He even had Janek in tears over the old times – twice. Oh, Arnold Sampson was good.

But he was not good enough. Janek had been searching too long and too hard to be fully duped. The alarm bells started ringing when the demands for money came. Then they really pealed out when these grew insistent, and all the while, Sampson's Joseph remained as nebulous as ever.

Money was needed to pay a contact to obtain an address.

Money was needed to arrange a meeting.

Money was needed to get a copy of Joseph's passport.

Money was needed…

Money was needed…

In the end Janek just walked away from the oily little man. He saw through Sampson's game, guessed why he was in Lisbon with a Sheffield accent, realised that a little Polish history could go a long way and remembered also, fielding a few clumsy attempts at the same kind of the thing the last time he had placed

Joseph's picture in *The Times*.

It was tempting to strike Arnold Sampson, to club him to the ground, but Janek remembered his two recent fist fights. Brawling wasn't really him, so he turned from the con man and set his jaw and his step for England. There were a few possible Josephs he had to check out on home territory, before returning to Orchard Road itself.

In truth, though, the Merida and Lisbon experiences had knocked the hope out of Janek. He fully expected a sorry parade of British red herrings and fuck ups next. Deep down he felt that he had had his last ever sighting of Joseph; the real Joseph. It was seared into his memory - his Joseph leaking blood from an awful head wound, in the deepest boondocks of the Polish countryside, in the winter of 1943.

He was not wrong about the British leads. Another four days wrapped up the whole sorry business.

There were three brothers in Norwich who were convinced their uncle was Joseph, even though the man himself swore that he wasn't. The guy told Janek to 'piss off' when he turned up on his doorstep. Then there was an old, deranged lady who wanted to back Janek into a corner with photograph albums. There was no doubt that her husband did look strikingly similar to Joseph, but there the matter ended - for he was called Stanley and had been dead since 1932. Another possible fellow was too ludicrous to warrant even a heartbeat of Janek's time and the last was another attempted deception, although much less sophisticated than the Lisbon con.

Exhausted, Janek took the train home. It was a

miserable journey; throughout he was haunted by the memories of his earlier expectations. They had buoyed him so much, just a little while back. Also, he could not get rid of the head-wound image. It dominated his mind's eye. It was there when he looked out of the train windows and it was there when he stared dully at his food. Always the blood was there, accusing him…'Well I tried,' he shouted out at last, losing control at a point in the journey just past Peterborough and his fellow passengers turned to stare at him.

Phil had taken good care of the house, and of Oskar. The cat rumbled like a sooty old motorbike at his owner's return. Janek reckoned that the cat's welcome was the one good thing about his trip away.

Phil had enjoyed his time cat-and-house-sitting. More than anything else, he had been amazed at the coins littering the carpets and stairs and kitchen table and surfaces generally.

'I picked 'em up Mr Lipsz. There's pounds and pounds. They're all there on the table. I didn't take none.'

Janek nodded.

'Not one,' repeated Phil, unsure if Mr Lipsz believed him.

'I know you didn't Phil. I believe you, and thanks for picking them up.'

'There was pounds. Every penny's there. You'll be able to get yourself something with it.'

'No doubt.'

'So how come there was so much change everywhere? Do you run a shop down in your garage, too?'

'No, Phil, it just builds up in my pockets and then

I empty them and then they fill up some more and I empty them again and so on. If you look carefully you'll even find some coins from when it was still old money, and it's five years since we changed over now. You can keep those if you want…in fact, take a handful of whatever you want - new and old - but will you do me favour, and just leave me be? Will you? I'm very tired.'

Phil didn't move an inch closer to the piles of coins, or the front door. He did open his mouth, though…only to close it again.

'Oh, and thanks very much,' added Janek. 'Very much…I'm losing my manners. That should have been the first thing I said.'

Phil found his voice. 'Didn't you find him then, Mr Lipsz? Your Joseph?'

'No Phil, I didn't. Not at all. I just trailed round the world on a massive great wild goose chase.' He brought his clenched fist down on the kitchen table with an almighty crash. The coins scattered everywhere once more and Oskar, the cat, bolted for the security of the upstairs airing cupboard. And then the old resistance fighter and pub-brawler and traveller and proprietor of The Disappearance Club broke down in front of his twelve-year-old cat-sitter…great noisy sobs which scared and embarrassed Phil at the same time. 'I got no closer to him,' Janek sobbed, 'than I ever have sat here in my own back bloody garden, and I feel like old, stinking, dried-up shit.'

Phil extended a timid little hand. He patted Janek on the elbow. He had seen his dad hug his mum when she was in a similar state - when her brother was locked away for nickin' and when Aunty Flo had died -

but it didn't seem right to hug Mr Lipsz, him bein' a man and everything, so he just patted his elbow. Janek nodded recognition of the gesture.

'When I've sorted myself out, when I don't feel so bad,' he sniffed, 'I'll pick that money back up, put it in a big cardboard box, and you can have the lot.' Then he stepped towards the door. Phil followed.

At the mat the boy turned. 'I liked it in your house, Mr Lipsz. Through your kitchen window, I watched the birds on their feeders – in the cherry tree. It's really good that it's so close to the house. Till I sat and watched 'em with your cat, I had no idea that garden birds came in any colour 'cept brown.'

Janek smiled his tears away. 'Make sure that you open your eyes to the colour of the world, lad, for there is more than enough in it that is drab as it is.'

Phil stepped lightly down the path, trying hard to understand what had just been said to him.

The next few days were difficult for Janek. He manned the Disappearance Club office, but his heart was not in it. All the time, Joseph peered down at him from the back wall, his soulful eyes hard on Janek's neck.

In a very amateur way, Janek tried to work out the odds of the boy being dead by now: average life expectancy – sixty-nine. Counting from the end of the war, then, he would be about forty-seven now. There were twenty-two years between those two ages, but flash floods and house fires and muggings-gone-wrong happened all the time. And what about complications from old injuries? Couldn't they carry a man off? Janek saw again Joseph's gore-soaked head and his blood leaking onto the floor.

But surely the Dymek woman had seen him alright? She had patched him together, hadn't she? Joseph had been alive in 1945 - when he left her. Janek knew that much for sure: old friends had found that out for him. That was two years after...after...after he had...

Janek sucked in air, stared bug-eyed, clutched the edge of the table with trembling hands.

...It was a hell of a blow the boy had been dealt - with a heavy wooden rifle butt: there might well have been further physical consequences, even years after. Maybe fatal ones. Janek felt down by his own left kidney - it had never been the same, not after the beatings he had received in the Gestapo cells at Cracow. Hadn't the doctors told him that he would suffer down there all his life?

Janek shut his eyes as he remembered the pick-axe handle blows he'd received - one after another after another. And couldn't a rifle butt do as much damage as a pickaxe handle? Maybe more - to a fourteen-year-old body. Janek vomited, great yellow gobs over the desk and over his papers and into the eyelets of his shoes. And then he vomited once more.

For an hour he just sat there in the cooling yellow smell. The search for Joseph had taken it out of him. To his core he felt like one of those old, clapped out animals which merely exist; just shitting, pissing and dribbling in their own dens, knowing that the game is up and waiting for a cold snap or a passing predator to make an end of them.

It was Phil who roused him from this pathetic state. He had been knocking for the return of his ball for some time. Then after receiving no reply, and buoyed with the confidence of having been allowed within the main house itself, he had just reached over, flicked the latch to the double doors, and slipped into the garden.

It was a warm day and Janek's office door was wide open. Immediately, Phil saw that the old man was in terrible state. He was just staring, he hadn't heard Phil, the vomit thick about him.

'Mr Lipsz,' he gasped, 'Mr Lipsz?'

Janek jumped. His own smell hit him for the first time. He jerked out of his chair. 'What the hell are you doing here?' he cried, suddenly embarrassed.

'I'm sorry, sir,' stuttered Phil, employing the manners of the classroom in his discomfort.

The little word galvanised Janek yet more, also it cleared his mind of all embarrassment. 'Don't ever 'sir' me, lad. There's nothing in me worthy of it. I'm just an old criminal with a few war stories, that's all. There's nothing special about me.'

Phil knew that he should offer to help the man: clean him up, fetch a towel, a glass of water, maybe a drink of something stronger, but he didn't. He just sat down and returned Janek's gaze.

'Then tell me about them…them old war stories.'

Janek smiled thinly through the nobs of sweetcorn and bile about his mouth. 'In here, like this?' he said. 'Come on!'

'So wash that stuff off your face and then tell me.' Phil looked up at the big black and white photograph and then back down at the man before him…'You're not ill are you Mr Lipsz?…It's yourself you're sick at, isn't it?'

Janek lunged at the boy, but Phil dodged away fast

to the other side of the table.

'You little bastard. You ungrateful, little bastard,' thundered Janek.

'I see'd my brother just like you one day,' blurted Phil, ' when his dog had puppies and he drowned them all, rather than pay vet's fees like 'e should of and me mam found out…'

Janek stopped chasing him.

'…And afterwards he was sick like you and stared at the wall and did nothing and was no good to nobody. They sacked him from his work in the end. And all cos he drowned them puppies that he could've found 'omes for anyway, with a little bit of effort.'

Janek wiped his mouth with the back of a dirty hand. Phil stood still. He stared at the begrimed and bent-nosed old man. They were both, man and boy, blasting out their breaths.

'I'm sorry Mr Lipsz, I don't know where all that came from. I shouldn't 'ave come in here like I did, shooting my mouth off. You probably are sick. Probably ate something bad when you was away.'

'Crap,' snapped Janek. 'You were right the first time, I'm not ill.' He returned Phil's gaze; not aggressively.

'I don't like it, Mr Lipsz. You've been good to us, us kids: most people round 'ere think we're a nuisance. There's half a dozen gardens down this street is football graveyards - there's not one of 'em we would even try getting our ball back out of. But you, you actually work out of yours and it's still ok. It's not right that you should be so unhappy….' Phil paused as if weighing up whether to say more. '…Unhappy with yourself,' he hazarded.

Janek wiped the dripping vomit from his chair.

'Alright, detective, you got yourself an audience with Janek Lipsz,' he said, sitting back down…'You ever play soldiers with your friends?'

'Yes, Mr Lipsz.'

'Going rat-a tat-a tat?'

Phil nodded.

'Well there is rat-a-tat-tatting in war, but all that stuff in uniforms with pitched battles and tanks and planes and all the kit, that isn't even half the story.'

Phil nodded again.

'Three quarters of it is dirty, underhand and crude. It makes the gutter look clean. There are no uniforms and the kit is…'

'What did you do, Mr Lipsz?' asked Phil cutting through.

Janek stared hard at the young lad.

'You heard of Reinhart Heydrich?'

Phil shook his head.

'He was Adolf Hitler's blue-eyed boy; the fellow all set to succeed him one day. Stationed in Czechoslovakia, he was. That's the country that neighbours my Poland. Heydrich was the Nazi ruler of the whole of it. Well, one day The Resistance ambushed his car - shot him up, dropped in a couple of grenades to make sure of him too. Killed him stone-dead they did. It was one of The Resistance's biggest successes of the war, not just in Czechoslovakia, but throughout the whole of the occupied territories.'

'And you was in The Resistance,' trilled Phil, wide-eyed.'

'Yes. And do you know where I was that day and what I was doing?'

Phil waited.

'I was way down in the south of Poland, burning someone's house down. Me and my little band of men were nothing to do with the biggest assassination in all Resistance history.'

Phil shifted in his chair.

'We had heard reports of a woman consorting with a German soldier. She was allowing him certain freedoms – you know what I mean?'

Phil said that he did.

'For sausages and butter.'

Janek shifted in his seat too.

'So, we, The Resistance, we drove ourselves down to her little one bedroom house and burnt it to the ground. We allowed her one dress and one blanket to shuffle off in, that was all, and then we set fire to her pathetic little hovel of a home. Not before we'd stolen all her sausages and butter, mind.'

Phil looked down at the ground.

'And that's not the worst of it: the people loved us for what we'd done and shunned that poor woman. They turned their backs on her when she stumbled through the cold streets. But the Czechs hated their resistance fighters who had had the guts to take on Heydrich, because Hitler ordered thousands of those same ordinary citizens killed in retribution for his favourite's death - just pulled from their houses and shot on the spot. That's real war: being hated for daring and honourable actions, and being feted for cowardly destruction.'

'What happened to the woman?' Phil asked in a tiny voice.

'I don't know. The usual.'

'The usual?'

'Turned to her German officer for protection, or found a Polish man who didn't know her past, or found one with a warmer heart and a more forgiving nature than most. Or hanged herself. There were always a few of those.'

'What was her name?'

'No idea. Didn't even know it when I was burning her house down, and I couldn't tell you what she looked like either - except that she was good-looking. She must have been: the people were always less forgiving when it is a cracker who strayed to the other side.'

'Is the Joseph you look for her son?' asked Phil.

Janek smoothed down his hair. 'No, no. Not at all.' Janek rose. 'I think you've had enough war stories for one day. And I do feel less sick with myself. Thank you. We all need to unburden ourselves occasionally. I am sorry that I called you an ungrateful little bastard. It is sometimes easier to be rude to someone than to face truth with him.'

'That's alright Mr Lipsz. I've been called worse.'

'Your ball,' cried Janek, jumping up, 'they'll be waiting - the other boys.'

'Not today. I was playing on my own.'

They ducked out from the garage and collected up the ball nonetheless. The lamps were just beginning to hum in the street as Phil flicked the latch to leave. 'My granddad told me once, that men do many things in times of war which they would never dream of doing sat at home in peace times...I mean times of peace. That's true isn't it Mr Lipsz?'

Janek leaned self-consciously against the doorjamb, 'Phil, there are very few men who survive wars and have no shameful secrets.'

Youngster though he was, Phil made a difference. Janek felt happier in himself after their discussion; a little more bothered to get back on. He received calls, he made calls, he arranged transfers of money: to West Africa one day, to South East Asia the next. He even responded to a couple of new Joseph letters - the last of the correspondence from the newspaper appeal - they seemed unpromising little things, but he did follow them up, requesting more information.

And he found that he could look at the office photograph once more. For the first few days back, it had been impossible to look Joseph in the face. Guilt, disappointment, fatigue, shame; they all conspired to turn his head away. But after Phil had got him talking, Janek found that he could look at the back wall of his own office once again.

And then one windy evening The Reverend Tony Collier called round. He had tried a few times while Janek was away and now he had caught his man at home. The two of them sat down in the living room.

'How are you doing Janek?'

'Ok.' It was only half a lie: a week before it would have been a complete lie.

'We've missed you at the drama club, old boy,' said the clergyman.

Janek nodded.

'Bill and his mates never showed up again.'

Janek nodded once more.

'So we had to get some new people in and start up from scratch. I reckon there's still a part in the play for you if you want it.'

'Tony, I'm not really doing people at the moment. I went away for a bit recently and it was a very depressing affair. Not the kind of thing a man gets over quickly,' replied Janek.

'A bit of company might be just the thing then…Clara and her mother have been asking after you.'

'That's nice. But really, I don't think I'm fit for company. Thanks for thinking of me though.'

'The play's just not the same without you as Big Daddy,' said Tony, refusing to give up.

Janek picked a yellow speck out of the corner of his eye. 'How's God doing?' he asked, 'Still looking down?' It was a rude little question, but Janek wanted to effect an immediate change of subject.

'I'm quite sure that He is,' laughed Tony, tolerantly.

'Then I reckon He's not got his glasses on when He peers over in my direction.'

'So what shall I tell Dorothy and Clara?' replied the reverend, changing the subject back again.

'That the mother's too fat for me to be interested in and that I'm too old to interest her delicious daughter?'

'I think it might be better if I just said that you are too busy to attend.'

'Right.'

Janek rose to shake hands with the clergyman. 'Sorry about the rudeness and the blasphemy Tony - like I said, I'm not up for social contact at the moment. But I do appreciate that you came to call.'

'May I again, some time?'

'Yes. Although not often, if you don't mind.'

'I do pray for you, Janek,' the reverend said when they reached the front door, 'Most mornings.'

'Will that make a difference do you think - if I don't?'

'I reckon it might turn out to be the best insurance policy you've got, my friend.'

Janek raised an eye brow, 'Thank you for calling, Tony, and all the best with the production.' He closed the door as God's representative sniffed one of his front garden roses.

'Nice man, but he can smell the guilt on me,' Janek said quietly to himself.

Soon it was mid-October.

When he was a boy, Janek's mother had always told him that the autumn days were a giant snail, slowly drawing in the light of day, which was held at the end of their stalk-like eyes, getting ever shorter, till finally they snapped completely away - and then it was the dark of winter. Janek laughed out loud at the memory and realised it was the first time that he had laughed since returning from his trip abroad.

And as more weeks went by, a rush of work came his way, which kept him busy. Janek had a theory that the short nights brought the escapees out. During the summer months they managed to cope, but the year's waning light acted as a final straw on the backs of their tired, frustrated lives. Then they came knocking on his door, all set to disappear. There had to be something in it: numbers always doubled in November.

In contrast, his own mood lifted: enough to nail down business and agree terms with the new clients.

He was pretty stable emotionally when raising the issue of Joseph with them too, although it was rather a strain at first. But Janek soldiered on and the upshot was - a fresh crop of escapees with instructions to keep a sharp look out. Janek wasn't very hopeful anymore, but he did his duty by Joseph and got the new recruits out there searching.

Drink helped him cope too. He had started taking a bottle of gin down to the office. Some days, after a few liberal shots, he even forgot about Joseph's head injury and in between clients, he would take in the garden. The last of the autumn berries were still on the trees, and the apples. Everything seemed to be in a race to finish them, before the first frosts did: jays, robins, finches, blackcaps, squirrels. And in turn, sparrowhawks would fly low on a daily swoop-by to hunt them.

Janek watched all this and delighted in it and slowly the entrancing rhythms of Nature softened the discordant clangour of disappointment.

CHAPTER 8

To the footballers, the blue Renault and its female occupant were part of the street, like the trees that lined it, like the weeds that pushed their seasonal way up through the pavement and like the streetlights that blushed rose-pink at dusk. Now and then they wondered whether she had died - there in her car - for she never reacted when the ball struck her windscreen, but the tears upon her were always so fresh that they dismissed the idea as soon as ever it occurred. So one day, when a woman appeared who was not part of the landscape and stood at the head of the street - just stood there - and did nothing more, they stopped their game and took notice.

'Copper?' volunteered Phil.

'Nah, too old,' a voice retorted.

'Forgotten where she's going?'

'Uh-uh. She's not going anywhere. Look...she's rooted to the spot.'

'Lost something then?'

'Or someone?'

'Maybe.'

'Hey, Mrs! You lookin' for someone?'

The old woman flinched at the question, as if it had been bellowed an inch from her ear, when actually Phil had asked in a quiet, polite manner. 'You lost?' he

147

persisted.

'No…thank you,' the stranger replied at last. 'I'm exactly where I want to be.'

She was staring up at no.33.

Phil shrugged, taking her in as he did so: frumpy clothes, about sixty-five, sweet little face; actually rather pretty in a mature kind of way, but tight around the mouth as if suppressing an oath - or something worse. And there was the same puckering about her eyes too, which rendered them stag-like rather than doe-like. Phil followed her gaze.

'He's never in the house, you know…not during the day. You'll find Mr Lipsz at the bottom of his garden. If that's who you're after.'

Phil's articulation of this name acted upon the woman as a morning worm does a bird. She twisted her neck, narrowed her eyes, jerked her body in the boy's direction. She moved purposefully over to him. 'What did you say?' Her voice was hot and forcing.

'Mr Lipsz. If you're looking for Mr Lipsz, don't bother knocking at the front door, just go straight down to his garage doors. Look down there, you can see them from here,' pointed Phil. 'He always comes out. He'll probably just think you're me after my ball.'

The lady nodded her head.

'Is it him you're after then, Mrs?'

The woman did not reply, just shifted her tight gaze from the house to the indicated double doors.

'Is it?' he persisted.

Still she did not answer and Phil's friends became impatient; he had the ball under his arm.

'Ok then,' he said by way of conclusion and walked away from the woman. 'Completely barmy,' he told the other footballers, 'Got an accent like Mr Lipsz mind.'

For a few minutes the lads played 'keep it up', with their eyes as much on the woman as their ball, but then they tired of her strangeness. For her part, she shifted ten metres closer to the double doors, shilly-shallied over the eleventh, and then came to a halt again. Her eyes took in every bolt and panel and knot of the wooden doors.

Suddenly a man appeared, dark under a hat and carrying a brief case. It was one Lawrence Garlic, brother to Graham Garlic, a man Janek had helped disappear a decade before. Every six months he brought money and news for Janek to pass on to Graham in Panama. The woman did not know this and her eyes narrowed further, like the livid tightening of a bull's immediately prior to charging. She scrutinised every line of the man's face. Also she snapped her handbag open. It was a big, square leather one; almost a satchel.

These little trips to Janek were the only days Lawrence Garlic ever took off work - half days really. Always he came post-lunch, two afternoons a year, after he'd spun his boss a line about hospital appointments. And always, on the way to Janek, he started at shadows and jumped at noises and looked sheepishly about, terrified that he would be noticed by someone from work...all for fear of a boss who played golf every afternoon and the boss's secretary who told the big man everything she saw upon his return at eleven the next day. He did these things for a brother he had never really liked, because family is still family, regardless of bosses and secretaries and likes and dislikes and personal inconvenience.

Only once in the last ten years had he seen Graham - in British Honduras - to inform him of their mother's death. And they had cried together and had promised to be better brothers to one another and to keep in closer touch, but now, some four years on, as before, their only contact was at a remove, through Janek, courtesy of fictitious hospital appointments.

The strange woman knew none of these things either. Tentatively, she covered the eleventh, twelfth and thirteenth metres, which brought her closer to Janek's double doors and the nervous Lawrence, who was approaching from the opposite direction.

She delved into her bag. Inside was a large hunting knife, twelve inches in length. There was a groove down the blade, designed to channel the life-blood out of anything, or anyone, stabbed. The woman traced a trembling finger down it and then grasped at the heavy firmness of the hilt. Her hand shook and a lipstick tumbled, unnoticed by her, to the floor.

The footballers had stopped for the woman - step thirteen had encroached upon their game - and were watching her rummaging about in the bag.

'Is there an animal in there?' joked one.

'Doesn't she know she's dropping things?' added another.

''S a lipstick innit? And a pen, look, the pen's about to fall now!'

A biro bounced off the woman's instep, but still she remained oblivious to her littering. While her hands fumbled, she had eyes only for the behatted and briefcased man ahead.

Suddenly he noticed her; maybe on account of her

unflinching stare, maybe on account of his own skiver's jumpiness, which impelled him to mark everyone. Their eyes met. Hers hostile, his fearful…At the same moment Phil took a couple of steps forward and scooped up the woman's lipstick and pen. 'You dropped these, lady,' he said, offering them to her. 'Right out your bag.'

She jumped as if barefoot on coals. Her hand jerked off the knife and out of her handbag. She rounded on Phil, snatched up the offerings then pushed past him to keep sight of the man. Not a word of thanks did she give. Not one word, but she did protrude her tongue an inch, animal-like. Then Lawrence knocked on the double doors and she snapped it back in.

The doors opened.

She strained to look in - saw the fringe of Janek's hair, one cheek and an ear. Then swore - the kind of language Phil only ever heard when his father lost the rent money on a dead cert. Next thing she stormed off. And Phil was left open-mouthed, like a comic-book illustration of himself.

Mr Garlic spent two hours in with Janek. The two men liked one another and Lawrence felt secure in the little office. It was one place he was sure he would not be seen. Their business was concluded in under an hour, but Janek knew that Lawrence liked to stay behind until usual office hours ticked by, so for the last hour they sorted through the day's banking returns together. They talked current affairs and they talked about Lawrence's brother:

'He was forever in trouble you know, even when

we were young.'

'Really?'

'Oh yes. One of my earliest memories is of Graham being beaten for giving Grandma Josephine an overdose of laxative…'

Janek laughed.

'…We had a farm in those days and dad kept a couple of horses. He had this thick syrupy stuff from the vet which he'd spoon into them whenever they were constipated.'

Janek's eyes smiled. He loved the past, so long as it was not his own.

'Well, gran was entirely costive-bound, blocked up to bursting, and Graham ladled the stuff into her, more even than we'd give a sick horse. He said that he didn't know what he was doing, but he did. Dad said that Graham had treated the horses before - all on his own. Boy did he get it. Gran didn't even get one foot up the stairs before the floodgates opened.'

Janek sniggered.

'And another time he tied Uncle Ben's shoelaces together - the old fellow cracked his head open on the hearth. Uncle Ben swore that the boy would die on the scaffold one day.' Lawrence laughed, 'Actually, Graham was quite relieved when they abolished capital punishment here in this country. I remember him saying so.'

'Have they still got it in Panama?' grinned Janek.

'Now that's a thought. I suppose Uncle Ben would have the last laugh if they strung Graham up over there, although the old fellow has been dead himself for quite some time.'

'So what did your brother run from in the end?'

asked Janek who, while always remembering his duties to the disappeared, did not always remember why they had had to disappear.

'Oh the usual…money problems, women, aggressive creditors, the law breathing too hotly down his neck.'

'Do you miss him?' Janek asked suddenly.

'He was great with the kids. They miss him. Or they did. He knew the woods like the back of his hand and could find anything in them, just for the asking: a grass snake here, a fox cub there, a hibernating hedgehog elsewhere, one of those red toadstools with the white flakes on top…the ones that all the other adults in their lives could only ever find inside an illustrated book of fairy tales. He always had time for my children - I'll give him that.'

'But that was not enough to make you like him?' quizzed Janek, seeing the animosity through the reminiscences.

'When he left, he took with him a good deal of my money. Said that he would pay it back, but he never has. And now I ferry money from his account out to him every year. Money that is, by rights, mine. And that makes me feel weak and stupid.'

'Why do you do it?' asked Janek.

'Because I could never stand to think of him starving, although I'll bet he's been doing better than me for years. He was never one for falling on his face, our Graham,' said Lawrence - rather bitterly, Janek thought.

'Then why didn't you let me take the whole job on - the collecting and the ferrying of the money and everything else?' questioned Janek.

'Honestly? I didn't know whether I could trust you at first. And now that I know I can, I just keep coming anyway, in case you've heard news of him: older brothers are never forgotten.'

'Or forgiven?' pressed Janek.

'Maybe one day…when I'm too old to be proud any more…Any luck with your Joseph?' asked Lawrence, changing the subject by way of a nod at the enormous photograph in front of him. Over the years Janek had told him something of his search.

'Bloody disastrous newspaper campaign to find him. Waste of money, waste of time. Just a load of red herrings and con artists trying to fleece me,' complained Janek.

'You're not losing hope though?' asked Lawrence.

'I mustn't. I have to believe that he's still out there.'

The woman was angry. She had come straight to the park after failing to get close to her man…the hateful man. She had not factored in that bloody boy. Why couldn't he have just kept his nose out, instead of grubbing about for her lipstick and pen?

She unfolded a sheet of paper from her bag. It was a leaf out of the electoral roll. A sharp red line bisected the page. The woman stared at the details immediately above it: Mr Janek Lipsz, 33 Orchard Road, London, SE9 4PW.

She hadn't even managed a good look at her man. She still did not know whether it was really him. Tomorrow. Tomorrow would be the day.

At nine-thirty she was back. It was too early for the footballers so she had Orchard Road to herself.

Slowly she walked to the double doors and then back to the head of the street. The fellow yesterday - the shifty one in the hat - he had simply knocked on them.

Could she really have found her man, after so many years? Was he really just a few yards behind those doors? It seemed incredible.

All of a sudden she no longer had the street to herself: a short, pudgy man hurried straight up to Janek's double doors and went straight in – another client. The woman held her breath, fumbled for the clasp on her bag. This was not as she had imagined things: her plans had not included scurrying little fat men. She felt powerless. She paced the road, up and down, sometimes turning a few metres up the adjoining street too, for she knew that she had made a static spectacle of herself the day before - and in front of little boys. She had been anything but subtle. Today there was to be no standing in one spot, gawping.

It was more than an hour before the stout man came out. He was twenty paces from her, she had her bag open. She could see the red blotches on his pinched face and hear the shortness in his wind as he approached.

'Excuse me?' she said, when he drew level.

The portly man stopped.

'Excuse me,' she said once more.

The fellow looked impatient.

'Have you got the time?' she gabbled.

'Eleven o' clock,' he replied then shot off on his busy, fat way.

She grimaced after him - but not at him - she was exasperated with herself and kicked out at an ash sapling which was trying its luck on the grass verge.

'After thirty years, is that the best you can do?' she goaded herself… 'Wait,' she cried, running after the man.

He stopped, obviously irritated. 'Didn't you hear? I said it was eleven,' he snapped.

She was less than a metre from him now.

'Please,' she said. 'What goes on in there? What does that man in there do?' She indicated Janek's garage.

'You a private dick or sumpin?' hissed the man.

'A what?'

He looked her up and down and then scoffed an answer to his own question, 'Nah, I guess not. He's a facilitator, love. That's what 'e is. Now if ya don't mind...' And he was gone, like a squat little badger caught out in daylight.

Tears streamed down the woman's cheeks: she wanted to take out her knife and lay the point against the man's eye and make him tell her exactly what went on behind those closed doors. But that was out of the question, for her fight was not with him, and deep down she knew that as a woman, and an old one at that, there was only one knife fight in her, so it could not be wasted.

Then her subconscious called to her; great melodies of hope. Suddenly she became aware that she was not the only woman crying in the street. Ten metres distant, a woman was sobbing in a blue Renault. And some power of delayed observation told her that this car and this woman had been there in the road the day before too – watching and waiting like her.

Slowly she walked up to woman and car, drying

her eyes as she did so, trying desperately to compose herself. She approached from behind and could see the occupant's heaving chest and auburn hair. Timidly, actually scared of this stranger's weeping, she knocked on the driver's side window.

The seated woman spun round like a wild animal disturbed in its den. There was anger in her eyes, as well as sorrow, but when she saw the empathy of another female face, the anger receded; only the tears remained. 'Yes?' she said hollowly, rolling down the window.

'I'm sorry, I'm so very sorry to disturb you like this, but do you, by any chance, know what goes on in there?' the Polish lady asked, indicating Janek's garden. The words acted as a floodgate. It was fully five minutes before she could understand anything through the wracking sobs. For years Renault woman had waited alone and it was very nearly too much to be called on now to account for her lonely vigil.

At last she choked out a coherent answer. 'That is where they go to leave, but never return. That man in there, Mr Lipsz, he is an evil man…he arranges it for our husbands and our loves to run away and then he helps them to stay away from us, forever. He knows where they are…all of them…but not a thing will he reveal. Not a clue does he let slip. Through him they get away with everything: the money, the mistresses, the desertion, and most of all, they get away without having to explain themselves and face truth with us. And we are left here not knowing whether they are happy without us, or sad without us, or miss us, or loathe us. You know, I don't even know whether my Clive is dead or alive. But that man in there, he knows, and there's not a power in the land can force him to tell me. Believe me – I have tried them all.'

The Renault woman seemed to swell and grow while she said all this. Then, suddenly silent, she shrivelled back down to steering wheel-level.

'I'm very sorry, I really am,' came the Polish accent, 'But do you mean that the man up at that house actually helps people to disappear, away from their lives here?'

'Yes, that's exactly what he does,' came the tiny reply.

'Only men?'

No answer.

'Please. Is it a male-only service?'

'Twice. I've seen two women go in. That is all - in six years. The seated woman sank yet lower, reduced to nothing. She was as shovelled earth. For a moment the questioner hated the Renault woman's passivity and then she realised that what she actually hated was her own inaction. 'Thanks,' she said, at once resolved. Determined strides carried her across the road to Janek's double doors.

She rapped firmly then unclasped her bag. She let her hand rest loosely upon the contents. A headscarf was uppermost and covered everything else from view. The sweat stood out on her as on a horse in the chase; her breath snorted out in great shotgun blasts.

Slowly the bolt drew back, the hinges complaining.

The woman swallowed down a thick phlegm of fear.

'Phil? Is that you?' asked Janek, as he levered one of the doors open…

The woman took in every pore of the face before

her: the lively eyes, the strong chin, the fantastically broken nose. It was him - definitely the man - not just on account of that signal nose, but in every line and every angle of the face before her.

'Hello,' Janek said kindly, 'I thought you were the boy from across the road. How can I help?'

The woman opened and shut her mouth like a fish mouthing a hook. Janek smiled tolerantly, moved a little to one side so that the newcomer could see the way through to his office - if indeed an audience with him was what she wanted. It was rare for women to call. 'What is your name?' he asked softly.

'Sarah.'

'I'm Janek Lipsz. Have you come to see me on a specific matter?'

Janek Lipsz…the name whipped her blood into torrid waves.

'I have heard that you do not do women,' Sarah spluttered, almost at a loss what to say. It was a terrible opening and her hand dipped beneath the headscarf. Janek looked at the woman, saw that he would have to be supportive and sensitive. He stifled a risqué rejoinder: 'In my capacity as a disappearer of people, you mean?'

Sarah nodded, unsettled by her own verbal clumsiness. Whenever she had visualised this moment, through the long, agonised years of waiting and searching, she had always imagined herself cool and focused before her quarry.

'Please come in,' Janek smiled. 'Careful, there is an exposed root there.'

As he led the way, Sarah eyed the side of his neck, where the artery was at its thickest, and her handbag-hand tensed.

Janek turned.

She jumped.

'Have you come far?' he asked.

'Many miles and many years have brought me here to you,' she replied.

Just what I need - a bloody riddler, thought Janek, but said nothing.

Once inside she was reluctant to sit. Janek offered her the usual client's chair - three times - but each time she remained standing. He noticed too that she wore her handbag wrapped tight about her, as if for protection, with her right hand deep and secure within it. It was just about the biggest handbag he had ever seen.

Janek did sit down. He could not conduct business as if across a chip shop counter, but did not mind Sarah standing: over the years he had come to accept that it took all sorts to turn the world, and many of them, none too stable. Also, as a general rule, people only considered fleeing their lives and everything familiar to them, when the familiar had started to do funny things to their heads…so if this woman's fatigue with her existence manifested itself as chair-aversion, then he would go along with it.

She stood silently; Janek set the ball rolling…

'I help people to disappear - without trace if need be. But also I lay down the framework for their eventual return, so that they can exercise that option too…should they ever wish to. It is an insurance I advise my escapees to take up.' Janek paused. The Sarah-woman didn't seem to be listening. 'Is that what you want?' he pressed. 'Is that why you are here -

because you wish to disappear?'

Sarah clutched her bag to her body even more tightly and Janek noticed that her right hand had all but vanished into it.

'Yes that is what I want,' she replied - in a voice which seemed wrenched from somewhere unnatural…Maybe from within that bloody handbag of hers, thought Janek.

'I can help you with that,' he said.

'It is what I want,' she repeated woodenly.

Janek had thought so, and there it was for sure - her accent. The woman hadn't said enough for him to be sure before. But this time he had picked it up, definitely picked it up. She was from his home country - originally. Years away had softened the vowels, as with him, but they were Polish vowels, unmistakably Polish vowels.

'You are from Poland too. Which part?' he asked. It seemed a fair enough question…not overly personal. Janek fancied it would serve as a bit of social cement between them. So the response he received surprised him.

Absolute silence. Not even Sarah's breath seemed to break it.

'It's none of my business of course,' said Janek, backtracking…'If you wish just to stick to business we can settle terms…' He tailed off.

She was not listening.

Janek felt a flash of anger - which he extinguished just as soon as he registered it. He had had some real kooks come to see him over the years. They were part of the territory, as was not being offended by them. He peered curiously at the woman. She was not looking at him, but directly behind his head.

'Why is he there?' she rasped-half-gasped, her Polish accent broadening. 'Why here on your wall?' The woman was taking in every little detail of the photograph behind Janek. Suddenly she stepped closer to the image, as if attempting to absorb it via osmosis.

'He is better viewed from a distance,' interrupted Janek, disconcerted. He was not used to visitors being more affected by Joseph than he and he felt uncomfortable with it. Also, it usually took a while for him to build up to the matter of his lost boy. This woman was jumping the gun. He felt emotionally mugged…and by a loon to boot.

A muscle in Sarah's cheek pulsed, but she didn't move a millimetre farther away from the photograph. She took her hand out of her handbag. Indeed, she extended a shaking finger to touch Joseph's face and then actually traced down his nose with it.

Janek decided then to class her alongside the nuts on park benches who shout at passers-by. Strangely, though, her unusual intensity served to calm him and he felt free of his usual reticence concerning Joseph. 'I lost him,' he explained, 'In the war. Been trying to find him ever since.'

'Beautiful boy,' murmured Sarah.

'Yes, I suppose he is,' replied Janek.

'Beautiful, beautiful boy.'

Janek sat there, not saying anything.

'Then you think he is alive, still?' Sarah whispered into the silence after some time.

Janek was brought up short - put on the spot to account for his own assumptions. 'Well, I know that he survived the war and I am as certain as I can be that he left Poland. But where he went, I have no idea. I have been trying to find that out now for over thirty years.'

'But you do think that he is still alive?' persisted Sarah.

Janek twisted in his seat. 'Yes. In my heart I think he is still living, but I do not know whether that is just my heart willing it so.'

Sarah hung her head; it was the first time she had averted her gaze from the picture since first noticing it. 'Joseph is out there,' she said to the floor.

'What did you say?' shot back Janek. 'Did you just say Joseph?'

'Yes,' said Sarah, colouring a little.

'But I didn't tell you his name.'

'Yes you did,' she replied matter-of-factly, but her cheeks coloured more deeply. Her hand reached for the open handbag once more and disappeared within it.

Janek tried to remember. Had he told her? It had been a strange few minutes…maybe she was right. How else could she have known? He must have.

'It is in the hope that he is out there somewhere that I find the energy to carry on my work here,' said Janek with an expansive wave of his arm. 'If I ever really thought that he was no more, I would shut up shop, forever. If I definitely knew that this world was without him, then I would answer no more knocks at my door. When that time…' He stopped mid-sentence, still trying to sift back through exactly what he had said to this strange woman. Had he mentioned Joseph by name?

'You did,' returned Sarah, reading Janek's thoughts

in the wrinkling of his brow. The colour had receded from her face and she replaced a loose strand of hair with her one free hand. The other remained deep within the capacious hand-bag.

Janek shrugged, then wondered at himself: he never shrugged when discussing Joseph - never. The subject was too raw. What was going on? How was it that everything was being turned upside down? What strange effects this woman was provoking. Janek noticed a little bit of knuckle protruding from the bag. Why didn't she just stand like a normal person?

'Why do you search for him?'

He was a bit put out by the question. Always before, it had been his place to advance the conversation about Joseph, to introduce the whys and the hows and wherefores. Always he chose a comfortable and convenient moment, or rather, the least uncomfortable one, usually at the end of proceedings, but today, here was this fruitcake, who looked like Nelson with one hand tucked away, conducting the whole show from the start.

'You do want to disappear don't you? That is why you are here, isn't it?' asked Janek, hissing his 'esses' rather.

'I am desperate for peace,' replied Sarah. 'But please, why do you search for Joseph?'

Janek gave in. Did it really matter when a client heard the story - at the beginning or at the end of proceedings? 'I was entrusted with his care in 1943, in Nazi occupied Poland. I did a bad job of it and the boy almost died. Since the end of the war I have been searching for him so that I can make up for my negligence…and for my sins…'

'Have you ever come close?' interrupted the woman in a feverish voice. 'Ever just missed him by a little?'

Janek looked strangely at her. 'I have been without luck these last thirty years.'

'But you have never stopped searching?'

'Never. It has been the focus of my life since 1945…'

Janek registered a couple more knuckles peeking out of the handbag.

'…When I arrived here in Britain, after a brief stint as a school caretaker, I set myself up as a private detective, above an optician's in Beckton High Street. I had developed certain investigative skills during the war and there was a market here: displaced people who needed help in finding one another, families split up, valuables lost, rackets to be investigated. I reckoned that the business would pay my way in this country and help me to find Joseph. In those early days I was confident that I would turn him up in no time. That did not prove to be the case. I learned that sometimes people just disappeared, without trace. I…'

'Why England?' interrupted Sarah.

'Sorry?'

'Why settle in England to look for Joseph?'

Janek looked up at the big photograph before answering, 'I still had contacts in Poland and they had turned up no sign of him back home. And a lot of Poles who could get out of the home country came here. I did. I thought that Joseph might have done the same - just an idea really. I had to get out anyhow, away from the Russians.'

'But you didn't find him here?'

'No. But I did study every disappearance case which came my way, until I ended up something of a specialist in the field - and more and more frequently, I was asked to trace people: sometimes long-lost relations, sometimes embezzlers who had fleeced the companies they worked for. I was good at finding them. I got a name for myself. And over time, by immersing myself in these vanishings, by really poring over them, I became an expert in the theory of disappearance. On paper, I could map out for any one man how best to cover his tracks – and still keep some contact with his old life. That is the hard part; one or other is easy, it is doing both which requires skill. Then, as I became more and more frustrated with my own lack of success in finding my Joseph…'

Sarah seemed to wince.

'What is it?' asked Janek.

'Tooth-ache,' she replied quickly.

'…And as I became more and more frustrated with my own lack of success in finding Joseph, I settled upon the idea which was to become my sole trade - helping people to disappear - for a very reasonable fee. In place of expensive rates, I imposed a condition: my clients had to assist in the search for the boy. Every person I helped quit their old life for a new one was given a small copy of that photograph up there and an artist's impression of what Joseph would look like as a fully grown man. And they were instructed to keep an eye out for him. Within three years I had escapees in twenty-one different countries. I was sure that one of them would turn something up. And they did, for most were very loyal and valued the discreet job I did for them, so it was not long before I was notified of sightings. I followed up all leads in those early days, but nothing came of any of them. There were lots of lookalikes, mistaken identities and sometimes, I just arrived too late. Not one definitive sighting of Joseph did I get…

…Time went by, I moved to this place, and I became more discriminating. There had to be a balance: when I travelled to check out sightings I was not here to receive more custom and I needed to maintain the numbers of searchers. Also, I was not here to receive any fresh information on Joseph. I feared Sod's Law, the law which said that the real red-hot stuff would come in while I was away. So in the end, I graded the quality of all leads and responded only to the best. Thirty years on, I am still doing the same, and one day I hope that the big one will come in.'

Janek sighed out his breath. He took in Sarah. She was wringing her hands, actually wringing them. It was a shock to see them both out in the air together: her bag was hand-free.

'Wh..wh..what happens now when you are away? When you are off on the trail? Who is here to receive the news of Joseph that might come in? The red-hot stuff?' Sarah asked, and Janek thought that he could hear panic rising in her voice.

'No one. That is why I only travel for the best of leads these days. There is always the chance that I might miss the real McCoy while I am away.'

'So the real evidence might arrive here and you would never know?' Sarah spluttered reedily, her voice breaking. 'Never, ever know?' she repeated.

For a moment Janek was unsettled, even a little

intimidated, by the depth of her feeling. 'Yes, I'm afraid so,' he replied quietly. 'I have someone feed the cat and mind my house, but no one mans the office when I am away…'

'I understand,' she whispered and Janek could see from the set of her face that she was lost in grim thoughts. For half a minute neither she nor Janek spoke. Why was this woman's response so extreme? And why was she affecting him so?

At last she spoke. Once more it was in a tiny voice, shaking with emotion: 'Please, Mr Lipsz, please may I see the artist's impression?' The last two words were actually gulped out.

Janek was taken aback once more, by her intensity and by her pre-empting of him. 'Of course,' he said after a pause. 'Always I show it to my disappearees, always. Indeed, they have a copy to keep. That is the whole point.'

Janek slid open the relevant drawer. The usual timings and order of the whole Joseph business were being completely reworked. He took another look at Sarah's face. He sensed that it would be an unpleasant, even dangerous, business to contradict the emotions which lay behind her eyes.

'Nowadays I do no broader detective work, only my Disappearance Club, as I call it…that and poring over every lead that ever comes in concerning my missing person. See, here. This is what Joseph would look like now.'

Sarah groped greedily for the artist's impression and Janek noticed that her lower lip quivered. Her hands closed around the image. Janek started to speak, but she silenced him with a passionate shake of her head. She traced the contours of the face and gazed into the carefully drawn eyes. Janek did not know quite what to do. Was this woman responding to Joseph, or would she have reacted like this whatever the person or image before her? If he offered her a slice of cake would she stare at that as if it were made of solid gold too?

'Would you like some cake?'

No answer

'A biscuit?'

Not a flicker.

'I have some…'

'His chin is too square,' Sarah stated, still examining the face. Her voice was shaky, but carried authority, 'It would never have grown so blockish.'

Janek opened and shut his mouth, stopping himself just in time from saying that the artist's impression had always been good enough for him, and for every other person who had ever seen it.

'Your artist put in too much jaw.' Tears filled Sarah's eyes, until the lids and lashes were bristling with them, but they did not drop. Her eyes were magnified. The size and brightness of them had the effect of making her appear decades younger. For a second, until they fell, she reminded Janek of someone. Then they spilled and the memory was lost before he could put either a name or face to it. Janek was confused and then, just as suddenly, shocked into a wild, hopeful thought:

'You don't know a man who looks like that do you?' he asked passionately.

Sarah shook her head with sorrowful little movements. 'No…You must forgive me', she added. 'I suffered my own tragedy in the war. Your tale of Joseph reminded me - yours is a very moving story.'

Sarah saw the softening in Janek's face. She slipped the artist's impression into her bag. 'You do not get many women coming into your office, Mr Lipsz?'

Janek said that he did not.

'We can make rather a spectacle of ourselves, when something pulls at our heart strings. If you had had more of us in here, you would have had to pass the tissues more often.'

'Oh I am sorry,' gabbled Janek and passed her half a dozen.

'Thank you,' she sniffed, 'There's not one of us Poles came through that war unscathed. They don't understand that in this country, do they? Doodlebugs and air raids, they are not the same as invasion and occupation.' Her hands were by her sides now. Both of them. 'I hope that you find him, with all my heart, and may God be with you in your search.'

Then Janek was ashamed that he had ever allowed the woman's interest and passion to irritate him. He recalled attacking Francis Teak, just three months earlier, because he would not take the matter of Joseph seriously…'There is a pub down the road. Shall we go and get a drink there together?'

Sarah flashed her eyes back up at the framed photograph and shook her head, 'I couldn't.'

'I have a little gin here.' Janek indicated one of his cabinets.

She locked eyes with Joseph again, as if trying to find her answer in him…'It is a little early for me,' Sarah replied stiffly.

'Then coffee up at the house?' pushed Janek, keen

to make amends in his own mind for the uncharitable thoughts that he had had earlier.

Sarah's eyes flickered from one face to the other: Joseph's to Janek's, Janek's to Joseph's. 'Very well,' she nodded.

Janek led the way up the garden path. It was slippery with leaves and there were muddy patches. Half way up, at a particularly tricky patch - one where he had slipped before himself - he reached gently for Sarah's arm. She jumped at his touch as if he were red-hot.

'Sorry,' he said simply, 'Watch your step, the ground is treacherous here.'

They went in through French windows. There was a rug on the floor and books on shelves and books in piles. Five seconds after entry, Oskar the cat twirled himself around Janek's legs then threaded himself this way and that against the newcomer's shins. Janek noted that Sarah seemed much more comfortable with the cat's touch than his. Maybe it was a man-thing with her. He led the way into the kitchen, wondering at the abuse this woman might have suffered - at the hands of men.

When the coffee was made she clasped it with both hands, taking in the heat as well as the taste.

'I've popped the heating on, but it takes some time before you feel it in this place.'

The woman had discarded her handbag, fully zipped up now, and Janek took this as a good sign. He tried to guess at the various emotional props she probably had secreted within: locks of hair, a bit of fluffy cloth, a precious photograph of her own?

Still Sarah did not want to sit, so they stood and

talked.

'So where is it you wish to escape to?' asked Janek.

'I have no idea,' returned Sarah, still cradling her mug. 'Somewhere I can breathe once again.'

'Well there is air everywhere,' joked Janek then remembered that Sarah was not big on humour. 'Usually I like my clients to decide on their own destination - that way they can't blame me if it all goes tits-up….wrong,' corrected Janek, unsure where this woman stood on coarse language either. He mused silently that things were much easier with men. 'This country or abroad?' he continued.

'I think abroad. Yes, abroad, that would be best for an entirely new start wouldn't it?' asked Sarah.

'It certainly helps make a clean break with the past, if that is what you want.'

'My past is a barren land. It has broken me and now I wish to break with it,' she replied.

'Abroad it is then,' said Janek, trying to sound upbeat. He paused, waiting for her to ask where, or even to hazard a few countries herself. She said nothing. The central heating clunked into action. A wood pigeon landed heavily in the cherry tree by the window. Janek cleared his throat: 'America is not a bad place. There is a lot of it, both to see and to hide oneself in, if need be. And more than anywhere else in the world, there is a highly developed and protected sense of the individual; an individual has more rights there than anywhere else in the world. That makes a person in the States very hard to touch - legally. I would advise there, if you have no objection to the country.'

'America it is then,' said Sarah.

She looked over to her bag. Oskar had curled heavily on top of it, his head and paws comfy, his belly flat against the soft leather. For a moment, Sarah looked disconcerted. Then she turned a smile on Janek, the first to have cracked her intense, worried face. 'I am sorry to be so cheeky, but have you an apple, or something?' she asked. 'I am feeling rather faint after this morning. I fear that I have been far too emotional.'

'But of course,' Janek replied.

He handed her an apple of the most exquisite crimson. 'Would you like something more substantial? Cake, biscuits, ham and pickle?'

'No, no,' replied Sarah, but she did breeze past him into the body of the kitchen, where the stove and cupboard units stood cluttered and grubby.

'Sorry about the mess,' Janek said.

Almost before the sentence was out, Sarah had snapped open two drawers. Out of one she pulled a kitchen knife, about a foot in length. 'I hope you don't mind,' she said, noticing Janek's eyes following her. 'My teeth are not so very strong these days and I can't just bite into apple anymore. I need to slice the portions off.'

She proceeded to carve a slice, holding the apple in her left hand, the long knife in her right. Then she stepped closer to Janek.

'Be careful,' he said. 'There are much smaller ones in the same drawer you know; I joint chickens with that bugger! You could do some damage with that.'

Sarah smiled strangely and continued with the outsize blade.

Janek shrugged and his elbow actually brushed

against her arm. She did not jump or flinch at his touch, unlike in the garden. Bloody good job, thought Janek, she'd have sliced a lump off one of us with that thing in her hand.

'Will you ask me to look for your Joseph?' asked Sarah through a mouthful of apple.

'Yes. It is an absolute condition. Of course, I have no control over what people actually do once they arrive at their destinations, but I only take on as clients those who show willing at this end - in terms of keeping an eye out for Joseph, that is. Just this summer I attacked a man who demanded my services but made clear that he would not do what I asked in return.'

'Attacked him?'

'Yes,' said Janek, wondering why he had told Sarah. Deep down, was he just a schoolboy trying to impress the girl with how tough he was?

'Physically attacked him because he would not help find Joseph?' persisted Sarah.

'That's right,' Janek replied, colouring a little. 'Nothing too brutal, but I did shake him up a bit.'

'Where, down in your office?'

'No, it was out in the street actually.' The colour spread to Janek's neck.

Sarah put down the big knife. It clunked heavily against the wood of the kitchen table. 'It is a good thing to carry such passion in you for your cause.' She paused, looked at the knife on the table then at her bag. Oskar was purring into its leather folds. 'Mr Lipsz, may I come to you again tomorrow? I am afraid that today has been very emotional for me. I am afraid that I have made rather a fool of myself and...'

'No, no, no, no,' Janek interrupted.

'Oh but I think I have. Would it be alright if I returned to you tomorrow? I have some things I must think through?'

Janek smiled, his best comforting, tolerant, sensitive smile, 'Certainly. I am here all day.'

'How about two o' clock?' she asked, eyeing the skewed nose which had remained such a constant over the years.

'Absolutely. But you may come at any time.'

Sarah seemed happy and took an enormous bite out of her apple, as if to seal the arrangement. Janek looked on, confused: a horse couldn't have taken a bigger, better, cleaner, more powerful bite. Hadn't the woman said that her teeth were weak? Wasn't that why she had needed a knife?

CHAPTER 9

'I couldn't wait,' she said, bursting in on Janek at ten–thirty in the morning. Sarah was beaming.

Janek put down-cum-hid the G&T he had just mixed for himself. The disappointments in Mexico and Portugal had driven him to the hard stuff. Now it was purchased on every shopping trip.

Sarah did not seem to notice the glass. In contrast to the day before, she no longer seemed in urgent need of a psychiatrist's couch: gone was the quavering voice, the obvious sorrow, the handbag as shield against the world. She had dropped it into a corner upon entry.

Janek looked wistfully at his drink and considered asking Sarah whether she had ever heard of knocking; Janek's drink habit was one thing he did not like his Disappearance Club clients to see.

'Couldn't wait,' she said again.

Nor could I, thought Janek, but actually said, 'So I see,' and tried to bury his pre-drink irritability. He was glad that she had come in this new, light mood, though. Maybe she was a morning person? And whatever the drawbacks in terms of his enforced sobriety, it would be better talking to her when she was like this…besides, if his craving grew too insistent, he could always just swig the drink down regardless and she could think whatever she liked.

'Changed my mind,' she crowed.

'Everything's changed about you, if you don't mind me saying so,' rejoined Janek.

'I know, I've been doing some thinking.'

'Right,' said Janek.

'And I've changed my mind.'

The conversation was proving hard going for Janek - before his morning measure.

'Can you be more specific?' he asked.

'I'm not going. I don't want to disappear anymore.'

'Right,' repeated Janek and reached for his drink. There was only so much a man could take…The lovely cool gin hit the spot splendidly: he breathed it in and drank it down at the same time. In a trice the ice cubes were tinkling loudly against one another at the bottom of an empty glass. Then Janek tipped in another shot and tonic with the practised hand of a heavy drinker. The whole process, from first tonsil-freshner to refill, took no more than twenty seconds.

'Don't you want to know why?' enthused Sarah, as he was in the process of setting down his second glass.

'Yes, yes I do,' Janek replied, this time with genuine interest.

'You. It was you.'

'Janek turned about, pretending to look to see if there was another person in the room. He laughed - he was pleased for the dippy old bird - and if he had played some part in her new-found happiness, then that was great.

'It was marvellous to see someone living and breathing a cause. You work towards an admirable objective. No…you are driven by one. And just witnessing your intensity...'

Janek felt like saying that it was nothing compared to her intensity.

'…And just witnessing your intensity yesterday and your determination, has filled me with new hope. I realised last night, after talking to you, that I just did not have to run any more. That the days of feeling as if I no longer fitted were over. All one needs is a cause…something to live for.'

'This is great. Truly wonderful,' said Janek, doing his G&T some serious damage.

'That is why I want you to give me a job.'

Janek nearly took one of his ice cubes down. When he had finished coughing, it felt as if his diaphragm had knotted about his spleen. 'What?!' he gasped, clutching at his side.

'Well you yourself said that there was no one here to man the office when you are off following leads and sightings.'

Janek frowned.

'Well didn't you?'

'I go away very infrequently now.'

'Then with two of us on the case, you could go more frequently.'

'Look,' said Janek, motioning the loopy woman before him into a chair, 'You don't really know what this business involves.'

'I could learn,' interrupted Sarah, her face irradiated with girlish enthusiasm.

'No, no…listen…please listen to me: the last time I had genuine, quality leads to chase, you know what I had to do to get them? Huh? I had to commission a double-spread in *The Times*: one page with Joseph's 1943 photograph on it, the other with the artist's impression I showed you. And my contact details were printed beneath both. People all round the world responded to that double-spread and then I had to sort the sightings. The vast majority were complete bollocks. In fact, less than half of a percent were any good and I followed those up - even went to Mexico and Portugal to check two of them out. But in the end, they all turned out to be crap. It is a demoralising business, this, believe me. I plod on because it is all I know and because I have been doing it for decades now. Anyone else would be driven crazy by it. Mine is not a career I recommend.'

But Sarah was looking at Janek with unblinking eyes of fascination.

'And I am an old man who is used to his own company. I do not share space well.'

Sarah heard none of this, 'I am an old man' stuff for she was stunned by Janek's double-spread revelation. 'You actually did that? Went to such lengths?' she said in a respectful whisper. 'It must have cost you a fortune.'

'Twenty thousand pounds for the ad, that's how much.'

Sarah's eyes blinked.

'That's right, the price of a new house - cash. And all that money didn't get me one step closer to Joseph.'

'What about the club members? They're out there searching. I could help with the leads they send in.'

'The disappeared? They don't come up with enough quality sightings,' replied Janek, 'Certainly not enough to warrant another pair of hands here.'

'But are there no more leads and sightings yet to come in from this *Times* double-spread?' asked Sarah, the first cracks appearing in her enthusiasm.

Janek hated to be the one to widen the cracks - he feared a return of the other, manic Sarah: 'How many three-month-old newspapers do you pick up and read?' he said.

For a second Sarah was entirely deflated and Janek saw in her eyes an awful sadness, like a child's when love is withheld and they rolled pitifully over in the direction of her outsize handbag. Then, just as quickly, she rebounded, like a child will when love is bestowed once more. Her eyes were bright again and snapped back round to Janek. 'But the disappearees - your clients - aren't they duty-bound to look out for Joseph and to contact you when they think that they've found him?'

Janek nodded, 'Some take my request seriously.'

'Only some?'

'Quite a good proportion. They are not bad people, by and large, and even the bad ones do have much to be grateful to me for.'

'So there you are then,' crowed Sarah triumphantly. 'Together we could ship more of them out and with me here, there would always be someone around to receive new business as it comes in, even when you are away in countries like Mexico. That way the number actually searching out there would always remain high and you wouldn't miss any hot new leads either.'

'But Sarah, Sarah, I told you, I go off chasing leads very infrequently these days. Also, mine is not a high turnover business. There is just not the workload for two people.'

'But we could generate more - together.' Sarah

snatched a look at the photograph behind Janek. 'Let me see, now…how do your clients find out about you and your service?'

'Word of mouth mainly.'

'And?'

'And?' repeated Janek.

'Yes…And?'

'I occasionally advertise in Private Eye magazine.'

'And?'

'There is no other 'And'.'

'But there must be thousands of other avenues and opportunities.'

'I dare say, Sarah, but I am tired, my dear, and I have had so many disappointments. This is a young man's game.' Janek's words rattled through his head and he was shocked at them. Was he giving up?

'Then you will die without finding Joseph,' rasped Sarah. And her eyes were glowing coals upon him. Janek was shocked at her intensity, then he felt shame that someone, anyone, should care more than he did; that another could show him where he might be trying harder in his searching, and he shrank a little under the heat of Sarah's stare. 'Why do you care so much?' he asked in a quiet voice. 'What is it to you?'

'I came here yesterday so low, lower than I have ever been. But you raised me up by showing me how one can live for a cause and now I wish to take up that same cause. Your search speaks to my soul; I want my life to be given direction by it.'

Janek did not doubt that she was in earnest. He did not doubt that she would do a thorough job for him. But there were other considerations…his had always been a one-man show. How could such an old dog learn to work with another and to share space? Sarah seemed to have ignored that point, even though he had raised it. And there were other things…

'Ok,' retorted Janek, getting second wind and sounding more forceful. 'Let's not beat about the bush: you're here on a thoroughly uninvited job interview, and quite frankly, on the evidence of the twenty-four hours I've known you, you're about two jumps short of the loony bin. So why on earth should I employ you in my thirty-year-old business?'

'Because it's only a lunatic would drop everything to help you search and because you won't be employing me: I don't want a penny. I'll do the job for free…no…I'll do it for the satisfaction it will give me.'

Janek looked at his empty glass and wished it full.

'Do you want a G&T?' he said.'

'No, definitely not. And that's another reason why you should have me working here – to get you off that stuff and back putting all your efforts into looking for Joseph.'

Cheeky bitch, he thought, but deep down, Janek knew that the drink was affecting him adversely. For months he had been less professional, less on the ball. He looked longingly at the bottle…

…She might just make the difference, this nutty woman. And anyone who was prepared to work for nothing was likely to do a bloody good job. Didn't he owe it to Joseph at least to try her out? Was this barmy cow one of fate's little helpers? Janek rubbed his tired ginned-up eyes…

'Ground rules,' he said, springing up from his seat, 'and I don't apologise for any of these, on account of the fact that I don't know you from Eve…First, I want no kind of relationship with you beyond the professional, second, you must never try to tidy me up, third, and this is the most important one of all, if it doesn't work out, and I tell you to bugger off, then you bugger off - pronto.'

Sarah beamed, 'So you are saying yes.'

'I am saying yes. On those terms.'

Sarah clapped her hands together. 'And Janek...'

'Yes?'

'What does pronto mean?'

'It means straight away,' Janek half-shouted, 'If I tell you it isn't working out with you here then you must leave at once. Got it?'

'Got it,' nodded Sarah, her head jiggling wildly. And as she nodded hers, Janek shook his, wondering how on earth an old dyed-in-the-wool, stick-in-the-mud like himself could have been so acted upon. He looked up at the heavens - no point - relief was not often vouchsafed from there. He looked at his gin bottle; it seemed that relief would not be accessible from there much longer either.

The sun careered in through the windows, much more fulsomely than was usual of a November morning. Janek's spirits were fired by the rays. It might just work, he thought, in spite of Sarah's obvious instability - maybe because of it. He set to working through the practicalities.

'This is a small office,' he said to her, 'Too small for both of us, particularly when clients call.'

'I've thought of that,' interrupted Sarah eagerly.

'Oh!'

'I could work from the main house.'

'My house?'

'Yes. Your house,' Sarah replied, a shade more gingerly.

'You could, could you?' returned Janek, imparting caustic spin to his voice. 'You have seen little of my house other than the kitchen. There is not much more room inside it than there is in here. I live a cluttered life.'

Sarah stayed silent. Janek twiddled his pen. Her eyes flitted from the pen to his face and back again. After twenty seconds he spoke, 'There is one room I suppose, upstairs, which is full only of junk. We could clear it out. It might make a passable office.'

'Let's go up and see it,' enthused Sarah, breaking her silence.

'No. I couldn't, not right now…'

Janek could see that Sarah was suppressing a rejoinder, keen to be on good behaviour at this early stage. '…Not when a client might call,' he fudged, knowing deep down that his reticence had much more to do with not being able to get in through the door of the room in question than with keeping strict office hours. A blackbird called. Another answered. They could both hear the gurgling of the stream. He looked at the side walls. Sarah glanced at the huge photograph of Joseph then stared at her own hands.

'Right then,' said Janek, stirring up the silence, 'Where to start?'

He pulled his eyes down from the walls and started riffling his correspondence. Before actually finding the things he was after he started in, 'These came yesterday: two letters that got lost in the post. They are the last of the replies to my newspaper campaign.'

Sarah's eyes widened till they were as big as a fox

cub's in their curiosity. Then they grew still larger as she continued watching Janek's nimble fingers root through the papers of his desk.

'Here,' he said, at last, and for the first time noticed the huge orbs turned upon him. Internally Janek jumped. 'There's nothing to get worked up about,' he assured the eyes before him. 'They're both crap. I'm showing you what not to bother with.' The eyes dimmed a little and Janek turned the contents out. 'See here,' he continued, 'this one is asking for £50 in advance before he can send any solid information - just someone on the make. And the other, seemingly solid at first sight, is just the ramblings of a fool. He has included a whole list of sightings and dates beside the sightings - looks good doesn't it? But on closer inspection, the details are contradictory! They simply do not add up. The sender is a deluded fool, after a bit of attention. The first was a deliberate, if clumsy, con job; the second almost certainly just innocent lunacy, but both of them could waste days, even weeks, of a searcher's time.'

Sarah asked to hold the letters herself, turning them over for every little detail. Then she threw the con artist's effort to the floor. His return address flashed up at her, provocatively. 'We should inform the police. You should inform the police. He's a bastard, a bastard, and an arsehole - when he's not trying it on with you, he probably bills little old ladies thousands for trimming their hedges and kidnaps dogs so that he can charge the owners for their safe return.'

'No, no,' said Janek, interrupting this blue tirade, 'You have much to learn, Sarah. We never call the police here. They have a passing interest in my work as it is; many who disappear via me do so with debts to their name, company secrets in their bags, and court cases pending; that sort of thing. But the business requires that we preserve absolute secrecy and anonymity. We tell the police nothing and we tell the families of the disappeared nothing. That is essential, or the disappeared themselves will not trust us and then we will no longer have our body of searchers out there. So we cope with money-grabbing letters ourselves - or rather, ignore them.'

'Do members of the families of the disappeared ever turn up here?' asked Sarah remembering the woman outside in her car.

'Occasionally. They are the saddest of cases, but never a word of information do I give out - unless the disappeared have given their direct permission.'

'Is that quite fair?' asked Sarah.

'My loyalty is to Joseph first, always to him, then to my clients. Their families do not come into it. Or rather, they come last.'

'Have you always been so uncaring?' pressed Sarah, and there was more than a hint of pugnacity in her voice.

'That is the way of this office and the nature of the business you have chosen to be in. No - the nature of the business I am letting you dip your toe into,' Janek flashed back. It had always pained him that the Renault woman sat sentinel outside his house day in, day out and that for five seconds' breath he could tell her exactly where in the world her husband now resided. Sarah had touched a raw spot and he had bridled.

She looked not at him, but at the photograph of Joseph and to Janek's mind, seemed to be suppressing a sharp-tongued retort. After quite a pause she did speak, but it was on an entirely different subject. 'Was it really twenty thousand pounds you spent on that double-page spread?'

'Oh yes. Hard cash,' answered Janek, keen not to remain pissed off. 'It was less than half that when I commissioned one before.'

'Before? Then it was not the first time? You have put so much money into your search!'

'Many, many thousands over the years. It is not a cheap business, looking for someone who has left no trail. It is like searching for a needle in a haystack whilst dropping gold out of your pockets.'

'You cannot be a bad man, then. It is impossible. One so free and unselfish with his money must have a good heart,' announced Sarah.

Janek thought this rather faint praise, suggesting as it did that she had thought him a bad man before. He shrugged off her comment: she had probably got a bee in her bonnet about that 'not telling the families' business - he would have to watch her in relation to that. He added, 'I search because of my guilt; the money I pay *The Times* is the price of my conscience, although it does not come anywhere near the total required. Do not become too convinced of my goodness.'

'What did you do?' stuttered Sarah.

Janek shook his head. 'That conversation is for me and Joseph alone - if I ever find him. After we've had it, and when I have handed over to him a little something I have kept aside all these years, then my life will be done.'

Janek stayed perfectly silent and perfectly still for

quite some time. All the while Sarah stared at the photograph of the boy in question.

'You mean you will die, after finding him?' she asked, breaking the silence. Her voice was shaky.

'No, probably not. I mean that I will then be free to grow old and to shuffle and mumble and go deaf and drink my gin. But most importantly, I'll be able to look my guilt in the eye and maybe sleep at nights,' Janek sighed. He paused, aware that he was revealing more of himself to this strange woman than he ever had to any single person before…'Now a lot of the work here is as dull as can be, Sarah,' he continued in more professional fashion, 'There's a lot of financial juggling: ten pounds to be paid in here, a hundred pounds to be paid out there, another few hundred to be wired across the Pacific. Wherever people go, they need moolah.'

Sarah's brow furrowed.

'Moolah...money - in order to get by. And it is always the first couple of years away that are the hardest. If an escapee can manage those, then he is usually well set. In those early months, though, I have to advise them, organise their accounts, even arrange them loans sometimes. That's not an easy job, that isn't: obtaining credit for a person who is in hiding. It is no sinecure here in this office; I do earn my percentage. And with it comes a little dribble of quality Joseph leads…only a very few, really. I don't want you to be under any misconceptions about that. We are not going to be fielding Joseph-news like falling confetti.'

Janek paused. He had heard a sob.

'Why are you crying?' he asked. His eyes were hard on Sarah, not aggressively so, but it was clear that he meant to have an answer.

She opened and shut her mouth twice, looked at the floor, raised her eyes, looked down at her handbag, then after quite a little time, raised her eyes again, this time with an answer, ' I am just so overwhelmed at finally being a part of something - and such an exciting something.'

'I thought I was just detailing what a frightful bore the job is!' laughed Janek, but there was no mirth in his eyes, for he was sure that Sarah was lying. That was not what she had been crying about. He was sure of it. Her looking away like that and struggling to find an answer; they were textbook signs of an invented story, made up at speed. But why?

He did not take his eyes off Sarah and she did not take her eyes off Joseph. I may well live to regret this, he thought to himself, having this fruitcake here with me.

Sarah was too absorbed in the black-and-white face before her to notice Janck's suspicions. She seemed almost to revere the image. In the lines of her cheeks and mouth there was sadness too, beyond any measure of normality. Janek actually wanted to put an arm around her, but that would be all wrong - in front of Joseph. Also he was sure that she would flinch from his touch, as she had the day before when he had offered her his arm to negotiate the tricky bits of the garden. What secrets does this woman hold? he thought.

It was then that the first football of the day bounced off the roof of the little office. Sarah was jolted out of her Joseph-fixation.

'Ah,' Janek smiled, 'the other big job of a

Disappearance Club operative - the duty above all others which must not be neglected - the curling shot over the bar.' He sprang to his feet, took Sarah outside and introduced her to Phil.

After five weeks, Janek was pleased with how things had panned out. Sarah proved to be a whizz at the financial end of things. Also she set about contacting the existing Disappearance Club members, to remind them of the importance of keeping an eye out for Joseph. When she first suggested it, Janek had thought it rather an intrusive little ploy, but the letter she penned was very diplomatic and included a copy of the artist's impression, 'in case the original has been lost.' It was a neat piece of proaction: Janek liked it. The missive was sent to the last known address of every one of his clients.

And they received back fresh leads - two of them.

They were neither of them very good - to Janek's experienced eye - but that was exactly what made them so useful. He was able to show Sarah how to identify the weaknesses in a supposed sighting; how to sift for details of age, race, background, family. And she picked the information up and assimilated it as if lives depended upon her immediate proficiency. A raw recruit infantry man, bound straight for the front line, with a mere half hour to acquaint himself with his weaponry, could not have concentrated in more earnest.

And she cried too, when Janek proved to her that both leads held no water, but smiled soon afterwards as well, because she realised the value of the lessons learned. At that point Janek had wanted to take her hand in his - just for empathetic contact's sake - but with mere inches to go, he had remembered himself and drawn back at the last moment. In all areas Sarah had proved herself easy-going and adaptable, except the physical. Even five weeks after their first meeting, she was still like the feral cat which will sit comfortably in your home, but never permit your touch.

And like an independent cat, she did not impinge. In her upstairs room she beavered away silently and diligently, only coming down to see Janek when something needed explaining. But she was such a quick learner that this did not happen much any more.

Janek was not entirely happy about this. He had come to look forward to Sarah's little visits. After having been in two minds about the whole shared space and co-working idea, he now thought it a signal success. And it warmed his heart, really got it nicely heated through, to know that there was someone else who shared his passion and was proactive about it too. He liked explaining little details to her, he even liked how one side of her mouth rose relative to the other when she was concentrating - which was virtually all the time. Also she respected his expertise. That was obvious.

His clients respected his expertise, but only in so far as it might benefit them. Sarah was different: she seemed to hang upon his every word, particularly when the topic of Joseph came up - but Joseph's whereabouts was not an issue personal to her; finding him could not benefit her personally. How could it? So, intrigued, as well as feeling warm towards its occupant, Janek often found himself staring up at her little second floor room. Whereas before he used to look out for a woodpecker or a jay on his peanut feeders, now he craned for a sighting of the strange and elusive creature who grafted away at the top of his house. And whenever she did look down from her office window, Janek would snap his eyes away like a bashful schoolboy caught staring too assiduously at a pretty girl.

'You silly old sod,' he would say to himself and get back on with whatever it was he was doing: usually Disappearance Club work.

Janek was still the public face of the business. His clients expected one discreet man; another person in the room would not have been the done thing, especially not a woman. It wasn't that the escapees were all unreconstructed dinosaurs, it was that they were men…men who were generally in the middle of leaving their women in the lurch, or of discovering new sexual appetites - these details tended to come out when Janek established their reasons for absconding. Nailing down these reasons and motives was a necessary part of the job: a man could only be advised of his disappearance options when the facts of his individual case were known. And a female trainee sitting in, taking notes, as it were, would almost certainly clam up these male clients, 'tighter than a crab's arse', as Janek had put it to Sarah. He was quite candid in his explanation; and she, for her part, accepted with good grace that the clients might well be less forthcoming with her in attendance. So she stayed in the background and organised and ferreted and came up with initiatives.

She got advertisements out to a dozen new

magazines:

THE DISAPPEARANCE CLUB
DROP YOUR OLD IDENTITY AND START
A NEW LIFE ELSEWHERE
PO. BOX 7401 OR RING 01-302-0958

She even despatched flyers. According to her research, doctors and teachers were the most stressed professionals in the working world, so she had Disappearance Club leaflets produced and then delivered to surgeries and school staff rooms. It was a cheeky strategy, but it worked: the little garden office was abuzz with new clients.

And the increase in numbers thrilled Janek. The gin bottle no longer appealed to him. He even thought that the world was being cut down to manageable size by the army of searchers they were sending out to its four corners, and in his wilder moments, he found himself thinking in terms of success once more; actually believing that Joseph would be found. And most of this was down to Sarah, the woman who had turned up at his office, all kooky and with an arm permanently stuck inside her handbag.

'Who can blame me, if I sneak a look up at her window?' Janek mused to himself.

'Look at this!' shrieked Sarah bursting into Janek's office one morning near Christmas, 'we're in *The Daily Telegraph*. The bloody *Daily Telegraph*.'

Janek shot out of his seat as if a powerful boot had propelled him.

'What?'

'Here,' said Sarah, her fingers fumbling the pages in excitement, 'page 12.' She slapped the page down, tearing it a little in her fervour. She stood there quivering.

Janek stared at the title:

THE DISAPPEARANCE CLUB
TIRED PROFESSIONALS HELPED TO VANISH FOR A FEE

'Unbelievable,' yelled Janek. 'Un-be-fucking-lievable.'

He read the article; first at pace, then a second time, really taking it in. It was good, very good - no exaggeration, ninety-five percent of the details were accurate and there was nothing incriminating, which was lucky; the journos could easily have turned up a rotten escapee: one of the guys dripping with stolen pension bonds and the life savings of widows and orphans.

'How?' asked Sarah, voice trembling through a number of octaves in her excitement.

'One of these new clients I've been seeing recently - he must have been an investigative journalist. He probably taped me the whole conversation through, so then he had himself a scoop…I'll be damned: page 12 of *The Telegraph*! We'll have more business now than you can shake a stick at,' whooped Janek. 'There'll be queues like at the cinema!' He clapped his hands together and beamed at the woman in front of him. She was beaming too. Janek beamed back some more…Now why in the hell isn't she coming round this side of the desk and hugging me? he was thinking.

That's what a woman would normally do at a time like this. Nothing sexual, just a bit of shared high spirits. But this one, look at her, she's as far away as ever.

'But this is the best news,' he actually said, from behind his side of the table, 'Ever.'

'You know what I think, Janek? I think we're going to get a whole legion of people out there in the world, all searching for Joseph, and we're going to find him. We're going to find him,' enthused Sarah. Her eyes were bright and her skin seemed to have taken on a creamier quality. To Janek she was beautiful. It wasn't just looks, it was looks coupled with passionate energy. She had taken on the Disappearance Club work and had cleaved to it as if it were a child of hers. Janek was reminded of a bear and its cub - a comely and attractively vivacious bear.

'Today we are going for a drink together,' he announced. Janek had asked her half a dozen times before and every time she had fought shy of his invitations. But this time the air was pregnant with the euphoria of the moment. On the table before them lay the once-in-a-lifetime *Telegraph*. How could she refuse?

A little of the creaminess leached from Sarah's skin, although her eyes stayed bright. Janek saw the indecision in the contracting pupils, then saw them swivel away to look at the photograph of Joseph. What the fuck's he got to do with it? he thought, angry at the young man for the first time in over thirty years - and a little jealous too. 'After work,' he added, unable to wait for her answer in silence.

'Yes,' she said at last. 'We shall go for a drink, you and I, this is quite a thing to celebrate. When we are finished for the day - we will go then.'

The reply was about as emotional as boiled cabbage, but Janek grinned nonetheless. She had said yes - finally - that was what mattered. And ten-to-one, the alcohol would thaw her out a bit. Trying not to telegraph his feelings too clearly, Janek reined in his ridiculously toothy grin. 'I reckon we've got a day before the deluge descends upon us. The article actually specifies the address here. See? That means the punters will turn up at the door. But they'll have to be very quick out of the blocks to arrive before tomorrow morning. Unless there are lots of very desperate people living close by, I don't think today will be that different from yesterday. We might get some phone calls though - from the press as well as from prospective clients - I'm not ex-directory here,' Janek said. He thought a moment. 'Tell any new enquirers that we need to see them in person, that ours is not a telephone service.'

Sarah nodded.

Janek was still thinking hard when Sarah rapped on the desk for his attention. He realised that she must have said something which he had missed.

'Oh I'm sorry,' he said.

'What about the police Janek? Have we got anything to worry about there?' she asked, real concern in her voice.

'What, from the rozzers? Nah! I've told you before they've been on to me for years. This article won't make a jot of difference to the relationship I have with them. Absolutely not. Put that concern out of your head.'

'What about the neighbours? Have you thought about them?'

'I've never cared what the people down this road

think. Most of them are sure I'm mad anyway. It'll just serve to confirm their prejudices.' He laughed. 'My only real contact with the people hereabouts is with those footballing lads, and this *Telegraph* business won't change that any.'

Janek looked up and saw the relief in Sarah's face. Her head of hair seemed to lift as the tension eased at her jaw and cheekbones. He realised then exactly how much the job she did mattered to her. It was her life.

'You love what you do here, don't you?' he said.

'It is my blood. I merely exist when I am not here.'

Janek was startled at her vehemence. A little of the colour drained from his face: he had never really bargained on being so central to a woman's life - any woman's life - at such a late stage in his own.

She saw the colour being chased from his cheeks and panicked. It was ever Sarah's fear - since her early display of instability before him - that Janek would decide that she was too precarious, mentally, to have around. She controlled the rising hysteria in her throat; thought of cool meadows and mountain streams, managed to speak calmly. 'And what else would I do with my time, nick hubcaps?' she joked. Her smile was thin and forced - a sharp gash of incisors - but the quip had worked. Janek laughed out loud and the tone was lightened once more. To make sure of him, she added, 'I'm looking forward to that drink and the pub.' It was a lie, but Sarah knew that that was what the man in front of her wanted to hear. Therefore it was necessary for her to say it, in order that he dwell on their 'date', rather than run the risk of him dwelling on her foolish 'blood' comment. The excitement of the morning was causing her to make mistakes. She was keen to get back up to her little room.

For his part, Janek was enjoying her company and was not so very ready for her to leave. Also, it was a hell of a thing, to be covered in the national press. It called for a bit of social contact, social cement even. That's what he thought. So when he noticed her edging for the door, he racked his brains to come up with something to hold her. Luckily there was an obvious little something.

'You do realise that this will mean big changes?'

'How so?' asked Sarah warily, unsure whether Janek was referring to their going for a drink together, or Disappearance Club business.

'Isn't it obvious?' he said, pointing at the open paper, 'This article is not gender specific. We are going to be getting female clients; still not as many as men I shouldn't think, but the business will no longer be a male preserve, not after this national exposure. And don't you see? They will be more comfortable revealing their little secrets to another woman, just like our male clients are most comfortable revealing theirs to me. You will have to receive and advise them.'

Sarah felt her skin flush hot with excitement.

'If that is alright with you?' added Janek.

'Yes…yes,' Sarah replied breathlessly. 'Can we go through what I will have to say? Can we do it now? Right now?' Sarah was back in the centre of the office, no longer edging for the door and she was leaning forward, almost overbalancing in her childlike impatience.

'Of course, but please, sit down, before you trip over yourself.'

Sarah did, neatly and primly, in front of Janek.

Already she was composing herself, mentally and physically, for the female clients waiting in the queues of her mind. Janek stared at her seriousness, loving it, but he also took her in as a woman. She had a lovely face - once a fellow had allowed for its unnatural intensity and rather scary eyes. The various features all complemented one another. Her mouth especially, was…

'Are we going to start?' snapped Sarah.

'Oh yes…right,' returned Janek, bashfully.

They covered everything, from the different legal positions of various countries, to financial considerations and then back full circle to visa requirements and extradition law. It was quite a chunk to take in; all the while Sarah noted and annotated. The questions she asked were insightful and pertinent; even Janek's thirty years of experience were not proof against some of them and he was left groping for answers. In the end though, he managed to field them all.

'I can't wait for my first client,' gushed Sarah, 'And we could get a phone line put in between our two offices so that I can ask you anything I am not sure of.'

Janek betrayed a flicker of emotion - just a slight sagging about the shoulders. Why was she so very keen to be shut away from him? After all, wasn't it down to him that she had this passion in her life? Then again, maybe it was just her professionalism that wanted a phone line and the trimmings. He took his time to answer, 'At the pub, this evening, after we have had our chat, there won't be anything you don't know. And then you will be all set for your first client.'

Janek had underestimated the power of the press, though. It was one o' clock in the afternoon and Sarah had not been back in her own office twenty minutes, when there came a knock at the front door. Janek could hear the raps from where he was at the bottom of the garden. It could have been a meter-man or a religious nut, but instinctively Janek knew that it was someone who had read the article. He nipped out of the garage doors, walked up the side of the house and looked.

Yep: it had started. The rush had started. And the first to his door was a woman! She had the day's *Telegraph* under her arm. He was just about to hail her when the door opened. Sarah welcomed the visitor and the two of them started talking animatedly. He peered at Sarah through the white roses of his front garden. She looked lovely. Janek was all set to interrupt when something stopped him. It was embarrassment, and what was more, of the kind he couldn't remember feeling for about four decades. The door banged shut.

'This will never do, Janek Lipsz,' he muttered to himself and knocked stoutly on his own front door.

Inside he could hear Sarah taking three steps at a time. She opened the door without respect for its hinges.

'Come on. Come on. I thought you were down in the garden. What are you knocking at your own porch for? Isn't the back door still open? There's a woman upstairs, she's read the article. She's come all the way from Ipswich!'

Janek followed Sarah up, trailing in her wake. She had learned to negotiate the stairs with the speed of a mountain goat. One of his knees complained as she waited for him at the top.

In the room, though, Janek was as sleek a professional as ever graced a bedroom-office. He escorted their visitor through the various options open to her, he explained the nature of the service offered; he even left the room for ten minutes so that she might confide any sensitive details to Sarah in his absence. Then he returned with tea, biscuits and advice on how a woman could keep herself on the NHS books whilst still living it up in Costa Rica (Janek had already recommended this country as a lovely, stable Central American haven).

'They all understand English too and there is none of this business the French engage in - pretending not to,' he added. 'You'll be able to order your bread on the first morning and everyone will want to speak English to you so that they can practise the language.'

Normally, Janek was wary about recommending countries, but as this was such a special day - a female client directed to them via the national press - he had decided to stretch a point. Usually the clients chose their own destinations. This woman had seemed all at sea, though. Also, Janek had wanted to impress Sarah with his encyclopedic knowledge. He wanted her to know his brain was a data bank, one that was just a short walk down the stairs and up the garden path - always free and always accessible.

He got a good deal of information out of the new lady. Her name was Tracy Bourne. She was thirty-nine and her husband, Buster, had used her as a punch-bag throughout their fifteen year marriage: one beating had perforated an eardrum, another had broken a collar bone. Now Tracy wanted revenge, and a new life. The thuggish husband had got himself into trouble with the tax man and owed thousands. Consequently, he had put all their money into her sole name so that it could not be touched. Now it was Tracy's intention to do an even more thorough job of fleecing Mr Bourne than even the Inland Revenue could do, and then to disappear somewhere she could not be traced. She had dreamt of doing this ever since the money had first appeared as cleared funds in her account. Then along had come *The Daily Telegraph*. The article on page twelve seemed to have been written with her personal situation in mind. Half an hour after buying the newspaper she had boarded the London train at Ipswich station: first destination 33 Orchard Road, second destination somewhere warm to enjoy the zeros.

They concluded business with Mrs Bourne in a little under two hours. It was decided that she should return home one last time - to lay hands on six or seven more documents (it always surprised the novice escapee how many were required for a quality disappearance). Next, in two days' time, she would take a room at Sarah's lodging house (grubby, but with the benefit of a landlord who asked no questions) and then be on her way after one more session with Janek - and one with her bank.

Mrs Bourne made a note of Sarah's address. She was extremely happy. Scarcely could she believe that her fairy-tale plan was actually within grasp. All the way from Ipswich she had only half trusted the *Telegraph* story; had feared that it might be a bit of journalistic cobblers thought up by a blue-sky gazer in order to boost sales. It amazed and delighted her that the article had been accurate. She asked a whole rush of additional questions. They were all rather impressive as greenhorn questions went - the weeks of daydreaming revenge had honed her mind to the actuality of the task.

Janek answered her, but with only fifty percent of his mind. The rest was turning over and over what he had just learned: Sarah's address! Throughout the time she'd been working with him, Sarah had always been very cagey about revealing it. Now the truth was out: she was staying at a rough boarding house - Janek knew it well. It had an unscrupulous owner with a reputation for renting out to tenants who maintained only a passing acquaintanceship with morality. What was Sarah doing there? Of all places!

'I want to be gone by Christmas. It'll be a special festive gift for my Buster to realise that I've gone with all his money,' said Mrs Bourne.

Sarah's living there, of all places! thought Janek.

'I want to be gone by Christmas,' repeated his new client, more loudly.

Janek was called back from the world of dingy dives. 'But of course, my dear, we'll have you away in good time. Your husband will be eating crusts and lard by the 25th; you have my professional word on it.'

The two of them nailed down a few more details and underscored a couple more dates and then the abused wife from Ipswich left.

Sarah was cock-a-hoop. It was the first time she had seen this end of the business. She paced around the room imagining herself before the legions of women yet to come. Janek actually heard her repeating phrases to herself, trying to learn them by rote.

'We'll make sure of everything at the pub this evening. I'll write it down for you,' he said. Janek stressed the word 'pub' and waited for some answering enthusiasm. There was none. In fact, to his reckoning, Sarah seemed to turn a rather cold, snake-like eye upon him - actually, that of a snake contemplating a long slither on broken glass. 'What time shall we go?' he asked, more than a little deflated.

'At seven. We shall give it an extra hour today, on account of the newspaper article,' came the reply.

Janek nodded, then considered himself dismissed. He retreated to his garden office where he attempted a psychological profile of Sarah. After a while he gave up…

'Mad as a bassoon…but a sexy one.'

CHAPTER 10

It was nearly eight when they finally left for the pub because a car pulled up outside the house and Sarah insisted on waiting to see whether the person was a Disappearance Club caller or not. The man sat lumpily in the driver's seat doing nothing for about half an hour. Afterwards, he just drove off. Then, with no great enthusiasm, Sarah pulled on her coat and went down to Janek who was all ready and stroking the cat in the kitchen.

'Excellent,' he said, smiling broadly. 'Shall we go?'

Sarah tried a return smile - really a very good effort, she thought.

They walked together. Not too close; Janek had no intention of scaring her off before the drink. He knew what the safe subjects were too and stuck to them: club business, the newspaper article, Tracy Bourne and birds. Sometimes Sarah could be coaxed out of her shell a little on the subject of birds.

'A few years ago, there was a family of long-tailed tits nesting in the garden, right in among the thorniest recesses of the crab apple. But a magpie came and killed the mother on her nest. She probably succumbed defending her clutch. Just left her there it did and that's where I found her, atop eleven tiny eggs. The nest though, it was of the damndest construction:

moss and spiders' webs and hundreds of feathers. It was as springy and elastic as could be and the best insulator one could ever hope to construct. I read in a book that the nest is designed to expand around the brood as it grows and that it is quite unique in the animal kingdom.'

'Interesting,' nodded Sarah.

'I kept it you know, at home, in a sealed container. I could show it to you tomorrow if you wanted.'

'Ok.'

'They are tiny little birds, you know.'

'Ok.'

'The unhatched eggs are still at the bottom of the nest.'

'Ok.'

'All eleven of them.'

'Ok.'

Janek dried up.

The pub was about ten minutes away. It was a small place, tucked back from the road, about three hundred years old. Chestnut trees led down to it, and a bank of hawthorn. In the winter they stuck out of the ground like geriatric hands a-begging.

The two of them covered the distance in eight minutes; vigorous walking taking the place of vigorous conversation.

'The trees look like the hands at an old folk's home don't they?' said Janek, trying once more.

'Yes, they do.'

'And look,' he added, nodding to what looked like a milestone beneath one of them, 'That boulder marks the spot of the old gallows where they used to string up the highwaymen and murderers. It was a good spot, because the pub-road led to the main crossroads of its day - back in the seventeen and eighteen hundreds. Imagine the poor bastards hanging up there. Most likely they weren't all guilty, neither.'

Janek could not see Sarah's face because the meadow approach to the pub was not lit, but he heard a sharpness in her voice: 'There's been many killed who never deserved to die and many still living who should have bled for their crimes - but have not.'

Janek said nothing. Usually when he walked this stretch he liked to spook himself that the Grim Reaper was striding just out of step with him. Today the conceit didn't seem necessary: Sarah was morbid and serious enough to make the Grim Reaper redundant.

'Drink?' he said, when they finally ducked in through the pub door and had claimed a couple of bar stools. There was a warm atmosphere inside. Janek hoped that it would rub off on Sarah.

'Yes please,' she said, 'whisky and soda; a double if you don't mind.'

Mind? You've gotta be joking. I'd give you a triple and forget the soda if it was me doing the pouring, thought Janek.

He ordered himself a good, thick, pricey red wine, something that was weighty enough to be fully opaque. They had their first few sips in silence, taking the place in. Janek had been many times before, but one always takes a place in afresh when showing it to someone else for their first time. The ceilings were low criss-cross beams of oak separated by discoloured wattle and daub. The tobacco stains seemed centimetres thick; half of the windows would no longer open because the walls had shifted relative to their sashes. The central fireplace was an enormous open one, more than broad enough for the roasting of an entire ox, and the flagstone floor was barely truer than the hawthorn bank outside. Janek had always loved the place and of late he had grown to love it even more, as he was still banned from the high street pub.

Lying beside the fire was a white-muzzled and rheumatic dog of great antiquity. It stank rather - a mossy, oozy smell redolent of decaying logs and leaf mulch. In a more modern place it would have been too earthy, but here, at *The Leather Bottle*, it was not incongruous and the nostrils remained unoffended.

'The pub is called *The Leather Bottle*, said Janek, 'because they found one here, hidden, with dozens of gold coins crammed inside it. Dated back hundreds of years they did. The kitchen was being modernized - the only room in the whole pub that has been - and the builders turned up the leather bottle beneath the old stone floor. Before that the pub used to be called *The Noose and Knot*, because the drinkers could see the meadow gibbet out of the upstairs windows.'

Sarah nodded into her drink.

'Must have reminded the old timers to keep their noses clean,' Janek added.

'Have you always done that?' asked Sarah suddenly.

'What?'

'Kept your nose clean?'

The question surprised Janek, not in itself, but on account of the accusatory roughness in the voice asking it. He stared at Sarah: she had already downed three quarters of her whisky. Oh Christ, he thought, she isn't one of those drinkers who wants to fight after a few sips of the strong stuff is she?

He met her unflinching gaze. 'Yes. Yes, I have. My nose has stayed pretty clean - considering the business I am in.'

'What about during the war?' pressed Sarah.

Janek stuck out his lip and let his glass play against it. 'There aren't many clean noses from that time,' he said after quite a pause. He stared into the opaque redness of his wine. This wasn't the direction in which he wanted the evening's conversation to turn.

'Speaking of noses, can you smell that dog?' he asked, pointedly changing the subject.

'Yes, he's like old cheese. But it doesn't matter in here. It would be wrong to have a well-scrubbed young dog in this pub.'

'I know what you mean. It's not a 'best in show', prime of life, kind of place is it? And it's funny, I can't remember that dog ever being anything other than incredibly old, although I suppose he must have been young once,' replied Janek.

Sarah finished her drink. 'Another?' she asked, slightly thick-tongued.

'Mmm,' gurgled Janek, finishing his glass. 'Yes please.' This was a bit more like it - if she was going to knock 'em back, then he was going to match her. Maybe she went through a whole range of personalities until there was a final, sweet, approachable one? But what in hell had happened to her to make her such a funny old stick? he wondered. She had told him something of her war experience: that she'd been captured by the Nazis and forced to work on the home farms in northern Germany, hacking and packing swedes and sugar beat and turnips. That was back-breaking work…Janek knew; he had friends who had never made it back afterwards. What of her experiences after the war though?

'What did you do after 1945?' he asked suddenly, as she was trying to attract the barman's attention.

Sarah busied herself waving her money, but Janek could tell that she had heard; the tenner was just a prop for evasiveness. He asked again, closer to her ear this time. She moved a whole foot away, as if his breath scorched her.

'I spent my time searching,' she growled, actually rubbing her face, 'for the man who robbed me of everything I ever loved; of my blood. I have vowed to hunt him down till the debt is repaid - with rivers of his own blood. My search has taken me to many countries.'

Janek swallowed hard, 'Then why have you stopped here with me?'

'Because I will learn things from you, then at last I shall be able conclude my search.'

'Do you think that what I have to teach will be so relevant to your personal case?'

'Oh yes, I am certain of it.'

There was then a wildness about Sarah and Janek felt unnerved by it. So did the barman who had come to serve her. He stood at a respectful distance and ahemed quietly into his beard.

'Ahem. Ahem.'

'A double whisky and soda and a large red wine, please,' she said, putting the man at his ease with an unexpected lightness of tone. Sarah smiled at Janek, for she could see that she had unsettled him, as well as the barman.

To Janek, 'rivers of blood' was something Enoch Powell said, not comely ladies he took out for drinks.

Sarah made a conscious decision to lighten up, to don the mask. It was of paramount importance that Janek not be scared off. She could not afford to lose her job, voluntary though it was. It was far too good a position from which to learn.

'So you are using me, then?' said Janek, 'That stuff about feeling energised by me and my search wasn't true?'

'Oh don't be so ridiculous,' Sarah scoffed. 'While I am here, your search is my search. There is nothing nobler or more important that I could do with my time. It is just that my job will not be over when Joseph is found, that is all.'

She saw Janek look confusedly out of the window. 'Your search is my search'...He mulled over the words. 'You're not like other women, Sarah,' he said at last, pulling himself away from the fantastic shapes of the hawthorn trees, 'Do you always speak in riddles?'

'When necessary. We are not so very different, you and I, Janek. We riddle because the truth is too painful. Isn't that the case?'

'I used to drink gin for that problem, but you stopped me,' retorted Janek. He stared very directly at his companion.

'And don't you work ten times more productively now?'

'Yes, yes, I suppose I do. But isn't it strange that you should exert such wifely control over me? Especially when...' here Janek paused...'when sometimes you seem barely able to tolerate me.' Janek was becoming bolder now: the wine was beginning to fire his system, the ruby fingers of intoxication to work away at his brain. He had completely forgotten that she had unnerved him just a few moments before and he was cheered too, by the fact that she was calling him by name. Often, even that seemed an intimacy too far.

For her part, Sarah knew what was happening. In the post war decades, in the course of her long search, she had drunk with a good many men, probing for clues. And a good proportion of them, at some time or other, would nail her with that same stare Janek was turning upon her now. Lately, she had seen it in his eyes quite a lot. He desired her, she knew that, in spite of his cautionary speech when they first agreed terms. It was a repugnant thing for her to countenance - closeness to him - but the infatuation itself might prove useful. Besotted men tend to let the object of their affections stick around and, in addition, they often reveal more about themselves than they ever intend - especially when drunk.

'You're letting me catch you up,' said Sarah, pointing at Janek's glass. She raised hers and he followed suit. 'They always mirror your movements, if they want you,' Sarah said to herself. Twice she repeated the action and twice Janek acted as her shadow. Then their glasses were empty.

'I'm game for another,' he grinned. 'What will you have?'

'A G&T this time, I think.'

Janek rose in order that he be noticed behind the bar. Sarah looked about her for the next domino in her plan. She saw it, over by the fireside tables. Excellent - he would have to negotiate the dog in order to get one.

As soon as Janek sat back down with the drinks, she started in, 'Would you mind, Janek, getting me a menu? I really think I ought to eat something, to soak up all this booze.'

'Of course,' said Janek, springing up. 'They're over there aren't they, over by the dog?'

'I don't know,' Sarah lied.

'Yes, look, there they are.'

Janek stepped carefully, in between twitching paws and past a pair of quivering, dream-worried ears. And as he negotiated his tricky way, Sarah, quite deliberately, tipped her gin into a standing plant pot and then rapidly charged her empty glass with the full shot of tonic water. 'Piss easy,' she thought as Janek toddled back with the menu.

The next two hours involved quite a lot of this pantomime, with Janek the unwitting fall guy. By the time he had been to the lavatory twice, ordered their meals, eaten his, one third of Sarah's, suggested that they return to their original stools after dessert, and had checked the night sky for stars (he thought this romantic), the bar plant was absolutely reeling. And so was he.

'So, why are you staying at that shit hole in Paddock Road?' said Janek, finally drunk enough to ask. 'Last I heard there were prostitutes upstairs and cannabis plants downstairs. What kind of a place is that to stay at?'

'A cheap kind of place,' Sarah replied, 'Very cheap. You do not pay me, remember? That is not a suggestion that you should, just a statement of fact.'

Janek slurred that he did remember and that, by God, he should be able to do something about it - if the punters really did start queuing up on the back of the *Telegraph* article. Then he recalled that the two of them were supposed to be discussing Sarah's new role, now that dozens more women were expected at the Disappearance Club. They rolled the marble of jobs and responsibilities between the two of them and jawed over issues, until Sarah noted that Janek was repeating himself, then she moved her stool closer to him, settling it between his splayed legs.

'So Mr Resistance man, tell me your story. You were in The Resistance in the war weren't you?' she cooed.

'Um-hum,' Janek nodded. 'For five years, until the fucking Soviets turned on us and we had to flee our own country. They wouldn't tolerate any organised groups at all. And we couldn't resist any more; we were too exhausted after the long years of war. They had a pretty clear idea who we were too - tortured the information out of our neighbours, as well as the retreating Germans they captured. I was lucky to get out when I did. I saw the worm turning. Some of the others were too slow cottoning on and thought that the Ruskies would just let them tend their farms and man their shops as before. Not a bit of it, they were rounded up and shot. Weren't even given the time to shit 'emselves with fear.'

'What about before that? Did you ever kill anyone?'

'What kind of an arse-wipe question is that?' spluttered Janek. 'Course I did! There were little old ladies, twenty years older than you, killed grown men with their hatpins in those dark days. Did I kill anyone! What a damn fool question!' Janek sneered, forgetting for one moment that he wanted to get it on with the woman in front of him.

Sarah tipped her stool so that she came to rest a few inches closer to his crotch. 'But what about someone who didn't deserve to die, who you just knocked off in the heat of the moment because you could and because the years of killing had turned you hard and uncaring?' Sarah asked, in a voice like honeyed summer.

Janek choked a little. The liquor irritated his throat. He caught his breath. Sarah could see that images, sharp and horrible, were flashing across his mind's eye.

'No,' he coughed out hurriedly. 'Never. I never killed anyone like that.'

'What about nearly? Did you ever hurt someone in that unfeeling way?'

'I never killed anyone like that,' shouted Janek, 'Never!' He was standing now and booming out his reply, and the other drinkers were staring at him in silent shock, listening to his alarming words. The pub dog woke with a deep bark, roused from the squirrels of his dreams. For a moment they were both, man and dog, baying at the pub regulars. They continued this duet for about twenty reverberating seconds then the landlord came over - a powerful-looking man with cold eyes and a no-nonsense moustache.

'Sorry,' said Sarah quickly. 'Some bad memories from the war: these old boys saw things no man should ever have to see. He'll be alright now. It only happens a couple of times a year; I'm sorry it had to be here.'

The landlord harrumphed gruffly. 'Ok,' he said. 'But he's had enough for tonight. No more drink.'

Sarah nodded and Janek sat gingerly down.

'That was your fault,' he said, stingingly. 'I came here for a nice night out, not a how-do-you-do with my past. What made you bring up all that shit?'

'Sorry,' said Sarah simply, but was all a-quiver within: obviously she had touched one hell of a nerve. Another little push, and maybe a mouthful more booze, and she was sure that he would have spilled the beans. How dearly she wanted to hear that story.

Janek shrank down into his seat, aware that people were looking at him. The dog was watching him too and the landlord was glowering over. Mentally, he closed out everything pre-1945 and just sat heavily on his stool, like a toad on a bucket. Sarah saw his shutters come down and realised that there was no chance of getting anything more out of him. She would have to bide her time for another opportunity.

Conversation after the event was drab to non-existent. Sarah talked 'Telegraph' at Janek; he stared moodily into the bottom of his empty glass. The outburst had killed the wider atmosphere of the pub as well. Three stout old boys were whispering about whether the 'foreign geezer was a war criminal'. No one else was speaking at all. So oppressively quiet had it become, that a deaf old woman, sitting in the pub's prime window seat, was actually fiddling with her hearing aid in order to turn it up. Then the aged dog decided to start barking once more, with the utmost vehemence, and the old woman almost fell off her seat. She clutched at her ears as if the IRA and the SAS were having a ding-dong inside them.

Janek stood to go. Sarah did the same. They felt the hot intensity of eyes upon them as they pushed arms into coat sleeves. The dog shook itself to standing; it was the first time in five years it had done so before closing time. It too stared cataractedly at the couple. They stepped out into the night air, closing the door with the quietest of snaps behind them.

'Well, that's another pub I won't be welcome at,' said Janek gloomily.

Sarah said nothing.

The walk back up the hawthorn and chestnut bank was quite a strenuous affair, in the dark and with drinkers' legs. The ground was wet with winter chill and rocks jutted out treacherously. About half way up, Janek slipped and clutched at Sarah. It was in no way a clumsy pass on his part, just a clumsy fall, but still her sinews tensed at the physical contact. Janek could feel the rigidity course through her every muscle and joint. He didn't let go. Actually, he was offended and was enough in his drink to hang on. For a few seconds they jigged about the bank; Sarah trying to break loose, Janek holding tenaciously on.

'What the fuck's the matter with you?' hissed Janek. 'I just don't want to end up with my arse in the mud.'

'Get off me!' Sarah screamed, spinning around. 'Is that what you always do, you drunk, you animal thing, you. Take your filthy hands off of me. I'm not a little…'

Then she stopped. Janek could feel the rigidity in her recede.

'It is your arm I have hold of, nothing else. I would have fallen otherwise. The ground is uneven, see?'

Sarah nodded her head – just the merest of

movements. Then a light was on them; someone from the pub had opened the door and shone a flash-lamp up the bank. She allowed herself to be led.

'Bloody nutters,' they heard someone say.

Janek sniffed, 'See, it is me who should be offended at you! I've never got into any trouble at that pub before. Never.'

Sarah said nothing.

'And I've never seen that dog stand up before either. It'll probably have a stroke by the morning. Stone-dead it'll be.'

At the top of the bank Sarah disengaged. Janek tried to hang on a little longer, but she pulled free; there was no indecision in her at all. He let his hands flop by his sides, drunk enough not to bother masking his disappointment. 'I'm walking you home though. It's late and a lady must always be escorted home.'

'No, no. That is not necessary, thank you.'

Janek raised his hand. 'There is no point arguing. Even if you chase me away, I shall just follow at a distance. If you are going back to Paddock Road then I am coming; some of the streets around there are rather rough at this time of night.'

'Are you always so concerned for the females in your charge?' asked Sarah. There was a sneering growl in her voice, but Janek did not pick it up because a flat-bed lorry rattled past at the exact moment of her delivery.

'What did you say?' he asked when the six-wheeler had clattered by.

'Nothing,' Sarah said shortly, 'Nothing.'

It was a good half hour to Paddock Road. It was

situated deep within the seedy end of town. Two thirds the way there, the street lamps got fewer and farther apart and the stray dogs more numerous. Buildings showed clear signs of neglect and vandalism. There were fewer cars around. Young kids were playing outside even though it was past eleven.

The place itself could be seen from some distance away. It was a huge Victorian house, very ramshackle, arranged over three storeys and a basement. The upstairs lights were all blazing away. Downstairs, though, it was quite as dark as the meadow bank Janek and Sarah had traversed thirty minutes before.

They turned into Paddock Road then into the driveway of the boarding house itself. Sarah wanted no goodbyes whatsoever, Janek was gearing himself up for one; so she accelerated for the door, fumbling about for keys, while he followed at pace.

What the pair of them actually got was thoroughly unexpected.

A middle-floor window was thrown open, the sash clattering with a sharp crack. It was the landlord, purple-faced from cheap cider and pointing a quivering finger. 'What the fuck time d'ya call this? I said if I was gunna take foreigners then they'd have to keep to the 'ouse rules. Eleven I said to ya.'

Janek felt his anger rising and the alcohol in him began to boil. 'What?! You old bastard. You've got two whole floors of prostitutes in that house who bring up their maggoty men at all hours. You were raided for it last year and you know it.'

'Oh, another dirty Pole is it? Why don't you get the fuck out of my country?' the landlord screamed, recognising Janek's accent. 'And as for you,' he yelled, pointing at Sarah. 'You can get out of my house - tomorrow. Don't want your sort here. I'm sellin' up, I am. Going to a nice area…no fucking foreigners!'

Janek started searching about for a stone.

'Leave it!' snapped Sarah and she grabbed his wrist. It was the first time that she had ever caught hold of him and he thrilled at her touch. 'Leave it,' she repeated. 'He will forget by the morning. He always does. And he will tomorrow too…just so long as you don't leave him a broken window to jog his memory.' Janek ceased his search and let himself be led back down the drive.

'That's right,' jeered the face at the window, 'you can do your Polack-in-shining-armour-bit tomorrow, when I throw your whore out. Fucking foreigners.'

With that, the cidered-up old derelict slammed the window shut with even more force than he had wrenched it open. It cracked from lintel to sill. Janek looked at Sarah, she looked at the pane of glass, then hurried up to the front door and let herself in.

Janek stood at the end of the driveway. Just stood there, wondering at what had happened to the goodbye he had been planning then the same second floor window snapped open once more and the landlord launched a bedpan of water - or worse - at him. It missed by metres. There was moronic laughter from the room then the window was snapped shut once more. This time, along the line of the crack, the top half of the pane slid free and fell twenty feet to the ground.

Janek turned for home, just as the district dogs began barking at the rich crash.

CHAPTER 11

The landlord did not forget. Perhaps the smashed window reminded him; perhaps he really was planning to sell up. Whatever, at eight o' clock the next morning he hammered on Sarah's door to inform her that she and her stuff would have to be out by three the next day.

'Or I'll fuckin' burn it,' he added.

She knew that he meant it; normally his cider-head kept him in bed till noon.

Sarah's hands itched for her knife, but the desire didn't even come close to being acted upon: she had a far bigger fish to stab. The priority now was finding somewhere else to live. Her means were meager - hopping from country to country, bent on revenge, had not paid very well over the years.

She was due at Janek's by nine. A big post-article day was anticipated. Shit! That meant that there would be very little chance of ringing round letting agencies, nor of leafing through local papers. She performed a mental balance enquiry of her funds and didn't much like the figures. There was nothing else for it: she would have to ask Janek's help in finding a place.

The morning at Orchard Road was hectic. The two of them had seen four new clients each by eleven o' clock. No one case was similar either and Sarah was filled with a whole new respect for what Janek did for a living - now that she had experienced the cutting edge herself. In the lunchtime lull she sat slumped and dazed, feeling as if she'd done the Everest descent in a loose barrel. After a few minutes of ceiling gazing, she heard Janek's tread on the stairs.

'Hasn't bloody stopped has it?' he said as he came in. 'I've had one going to the States, one to the Bahamas and two off to Sri Lanka. All of them want to leave before New Year! How many banking days does that actually give us? And two of them just do not have finances which can be knocked into shape that quickly. What about your people? Were they all *Telegraph* punters?' He sat down heavily, legs akimbo. Sarah's client chair groaned under the strain. She pulled a little face.

'Oh sorry,' he piped, sitting more demurely.

'The face wasn't at that,' Sarah said, shaking her head. She did not answer his questions, but inhaled deeply instead. Three vast lungfuls. 'I've got a problem,' she said at last. 'I've got nowhere to stay from tomorrow. My landlord is throwing me out.'

Immediately Janek forgot about punters and articles and all other Disappearance Club business. 'You mean that old bastard is actually going to hoof you out? For what?'

Sarah shrugged.

'Can he do that?'

'Oh yes. There are no laws - that's part of the cheap rents game.'

She paused again, 'So I'd appreciate it if you could help me find somewhere nearby. I don't have much money - actually very little.'

Now it was Janek's turn to pause: he stuck his chin out as if he were mouthing an extremely hot potato. Cogs were turning and lock gates were opening in the canals of his brain. 'There is nowhere both cheap and salubrious in the area,' he said.

Sarah looked crushed even though she didn't know what 'salubrious' meant.

'But there is a way...I'm not sure what you'll think of it, though.' Janek ran his fingers through his hair; Sarah could see that he was building up to something. 'You could live here,' he said in a rush. 'This room is too small, but the one next door could double as a bedroom and an office, if we got one of those fold away mattresses. It would make up for the fact that I'm not paying you anything and you'd be better placed to address our increased business volume; I have a feeling that these new clients of ours will not be respecters of usual office hours, there will be too many of them for that. Then if I have to go away to chase up leads - there are bound to be some fresh ones come of the new wave of escapees - you will be here to man the fort. Also, and I was thinking this last night, that horrible dive is no place we can send clients, not even for one minute.'

Sarah tried to interrupt, but Janek powered on. 'Our Mrs Bourne, there is just no way she can stay at Paddock Road. We ought to put her up here. This office should be turned into a guest room, with you in the big room next door. It would work; I really think that it would. And then there would be no need to worry about shitty doss houses and psychotic landlords boxed out of their skulls on moonshine cider.' Janek paused for breath before starting back in again, 'And what about Christmas? These dingy dives are not the places to spend...'

'Yes,' said Sarah, getting a word in edgeways.

'And then we c...c...could...' Janek stuttered to a stop. 'What did you say?'

'I said yes,' repeated Sarah, 'I think it's a great idea, all of it. I want to take you up on your offer. And thank you very much.'

'N...n...not at all,' said Janek, rubbing the side of his head in surprise. 'You don't want to think about it at all?'

'No. But I do want you to help me bring my stuff over here later today. I haven't got much, but it is more than I can comfortably carry on my own.'

'Right,' said Janek, 'Then that's what we'll do then.'

'Good.'

She smiled at him. A genuine smile. It felt weird to her: half betrayal and half relief. She told herself to keep the ultimate goal firmly in mind - the one and only reason she had offered to work with Janek in the first place...

Sarah reined in her mouth; there was too much soul-searching involved in this smiling business... 'And there's another thing,' she said, changing the subject, 'I had a woman in with me this morning, can't have been a day over thirty, who was obviously just out to embezzle funds from her employer and then leg it abroad. What do we do with people like her?'

'Was she interested in Joseph?'

'Very interested.'

'And she gave you the impression that she would look out for him, thief and swindler though she was?'

'Yes she did. Definitely.'

'Then her wider morals are of no concern to us. Sign her up and ship her out. Charge her a bit extra though, if you think she's really going to be getting away with a fortune, otherwise, just the standard rate.'

Janek looked round at the walls, imagining the place done up as a guest room. It might even be made to look quite inviting. He told Sarah a few of his ideas.

'And Janek,' she replied, standing, 'I want a copy of the main Joseph photo in my new room - mounted and framed. Would you do that for me? I want it to be the first thing the clients see when they come in, like it is in your garden-office. Do you think you could manage that? I'll pay.'

'Of course, but you won't pay. You won't dip your hand into your pocket at all. If everyone who ever came through my office took the search as seriously as you, I would have found my Joseph years ago. Not one penny,' replied Janek, with his forefinger held aloft for effect, 'Now I'm fixing us lunch,' he added and let the finger fall.

'My Joseph,' Sarah mouthed as he receded down the stairs, 'My Joseph!' And a pain at her temples made her wince. Five hot times it shot through her like just so many hornets' stings and when she looked down at her hands she saw that they had snapped the fountain pen that she'd been holding clean through. There was ink all over the desk blotter - and blood. Her blood. She had sliced a nasty gash in her palm. 'My Joseph, my Joseph,' she soothed and her head cleared and the blood slowed to a trickle.

The move was a piece of cake. Janek took his car

round to Paddock Road and he and Sarah loaded it up. The landlord was out, the cannabis plants were in, the prostitutes were making-up for the evening shift. As a parting shot, he did let fly with a stone and took out another of the old sod's windows. It was going to be cold December nights for the cider-bum.

The new arrangements at no.33 went smoothly. When Sarah's room was an office, no one could have guessed that she slept in it as well, when it was a bedroom, no one could have guessed that it doubled as an office. But all the time her huge Joseph photograph remained a constant.

In the week running up to Christmas, the Disappearance Club accepted seventy-three new people onto its books. Every man and woman of them was joined up, comprehensively advised, and given the Joseph prints. Mrs Bourne was sent on her way with her husband's money - and the taxman's share. She ended up staying with Janek and Sarah a total of four days and when she did go, she left behind an envelope full of cash. One thousand pounds.

Janek pocketed three hundred and handed the rest to Sarah. 'An early Christmas present,' he had said. She had tried to make him take it back and he had shook his head and set his jaw: 'That's for Paddock Road and for all the Paddock Roads you've ever had to stay at. Keep it. We all need a little safety net in life.'

And she had smiled again, another one of those genuine smiles...again it disconcerted her, just as much as the first.

It was funny living under the same roof. Janek had not lived with a woman since before the war. And he was still not very sure of this one. He wasn't stupid enough to try and touch her - he was playing a waiting game. In time, proximity would work its magic. Then there would be some results. He was ready for the long haul; besides he was waiting for news of Joseph. Something in his blood told him that there would be news. Sarah would bring it; her passion and her presence would bring it. And after that, things would happen between the two of them...

...And afterwards he could help Sarah with her own search, for whomsoever it may be, and whatever it might involve. She was cagey about that end of things, but one of these fire-warmed evenings he would coax the information out of her. Then he could start a few preliminary enquiries of his own. After all, he'd been a private eye for many years hadn't he? And almost certainly, all that 'rivers of blood' stuff in the pub had been the booze talking. If not, he would just have to talk her out of doing anything rash.

For her part, Sarah took to the domestic set up well: there were no more evil landlords and she was better able to keep her eye on Janek. When the work of the day was done, it was possible to maintain him under pretty close observation. Before, the two of them had said their goodbyes at the close of business and then traipsed their own ways. Now she could flit about and see for herself, the very nature of the man.

...It did not take long...he was kind and funny, in a self-deprecating way. The love that he bestowed upon the house cat, Oskar, was not of a normal order either. It was hard not to warm towards a man who cared so much.

Sarah had not been able to bring herself to spend

the £700, or even to pay it into her bank account. Most of the time it remained hidden away in a special place, but occasionally, just occasionally, she would take out the notes and stare at them. Then they would trouble her and the room would trouble her and Janek's softness would trouble her - all of his little kindnesses would trouble her - and she would snatch up the money and cram it angrily back into her secret place.

She knew that Janek wanted her; it was obvious. And he was so confusingly and irritatingly nice about it as well. For the first few days she had slept with her knife tucked beneath her pillow - just in case - but then she had snatched the weapon up and tucked it away in her secret place as well. And for the first time she began to doubt herself - could she be wrong about him? Was Janek even the right man? But then she would look at his nose and the rest of his face and remember his revealingly emotional response in *The Leather Bottle*. In addition, there was all the other evidence she had compiled before ever arriving at his garage-office. And why else would he be mixed up in the fate of Joseph? He had to be the man. He was the man.

She longed to question him - rather to hurt him - in order that the truth be out: to crush and stab and scald until she was quite sure that there was not one tiny piece of withheld information...And then the bastard would do things like give her £700 and bigger rooms and stroke the cat like it was a little child to be protected from the world. It wasn't how she had imagined things. None of it fitted and alone in her room she would sob at the incongruity of it all. Why couldn't Janek be a simple, grotty, wicked little man like her old landlord? Then she could have carved him up and buried him in his own back garden and given the killing no more thought than the squashing of a bug.

'Tea?' Janek called up. 'And I've got Bakewell tart too - as good as mother used to make - at least that's what it says on the box.'

It was the end of the working day and Janek always liked to mark it with a little something. There had been fewer clients - it being the 22nd of December. Janek didn't think people would bother now until after Christmas.

He brought everything up on a maroon tray. 'I think we should shut up shop,' he said entering, 'Until the 27th. What do you say?'

Sarah agreed. It had been a steep learning curve and the last few days had taken it out of her. Also, she felt battered emotionally.

'Good. Then there is no need for you to call your union in on me,' he joked, 'Christmas holidays for all - a universal right.'

Sarah couldn't suppress a little giggle. He really was a very funny man. Janek cosied down and set out the teapot and cups and cake.

It wasn't as good as mother used to make, in fact it wasn't as good as anyone used to make. The two of them howled with laughter as they tried to chew the rubbery sponge and looked in vain for the signature line of jam.

'The tea is good though,' smiled Sarah - another one of those smiles.

Janek looked at her…actually stared at her…just a few seconds longer than necessary and beamed back.

Then Sarah's smile was lost in confusion. She splashed great gobs of her tea, her cake bounced off somewhere, and instinctively, she looked over to where she knew her knife to be hidden. Quickly Janek averted his eyes from her face; it was obvious that the lady was not comfortable. He canned the idea of whispering sweet nothings. 'Another tea?' he asked sheepishly.

She did take one and Janek could see the tremors still wracking her hands. Also she had shifted focus and was now staring fixedly up at a point midway between cornice and lampshade. Janek had never seen quite so manic a gaze. 'Smashing being a straitjacket,' he said to himself. He was a bit angry really. He couldn't have been warmer to the lady - or kinder - and over rather an extended period of time too. That's what you get for taking in waifs and strays and wandering loons and showing a bit of human generosity, he thought. He did not say any of this, but out of the corner of one of her ceiling-fixed eyes, Sarah could read every word. They were there in his expression, as clear as the fantastically broken nose.

Slowly, terribly slowly, she looked towards him and then tentatively, ever so tentatively, she extended a finger. It was a quivering forefinger. The movement required great force of will. Gingerly, and with no more pressure than a cat's pad, she laid it gently against his arm then immediately withdrew the digit of physical contact. 'Please excuse me,' she said, 'I have a strange malady. It makes me unfit for company a lot of the time. And…'

Janek tried to interrupt.

'Please, I can say no more, not and stay here with you.'

Janek forced down one of the Bakewell tarts in spite of its armoured defences. He was thinking of something neutral to say…'I bought the boys outside a new ball,' he said at last, 'As a Christmas present. They've been knocking the same old one about for years. Last time I chucked it back to them, part of it came off in my hand.'

'That was a nice thing to do. They will appreciate it, I am sure. It is obvious that they like you,' she replied, calmer now that the conversation was not appertaining to her. 'I have noticed, when you walk down the street, their eyes follow you, with respect and warmth. That is a nice thing to see, across the generations, especially from boys who know that you are a foreigner.'

Janek smiled proudly at these observations, more at the fact that Sarah had made them, than that the boys rated him as an individual.

'They are even considerate towards me when I walk past them,' she continued. 'Always they stop their game and the little one with the blond hair, he never fails to 'good morning' me and 'good afternoon' me. He is a nice boy.'

Sarah neglected to say that she had deliberately stopped walking past them, and now took the long way round, along Shirley Avenue, because the boys had started calling her Mrs Lipsz, which had been more than she had felt able to take. It got her to thinking about her position. It was really rather an unusual one. What would her son say; if he found out? How could she begin to explain?

Sarah received a lot of smiles and hellos from the adults of the street as well. This had never happened to her before, anywhere that she had stayed. Of course there had been the usual nodding pleasantries at the old places, but here at Orchard Road it was different. The wives and mothers, in particular, beamed at her as they passed. Not a single one of them could ever have guessed at the compromised reality of her situation.

Sarah dragged herself back from the wandering alleys and mazy doubts of her mind to talk tea and cake and milk and saucers with Janek. These were the external domestic realities, but internally she felt like a cat left out in hammering rain. What a balancing act life had become.

One shopping day before Christmas, when she had been offered a lift by a whole gaggle of local women in an estate car, she told Janek about it upon her return.

'It's because they think you have saved me…from a life of filthy homosexuality,' he chuckled.

Sarah frowned.

'I first realised what they thought about me when Phil - you know the cheeky-faced chappie who comes round here for his ball - told me that his mother did not really approve of him mixing with me.'

'What exactly did they think?'

'Well…look at it from their little net-twitching perspectives. Here I am for twenty-odd years, a chap all on my own, single, and every other day, a new man comes along, a bit shifty looking, pops in the back entrance for a couple of hours and then buggers off, never to be seen again. Now what does your Johnny and Joan Average make of that?'

Sarah laughed out loud. She was doing more of that lately and it made Janek happy to hear it.

'And then you turn up, every day - a woman at no.33! Imagine them,' he sniggered…'A woman at number 33, a woman at number 33. Sighting: a woman at number 33! Raise all the nets, look out of all the windows, call Dorothy, call Joanne, call Norman, call everyone, there's a woman at no.33. A woman's reined in that old poofter at last!'

'Oh Janek, it must have been *The Telegraph* altering their opinions, not me.'

'Possibly. But remember, the article was published a good time after you arrived. That is how they will see it. And think: now we have both men and women turning up, front and back doors in use. It must seem a much more normal affair than before - if a business like ours can ever be considered normal.'

'So what about you, Janek, do you think that the people hereabouts respond to you differently now?'

'The men do. The women smile and good morning me, but the men actually stop for a chat. That didn't happen before. I suppose they are more comfortable with me now that they are sure I am not chutney ferreting among the plant pots. That or they are planning their own escapes.'

'Hey!' exclaimed Sarah interrupting, 'What would we do if one of the neighbours did turn up here?'

'What, all set to escape off into the sky-blue yonder, you mean?'

'Yes. What would we do?'

'Easy. Send him to Wolverhampton. He'd soon be back,' said Janek laughing at his own joke.

Again Sarah laughed out loud, big heaving guffaws.

Janek stared at her, maintained an unbroken gaze for a quarter minute - although Sarah only caught the last few moments of it - and then he stroked her arm. It was a simple little movement, but for him to do it took more courage than he could remember mustering in a long time.

She did not recoil.

She did not recoil, by Jiminy!

Janek felt like curvetting.

Sarah did not know what she felt like - possibly a lie down. Alone. She had seen it coming, the extended hand, and for quite a few seconds too. Immediately she had felt like shrinking away, but something had held her. And when the touch had come, the same something had stopped her from jerking away. It had almost made her return the touch as well. Almost. What was happening to her?

Then her mind was off, examining all sorts of possibilities. And she was not comfortable with any of them. Could this really be the man she was after? The one she had been hunting so long? What if it was all a mistake? Had she got her facts right?

Janek saw none of this in her furrowed brow, for he had stepped briskly into the kitchen to perform his usual rite of comfort when things were going well, namely, putting the kettle on. There was a spring in his step as he covered the floor and a snap in his fingers as he flicked the kettle switch down. For him, Christmas had come a few days early.

The actual Christmas gifts they got for one another

were easily chosen. Janek simply kitted out the whole of Sarah's new room - some things before the day, others wrapped for opening on the 25th. The gift for Janek was not so simple, until the weather worsened and made the decision easy.

Sarah knew that she had to get him something, but it was a strange affair, buying for a man about whom one harboured such deep and intense suspicions. So it was that the gale which blew through the area on the 23rd reflected exactly Sarah's troubled state of mind. She had been unable to get that little bit of physical contact they had had out of her mind. Even more perturbing to her was the fact that she had nearly reciprocated it. The storm rattled the windows, and anxious thoughts rattled around inside her head.

She looked out of her window at the swaying trees. They were the grand old men of the garden: enormous, spreading, unlopped. Now they leant majestically with the storm, their many branches intertwining; each lashing one against the other as if engaged in a vast grey cutlass fight. There was not a leaf left on any of them, but the ones from the lawn-floor were swirling everywhere, and to Sarah's mind they were like great coffee granules stirred by tree limb-spoons in the giant mug of a garden. But one tree was incongruous to the image - the willow down by the stream. It was flapping pitifully on its own.

In years gone by, when the other trees had grown rigidly upwards, it had sent out a massive horizontal trunk - a good three metres of knotty growth straight out to the side - before being seduced to the diagonal by the sun. And now it was in trouble. It was leaning dangerously close to its tipping point and the root anchorage seemed to be heaving. Even at her thirty yard distance Sarah could see a rippling and a submerging, a churning and a ploughing at its junction with the soil. The old willow was right next to the garage and its cement driveway. And in that instant Sarah read how one side of its roots must have been cut through to accommodate the original foundations of these two structures and so the tree was fighting the gale-force winds with only half the anchorage it required.

'Janek,' she cried out, fearing a death, for she knew how much he loved the old bank-side tree. But before he could answer, the colossal trunk heaved its last, right over to one side and then crashed down, bringing with it fence panels and half a dozen telephone wires...

Janek wept when he saw the old stream-guardian felled. He and Sarah went down the garden, in spite of the gale blowing. Along its length were the badges of Janek's long relationship with it: nesting boxes, bat boxes, bird feeders, trunk worn smooth where he had sat on it over the years, watching the brook silver past. He felt its fall like one might lament the passing of a friendly whale, or a stretch of dramatic and oft-walked coastline, suddenly lost forever beneath developers' tarmac. He raised a hand to brush away the tears and without thinking whether he should or not, very naturally, very gently, slipped his other hand into Sarah's. When he realised what he'd done, he didn't snatch it away.

Sarah tensed and then relaxed, a quarter tendon at a time. She stood stock-still beside Janek, not really sharing his grief: the tree was just a tree to her. She hadn't really known this particular one. But at her side her hand sizzled. His fingers were like acid, burning guilt and confusion into her. Whole, weighty seconds ticked by.

'Why didn't you whip your hand away? What were you thinking of? Now find a way to extricate yourself. Think of a way to break loose,' she was saying to herself, over and over, and all the while, time was passing and her hand was growing warmer and warmer inside Janek's.

'You must cut it into logs,' she said at last. 'One here, one here, and another there,' she indicated. Her hand was gloriously free now, tracing the lines where Janek's saw should be set. 'Then you could stand them in the garden. Their undersides will provide cool little spots for frogs and newts and in the autumn, toadstools will grow out of the wood.' Her voice was breathless and her face flushed. 'Frogs and newts and toadstools,' Sarah repeated, 'Frogs and newts and toadstools.'

She could see that the hands episode had cheered Janek. That little bit of closeness had gone a long way towards making up for the loss of his old friend. She plunged her hands into her pockets and excused herself on account of the wind and the cold. Once inside, Sarah went straight upstairs. There, she washed and washed her hand; soap lather five times on one side, five times on the other, and her tears sluiced it off as much as the tap-water. But come the next day, sleep, conscience's balm, equanimity's great restorer, had worked its magic: her hand no longer burned and she knew exactly what she would get Janek for Christmas - a replacement willow - if the local garden centre opened on Christmas Eve and had one in stock.

Before ten she had taken the bus up there and had brought a seven foot sapling back with her. The bus driver had tried to charge her double, so she had claimed that it was a walking stick. They had argued, she had told him to stop outside the police station which was en route and take the matter inside there; he had wondered if hers was the way people from Timbuktu always behaved. In the end she got back home with the tree on a single fare. She hid it at the back of Janek's garage-office. It was the best place - on account of their little break from disappearance work.

She did not switch the light on; Janek might see. It was to be a secret gift. But there in the gloom she caught sight of the big picture of Joseph. The young willow branches slapped against it. Immediately the old guilt came back, full flood. She traced a finger along his face, one finger from the hand Janek had grasped, and whispered: 'Forgive me.'

On Christmas Day itself, Sarah led Janek down to his garden-office. The willow sapling was there, propped neatly up. Joseph stared down at them, as through a coppice. Sarah took a bit of grit out of her eye, troubled once more, but hiding it well.

Janek was overjoyed. 'It is a lovely thought,' he said. 'The best present I have ever received', he said, 'And look, it's a vigorous young plant with a wide crown already.' He took in every aspect of its form. 'I'll bet the bus driver tried to charge you extra for carrying it,' Janek laughed.

'He did, actually,' smiled Sarah shyly, 'But I said that it was my walking stick.'

Then they both laughed together, and Joseph, the boy, looked down on their happiness. There in the garden office that was a shrine to him, he was forgotten for one Christmas moment and when Sarah looked up, she realised that she had forgotten him. It hit her as an awful gut-wrenching pain: she had forsaken the boy. But then she remembered the Christmas truce of the First World War when the British Tommies and the German soldiers had played comradely football against one another. And suddenly her Christmas actions and Christmas laughter and little Christmas gift didn't seem quite so bad.

They planted the tree there and then, right on the spot of the old willow. For Janek it was a labour of love; he set the sapling just so and with a dash of fertiliser. Lastly, he worked the wet ground in with the heel of his Wellington boot, so that the young tree was firmly set.

'Do you think it will grow outwards like the last one?' he said, patting down the displaced earth.

'Only time will tell,' Sarah replied.

'I reckon I have years enough left in me to find out,' Janek answered. He chortled at this little comment of his own, but this time the answering laughter from Sarah was muted. He looked over at her.

'You cold?' he asked.

'Yes,' she nodded and started to lead the way back in.

The rest of the festive break passed without highly-charged incident. Occasionally the two of them would talk about Poland and the old places they remembered. It seemed that the stamping grounds of their youth were broadly similar, although they had not known the same people. When not reminiscing, they ate and drank and stayed up late to watch golden oldies on TV, as well as a good deal of ropey new crap hosted by thirty-something young men with tidy beards.

Janek could just see the top of his new willow from where he sat. It tended to command his gaze as much as the television. Now and then he would steal a cheeky, silent peek at Sarah too. He felt that there was a calmer, rosier look about her of late. She was changing from the unstable, volatile woman of his early acquaintance - so he thought and hoped. Of course, she was still skittish, but being around her was no longer like being camped on the slopes of an ungrateful volcano. The lava below seemed to be boiling less intensely. The only times he really feared a relapse was when she was standing before Joseph - in her room, or in his office, or occasionally when he caught her taking a quick look at one of the small print versions of him. For some reason she became more distant then and a barrier seemed to form around her. At such times, he knew to leave well alone. Without these little reminders of her changeability, he would probably have taken her by the hand again - deliberately. As it was, Sarah did just enough to warn him off. Still, inside, he was heartened that she had not shaken him off that time at the bottom of the garden, instinctive and quite unplanned though his little action had been.

Maybe that was why she didn't shake me off, he thought, and he set to wondering how a man might engineer a planned-unplanned hand-holding!

In January the punters came flooding back: men who had resolved to flee for their New Year's resolution, women who had decided that they had cooked their last ever turkey in Britain; even a great-grandmother who could stand neither her husband nor the crime in the country any longer. By about the 8th, Sarah and Janek were back fielding their pre-Christmas numbers once more and, still, they were almost exclusively people who had read the *Telegraph* article. Janek calculated that that single half page had attracted more business than would otherwise have been drummed up in five whole years.

By the end of February there was still no let up. Nor March. The wheels of the business kept turning and turning and Janek and Sarah were the coal-stokers who kept the engine racing. Every day at seven-ten (they had been forced to stay open an extra hour) the two of them collapsed on the sofa in the living room. Janek was almost too tired to care that it wasn't into one another's arms. He would shake his head amazedly as they compared turnover - just as soon as they felt able to count after the rigours of the day. Between them they were averaging ninety clients a week.

With that level of throughput something had to happen.

It did!

On the 2nd of April, a letter dropped on the hall mat of no.33. It was Sarah who picked it up. The envelope was addressed to Janek Lipsz, the post mark from Montreal, Canada. Sarah had just said goodbye to a client. There was no one else waiting - for once. She turned the letter over. It was quite thick. There was a sender's address on the back: Robert Paley, Serendipity 2222, Montreal, Canada. Sarah looked out through the garden room window; Janek was just finishing with someone too. She would take it down to him.

She had stopped getting overly excited about every letter from abroad. At first she had felt sure that each missive carried pivotal news about Joseph, now she knew that the Disappearance Club clients wrote on all manner of subjects and requested all manner of objects - some wanted magazines posted, others M&S shirts, one even asked for his favourite brand of bog brush to be sent out. This one was different though: it was wrapped and taped as if it held important documents or photographs. There was a weightiness about it which the letters requesting shirts and bog brushes lacked...

'This just came,' she said to Janek, 'Thought I'd bring it down to you. Somehow it looks different from the usual ones.'

Janek reached for it. 'Don't get your hopes up too high,' he said, noting her excitement. 'I've had club members' death certificates arrive looking like this.'

He slid his finger along the seal.

No good.

He took out his envelope knife.

Better.

Sarah jumped as the contents spilled out. There was a lengthy letter, two photographs, and what looked like a business card. Janek and Sarah took up a photograph each; she was not about to stand on ceremony. Now that the letter was open, she considered it as much hers as his. The photographs were of a bald man, one who looked strikingly like

Joseph in all respects except his lack of hair. Robert Paley was one of the club's recently disappeared. He had sent them.

The man in the photographs really did appear to be a sleek-headed Joseph.

'It's him,' squeaked Sarah and she clutched at the table for support. Again Janek shot out an instinctive hand and clasped her hand. Again the contact was accepted.

'Wait, wait,' he said and then added, 'love.'

The word echoed strangely in the little office, but Sarah seemed not to hear it. Certainly she did not respond to it. 'There are billions of people on this planet. Many thousands of them look like our Joseph - it is a cold fact. Let us read the letter,' intoned Janek.

They did so, together. It seemed that Robert Paley had happened upon this likely looking fellow in Montreal. He was an optician: Paley had taken the two photographs of him at his practice, surreptitiously. And had then tailed the man to a house a few miles distant. He had included both addresses. They were both in Montreal.

'Why the hell didn't he ask him some questions?' spat Sarah. There was venom in her voice.

'Often they don't, Sarah…usually in fact. You have to realise that a lot of these people who flee do so because they have something to hide, or are escaping possible prison sentences. Once you are in that world, you often move in circles of similar people and, in time, it becomes hard to believe that other missing people don't inhabit the same world too. They don't ask questions because they wouldn't answer any themselves, if the positions were reversed.'

'What's to be done then?' snapped Sarah, losing none of her sharpness. Her eyes were brighter than Janek had ever seen them and her tongue protruded through her lips. Her breath came out in noisy jets either side of it. For once he thought her rather ugly.

'I will go,' he said simply. 'It is a good lead, as good a one as I have had in ages.'

'What about me?' she rasped.

'You must stay here - man the business. Woman it, rather.'

The little joke fell flat. Sarah had ears only for the Montreal affair and she did not look happy about staying behind.

'You remember that was the deal we made? I would show you the ropes here and then when the time came, I could go off and chase the quality leads, wherever they might take me.'

Sarah nodded, remembering the agreement, but not liking it so much after all.

'I will not be gone long. It will take no more than ten days to establish whether the man is Joseph or not, barring mishaps.'

'Barring mishaps?' Sarah repeated hawkishly.

'Yes, mishaps,' re-repeated Janek, becoming a little annoyed. 'Unavoidable events and delays.'

'Like what?' pressed Sarah, not giving a fig for his annoyance.

'Like he has gone away to see family, or he's buying a new line of spectacles somewhere, or he's been locked away in the state penitentiary, or he's choked on a bottle top, or I don't know what else…mishaps, ok?'

At last Janek's sarcasm succeeded in cracking

through the carapace of Sarah's crabbed intensity. 'Then I shall just have to wait here at home and hope,' she said sadly.

Immediately all Janek's peevishness evaporated, for Sarah had just called his old house her 'home'. In that one word he saw a whole world of hope. If this Canadian man could just turn out to be Joseph, the actual Joseph - their Joseph - then life's sunshine might really be his for the grasping.

CHAPTER 12

It was hectic - getting ready to leave and keeping the office going - for the numbers didn't tail off one iota. It was midday, three days before Janek was due to leave, and he hadn't even found time to brush his hair. It stuck up like a morning penis.

'I always thought that I would carry on the business…you know, after Joseph was found,' Janek said, 'but now I'm not so sure. If this fellow turns out to be him, really him, I might just jack it all in.'

'What and live near Joseph? And play with his kids - if he has any?' replied Sarah. They were questions calculated to provoke, although Janek did not know it. Sarah slid them out the side of her mouth and a sly smile played over that half of her face once they had been delivered. She watched Janek intently. He was struggling with his response, she could tell. Sarah did not let him off the hook. 'Well?' she pushed. 'Do you think that you will see much of him afterwards, assuming that you find him this time?'

'It is difficult to say,' answered Janek at last. 'We have a lot of issues to sort out, he and I.' He scratched a troublesome ear. 'I think that decision would be down to him.'

Sarah snorted silently into her papers, if it is possible to snort silently. Whatever, she took care that

Janek did not hear her.

Janek had thought this conundrum through himself, many times, although it was not a riddle he liked visiting: it might very well prove that Joseph would not want to see him at all. After all, Janek had never been able to forgive himself for what he had done, so why should his victim? But then again, decades had elapsed and Janek had contrition to offer, and the evidence of his years of searching, and the diamonds of course. They might make a difference. But he didn't like the way in which Sarah was able to see right into him. She had this uncanny ability to sniff out the most sensitive spots of his inner self. It had been disconcerting when Phil used to do it, after a fashion, but Sarah seemed to have the ability honed to a fine art - and she lived under the same roof. Maybe he just wore his heart upon his sleeve and the perceptive could read it there and pick away.

He went out to his garden-office, where he would be free from uncomfortable questions and where new clients might divert his mind. What he actually got was the first ball of the day, right smack against the side of his head. The football games had been fewer over the winter, but now that it had turned spring, the boys had started up once more. Janek lacked the skill to head the ball straight back over. It landed in a patch of daffodils and he picked it up.

'Hey,' he called good-naturedly, 'watch my flowers.' He unlocked the double doors and carried the ball out. Phil was there and a couple of other boys. They seemed to have grown. It was the first time in months that Janek had really taken them in, what with the reduced incidence of football and all the work he had been doing. 'Hello lads,' he said. 'First ball of spring, eh? Bounced off the top of my head.'

'I thought you said it landed in your flower bed?' replied Phil, smiling cheekily.

'I headed it there.'

'So it was your fault,' he teased. Then he remembered his manners, 'Thanks for the ball, Mr Lipsz, it's great. Me mum said it must of cost a pretty penny.'

'Yeah, thanks a lot for the ball,' trotted out the others.

'That's alright. We'll have you playing for Arsenal yet,' said Janek.

For quite some seconds there were rolling calls of, 'Err yuck' and 'Arsenal! Never!' and 'Millwall'…. 'Charlton'.

It had been a deliberate piece of goading and Janek enjoyed the frenzied response. 'Look monsters,' he said at last, 'I'm going away in a few days - for a week or so. Now I want you to try and keep that ball out of here while I'm gone, but if it does end up coming over, you call up at the front door. No more than a couple of times a day, mind.'

'Mrs Lipsz'll be staying then?' asked Phil.

Janek paused for a moment, licked his lips, once round one way, then round the other. 'That's right,' he said at last, 'the lady of the house will be staying.'

'So you won't be wanting me to look after your cat then, Mr Lipsz?'

'No, Phil, that won't be necessary this time, thank you.'

Janek took a step back towards his doors then turned again, digging into his pockets. 'Here,' he said to Phil, 'Come here.'

The boys had already started their 'keep it up' once more, but Phil dashed over. 'This is for you,' Janek said handing the boy a five pound note. 'Share it with the other lads. And make sure, if you see that cat of mine about, you stroke him for me…And only twice a day at the front door, right?'

'Sure Mr Lipsz.'

'And there's one other thing, Phil, when you do knock at the door, no calling the lady who answers Mrs Lipsz, ok?'

Phil grinned and his eyes sparkled. 'I understand Mr Lipsz.'

'Good lad. Now off you go. I want to see that ball stay up for a count of thirty.'

Janek stayed and watched them till the ball hit the tarmac at twenty-eight then he slipped back into his garden. Just as he was fastening the latch once more, Phil's voice called, 'I hope you find him this time, Mr Lipsz.'

Janek fumbled the mechanism.

'So do I. So do I,' he whispered to himself.

Sarah wasn't easy company as the day of Janek's departure grew closer. She seemed terrified that he would fail to see Joseph, or lose him, or somehow not tell her what happened if he did see him.

'You will inform me, won't you? You will tell me everything, won't you?'

'Yes, of course.'

'Because I'm not just working here to be kept in the dark when it really matters,' she continued.

'I said I'd bloody well tell you. Got it?'

Sarah snapped her lips together and looked unconvinced.

The day before Janek was due to leave, they saw six more clients between them, did the banking, filled in a tax return, and went down to the shops in Janek's car to stock up on everything Sarah might need while he was away. It was a tense, nervy time. Janek was really feeling the pressure of the occasion and Sarah was, if anything, even more edgy. They snapped at one another - so much so, that in the evening, upon their return, they kept to little zones of the house where the other was not. Now and then, Janek would visit the 'Sarah zone' and try to go through what would need to be done in his absence, but the internal demons they were both carrying made conversation difficult. In the end, Janek simply sat down in the living room, compiling for her, independently, a written list of instructions and 'just in cases'. It didn't take long to knock together. Then Janek was all alone, in the gathering gloom - all alone, except for his inner self.

An ugly little fellow.

It started to prey upon him, to ask questions, to needle and prod. Janek knew that this would happen. It always did - when it was near time for the safe to be opened, and the diamonds taken out. 'Would he take the photograph out? Could he bring himself to? Could he stop himself? Would looking at the girl bring good luck or would she bring bad luck? Maybe she would curse him from the photograph?'

When it turned truly dark Janek sprang up from the sofa, which had grown squashily warm from his hours of sitting on it. He stalked to the hall, flicked the light on. Immediately the bulb blew; he would have to make do with the little light under the stairs. Before proceeding any further, Janek looked behind both shoulders, as well as up the stairs, towards Sarah's room. She didn't seem to be stirring.

The door needed a sharp pull; the winter had stiffened its hinges. He clicked open the meter safe. His fingers were fumbling and he was making more noise than he wanted to. Quickly he snapped his head out from under the stairs and looked up them again, towards Sarah's room. It was still shut, a light from within framing it.

Slowly he eased the safe tray out. The diamonds were there, in their little sack. He looked only at this draw-strung bag. But his inner self, that nasty little imp with whom he had had so much trouble all evening, was taunting him:

'Open the chamois leather envelope. Go on, go on,' it chivvied, 'Open it. Open it.'

Janek remained resolute, 'Only the diamonds,' he said to himself. 'Only the diamonds,' and reached out a decided hand for them. He would snatch them out then whip the safe door shut with his other hand - one had to make a stand against a troublesome inner self.

He had drawn the precious bag from within and had half closed the 'meter', when the chamois envelope winked at him. His physical eye noticed it. Immediately his heart was rounding the last bend of the 5000m steeplechase. A twitch broke out just above his upper lip, and his hands could not support the weight of the precious stones they were holding. He dropped them into his lap.

Janek reached forward, a slave to his inner self. He could not help himself. The leather was as soft as ever he remembered it. He slipped a thumb under the flap. There lay the most precious thing in the safe. It took Janek thirty seconds to slip out the photograph - such was the jittery and trembling state of his fingers.

Its reverse side was smooth, but yellow-white with age. In pencil there was written upon it, 'Barbara 1942.' The blood swirled and surged at Janek's ear drums. He bit his lip, shook his head, screwed up his eyes.

When he opened them again, the photograph was the right way round.

He stared: that wave in the hair, those eyes, that innocence…the pity that should have been…

'Janek?' Sarah called

Jesus Christ!

The photograph flew into the air: Sarah's call had come from at least the fifth step down. She was actually looking over the banister at him. He was caught in the light from the understairs cupboard. Two diamonds spilled from their bag. Janek snatched at the photograph like it was his own falling soul.

Sarah reached step eight.

Janek lunged off balance. He caught Barbara in his hand. She crumpled in the act of his clutched at her. He stared aghast at the creased photograph…

'What the fuck are you sneaking about for?' Janek exploded, 'Snooping and nosing and fucking sneaking.'

Sarah remained perfectly still on the eighth step. Janek was shouting so loudly she could have heard him on the six hundred and eighth. She was shocked, actually white in the dim light from the cupboard.

'Is this what you do then, eh?' spat Janek with hateful force. 'Lock yourself away all day, to bide your time, then sneak out silently to snoop and spy?' He had jammed the photograph into his pocket and scooped up the diamonds, including the two spilled ones. He stood and stared at Sarah, all scarlet hostility, his fists balled. His eyes had become wolf-like: pin-prick pupils and all the top half of the iris lost beneath the upper lid. His mouth flared open, teeth bared.

Sarah was scared. For the first time since living with Janek she was genuinely afraid of him. She had no idea what he had been doing down there on the floor in the hall and had no intention of hanging around to find out. She ran back up the stairs and into her room. Immediately she rooted through her things and turned up her twelve inch knife. She clutched it to her, just behind her back, blade ready, expecting Janek's tread on the stairs at any moment. He had given himself away as far as she was concerned: she did have the right man, it was obvious now. That was the face and the anger of a man who was capable of anything. She had seen his predator's eyes. War would bring that side of a man out - and feed it. All that was required was for it to be there somewhere in him already...

...When he finally burst into her room, she would cut him a new hole to breathe out of...a new hole to piss out of...a new hole to shit out of...a new hole to scream out of. Her blood was up now. She thought she heard a creak on the stairs and there, in the middle of her room, she practised, quickly, the roundhouse motion with which she would stab him.

She was mistaken, though. Janek had not taken even one step closer to her room. He had simply finished gathering everything up and then locked the little safe door. He had shut it empty - had left the photograph and all the diamonds in one of his jacket pockets.

Next, he paced about in the perfect blackness of the living room, agitated. On reflection he felt very stupid. What could Sarah have seen in the half-light anyway? If he hadn't reacted so ridiculously, she would simply have assumed that he was tinkering with something dull and dusty under the stairs.

What a fool he'd been!

He sat and berated himself.

Upstairs, Sarah was thinking hard too.

She couldn't kill him. Not now. What about Joseph? Janek was still the man to find him, whatever other kind of man he was. And he was due to leave in the morning. Nothing must jeopardise that. 'Always focus that, Sarah. Always,' she mouthed to herself.

She slipped her blade away.

Then she looked to the heavens and whispered in emotional communion, 'One day, my dear, one day, I promise.'

Janek did come to her door, in the morning, early. He bore a tray, steaming with food and tea and contrition.

'Sorry about last night,' he said coming in, 'as you must have guessed by now, there are scorpions in my past. They sting me sometimes and the venom puffs and swells and froths and comes out of my mouth. I lose my head then and sometimes direct the bile at those I care for most, when really it should be directed at myself - the chief of sinners. It is always worst when I am about to go off and follow a lead. The anticipation gets the better of me.'

Janek had rehearsed this mouthful. He though it hit the right note. He also hoped that Sarah might recognise her unstable self in some of the description, and so cut him a bit of empathetic slack. She smiled. He took from this that she had and that he had been forgiven.

Only Sarah knew that the smile was forced, dictated by the demands of the Montreal sighting and Janek's afternoon flight there: nothing could be permitted to jeopardise the potential locating of Joseph. She started in on the breakfast, after buttering and jamming a crumpet for Janek. Hers was a well acted display of warmth. Janek took the crumpet with his left hand, keen not to get his right sticky with smeared jam: he had in it an envelope, thick to bursting.

'I have this for you too.' He dropped it on the bed, near Sarah's elbow. Twenty and fifty pound notes spilled out of it. 'I know it looks like I just threw a wad together after the row I kicked up yesterday, but actually I was planning to give it to you anyway. I took the money out when we did the banking last. Remember I took ages at the cashier's? That was why.'

With her hand Sarah riffled the money. With her head she was thinking, no amount of money will ever settle our score.

'There's two thousand there. It's all yours.'

Sarah's eyes did widen in spite of her bitter thoughts...He was a bastard, but a generous one.

'That's a year's wage,' she said. 'I've been here six months and we agreed that I would work for nothing. That's one hell of a pay rise.'

'We agreed terms before the *Telegraph* article. You and I have taken over ten thousand pounds since it came out. See, I'm still being a tight-fisted, blood-sucking employer: I've kept eight thousand plus for myself,' Janek said. 'Go on, count your share,' he added.

'No, I don't want to,' Sarah said from the comfort of her pillow. 'But I will finish this breakfast. Thank you very much for it.'

'Right-o.'

Janek gained some cheer from Sarah's well-shammed warmth, but the night before still weighed on him as a heavy embarrassment. Also, he was very jittery about the flight and the potential Joseph that he would be meeting…

'Egg ok?' he asked.

'Mmm, lovely.'

'Bacon?'

'Scrumptious.'

'Little sausages?'

'Haven't tried them yet.'

'Right-o.'

'I suppose I'd better finish packing then,' he said at last.

'Suppose so,' Sarah replied. 'And Janek,' she added. 'Thanks for the money. It is very kind of you.'

He walked backwards out of the room, looking for any little signs that Sarah's forgiveness of him was not complete. She gave nothing away, even thanked him once more, and then beamed him out of the room. Inside though, she was quite convinced. The night before's rage had been white-hot. Give a man like that a gun and a war and brutalising years of hard struggle and he would turn murderer, rapist, kidnapper, torturer…anything. Yes - she was convinced that she had indeed found the right man at last.

And Janek was convinced that he had been forgiven. And after only one night! 'What a wonderful woman,' he thought. Most, he reflected, would have made unlimited capital out of the hallway incident - and for aeons - snapping that they were 'fine' for interminable days upon days.

Actually, Janek had very little left to pack; his suitcases passed scrutiny every time.

It was the photograph that was worrying him. He had to get it back under the stairs. It burned in his breast pocket and he felt as if that side of his jacket weighed more than the other. He imagined the girl's lovely deep eyes carving through his shirt and skin into the essential him, cutting quite through to his soul. Indeed, the heavy, emotional load in his pocket actually made him feel physically sick. The little bit of crumpet given to him by Sarah was the only thing that he had not vomited straight back up all morning. Everything else, he'd been unable to keep down.

When he heaved that up too, at about noon, and flushed it spinning down the lavatory, he knew that he could delay no longer in returning the photograph of Barbara to its little 'meter'. But putting her back under the stairs was not an attractive option, not after the scene of the night before. But then again, nowhere else was as safe, because Sarah might look through his things while he was away - people did do that - it was a recognised perk of house-sitting. Not that the photograph would mean anything to Sarah, but Janek could not stand the thought of his Barbara being touched. He thought of tucking the photograph away somewhere in his car, but he was driving himself to the airport this time and that would mean leaving Barbara in a car park for days on end.

No.

She had to go back to her usual place under the stairs. He would just have to steel himself to the task.

In the end it was only a ten second job, although Janek's tongue was stuck to the roof of his mouth throughout, and his breath rasped in hoarse gasps.

He had not been able to resist looking at her face - to see exactly where his clumsiness had crumpled the image: one crease ran straight across her forehead, another bisected an eye. The blemishes pained him. Awfully. So it was that when Janek had re-locked the safe door, it was straight to the gin bottle he went - he still had a little left from before Sarah's time. How he wished that he had another photograph of Barbara: one that was not marred or damaged in any way. He could not stand to think of her loveliness sullied. He swigged down the gin, until he really felt the alcohol buzzing round his system.

After another few shots, his inner self surfaced once more, riding his bloodstream in tandem with the alcohol. It leered at him: 'You're a fool, Janek Lipsz, a fool to think that Joseph will ever forgive you - an old bastard like you. You should have been strung up like the Nazi camp guards were, on a short rope, in front of the people, in Cracow market square.'

Then he downed another gin before remembering that he was driving to the airport this time. 'Shit,' he said, wiping the beads of spirit from his lower lip. His inner self was sent back to its dark lair. Janek knew that Sarah would get up to say goodbye and wish him luck: looking for Joseph was so pivotal to her life now, that it would be inconceivable for her not to. He could not be under the influence when she appeared.

An hour later she did come down, red-eyed, clearly unmanned by the enormity of the impending trip. It was the fear of failure which was shaking her, and the recognition that this Canadian optician might turn out to be just another lookalike.

Janek had been pinching himself and downing coffees just so that he would pass for sober.

'Find him, please find him,' Sarah cried.

Janek felt himself welling up too.

They did not touch.

'Go now. Leave with plenty of time and God be with you,' she added.

Janek walked briskly towards his car. 'God!?' he repeated to himself, 'God with me!? Now wouldn't that be funny if it were true?' Then he waved Sarah goodbye.

CHAPTER 13

Montreal was very cold. The wind whipped through its wide streets. Janek couldn't help but think that London's narrow little alleys would impede the biting gusts. On the positive side, the address Robert Paley had given him looked like it would be easy to find. The fellow had provided a map and the roads on it were marked as clearly as blood in snow. Janek figured that he could get where he needed to be in about quarter of an hour.

He stopped when the lights turned red; he walked when the lights were green. He looked in shop windows, he checked the time on clocks, he engaged in people-watching. Then as the streets fell away and Robert Paley's directions started to become even more precise, Janek stopped noticing these things. Before, it had been a deliberate policy to register the sights, in order that his nervousness not overheat. Then suddenly, when Janek realised that he was just two blocks away from the target optician's, his emotional temperature started proving much harder to control. His strides wobbled out on gelatinous knees and each breath came blasted out of shotgun nostrils.

Janek stopped by the revolving doors of a big multinational bank. 'Oh God!' he wheezed, trying to suck back in a little of the air which was being so forcefully expelled. 'Please God, if this can just be my Joseph, then I will praise you for ever more.' He surprised himself with these prayer-like appeals. Where on earth had they come from?

Janek looked at his map. According to Robert Paley's annotations he had only two hundred metres to go. Fear played a little ditty down his spine. Then he thought of Sarah, at home; just as nervous as he. It was the first time in his thirty-plus-years of searching that he had ever weighed the emotions of another person - at the point of zeroing in on a possible Joseph. Realising this, he set off again. His strides were purposeful: he had scored a victory over the jelly-knee syndrome. The sense that he was searching for both himself and Sarah seemed to have vanquished the wobbles. Janek was reading off shop fronts: tobacconists, chemists, pornographers, bakers, coffee bars, fast food outlets, newsagents, book shops, optician...

OPTICIAN

Janek looked away from the letters. They scalded his eyes.

I dare not look at them...

I dare not look at them...

I dare not look at...him...

The wobbles returned.

He was shaking and there was not a drop of saliva in his mouth. His chin sagged pathetically.

A man barged into him as he bustled his busy way past. Janek shut his jaw with a dry clack. The hard physical contact had given him impetus. He looked up. And there in front of him, standing by the plate glass of the shop window was a quite incredible sight...

Sarah ran the business on her own as best she could. The numbers of clients had tailed off a little: she would not have been able to manage otherwise. However, she was seeing many more men than before - Janek not being present to receive them. The two of them had maintained a rather strict gender divide over the months, so the male of the species was pretty much new territory for her.

If she hadn't been so worked up about the 'Montreal Joseph' she would have laughed at some of the chaps who came by. Quite a few didn't give a stuff. They revealed everything, let it all hang out: they wanted to fuck cocktail waitresses…they wanted to fuck ladyboys in Thailand…they wanted to fuck tight young pussy anywhere in the world. One man said that he was off because he and his wife wanted different things: she wanted children, he wanted air hostesses. He had suggested younger air hostesses, but the compromise had not been enough to bridge their differences.

At the other end of the spectrum were the men who were stuffy about having a woman dealing with them at all and would barely divulge any personal details. Sarah was lucky to get name, rank and number out of these individuals. The two types were polar opposites and would have been amusing as such, but for the enormity of events which she knew to be playing out six thousand miles distant.

It was the old sweats who really missed Janek's presence - not the escapees themselves, but the people who had been assigned jobs by them, like depositing money or letters: those who had come to expect Janek down in his little garage, not a woman up at the house.

But nothing proved to be beyond Sarah, even though she had been a bit daunted by the male end of the business at first, and not a man-jack-of-them left thinking that she was not competent and thorough. It was actually a visit from a woman which gave her the most trouble.

For months Renault woman had noticed a greater volume of people coming up Orchard Road and stopping at number thirty-three. She also recognised Sarah as the person who had asked her about Mr Lipsz and the strange goings on at the back of his garden. And since long before Christmas, she had been trying to work out why this foreign lady visited the place every day. Then she wondered why it had become necessary for her to stay over at the house. Next, Renault woman had noticed that this same lady actually received callers herself - at the door - taking in new business as it were. And now she appeared to be living at the house with the odious Mr Lipsz...actually living with him. So Renault woman became convinced that there was aiding and abetting going on: that the foreign lady was in league with Lipsz. She had turned; she had cosied up to the enemy.

At first the woman entertained thoughts of murderous revenge: she would run the turncoat over, she would crush her skull in with something from the car tool kit. She would burn the house down and so render the bitch a charred husk. For a while these black imaginings cheered her. But soon she was back to sobbing in her car seat again, swigging Jameson's, because deep down, Renault woman knew that these were idle dreams, for she was not the murdering type.

She was just giving herself up to complete misery

once more when she noticed Lipsz drive off, with a suitcase and everything. He was going alone. The foreign bitch was actually waving him off. The Jameson's was dropped under the passenger seat: this called for a clear head.

After Janek left for Montreal, Renault woman watched the house for three full days - with even more diligence than ever before. The clients kept coming, the door kept on being answered, they kept leaving, they kept coming, coming-leaving, coming-leaving, and once every day the trim little foreign woman would head for the newsagent's, always to return to the house within ten minutes.

Renault woman decided to call.

Yes. She would call, now that Lipsz was gone; to appeal to this woman, the woman she had helped. Surely this person would have heart enough to return a favour? No woman could be so stony as to refuse, especially with Lipsz out of the way.

For an entire morning she sat heavy-breathing, trying to summon up the courage to knock, but it was only when she saw an old silver Saab crawling up the road that she finally acted. It was because the car was just like Janek Lipsz's. It took two horror-struck minutes for her to realise that it wasn't actually him returning. Then she jumped clean out of her own car, terrified into action - the job had to be done before the old bastard arrived back.

On shaky legs, much like Janek's in Montreal, she walked up the path. The twin threes of the house number appeared as if under water. Four times in her six year vigil she had knocked for information at the garage gates; four times she had been fobbed off. This was her first time at the front door.

Fifteen seconds later Sarah opened up. She smiled down at the derelict before her. Never before had she seen a woman who looked more in need of a fresh start and a flight to somewhere wholesome. Sometimes the punters came and they looked as fit as butchers' dogs, not this one - the poor love really looked as if she had something to escape from. Life had hollowed her cheeks and lined her face and replaced her hair with fraying straw.

'Good morning,' soothed Sarah. 'What can I do for you?'

'This is the Disappearance Service isn't it? Where a person can arrange to vanish without trace?' Renault woman quavered.

'That is right. We can help you to start over just about anywhere in the world.'

'I was wondering whether you could help me?' came the same broken voice. 'Maybe you have heard of me? I am Margaret Boyes; it is not a common name.'

'No. I don't think so, but please, do come in.'

Sarah led the way upstairs.

She didn't recognise Margaret as the Renault woman who had helped her before. That day, in the street, Sarah had been too wrapped up in her own business to take in faces, and the woman in the car had been a type anyway - a seated, shrunken, broken creature who leaked information, not a walker and a knocker on doors and an enquirer, albeit a decayed one. Besides, Sarah was functioning on forty percent - more than half of her was in Montreal with Janek.

She invited her 'client' to sit down, brewed up a

cuppa for each of them too. Seeing Margaret seated did jog a little memory in Sarah, but it was not a strong enough jolt to take her back to the Renault car and the pavement of Orchard Road and their previous conversation.

'You remember I helped you once?'

Sarah looked blankly at Margaret through the steam of her cup.

'…When you wanted to know what went on in this house, what went on down in that garage at the bottom of the garden.' Margaret indicated out back with a sweep of her cadaverously thin arm. A good measure of her tea splashed onto the carpet.

Suddenly Sarah did remember. She was shut in a room with the woman. Alone.

'I told you everything I knew,' Margaret continued, 'And you went in the double doors and now you have set up home here. Very comfortable.'

They both spilled tea. They both put their cups down at the same moment.

'I do remember you, now. Thank you for your help. It made a great difference to me,' stammered Sarah, fearing what was about to come; what was about to be asked of her.

'Now I need your help, my dear,' said Margaret rising from her chair. 'In 1969 my husband, Clive, Clive Boyes, disappeared from our home. It is not five miles from here. I haven't seen him since, nor have his two daughters, although he did ring our eldest in 1970 - once. It was her he told. Told her that it was a Mr Lipsz here who had fixed him up to flee his country and his family, and that she could always get in touch with him through Mr Lipsz. Since then: nothing.'

Margaret Boyes was crying, the tears great moonstones of misery. 'I have spoken to that Lipsz bastard and he will tell me nothing, but I can see in his eyes that he knows. He knows everything. Where my man is. Why he ran out on us. Everything,' she wept.

Sarah thought of Janek's eyes and the secrets she was sure were hidden behind them.

'I want to know what has become of my husband and I think that you can find out for me,' said Margaret Boyes, her reedy voice suddenly much stronger and more forceful. 'There'll be records here. Addresses, that sort of thing, I'm sure of it.' Renault woman stood up from her seat.

'I'm, err, um, you see, um, arr,' mumbled Sarah. This was an incredibly difficult situation. Outside of the house she could have coped, could have fielded the woman. Inside, she felt cornered, like a snail harried within its shell. Sarah decided to lie. 'I have no access to records. That is Mr Lipsz's area. He won't let me touch past cases. I am just a secretary and a caretaker while he's away. You will have to come back when he returns. I am sorry, there is nothing I can do. Mr Lipsz should be back by the end of the week.'

Sarah was talking so quickly she could hear her own lips smacking and spitting. A scream of visceral fury stopped her dead.

'You get that information now,' screamed Margaret Boyes, 'I am not leaving until I know where my Clive has gone.' Her face was puce with rage. She hurled her cup, catching Sarah full on the bridge of the nose. Sarah sprang up at the terrific pain. All sympathy for the woman evaporated. Sarah had to safeguard her own position. She could not give out information that

Janek had told her was to be kept secret. It was too pivotal a time to contradict him. She had to look to her own interests, especially with Joseph possibly found. She had to do something - fast. She hurled her own cup. It split the still screaming Margaret Boyes' forehead open. Blood splashed on to the carpet.

Sarah sprang round to the other side of the desk, took hold of Margaret's straggly hair with one hand and started punching, punching, punching the tired, lined, derelict face with the other. Not once did she let the woman flop or fall, but kept her bodily upright so as to keep striking her again and again and again: no one else's search could be allowed to muscle in on hers. The search for Joseph could not be compromised.

It was only when Sarah saw the wrinkles of the woman's face change from hard battle lines to the softer crow's feet of despair and defeat that she stopped. There was a moment's pity for her at that point. But a second later she hauled Margaret's light, depression-wasted frame down the stairs and out the door. Sarah pushed her so that she crashed face-down onto the hard tiles of no 33's front path. She had shoved with all the intimidatory might she could muster: Sarah had to protect her own plans. There was just no way she could take on another person's tragedy.

She did pity the woman more fully though, once they were outside. Sarah was able to feel Margaret's loss then, the access to sympathy no longer so obstructed by her own fears. But she had to ensure that there were no repeats - so Sarah said what she had to, although she hated doing it: 'Never, ever, come back, bitch!' she hissed. 'Stay in your car and weep your tears. If you knock on this door again, I'll break your fucking back!' And she slammed the door shut on the prostrate and sobbing form.

The footballing boys stopped their game at the sight of Renault woman passing. Never in over five years had they once seen her out of her car. She staggered and swayed past them, bleeding profusely. They stared at her, and up at the house from which she had been ejected.

'Look! Mrs Lipsz!' said Phil to the others, pointing up at a window. Then quickly he snatched his arm down, half on account of being intimidated by the wild intensity in Sarah's eyes, and half because he was dashing to help the Renault woman. She had collapsed.

Sarah watched the scene. 'There was nothing else I could have done,' she was saying to herself, 'There was nothing else I could have done.' Hours later she was still repeating the phrase.

CHAPTER 14

Sarah knew that Janek was back when Oskar dashed to the front door with a little Pavlovian purr.

She followed the cat.

The lock turned.

Janek entered.

Sarah didn't like the look of his face.

He raised a quivering finger. It matched his lip. 'Not one word, not one tiny, little word,' he croaked out and then fell to sobbing: huge, anguished sobs which heaved his ribcage up and down full inches. Sarah started too. And then, without making any conscious decision to, she was hugging him, hard, with one hand cupping the back of his head.

Her sobs were louder even than his. Joseph had not been found; that much was clear. She was no nearer to him than ever. But also she was hugging Janek Lipsz. How could that be? Hadn't he shown his true colours that night, in the hall, beside the understairs cupboard? What on earth was she doing?

'The optician was German. Spent the whole war in a little village near Bremen,' wailed Janek, 'Can you believe that? I went all the way to Montreal to ask a Kraut if he was a Pole…for fuck's sake!'

Sarah took his face in her hands - another intimacy which shocked her, even as she did it, 'You weren't to know. If he wasn't our Joseph, then he had to come from somewhere,' she said. She tried to make Janek's eyes engage with hers.

'Yes, yes, yes, I know,' he sniffed.

'Did he look like Joseph?' she asked, tremulously.

'Frighteningly so. I was sure it was him - until he opened his mouth.'

'We will just have to carry on looking then, that's all.'

'Oh right! Year number thirty-two of looking,' Janek scoffed, trying to free himself, 'I don't think I'll ever find Joseph.'

Sarah kept a tight hold on his face. She dug her nails in and even as he struggled, the fingers of her right hand found a little curl of his hair and tugged at it.

'Oww! Oww! What the fuck are you doing?'

'Don't ever speak like that again, do you hear? We will find him. We will find Joseph. Don't you dare give up, Janek Lipsz,' Sarah scolded.

Janek broke free, really quite roughly. 'What exactly is your stake in all this?' he demanded.

Sarah took a step back. She looked everywhere but Janek's face.

'I want to know why you're so goddamn interested in Joseph. It isn't normal for a person just to waltz in off the street and become fanatical about finding someone they don't even know. It isn't normal. I want to know what's going on.'

'I told you, I thought it was a beautiful cause,' replied Sarah, composedly.

'I know what you told me,' flashed Janek.

'And my life was empty. I needed something to fill

the vacuum - someone to fill it.'

'So you settled on a boy who hasn't been seen for over thirty years? A person who is probably dead…'

Janek paused. Sarah bit the side of her mouth in order to stifle a scream. A wave of hysteria threatened to overwhelm her.

'…When you could just settle on me,' he added in an embarrassed rush. 'Instead of us both wasting the few years we have left on this fool's errand.'

Sarah panicked, like a stag hearing the first hounds of the season. She could feel her gorge rising and too late she realised that she was powerless to stop it. She vomited: over the hall carpet, over Janek's shoes, over herself.

Janek was shocked speechless, his mouth actually left hanging open, and Sarah took advantage of the moment to run up to her room.

'So I guess that's a no, then,' Janek said to himself dryly. 'Jesus Christ, I've been turned down in the past, but never before has anyone actually puked a rejection all over me.'

He was too tired and too pissed off to clean up the vomit. Sarah, for her part, appeared to have disowned it, so Janek just dropped a couple of sheets of newspaper over the mess and went to bed.

He felt like shit.

In the morning the vomit was gone. Janek had fully expected to come down to the squelchy remains, and the stink, and the cat feasting on great gobs of it - but no. He looked where the hall had been most heavily spattered. It was a little bit wet and he could smell cleaning agents.

'Got it all up,' said Sarah, coming out of the kitchen. 'There's tea in the pot and the crumpets are almost done.' She disappeared again, obviously expecting him to follow her. He wasn't sure that he wanted to, after the night before.

'Janek?' she called and he stumped in after her. 'Sorry about last night,' she said, 'I'm afraid I got myself very worked up about Joseph. Maybe you were the same the first time you thought you had found him? You know, after the disappointment?'

Janek didn't answer.

'You must have been very upset about things yesterday,' she added.

'That was not why I suggested we get closer,' replied Janek. 'Rather, that just brought it out. I have had the idea for quite some time.'

'I know,' replied Sarah quietly. 'I am not stupid, or blind.'

'So does the prospect actually make you heave? I mean, are we to expect your breakfast to come up at any moment too?'

'I can't Janek, I just can't get any closer to you. I'm sorry. You have been very kind to me, but I need some success in my life before I can ever consider sharing it with anyone. And I have latched on to this Joseph business like a barnacle, I am afraid. It speaks to me. It provides me anchorage. You see, I have not been a very stable person over the years and it has given me the secure foundation that I need. And I really want to give it my all - before I can become emotionally involved in anything, or anyone, else. Do you understand?'

Janek nodded and did a good job of hiding his

disappointment.

Sarah had spoken very calmly: all night she had been awake, mulling over what to say. She thought the little story plausible enough and there was a little sliver of hope in it for Janek to set his sights on. Also, she had couched it in such a way that he would feel bound to resume the search for Joseph - if he ever wanted her to feel able to respond to his advances.

Janek cleared his throat. 'Got a bit of a cold; the Montreal wind was biting,' he said.

'Mmm.'

'My nose is streaming.'

'Uh-huh.'

'And I've got the beginnings of a sty coming. I can feel the bugger itching.'

Sarah could not play it cool: she could not wait for him to get round to talking about the search. The stakes were too high. 'Will you still look for Joseph? Will you still keep the Disappearance Club going?'

Janek raised his hands then let them fall.

'Please?!'

'Give me an hour. One hour. And I'll be back down at the bottom of the garden once more. Jesus - am I a man or a toad?'

They laughed together and for a moment Sarah forgot the Janek who had turned on her in the gloom of the hall. And she forgot that she had just lied to him too. Sharp sunlight irradiated the room, as if to match this forgetful instant.

'There's one thing you have to tell me though,' said Janek, stressing the 'have to'. Sarah caught her breath. Had he seen through her? Had she given something away?'

'Sarah?'

'Yes?'

'How the hell did you get two black eyes?'

'Oh those!'

'Yes those?'

'You know that woman in the blue Renault? The one who is always parked up by the side of the house?'

Janek's face darkened.

'Well I was stupid: I didn't recognise her out of her car and she knocked on the door. I let her in, assuming that she was a client. Once upstairs though, it became clear who she was and she started demanding information about her missing husband. I didn't give her any, so she hurled a cup at my face. See here.' Sarah ran her finger over a purple splodge on the bridge of her nose, 'The bruise spread and pooled under my eyes. Don't really understand the biology of it.'

Janek took two steps closer to look. Their faces were less than six inches apart.

'Is it true that she's been out there every day for six years?'

'Yes, although a daughter substitutes for her sometimes. It is a very sad case.'

'Can't we tell her a single thing?'

Janek shook his head. 'There is a trust between me and those I help disappear. Besides...'

'You're not a doctor, guarding confidentiality at all costs,' interrupted Sarah.

'...Besides,' continued Janek, 'Business would suffer if word ever got out that I had revealed an escapee's secrets. It is a risk I am not prepared to take. And bear in mind, I have been aware of her presence out there since her very first week's vigil. You've not even done a whole year yet. It is one of the pressures of the job.'

'She looked terrible, Janek.'

'Looks are irrelevant; if you want to find Joseph.'

Sarah was silent, but appeared to be hatching a rejoinder.

Janek hammered his point home: 'Don't be under any illusions about the business we're in, Sarah. You have sat up and taken note because one ruined, broken person, old before her time, has chucked a cup at you - but we make hundreds, thousands, of people out there unhappy. Many of them are desperate to know why a husband or a lover or a father - even a mother, since the *Telegraph* article - has run off and left them. Only twenty percent of our clients stay in touch with their families, you know, most are never heard from again, except by me. That's a hell of a burden to bear. I reckon that on average, for every person we help slip away, there are five or six left here in turmoil, with all the shit and mess to clear up, all pondering the whys and the whereabouts of their loved one's disappearance, as they struggle to cope. You might have seen that one woman, but there are many, many out there who look just the same as her and who want to hurl more than cups at us, I can tell you. You know, there are only two windows in this whole house haven't been smashed in since I set up practice here. Only two, I haven't had to repair. That's the business we're in - not so very different from your old landlord's is it?...You still want to find Joseph?'

Sarah was weeping big, pore-magnifying tears from her blackened eyes. She hated Janek for telling her all these dirty details - and because he was waiting for her answer. She could see the expectancy in his eyes.

'Yes,' she sobbed out, 'I still want to find Joseph.' It was horrible being made to face the human cost of her searching. She started sucking in air, in great, ugly lungfuls, like someone trying to resettle a thumped solar plexus.

'Do you want some gin?'

'No,' flashed Sarah through the gasps.

Janek nodded, 'That will come,' he said. It was a nasty little jibe, snapped out because he wanted some and held her responsible for having made his office alcohol-free. 'In half an hour we start back on then: Operation Joseph.'

Sarah knew that it was the disappointments that were making Janek so cutting, but looking at him, through her tears, she did wonder how on earth it was that she had ended up hugging him the night before.

They did knuckle down to the business. And Janek got some gin in too - as before. This time Sarah did not complain, for she understood more clearly the pressures of his position.

This meant though, as the weeks went by, that she, in her full sobriety, started to take on a bigger proportion of the work: she saw more people than Janek, she had a firmer grasp of all the names and figures; she could pinpoint information more quickly than he. The numbers coming to the door did tail off significantly however, so the search for Joseph was not compromised by Janek's drinking. By late May the *Telegraph* effect had worn off entirely: they had seen the last of the people who wished to act upon it. Business stabilised at a less frenetic pace.

Sarah started to come down more often to Janek's garden office. She told herself that it was to ensure that he remained fairly sober...that she was providing guidance necessary for the efficient running of the business: both of which were true. Deep down, though, she knew that something else was motivating her too. She appreciated the thirty-two year sacrifice of the man. Her mind was not so completely filled with the awful crime which she imagined Janek committing - the one which had prompted such a three decade marathon - but was able to consider that he might actually have atoned in some way.

She brought him tea.

She talked to him about things which were not Club related.

She ran odd jobs.

She began to doubt herself again and doubt the intelligence which had brought her to Janek's door in the first place, knife in bag. Now and then, Sarah thought that she might even like him.

And she had started to feel for him. He was getting old; she could see that in his face. Whether it was the gin, or the last disappointing trip, or simply Old Father Time's liver-spotted hand on his shoulder, Janek had begun to look pinched and stale. The skin of his neck sagged where before it had been taut, his cheeks flapped yellow where before they had been rosy, and the bags under his eyes were darker and shot with wrinkles.

More than ever, he would peer at his bird feeders, waiting patiently for the occasional woodpecker or cheeky jay. Sometimes Sarah would find him in the wider garden, tinkering with nesting boxes or fashioning lard balls.

She felt that he was losing heart.

Then she would pep him up, get him galvanized - for when the clients called. And he would turn it on for the callers, because he knew that if he and Sarah were ever to be anything more than just colleagues to one another, Joseph would have to be found. But he felt tired - so, so tired.

In spite of this changing dynamic in the day-to-day running of the business, Sarah still deferred to Janek in the matter of leads on Joseph - when they came in. He could sift the good from the trash like Sherlock Holmes could sort through criminal cases: little details missed by Watson would be picked up and made clear, vital clues for all to see. Sarah was Watson and she knew it.

One good lead did come in, towards the end of September. It was from Scotland, from a client who had not scarpered abroad, but had done his disappearing within the British Isles. His name was Martin Steele. He had had some business out on one of the offshore oil rigs, and had seen a fellow there who looked remarkably like Janek's artist's impression of what Joseph would look like aged a few decades. It was Janek's view that this client was trustworthy and solid. He had been gone eleven years and this was his first sighting, so obviously he was not prone to bouts of intense Joseph-spotting. All in all, it was a good lead. Only a few hundred miles away too.

'And he has noted that his man has a scar down his cheek.'

'But Joseph doesn't have one,' replied Sarah.

'He might have picked one up,' said Janek, 'Anyway, that's not the point; the good sightings tend to have a little something extra - like a scar,' explained Janek. 'They show a bit of thinking out of the box. Also, it means that our Mr Steele took the time to look at his man in detail. I like this one.'

'When will you go?' asked Sarah.

'Later today, I think. I'll drive through the evening and find a B&B somewhere in the Yorkshire Dales. It's nice up there. Then I'll get over the border into Scotland by tomorrow afternoon. Christ knows how to get out to this oil place - Dunlarssen Rig - but I suppose there'll be men with boats up there, like at every coastal town.'

'How long do you think it will take?'

'Not long, once I've found a man willing to take me out. I haven't got very good sea legs, but it was a boat brought me here to this country in the first place, so I reckon I can manage a few miles off coast.' He paused. 'It'll be funny if Joseph is there: all these years spent searching by air and land, just for him to be stuck out in the grey drabness of the North Sea.'

But through the flippant tone, Sarah could see that Janek was up for it. The old excitement was flushing his cheeks once more and his face seemed to have shed a few years. She smiled at him - one of those genuine smiles. They had started to become less of a strain for her to bestow of late.

'Do me a favour will you?' Janek said, returning one, 'Run along and get me an up to date road atlas from the petrol station. You know, from the place on the main road.' It was a short walk and Sarah turned for the door almost immediately. Within a minute of his request she was gone.

Straight away Janek sprang up and dashed for the hall. He had a perfectly good atlas under the seat of his car: his request had merely been a ruse to get Sarah out of the way. After the last time, he could not risk her being around when he opened up the meter safe under the stairs. It was the work of a moment for him to open it, whip out the diamonds and lock the safe again. There was no question of him taking out the chamois leather envelope and its emotional contents, for Sarah would be returning at any second with the superfluous atlas.

She had left via the Club's double doors, so Janek dashed down to the bottom of the garden in order to help her back in through them. They had become a bit sticky with the changing seasons.

'Bit of the wood has warped,' commented Janek upon her return. 'When I'm back, I'll plane it down, then it'll glide like it's on runners once more. You know, I put these gates on the day I opened up here, that's over twenty years ago now. They've served me and the business very well.'

Sarah could tell that it was all mere words - not that he wouldn't plane the wood down at some point - but that he was talking gates just to take his mind off the real task at hand. Indeed, after a bit more jawing about blown wood, he announced in a serious tone, 'About three o' clock, I should say. That's the time I'll have to leave. I reckon I better pack the same stuff I took to Montreal. It'll be cold out at sea.'

The reference to the Canadian experience dampened them both. They didn't say anything to one another for quite some time. An ice-sheet had formed in the garage-office, enveloping everything. Sarah stared up at the huge photograph of Joseph. A tear rolled down her right cheek and settled in a pore, arrested. It was as if it had frozen too.

Janek noticed. He felt impelled to break the silence. 'Come on. Lemon drizzle cake and strong, hot coffee were made for times like this. Ho for the kitchen!' he declared, with a forced chuckle. He rose quickly, hoping that Sarah hadn't seen through his fake jollity.

It was a sombre little snack, in spite of Janek's best efforts. Sarah could not be raised to any semblance of light-heartedness. And with him it was just an act anyway. He canned the pretence after ten minutes.

Twice Sarah dropped cake to the floor.

Janek looked at her hands; they appeared beyond her control. Her lower lip too, drew his attention - he was sure that she had sprung a cold sore. Normally he did not stare at people's disfigurements, temporary or permanent, but the funny thing with this one was that it seemed to have erupted in the space of only a couple of hours. He could have sworn that there had been nothing there when he'd first seen her in the morning.

She dabbed at it with a finger.

'Don't,' Janek ordered, snatching her wrist away. 'You'll spread it. Go and wash your hands.'

'What? What is it? I can feel something tingling,' asked Sarah in a cheerless voice.

'I think you've got a cold sore; probably because of the change in the weather,' Janek replied matter-of-factly.

'Really? I don't think I've ever had one.'

Her inflection was as dreary as before, but Janek

was barely listening. He was shocked: taking hold of her wrist he had felt the trembling that was wracking her. Sarah was like a little localised earthquake. He watched her jerk and jolt over to the sink. After washing she stood with her back to him, clutching the kitchen units, as if for support.

'You're not going to fall are you?' Janek asked solicitously.

'I'm fine,' came the clipped response, and from those few words, Janek could hear that Sarah had started crying.

Crying, shaking, cold sore? he thought. He sipped tea and ate cake, weighing whether to speak. In the end he rose and lay one hand against the middle of Sarah's back. She stared fixedly out into the garden.

'Why Sarah? Why does it matter to you so much?'

She gave no reply.

'Please, Sarah, tell me.'

In the refection of the window, Janek could see her mouth open as if to speak and then shut and then open again.

'Go on,' he said, encouraging her.

'I lost two children in the war,' she said at last, in words torn from deep within her. 'Two lovely children. Now take your hand off me, Janek.'

Janek snatched away the offending hand.

He nodded his head - so that was it - she searched to dull the pain of her own loss. 'I see,' replied Janek.

'Do you, Janek? I'm not so sure that you do.'

They stood there like that for quite some time - she with her back to him, staring blankly into the garden, he, stock-still, maintaining a respectful twelve inches distance. It was an uncomfortable situation.

Janek felt locked in the silent part of a game of musical statues. Also, he had the feeling that Sarah might erupt if he tried coaxing anything more out of her. There had been a sharpness and a bitterness in her last comment which daunted him.

'I'm getting ready for the off then,' he said at last.

Sarah did not reply, just kept on staring out.

'Right,' Janek concluded, turning on his heel and exiting the room.

Upstairs he mulled over what Sarah had said. It explained a lot: her moods, her intensity, her latching on to Joseph and the cause, her living in squalid little dives, her resistance to getting close to anyone. Janek longed to know the details though. Quietly, all alone, he actually admitted to himself that he loved Sarah and it was natural, therefore, that he yearned to know everything about her. 'One day she will tell me all and then I will tell her all,' Janek said to himself, as he looked for his warmest clothes to pack, 'And then, maybe, one day, she will grow to love me back.'

Janek drove off just after three. Sarah had prised herself away from the kitchen sink and actually did quite a respectable job of waving him off and wishing him luck. In waving back, Janek narrowly avoided crashing into Renault woman in her car. She was sat hunched over, glowering. It was a little infusion of guilt that Janek did not need. On the long drive up it added an extra spin to the occasion: if he could just be successful this time, then he might wrap up the disappearance game and get himself a little cottage somewhere. He could maintain the existing files and escapees, but not bother with any new business. That way, he'd be free of mad women hanging around - except one. He hoped that Sarah would come with him. 'What,' he wondered, 'were the chances of swinging that?'

It was a straightforward, clear drive up to the Yorkshire Dales. It was a part of England he'd visited upon first arriving in the country. He had loved it then: its wildness and tumbling crystal streams had reminded him of Poland. Subsequently, the rest of Britain hadn't, so the Dales had retained a special place in his heart.

It was nearly eight and he was looking for the same B&B-cum-pub he had stayed at as a young man, newly arrived, speaking no more English than one of the sheep in the fields he passed. It could be, he knew, that the establishment no longer existed, or it might very well have been sold and turned into a private house. In which case, he would simply drive on through the night and reach Scotland all the sooner.

It turned nine and he was still searching little lanes and dark corners for the welcoming light that he remembered. Then, just as he was losing hope, Janek took a sharp right and crunched to a gravelly halt right in front of it.

The Dancing Bear.

There it was. Not one thing seemed to have changed, and there was a 'vacancies' sign in the window. Perfect. Janek didn't bother with his case, toothbrush or flannel - nothing at all. He went straight to the bar.

There was a lively, nutty young ale on, which frolicked about his taste buds after the long, dry drive up.

'Good?' asked the man behind the bar, in a Yorkshire brogue as broad as any Janek had heard upon his first visit to the place, thirty-plus years before.

'Medicine for weary travellers,' came Janek's answer through the refreshing glugs, 'I didn't think I was going to find you.'

'Arr. It's a windy road in the dark, that's for sure.'

'I came this way once before, over thirty years ago. I was walking back then; I'd done twelve miles under a hot sun and by the time I found this place I was ready to swap one of my kidneys for a pint. In the end though, the chap behind the bar just wanted thruppence.' Janek took in the man standing before him. He was towelling a pint glass dry. His eyes were widely spaced and there was a very fulsome beard about his face - not overly long - but broad and high upon the cheeks.

'My father,' replied the man, reading in Janek's gaze the attempt to place his looks relative to the previous landlord. 'He's upstairs; not strong enough now to stand a-serving. I'll tell him there's an old timer passing through, though. He is always pleased to hear when that happens.'

'Actually,' said Janek, interrupting, 'I was hoping for a room for the night. I'm on my way up to Scotland and I've done about as much driving tonight as my eyes can stand.'

The bearded man put down the glass he was drying and charged Janek's back up to the top. 'You've come up this way, just to visit the place, then?' he said, his big beard cracking into a grin.

'Yes,' nodded Janek.

'In that case, I'll see if I can get the old man down.

He likes a pint last thing and loves chinwagging with the folks from his time.'

'And the room?'

'Oh yes, yes. You can have a room alright, and we'll only charge you for your breakfast before you go. The room's no problem at all.'

The father did come down, leaning on his son, William, for support, and he remembered Janek; not his face, but his accent and they fell to talking about old times. He wore an enormous bush of a beard; Janek thought that it might be compulsory for publicans in their part of the world to grow one - as some kind of ancient tradition.

After four pints he said so. The three of them roared at the idea and carried on drinking way past closing time and into the early hours.

It was ten when Janek got up. He knew that Sarah, if she'd been there, would have been on at him to start out earlier, but the drink of the night before dictated his rising. He wanted the breakfast before leaving too.

It was a right royal spread: rather fatty for a normal morning, but perfect post-skinful. The old landlord was not up in time to eat with him, but his son was. Janek told him a little of his travel plans - no details, just an outline - and the younger man mapped out a few short cuts for him.

It was midday when he set off, warm goodbyes and invitations for the return journey ringing in his ears.

Thanks to the privileged travel information Janek had received, he was clear of windy lanes and cowpats within ten minutes and driving down roads altogether wider. The sun was out, there was not much other traffic, and he had had a lovely little interlude. What were the chances of his being so warmly received up on the oil rig, he wondered?

The sun was still directly overhead when he turned back onto the A1. It was twelve-thirty…even Sarah couldn't have complained much at that.

For two hours Janek barely used his brake at all. It was a dream run. A couple of times he saw police cars and slowed down for them - that was all. Then the thoroughfare became less of a trunk road, more provincial. Roundabouts became regular features and Janek was aware of changes in the countryside: oaks and beeches were much less common. Everywhere they seemed replaced by close growing birches and pine trees. The smell of manure didn't fill the car anything like as frequently and Janek had to steal peeks at his atlas.

Half an hour after he'd sighted his last, lonely oak, Janek saw a sign for Berwick-upon-Tweed. According to his map and William and the regulars at *The Dancing Bear*, the turning he wanted was sixty miles farther on. That meant about an hour more.

Janek wasn't nervous. Not yet - maybe because he was in control behind a steering wheel and not flying - maybe because he had yet to engage a boat at the little port town towards which he was heading. He was still at a couple of removes from actually landing rig-side. But he knew that the nerves would come. They always did.

Montrose was the nearest coastal town to his wind-swept destination, the Dunlarssen oil rig, three miles out in the North Sea. Janek planned to engage a man with a boat to take him onto the waves and wait for him until he had checked out his Joseph. Almost certainly, he would have to find somewhere to kip down for the night and then hire his salty old sea dog.

The town of Montrose was all little grey Victorian houses and pretty sky lines. Janek clocked four fish and chip shops, also scores of bobbing boats at anchor. With any luck one of them - and its skipper - would be for hire.

The sea was black as molasses. Gulls wheeled above, dogging porpoises invisible to man, and the salt wind inched its nose into the crannies of Janek's car. He turned the heating full up, looking for a 'Vacancies' sign in the windows of the grey terraces. In the end he found one, suspended by a single wire, actually outside a detached place fronting the town square. He had passed the building twice, but had not noticed its sign.

He parked.

Inside was a stiffish looking woman; well preserved for a centenarian, withered for an eighty-year-old. She did not appear glad of his business and peered at Janek as if he reminded her of dockyard waste.

'Excuse me, do you have rooms available?'

'Rooms? Of course I've got rooms.'

'You're not full then?'

'I told you, I've got rooms. We're never full. Never.'

'Then may I take one?'

'Take it? By all means take it. It's five pounds, mind, in advance.'

Janek proffered the money. It was snatched from

his hand by a kind of claw and tucked away in an invisible spot. Afterwards he was shown to his room. There was a bed in it, a chair and a rudimentary wardrobe. It was as cold as ocean-going fog.

'Is there any heating?' Janek asked, fearing that he was pushing his luck. He was beginning to feel like an extra in a Hammer House movie.

'Heating is a pound extra. Hereabouts we find the sea air bracing.'

Janek took one look at his landlady's pinched face and decided that her last comment explained a lot. He said nothing, but did root out a pound note. 'For the heating,' he said, handing it over, 'And a hot cup of tea, if that's not too much trouble.'

The lady gave him a look which proclaimed that it was too much trouble, but in the end nodded her head to the request, in an Addams Family sort of way. Fifteen long and cold minutes later she brought the tea up and set it down, as if positioning a candle in a morgue.

'And might I trouble you still further?' Janek asked.

The landlady grimaced and looked at her watch in histrionic fashion. Janek thought that she might be late for a haunting somewhere damp.

'I want to hire a skipper and his boat,' he stated, refusing to be daunted. 'Is there anyone you recommend?'

'No,' came the sub-zero answer. 'I do not consort with sailors. Dirty people.'

The mouldering Morticia departed and Janek was left to his lack of mod cons.

The house rules were clear - he was permitted out

until eleven. That meant that he had a few hours in which to ask friendly locals where a boat might be hired.

The town fish and chip shops turned out to be staffed by warm, approachable people. Also they were supplied by local fishermen and their boat-hauled catches - so Janek was told. He enquired after these men, explaining that he wanted to hire a good sailor and his boat. Within ten minutes three separate shop owners had named the same pub as a likely place. So, having bought fish and chips from the last, Janek set off for *The Blue Admiral.*

'Last pub before you actually step into the sea,' were his directions.

Janek found the pub just as his final chips slipped down. The lady behind the counter had been right: another stride and he would have been in the sea. He tried the pub door. It was unlocked, but Janek needed to push hard against its brine-rusted hinges to gain admittance.

Four fifths of the bar conversation ceased the second his head was visible, the last fifth by the time the rest of his body caught it up. The place was full of flat-nosed blokes with missing teeth. On the floor three drunks lay curled up, two with dogs standing guard over them. They fixed their livid eyes upon Janek, like every other living creature in the pub, and bared their teeth at him - like every other living creature in the pub. The nearest dog growled, daring the stranger to touch its comatose charge.

Janek gulped. Clearly this was not the kind of place where one approached individual drinkers. He would have to try to enlist the help of the bar. Janek summoned up all his courage and strode to it. 'Whisky,' he said, thinking that that was the drink to be ordered in such a place. He added a politic 'please' and made his Polish accent as strong as possible, hoping that the regulars would notice that he was not English.

Everyone picked up on the twang, even the dogs. They started barking. The drinkers seemed to take an aggressive step closer towards him; the publican didn't move one step closer to the whiskys. Janek realised that the 'newly arrived foreigner' card was best not played in Montrose. He spoke quickly to the man behind the bar, dropping the accent so that he was sure to be understood. 'I want to hire a man and his boat for tomorrow morning, to take me out to the Dunlarssen rig.'

The growling stopped - human first, then canine.

Janek's whisky was placed before him.

'No problem laddie. We'll see you alright. Jim there, he'll help you,' said a voice.

Two drinkers on from where Janek was standing, a large man with a face as hard as sea air and hard drinking can craft, was addressing him. He beckoned. Janek went over, with his whisky and his heart in his mouth.

'There's the man you want,' the granite-faced fellow said.

'Sorry?' replied Janek, trying desperately to attune his ears to the man's guttural rasping.

'There's the man you want,' he repeated, gruffly, and with more than a hint of impatience. He pointed. His finger indicated a prostrate form, wheezing gently into its own blue cap. It was one of the men over whom a dog stood. The animal was one of those clever-looking Norwegian hounds with sickle-shaped tails. Obviously, its job for the night was to stand guard over the pickled master.

'His name's Jim - best man on the sea. He'll take you wherever you want to go for a tenner, so long as it's not another country. It's eighty pound for Norway and one-forty for Iceland,' stated granite face. His stony mug cracked into a smile, the first Janek had received from anyone in the pub.

'Dunlarssen rig is as far as I want to go,' explained Janek.

'Prod him on the shoulder then, tell him exactly what you want.'

Janek looked down at the man. 'He's flat out.'

'Och, do-nee be taken in by that…one prod from you and he'll be right up to know exactly what it is ye want doin'.'

'But his dog is standing over him with every tooth bared!' exclaimed Janek.

'Just so. But she's as soft as baby's shite really. See look,' the big local said as he stuck out a determined hand and caressed the dog's left ear.

'You got to be bold about it, though, like I was,' he said. 'No fannying around. Go straight in and get hold of Jim's shoulder and give it a good tug. Then the dog'll not suspect you, and your man will be right round in a jiffy. But if you pussyfoot around, she'll have you.'

Janek gulped down a scotch of fear. All eyes were on him. Everyone seemed to have heard what he had been told. The dog was watching him too. She was fully astride her drunken master, one leg at each corner of his collapsed form and showing clear inches of teeth.

'Maybe I should wait till the morning?' Janek opined.

'No man, now's the time to settle it all with your skipper. Do it now and he'll probably only charge you the price of a drink.'

'I'm happy to pay ten pounds.'

'Get it done, man. It's for the best, I tell you. Like I did…confident like.'

Janek drained his glass and set it down on the bar, exhaling with trepidation as he did so. 'One good prod you say?' he asked to make sure.

'Good and hard. And take no shit from the dog. Show it who's boss and she'll love you like a puppy.'

Janek steeled himself and formed a fist so as not to offer the animal a finger to bite off, just in case this man had got it all wrong. He bent closer to Jim. The bar turned silent. He tensed; the dog tensed too. Then Janek moved six inches closer. The animal's growling swelled to fill the vacuum of silence...

Quickly, forcefully, Janek nudged at the man's shoulder. The dog launched herself at his balled hand. Its teeth snapped shut just as he whisked the fist away. They missed by millimetres. The whole bar heard the sharp clack. The place fell about; the granite faced man dissolved into a thousand flakes of laughter. Quickly Janek made for the door.

'Wait,' shouted the man through his guffaws. 'Wait, man…you're alright you are. I'll set you a drink now that we've had our little laugh at you. And hand on heart, Jim ere's your man. You have my word on it. He'll be up and waiting for you at ten o' clock tomorrow mornin'…outside this pub. I lodge with him and I'll make sure he's up. Jim drinks more 'an anyone here, but he recovers from it ten times quicker too.'

Janek sat back down, as far as possible from the dog.

'What made you touch him with that animal standing guard there?' laughed another man farther down the bar.

Janek shrugged.

'Cos he's got balls,' answered granite face. 'Balls the size of coconuts.' 'Here fella,' he said, handing Janek a double. 'You're only the third person has ever touched Jim with his dog standing over him, and I've bought each one of you a double afterwards. One fella needed stitches, mind, before he could drink it.' The whole pub seemed to find this uncommonly hilarious. Janek swore into his liquor.

After downing the whisky, he decided not to spend long at the pub. The people were obviously arseholes and the door at Morticia's was due to shut at eleven sharp. He made his apologies and said his goodbyes. A couple of salty old Jack Tars clapped him out and his 'chum' who had stood him the drink reminded him to be outside the pub at ten. 'I room with Jim,' he shouted, 'I'll tell him and I'll make sure he's up in time to meet you.'

Janek nodded, although unsure whether to believe a word.

CHAPTER 15

It was a cold walk back to his lodging house so Janek set a lively pace and reached the B&B steps in good time. The key was a bit sticky, but he managed to let himself in after a bit of coaxing. All the time, he wondered whether he would actually see Jim waiting for him at ten the next morning. It was as likely as not just another set up. There would be the same old bar crew, propping up the grey pub wall, all set for a good laugh at his expense.

Morticia was no help whatsoever: the next morning, at breakfast, Janek asked her if she knew anything of a local man named Jim who frequented the *Blue Admiral*. Mention of the two names made her serving hand shake. It was a close run thing whether his plate or his lap received a fried egg.

'Here, we do not pollute the air with the names of the wicked. Ever.'

There was not much to say to that, so Janek ate in silence. The breakfast was actually rather good, which surprised him, although not good enough to make up for the company or the butterflies in his stomach - they had come, as he knew they would. Half were on account of the ten o'clock meeting, and the other half, due to his usual trepidation in respect of Joseph. If Janek was honest with himself, he couldn't really imagine his Joseph living among these Jack Tars and Medusas, but maybe the oil rig community was different.

He was at the pub by 9:50.

There was no one else there. Away to his right, though, were half a dozen men putting out to sea in little boats. It was a good fishing day: bright, clear and cold. Janek was tempted just to run over and ask one of the men to take him to the Dunlarssen rig. Also, he realised that he hadn't even seen Jim's face the night before – he was waiting for an unidentifiable person.

Janek was within an ace of hailing the nearest fisherman on the beach when he saw a figure striding towards him. He had a face as red as cranberries and hair which had not seen a brush, all atop a thick neck. There was an easy strength in all his movements and not one hint of a hangover.

'You the man wanting to get to the Dunlarrsen rig?' the fellow asked, drawing level.

'Yes. Are you Jim?'

'Aye. That's me. I understand you met my dog last night?'

Janek nodded at the memory and hung a paper-thin smile.

'Good guard dog,' commented the fisherman hoiking up rich morning phlegm. Jim whistled. Immediately the dog of the evening before came helter-skelter over the brow of the high street hill. She ran with sinuous joy, the crisp morning air licking at her coat. The animal bounded alongside them - in about five seconds. Janek was unconcerned: he could see a sweet, tolerant light in her eyes.

'She'll be coming with us - best bosun I've ever had. And don't worry, she'll not bother you, not one jot, assuming I don't keel over. If I do, mind, you'll be stuck out on those waves forever.' Jim seemed to find this prospect monumentally funny and it was some time before he could do anything but laugh. 'Come on, laddie,' he said at last, 'It's a good mornin' for it.'

The sea they put out on did not have one bit of picture book-blue about it. It was greener than apples. Brown seaweed and grey driftwood bobbed vigorously all about, and Jim's white and russet boat bobbed on top of the lot. It was a sturdy little vessel which Jim tossed about with consummate skill. His dog stood at the very front of the prow barking at each wave as it hit. After fifteen minutes, Janek hoped that one of them would claim her: the noise was cutting right through him and he was developing a sea belly. With every lurch, his gut seemed to heave two seconds out of sync with the rest of his body. There was no luck with the dog: its quick legs waltzed it beyond the reach of even the highest waves.

Janek caught sight of Dunlarrsen rig just after vomiting for the first time: he was raising his head up from delivering his load into the water when a monolith, even greyer and drabber than the sea air, hove into view. He couldn't feel nervous, he was too sick.

'Half an hour,' said Jim, reading the whites of Janek's eyes. 'You'll be sick a few more times before we draw alongside.

He was right on both counts. They heaved to thirty minutes later. Jim made fast. Janek chundered one last time and wiped the sides of his face. He had no idea what to do next - did one whistle or blow a foghorn or just wait in the bobbing green?

'Right, up we go,' said Jim.

Just above them, like a steel beanstalk, snaked a ladder. Janek looked skywards and lost it in mist and spray about a third the way up its length. 'Oh Christ!' he said out loud.

'There's no other way onto her except up,' stated Jim, not without sympathy. 'For royalty and the dead there's a helicopter, for the rest of us, it's this ladder.'

Jim went first, leaving his dog to bark after him on the boat. Janek followed, rung after frightened rung. His hands and hair were sopping with the salty spray. He peered through the fast-thickening sea mist for each hold. If he had not been so scared he would have stopped to marvel at the rapidity with which a clear morning could turn into foggy haze. The descending blanket closed out everything, even the dog's barking.

Janek knew that he had reached the top when a hand helped haul him up. It was Jim's. 'Not to be recommended after a couple o' pints,' he said, 'Now we'd better find the gaffer, I suppose. On a day like this he'll be tucked away in his cabin, tight as a spitball. Come on, I know the way.' Janek was led along half a dozen perilous walkways; anything he could clutch on to he grasped until his knuckles stood out white against the strain. And he swore with abandon, employing the expletives as a mantra with which to guard against falling. So it was that when he walked through an open door, he was swearing freely into the new, warm space which greeted him. Jim had gone on ahead, had knocked, and had introduced him before Janek even realised, so complete had been his concentration on not slipping.

'Good morning, Mr Lipsz. You have come a long way to see us. I am Manfred Orssen, the manager here. What can I do for you?'

For a couple of minutes, Janek could explain nothing but how low his internal temperature had fallen. There was a fire burning in the corner of the room which he headed straight for. He breathed in the lovely warmth.

'I am looking for a man,' he said at last and handed Orssen the black-and-white photograph of Joseph and the artist's impression.

The manager nodded. 'Looks like Max, although he's got a scar on his cheek now - picked it up here on the rig, about six years ago when a cable sheared in two. He was lucky not to lose an eye.'

Max? That is not good, thought Janek…although I suppose Joseph might have changed his name.

Orssen paused and looked serious. 'Has he done something? Are you here to arrest him? I mean, I do have a duty to my men…isn't some kind of warrant in order?'

'No…no…no. It is nothing like that. I am a private individual, I am not acting for any organisation or company or prosecuting body.'

'You are quite sure?' pressed Orssen.

'You have my word. Besides, I am past retirement age. The police and the courts do not send out men as old as me - if it's the authorities you are worried about.'

Manfred Orssen looked convinced. 'Ok. Then I shall get him. Umm…who shall I say is asking to see him?'

'Just say that Janek Lipsz is here.'

'Just that?'

'Yes, please...Oh, and when he comes, would you both be as good as to leave us to talk in private?'

Jim obviously didn't care; he started scratching his stubble. The manager on the other hand seemed perturbed - he was clearly a boss who liked to look out for his men. 'Well...I'm not sure about that...'

Janek gave Orssen his most 'I'm frozen' look, followed by his most 'I've come a long way over land and sea just for this meeting' look.

'Ten minutes alone then, but Max is free to leave any time he wants,' stipulated the tall Orssen.

'Of course,' said Janek, his tongue sticking to the roof of his mouth with apprehension. Suddenly, his nerves, which had been frozen like the rest of him, started to assert themselves most vigorously. It was about to happen: the meeting.

During the five minutes that he waited alone, Janek took in the precise details of the office. Adrenaline heightened his sensory perception: he noticed the green eyes of insects long dead between panes of double glazing, he discerned a spot of flicked jam on the ceiling, and he heard a stray wire scratching one of Orssen's mounted oil paintings. It was grating against the vermillion dress of a gypsy dancer. Janek stood up to tuck it back from the canvas - he had to do something with himself - when the door opened. In walked a tall man: mid-forties with a substantial scar down the right side of his face.

'Hello Mr Lipsz! This is a surprise...'

Back at the B&B, Janek wasted no time in calling

Sarah. He was very emotional. He did not trust himself not to create another scene in his own hall - if he just turned up at home with the news like last time. He rang on his landlady's private line. She was standing close by, ready to exact payment.

'Hello? Janek, is that you?' Sarah's voice was tiny with apprehension.

'Yes, it's me.' His voice was thick with exasperation and disappointment. Immediately, Sarah knew that it was not good news.

'How was it?' she asked timidly, fearing the response.

'You won't fucking believe it…I don't fucking believe it.'

'What Janek? What won't I believe? He was there wasn't he? You didn't miss him did you?'

'Oh no…I didn't miss him, he was there alright.'

'Well what then?'

'I'll tell you what - the guy I've driven the length of the country to see and nearly had my hand bitten off for…'

'Your hand bitten off?'

'Yes, my hand bitten off…he's only a guy I helped disappear fifteen years ago: me. Max Cunningham it was - a client. Went to work on the oil rig. I didn't even remember his name at first.'

Sarah was absolutely silent.

'Can you believe that? I'm calling on guys I've actually helped run away myself, to see if they're Joseph or not. Now how fucking crap is that? Sarah? Sarah?...Huh? Sarah, you there? I said how crap is that?...I tell you I'm ready to jack this game in, Sarah. Straight up…I don't think I'm even up to finding my own arse. You any idea how embarrassing it is to stand before a man who is supposed to be one of your own clients and then ask him who he is?'

There was a little strangled sob on the other end of the line.

'The poor bastard thought I'd gone up there to tell him that his mother had died…I tell you love, this time, this time up here, has made me realize I'm past it. I mean, Max Cunningham did look a bit like Joseph, but only a bit. The truth is, I just can't cut it anymore…Sarah, Sarah, you there? Sarah? You still there? SARAH?!'

But Sarah wasn't there at the end of the line, for she had fainted, onto her bed, and Janek was shouting down the phone at a dangling receiver: 'Oh great! Oh fucking great! Now I've got to drive straight fucking back without stopping, just to see if she's ok,' he swore, slamming the phone down. 'What a shhhhitty day - what a shitty, shitty day.'

His landlady was looking at him, revolted. Her mouth was lopsided-sickened, like a bulldog's after a nettle breakfast. She was bellyaching something about 'language' and the 'Devil's words.'

Janek took out the one pound he owed her for breakfast and another one pound note to cover the phone bill and he rolled them together into a stiff little column. 'Now,' he said, 'You take this money and you hold it tight in your grasping little hand and you shove it right up your arse, you ugly, piss-faced old sow.'

And with that he left the house, started his car, and was gone.

CHAPTER 16

Janek burst back through his own front door ten hours later.

'Sarah? Sarah?' he bawled; worried, pissed-off, tired, lower back complaining after such a long drive.

There was a thump and a scurrying upstairs.

'Janek, Janek? Is that you?' Sarah appeared at the top of the landing. Her eyes were scarlet with crying, her face puffy.

'So you're alright, then?' he growled.

She dashed down the stairs.

'I thought you'd collapsed, but here you are - sprinting about,' he snapped.

'Oh Janek, it wasn't Joseph. It wasn't him…' Sarah wailed, becoming unintelligible in the higher octaves of her weeping. She was a nose's length from him. Their hands brushed. Their breaths comingled: hot disappointment.

'No. Just another cock up…' He leaned his shoulder into her, '…I've had it. I've had it with these searches. I'm completely buggered. Failure after failure after failure. Year after year.' Janek was crying. There was exhaustion in his tears and frustration. Also the siren call of alcohol. 'I'm getting a drink. A bloody big one,' he croaked, disentangling their breaths.

On the kitchen table was a bottle of gin. Janek

splashed half of it into a chipped mug. He drank with his head right back, grimaced at the strength of the dose then started in again. His cheeks were flushed when he next spoke to Sarah: 'He's dead you know. No chance of finding him now. I've wasted decades.'

With a moan Sarah reached for Janek. He palmed her off. The alcohol was already riding him; he had taken down nothing else but his Montrose breakfast all day. 'Don't think you're going to start tugging at my hair again. Joseph's dead. Dead, I tell you.'

Sarah shook, put her fingers to her mouth, moaned pathetically, but Janek carried right on. 'Buried somewhere out there he is, somewhere in this shitty world.' The gin lit Janek's system yet more. He railed that Joseph was definitely dead. That he had to be dead. That there was no way he could still be alive.

His words cut deep, deep into Sarah. She felt herself growing faint again, sensed the kitchen beginning to blur. She thought that she heard herself scream. So she turned from Janek and dashed back up to her room.

For half of an hour, she could hear him sobbing. Then there came only silence, which proved harder for her to bear than the weeping. So careful step by soft step she descended and found Janek asleep on the sofa. The tired, disappointed man was flat out. Sarah stared down at him, a woollen tangle of conflicting emotions. She shook her head - things weren't getting any easier.

Janek shifted in his sleep, said something about a dog and kicking it and waves. He was having quite a conversation with his dreaming self.

Immediately Sarah was transported back sixty

years to a big Polish house with her father sleeping on a vast, comfortable bed. She was kneeling beside him with her sister, Miriam, and they were both teasing him, asking him questions which he was answering in his sleep. Most of her father's replies were nonsense, but some made sense: the two girls were laughing uproariously at them. An idea burned, phosphorus-like, in the heady oxygen of Sarah's reminiscence. She turned to Janek, twitching on the sofa.

'Janek?' she said in a low, soothing voice. 'Janek? What did you do in the war?'

'What? Who?' replied Janek. He scratched irritably, anxiously, at the side of his head, but remained fast asleep.

'Janek! Weren't you supposed to protect someone?' Sarah pressed.

'The diamonds,' nodded Janek, mouthing the words a couple of additional times. He folded his hands, as if in prayer, and laid them both under one cheek.

'The diamonds?' asked Sarah, in an even more insistent tone.

Janek flinched at the force of the question and mumbled something unintelligible.

'Was there something you had to do in return for them?' she continued, gentle as trickling water this time.

'Yes. Yes. Yes. Yes. Yes,' nodded Janek, seemingly annoyed at having to declare the obvious. He scratched his nose; a little unconscious tic.

'What Janek? What did you have to do?'

'Safety,' he nodded into his hands. 'To safety.'

'Was that at Roza Dymek's?'

'No.'

'Not there?' questioned Sarah.

'Not at that bitch's!' snapped Janek, suddenly urgent in his sleep.

'Where else? Where was safe?'

Janek jolted his arms out, thrashed his head from side to side then shouted in panic, 'The children. The children.' He jackknifed, bolt upright, his eyes staring. Sarah flinched involuntarily at the sudden movement.

'Barbara, Joseph!' he screamed. The names were shrieked in soul-deep pain, as if tortured out of him. He was awake, looking about the room with blind eyes, calling both names.

Then Janek was no longer shouting, but instead mouthing the words as if they were live coals searing his tongue:

'Barbara, Joseph!'

'Barbara, Joseph!'

'Barbara, Joseph!'

Suddenly he saw Sarah, no more than three feet from him. He stretched out his arms. She submitted to the hug - woodenly.

'You were talking in your sleep. You were shouting about Joseph and Barbara. What happened to Joseph and Barbara, Janek?'

'Nightmare,' answered Janek, 'Nightmare.'

'But what about Joseph and Barbara…in the war? Don't you want to tell me?' pushed Sarah, desperately disappointed that her man had screamed himself awake.

'Just a nightmare,' muttered Janek already nine-tenths asleep again. 'Zss a nightzmarez,' he slurred out of the side of his mouth and nuzzled his head against one of Sarah's breasts. Immediately, without calculation, she pushed him away – hard.

Janek's head bounced against the sofa arm. He sucked in a sharp rush of surprised air, his arms jerked up, and then he subsided once more into the warm bosom of sleep. Sarah gave him two minutes to lose consciousness completely then began the questioning once more.

'What did you do to Barbara and Joseph, Janek?'

Silence.

'Janek, what did you do to Barbara and Joseph?'

Silence.

'Janek?' she hissed.

He snored.

This was obviously a different kind of sleep. A huge tear of disappointment trickled down Sarah's cheek. She was angry too…angry at not having made more of her chance, angry at Janek for dismissing Joseph as dead earlier in the evening, angry at the sleeping man for all the secret things he had done.

Not angry; wrathful. She glowered down at Janek. Sarah took in his whole form, just as she had upon entering the room. This time, though, her mind turned to their first meeting and how she had held her knife ready throughout almost all of it. How easy it would be to gore him now. She reckoned that she could stab him four or five times before he even woke properly. Once in the neck, once in the chest, once in the belly, once in the bollocks…no, twice in the bollocks…

…She knew though, that it could not be done. There was so much yet to accomplish - Joseph was still out there to be found. She really believed that. He wasn't dead, not at all. And Janek had to be made to see that; when he was awake and not so sunk in his drink.

So there would be no stabbings. She still needed Janek. It was necessary, however, for Sarah to go into the kitchen and pick up the biggest knife she could find, just to be sure that it was not the right time to stab him. Deep down she knew that it wasn't; or she would have gone upstairs for her own knife - the one she had practised so long and hard with.

It was a strange feeling, standing there in the dark, gripping a twelve inch carving knife. Sarah's hand was shaking: it hadn't ever done that before, not in all the times she had rehearsed with knives, not even in the early days when they had seemed big and unwieldy objects to her.

She wanted to walk through to the living room and stand immediately over Janek with the sharp point of the blade - just to see what it felt like. But her feet rebelled. They would not move her. Again and again she tried. She was telling them that she would not actually do anything, but still they would not move her one step closer to the sleeping man. In the end Sarah threw the knife down with a curse. It clattered in the sink and she ran sobbing through the hall and took the stairs three at a time up to her room.

It was fear, not anger that woke Sarah, long before it was properly light.

She was scared of what she'd done…scared of what she she'd done while Janek had been driving back from Scotland. Scared of what she'd said…to the papers. To one newspaper in particular…

After Janek had rung from Montrose she had

dreaded his disillusionment; that final switch which might turn off his searching for Joseph once and for all. And the night before, when Janek arrived back - the things he had said - they had seemed pretty close to that point to her.

'So I was right,' she said to herself, dressing. 'It had to be done,' she continued, arranging her hair in the bathroom mirror, 'I had no choice.'

Ten minutes later when she slipped out of the front door she was still engaged in furious self-justification: 'I had to do it.'

The Yale lock clicked shut.

Outside it was first warm of what would be a hot day. The sky was lightening almost by the second; the birds were noisily about their business. A milk float was crawling up the road. Twenty minutes' walk away was a newsagent's which opened earlier than all the others in the area. Sarah strode off down the path which led to it.

There were no other pedestrians about, except for two scavenging foxes which bolted at her muttering. They flashed past a tight corner where a door was set ajar and a light was on: the newsagent's.

'I had to do it - but what will Janek say?' she groaned, pushing the door to the shop fully open. The bleary-eyed proprietor behind the counter looked up at his first customer of the day.

'You're early, love. Up with the lark today.'

Sarah smiled weakly, 'Has *The Telegraph* come in yet?'

'Over there, love. Big pile by the magazines.'

Sarah picked a copy up, leafed through a couple of pages, folded the paper over at another. Her hands were shaking, trembling the big sheets. She picked at her lip with nervous teeth. The lip quivered red against the sheet-white of her face.

The man behind the counter waited and waited. He waited some more. 'Usually people pay for their paper before they read it,' he snapped at last.

Slowly, whitely, still-reading, Sarah handed over the coins then turned silently from the counter.

'Oh, not at all, not at all,' grumbled the man to himself. 'Some bloody people.'

Sarah heard nothing. The door to the shop snapped back. She read the page through again, walking as quickly as her absorption would allow. Half way home she creased *The Telegraph* shut and clasped her hands to her face. The paper ink smudged down her cheeks.

'What the hell is he going to say?' she croaked then set off at speed for no. 33.

When she arrived back, Janek was still asleep, still on the sofa. It would be hours before his sore head and full bladder became insistent enough to rouse him. Sarah slipped straight upstairs - with her guilty paper. She spread it on the bed, open at page two.

The headline was too alarming, too unnerving, displayed like that. She snapped the paper closed and wrung her hands. 'He's going to hit the ceiling.'

After Janek's distressing phone call from the Scottish coast, after he had told her that he was ready to 'jack the game in', after Sarah had fainted away at the prospect of him finally giving up on Joseph, she had decided to find a way - a way to keep him searching for the boy. Upon coming round she had set to, directing all her mental energies to the problem.

There had to be a way of keeping Janek going…

Within half an hour she had come up with the idea of manipulating the press; of ringing *The Daily Telegraph* with red-hot information on The Disappearance Club - not as herself, but as a plausible-sounding public official. Entirely fictitious, red-hot information.

Sarah remembered reading in an old *Cosmopolitan*, something about a female police officer dying in a car crash. It was a magazine she had saved for a quite different piece, but suddenly this article had spun to the surface of memory, almost as a direct answer to her personal predicament.

So she had decided to contact the paper as this woman, rather than a living WPC. Somehow this seemed less illicit; more a hoax than a crime - should anything negative come of it. As soon as she had honed her 'scoop', she got hold of the direct line for *The Telegraph* editorial team.

After just a few words, it became apparent that everyone there considered the original Disappearance Club story a real hoot - and a seller. Sarah rode this. And it proved a short, bullshitting jump from there to them agreeing to run a whole new story; a juicily sensational one. They lapped up Sarah's fabrication.

When *The Telegraph* people said that it would be on page two she had been euphoric. Then, after a while, when she was off the phone, doubts had started to spin into her head:

Had she committed a criminal act?

Was impersonating a dead police officer an offence?

Could the story be traced back to her?

Could *The Telegraph* people sue if they found out

the truth?

And most importantly: What would Janek say? Would he kick up a stink?

Janek's mood upon crashing back through the door after his long evening drive had not been conducive to making a clean breast of things. But here she was now, on her bed, with the paper itself, and clean breasts seemed just as daunting by morning as they had the previous evening.

Still there was no sound from downstairs.

Sarah toyed with the edge of the paper. She had settled on newspaper coverage. And here the newspaper coverage was. The physical reality of the copy scared her. So did the physical reality of Janek, who would not remain asleep for ever. But she had done the right thing, she told herself; the only thing, she told herself. She hadn't acted too quickly or rashly, she told herself. Everything Janek had said just the night before about Joseph being dead, and what a waste of time it was searching for him, proved that she hadn't acted too hastily.

Didn't it?

Daring herself, she flicked the newspaper open once more.

For ages she sat reading and rereading. Part of her, a large part of her, was amazed at how one call to *The Telegraph*, just the previous afternoon, could result in a solid article in her hand the following day - even though the editorial team had assured her that it would be printed in the very next edition.

Sarah closed the paper only when she heard Janek walking about. Then she tucked it under her arm, swallowed hard and headed down the stairs. In the kitchen, Janek was rooting about for pain killers. His head was complaining about the night before.

'Hello,' he said as Sarah entered the room, 'Got a bit of a head on me today. Haven't seen the aspirin have you?'

Sarah shook her head.

'Oh…and don't leave knives in the sink, will you? They're dangerous if dishes or soap suds cover them over.'

Sarah nodded her head.

'You sure you've no idea where the pain killers are?'

Sarah did nothing with her head.

'You alright?' Janek asked.

'Uh huh.'

'Good.'

'What you got there?'

'Today's newspaper.'

'You went out early for it?'

'Uh huh.'

'You've got half of it smudged on your face. You look like a badger,' laughed Janek, hazarding a joke in spite of the white-hot rivets being driven into his skull.

'Janek,' said Sarah, her voice reedy, 'I've got something to tell you. Something to show you. Please sit down.'

Janek stopped opening drawers and prising open plastic containers. He didn't like the sound of this. It looked like one of Sarah's mood swings: Gale Force Ten Imminent. He pulled back a chair, sat himself at the kitchen table. 'What? What is it?' he said.

Sarah unfolded the newspaper. 'This.'

Janek had the copy of *The Telegraph* in front of him. He held it in balled fists and was reading the article for the umpteenth time.

'Sarah! How could you do this?' he shouted - also for the umpteenth time. He tore part of the headline:

LORD LUCAN ASKED
DISAPPEARANCE CLUB FOR HELP

'Sarah, what possessed you?' he glowered. 'It's not true, not one tiny bit of it.'

'I know. I know. I'm sorry,' she said, actually hanging her head.

'But why? Why did you do it? It's the most stupid thing ever.'

'It's just...I thought...'

'For Christ's sake, we have a finely balanced relationship with the police as it is without giving them this shit to sniff at!' Janek thundered.

'But I've already refuted it. When the *Telegraph* people rang here I made sure I did that. See, even in the article I refute the claims.'

'That's not the point. The police ignore me because I keep a low profile. You can't be low profile and part of the Lord Lucan circus. It isn't possible...Oh Sarah, how could you do this? There'll be half a dozen coppers here by lunchtime.'

'It's just,' she started, 'It's just...'

'It's just what?' spat Janek.

'I was just...scared that you were about to drop Joseph; you know, not look for him anymore,' Sarah said in a low voice.

'What?'

'When you rang from Montrose, you were so unhappy and telling me that you were past it, and not up to finding anyone, and so on, that I decided I had to come up with a way of keeping the club going. I was so upset, I just acted the second I had the idea. And you must admit that the last *Telegraph* article did help us get hundreds of new searchers out there,' she replied.

'But Lord Lucan…actually cold calling the papers to talk about our involvement with Lord Lucan!?'

'I didn't ring as me though, Janek, you've got to see that. That's how I was able to refute the claims - when the paper people called here.'

'Well who the bloody hell did you first ring as then, Arthur Scargill?' exploded Janek.

Sarah mumbled her response, scared for the first time that Janek might actually send her packing from his house. 'A WPC from Northumberland.'

'What?'

'A WPC from Northumberland.'

'Oh bloody marvellous!...Why?' whined Janek.

'So that the papers would bite. I couldn't just contact them as some little old lady from nowhere, could I?' implored Sarah.

'Shit! That's all we need: a copper from Northumberland, where there's no crime at all, so she'll have all the time in the world to get her buddies down south to harass us.'

Sarah shook her head.

'And then we'll really be in the soup.'

Sarah continued shaking her head.

'What? What? What the hell is it?' hissed Janek suddenly noticing. 'You look like a bloody dog with water in its ears.'

'She's not going to do anything – she's dead.'

Janek tore the rest of the headline, 'You mean to say that you impersonated a dead police officer, just to get us national coverage and thereby keep me plugging away?'

'Yes,' replied Sarah, staring Janek back full in the face this time. 'That's exactly what I did. I read in an old magazine that this woman police officer had died in a high speed car chase, so I pretended to be her and I took my chances. And I think it's paid off: we're on page two of *The Telegraph* this time.'

'Oh it'll pay off alright, assuming that I want to carry on the search, and I want to work twelve hour days fielding all the new business, and I want to be hauled in by the cops, then yes, it'll pay off,' growled Janek.

Suddenly, above their argument, they could both hear a sharp rap at the front door…Then another…'Well,' spat Janek, 'It looks like it's fucking well started already…if that's the police, I'll see them. If it's a new client, then you're dealing with everything,' he scowled, jabbing his finger at Sarah. They walked together out of the kitchen, arriving at the door in time for the third resounding knock.

Sarah opened up. 'Sorry, we were stuck with something in the oven,' she lied.

A small, neat woman of early middle age was standing expectantly. 'Oh that's quite alright. I've called because of this morning's *Daily Telegraph* article.' She brandished her newspaper at them. 'I was on my way to work in The City and I found that I just couldn't go one stop further. I'm not very happy you see, so I just hopped on the next train going in the opposite direction and determined to come and talk to you at once. I hope you don't mind me just turning up like this, unannounced, and without an appointment or anything?'

Sarah twisted her head to look at Janek. He saw desperation in her eyes and a deep, deep longing to succeed in their search for Joseph. Immediately, a warmth for her spread throughout every part of him, even the bit which was telling him that he should know better.

'That's quite alright,' he smiled at the new client. 'We are always ready to receive the tired and the unhappy.' He smiled at Sarah too, before turning back to the neat little figure on his doorstep. 'Sarah, here, will talk you through the various options available to you. Generally, she sees the female clients and I see the men.'

The woman stepped into the hallway and Sarah showed her up the stairs. Janek was left standing with one foot on the doormat and one on the bottommost step. He was still there when Sarah popped back down to him ten seconds later. 'Thank you,' she said and planted the slightest and chastest of kisses on his cheek, 'It'll be all right, you'll see.'

'Yes,' sighed Janek, 'Maybe it will – because I'm going to go to my office right now and put in a pre-emptive phone call to the District Superintendent Larry Oakes. If he calls on the house phone before I get down the garden, tell me at once, ok?'

'Ok,' agreed Sarah.

'Now go and see that unhappy little work-refuser upstairs and find out where in the world she wants to disappear to.'

Superintendent Oakes wasn't particularly interested, which surprised Janek.

'It's social services you want to worry about mate, not me - helping all these ne'er-do-wells escape their responsibilities to their wives and children. I got too many stabbings and bovver boys to worry about you - or Lord Lucan,' he laughed. 'Bit of free publicity was it?'

'It wasn't me actually.'

'Yeah right.'

'No, really, it wasn't.'

'Course it wasn't…and next you'll be telling me that it wasn't you fighting Billy Marsh up at *The Seven Stars* last year. Keep your nose clean boyo. Toodle-oo, Janek.'

The phone went dead and Janek stared into the receiver. 'Boyo! Bloody cheek. I'm twenty years older than you, Larry Oakes,' he said down the empty line. Then he replaced his handset too.

Perhaps Sarah would be proved right. Perhaps things would turn out all right.

Janek did not have much time to wonder how Larry Oakes had learned that it had been him brawling in *The Seven Stars*: by three o'clock he was seeing his fifth client. The last time the Disappearance Club had been featured in print, the solid rush of clients had only really started the day after circulation. Not this time. It appeared that people who had read the first article, but not acted upon it, were now reading this latest one and being tipped into action without further delay. They were all serious people, very clear in their plans and expectations: the interval had given them thinking time.

At five o' clock Janek collapsed into his office chair. So much for retirement plans. On the A1 back from Scotland he had been pissed off, really dreadfully pissed off, and in addition he had caught sight of his own face in the rear-view mirror - about twenty thousand times. He had not much liked the old, haggard, gaunt mug he'd seen reflected back at him. So he had decided there and then, on that southbound road, that the wild goose chases had got to come to an end and that he ought to lock the Joseph photographs away once and for all. Also he thought that it would do him good to spend less time in a souped-up garage and more time enjoying the comforts of his actual home…

…But here he was, back at it, back at the bottom of the garden, taking on new clients again. In his desk drawer lay nearly a thousand pounds in upfront fees. He reckoned that Sarah must have taken the same, judging by the number of callers. The business had never before done much more than tick by: whatever else Sarah had done, she had made them rich – in less than a year. Janek mulled over that word, 'them'. He rolled it on his lips; he weighed it on his tongue. He said it out loud to Joseph on the wall. 'Were they a 'them'? If not, what in the hell were they?'

Janek didn't have time to answer his own question: a man with a shock of red hair arrived to see him. He had called at the main house and Sarah had sent him down.

Janek gave the man a great deal of time and all of his attention: he had lost his six-year-old daughter, two years before, when a lorry had mounted the pavement.

Since then, the man had not been able to function properly within society. He could not hold down a job, in fact he had become quite incapable of dealing with any of the drudgery of life - bills, taxes, mortgage payments, weekly refuse collections - none of it mattered to him anymore. Now creditors were after him and his most recent employer was threatening to sue him for breach of contract. So the man had decided to do a runner, away to somewhere quite different, where he might have a chance to start over.

Janek felt for him. He suggested a few places in the world where the pace of life was slow-to-non-existent and where a fellow could get by on next to nothing in his wallet. And he determined not to charge the bereaved man anything; even to make sure that some of the crisp notes in his own pocket saw their way into an offshore account for him.

When the red-headed father smiled goodbye, Janek was deeply cheered: he felt that it was probably the first smile to have graced the man's lips in months. He felt that he had done some good. It was well after seven when they concluded business, so Janek locked up after him and went up to see Sarah.

'How many did you see?' he asked, treading wearily into her room.

'Six and a half.'

'Half?'

'Yes half; the last one was too stupid to be counted as a whole person. She wanted to know whether we could forward housing benefit to her in New Zealand. What about you?'

'No one congenitally stupid; one very sad case though, as sad as any I've dealt with over the years.'

Janek told her the story of his last client. Before he had finished, he knew that he had done the wrong thing: Sarah filled up with tears and turned from him. She stood looking out towards the gloom of the garden, her shoulders heaving. Janek remembered her war-time loss - the children she had mentioned. He swore at himself, but mentally he swore at Sarah too: if you would give a bit more of yourself and your past, I would know more clearly where not to go and when to tread most carefully, he thought. He left her, saying that tea and cake would be ready downstairs whenever she wanted them.

He was surprised to see her only five minutes later, in the kitchen.

'Were you always so caring and sensitive?' she asked, clearly referring to Janek's final case of the day. 'Or were you hard and mean and nasty as a young man?' It was an impertinent question and Janek laughed at it, but he was careful not to guffaw too fulsomely, because Sarah's eyes were still pink with the potential for fresh tears.

'Until the war I was a sweetie. I even stayed pretty much a sweetie for the first half. It was in the last few years of it that I slipped,' he answered with disarming honesty.

'I would appreciate it if you would tell me what you did.'

'I've told you some of it.'

'That's the point. I want to hear the rest.'

'I might ask you the same,' Janek replied, feeling uncomfortable.

'Yes. But I asked first.'

Janek was wary. He had no intention of being

forced to divulge things against his will, but then again, he had upset Sarah ten minutes before and did not want to do so again.

'Mine is a long and upsetting story,' he said at last. 'It would not make you like me any the more and probably a good deal less.'

'What? Am I not old enough to hear your story?' Sarah scoffed, really quite aggressively.

Janek sucked in his breath, 'There's no one old enough to hear my story.'

'I won't be put off forever, Janek. I won't be. You want to get closer to me don't you? Well that can never happen while there are secrets between us. You do know that don't you?'

'I reckon I do now,' nodded Janek. 'You have been very clear.' There was a sharpness in his voice which he did not want to end on: 'It's because I try to forget my past that I do not tell you - or anyone else. I am protecting myself,' he said.

'But you want me to carry on working here for you, don't you...without telling me what led to your thirty-two year crusade.'

'You work here for your own reasons, Sarah. That has been abundantly clear from the very first day. And I demand nothing of you; you could stop right now.'

'But you know I won't.' Her eyes were hard on him; his were hard on the cat which, mercifully, had just entered the room. He picked it up with an ostentatious sweep and rooted about in his mind for a change of subject...

'...Sarah, I want you to keep whatever money you take from your half of the clients,' he said at last.

Her gaze did not flinch. 'Do you want to die

holding on to your secrets, Janek?'

'Perhaps. I hadn't really thought about it,' he replied with some fire.

'Then maybe you should,' Sarah countered and stalked from the room.

All the warmth Janek had felt on account of assisting the red-headed man was turned to glacial chill. 'Last time I discuss my day at the office with you,' he said to the frigid air, then put Oskar down and went to the ground floor bathroom to take a look at his face. He was worried that Sarah had seen something in his pinched features which he had missed. Had that waspish little comment about dying been her way of saying that she could see the Grim Reaper's mark upon him?

The next morning a sparrowhawk landed in the garden and Janek called Sarah to see it. She arrived while it was removing a starling's head.

'Very nice,' she said.

Janek looked at her from under an arched eyebrow.

'No really,' she replied, 'the barred markings are striking.'

Janek was fully up for the quarrel if she had been at all off with him, or had pretended not to hear him. He had been thinking about the evening before, and was rather pissed off that Sarah had been so shitty: after all, he was the one who had had to deal with the shock of the Lord Lucan article, not to mention the nine-till-seven days it was generating. He reckoned that they would get at least four months of them until things started to tail off again. But true to her changeable style, she was not off with him. The new day had brought out the warm Sarah, as it had brought out the sun.

'How busy do you think it will be today?' she asked.

'Very. I reckon we'll have them queuing.'

Janek was right. The punters arrived in their droves. The usual policy of gender division had to be jettisoned by eleven. Sarah was instructing hoary old blokes who wanted to escape maintenance payments and Janek was advising women who wanted to escape on account of their husbands' sexual demands. Many of them had questions about Lord Lucan. A few even asked to go to the same country as him. They reckoned, quite reasonably, that it was one place where they were sure not be found. There were a number of criminals too – the 'widows and orphans trust fund plunderers' or 'WARTS' as Janek called them.

Also tempted by the article, were youngsters seduced by the romance of disappearing into the great blue yonder. To them it seemed like latter day running off to sea - which it was - except without the lash, the sodomy and the falling from the rigging. Janek did see the attraction, but tried to dissuade them. His view was that they should give life the chance to actually burn them first then, maybe one day, they'd really have something to run away from. Generally, he sent them off with a promise to review their cases in five years. Sarah simply dispatched them to Wolverhampton in order that the silliness be bored out of their systems.

The lowest form of escapee life were the stroppy teenagers who had just argued with their parents - they were just sent home with a flea in their ears.

It was six o' clock and Janek had one of his least favourite species to deal with: in front of him was a man who had made a mint out of worthless land in the boondocks of Africa and the south-western US. His scam was to set up mining companies, pay unscrupulous geologists thousands to confirm that his land holdings were heavy with cobalt and copper and then to list the companies. Immediately investors would pile in to snap up the attractively priced shares. Then as soon as the authorities became suspicious of his unproductive mines, the man simply disappeared with all the money. Now he wanted to do an even more thorough job of the disappearing and was unrolling huge wads of money at Janek in order that he facilitate the process. As a rule, Janek didn't like cases of this sort - unless the con man showed an above-average interest in Joseph - then the dirty money was worth it. He had already decided that this guy would have to be pretty damn interested, not least because the Lipsz coffers were already overflowing.

So it was that Janek was just staring out of his office window as the fellow told him about copper prices and land prices and share prices. He was quite happy to reveal every detail of his criminality, no matter how low-down and dirty. 'Some of these losers put in fifteen thousand each! Can ya believe that?' the man crowed.

Janek could believe it and said so, but his mind was already on the next case: a young couple who were waiting outside, actually walking around the garden. They were very much in love. Janek could read their story just by looking at them - bright young things who had met at university, but now they were languishing in jobs that they considered beneath them. So why not piss off together to Honduras with a few bank loans and as big a bag of condoms as could be squeezed through customs? A nice idea - if they had cobbled together enough money.

His mind drifted and started to invent scenarios: maybe he should accept the rich bloke sitting opposite and then give some of his money to the young couple? They looked like the sort who would keep their eyes peeled for Joseph - in between the bouts of sex.

'Hey, you listening pal?' enquired the con man who was still explaining how clever he was.

Janek had a really cutting reply to throw back at him, but he never dealt it: the phone rang. Normally he wouldn't have answered it in the middle of a consultation, but as he disliked the man across the desk intensely, and was still half-expecting some kind of fallout from the Lord Lucan article, he did not hesitate.

The con man fell silent. For all his brashness, he knew that he needed Janek.

The couple outside kissed under the alder tree.

'Hello…yes, that is right, I am Janek Lipsz…From where? From Paraguay?...You're ringing from Paraguay, South America?…Yes…I do remember the newspaper, I commissioned the appeal myself. Yes, a little while ago now. It was a double spread…And you are?...The person in the photograph!?...Did you say that you are the person…The person?' Janek tried to lick away the dryness of his lips…'I see…Your address…And your name is?...Right.' The dryness extended into Janek's mouth and throat…'Forgive me,' he said, 'but do you have any proof?...I see...I see...And may I ask, have you ever sustained a head injury?...You have?...Right...And how did you come by that injury?...'

The mining man was mightily bored listening in to this conversation. He made out something about the caller on the other end being knocked down a flight of stairs and having his head split open with a rifle butt...

Janek let out a feral howl and his phone-free arm jerked outwards, knocking a sheaf of share certificates and mining stock bonds to the floor. He bit down involuntarily on his lip and bled over a whole batch more.

The copper con man sprang up to save the documents: 'Hey watch out there, fella,' he said.

Immediately Janek snatched up the stick that he always kept by his chair and thrust it an inch from the man's face, still listening hard to the caller. He covered the receiver momentarily and snarled, 'Fuck off!'

The mining man was used to conflict, it was clear from the set of his face, but there was so much raw emotion in that one pregnant 'Fuck off' that he knew not to mess with it. He collected up his money and his bogus share certificates and all his other bits and pieces and left without another word.

'Where in Poland?' quavered Janek down the phone, not even noticing that he now had the office to himself: his right hand was still holding out the stick in threatening fashion. The tip was shaking.

'I see...And who am I?...Well...' he continued, still brandishing the stick at thin air.

Outside, the two lovebirds had noticed the bloke with the papers and the money and the loud suit leave so they had started to wonder whether it was their turn. It was getting dark and winged creatures were barging into them. They had snuck as far as the garage-office door, but being young and middle class and not brash con artists, had not intruded any further. They were still holding hands and the man was whispering to the woman, 'He's on the phone. I can't make it all out, but he's talking to a bloke called Joseph…I think. He seems pretty steamed up about something; he's waving a whacking great stick about.'

Twenty minutes later Janek staggered out. He was still bleeding from his cut mouth, the muscles of his stick arm were cramping and he was exhaling in great bulldog blasts.

'Hi there,' smiled the young woman, 'Is it our turn to see you now?' Then she took Janek in. 'Golly! Are you all right?' she asked. Her lover disengaged from her and took a step closer to the bleeding and quivering old man. 'Can we help?'

Janek tottered past him on legs of cold asparagus. His eyes were unfocused whorls. Not one word did he reply, for he had not heard either of them. Indeed, he was quite unaware of their presence. The young couple watched him mount the garden steps back to the main house and disappear within it.

Sarah was in the hall. She was closing the door on her last client of the day. The snap of the lock made Janek jump.

He saw her.

She saw the blood around his mouth and his huge staring pupils, like those of a man coming round from surgery.

'Janek!' she gasped

Janek tried to steady himself against the hall wall. His legs were doing their cold asparagus thing again. Above his head the door bell sounded. It was the young couple. They had had enough of waiting; also they were good people and wanted to know if the old man was all right. Janek raised a trembling hand in the air and shook his head, forbidding Sarah to answer the summons. His mouth hung pathetically open. Momentarily aware of what a shocking sight he had become, he snapped it shut.

'What is it, Janek? What is it?'

'It's him.'

Sarah furrowed her brows. 'At the door? Who's at the door?'

Janek shook his head, much more firmly this time, and little bubbles of blood foamed at the corner of his mouth. 'Him,' he stressed, 'On the phone.'

Sarah put her hands on her hips. The door bell sounded again. The lovers without could hear the two within.

Janek sank down the wall to the floor. 'Joseph,' he said quietly to Sarah and to his own chest.

'What!?' she replied sharply.

'Joseph,' Janek replied, 'on the phone just now, from Paraguay. Paraguay - I never thought of Paraguay. It is so out of the way…'

Immediately Sarah squatted down beside him and took his face in both her hands. 'Tell me exactly what you mean,' she implored.

'He called me when I had a client in. I wouldn't have answered 'cept I thought it was the police or the papers. Do you see? I wouldn't even have answered?'

Janek was crying now. 'Wouldn't even have answered,' he whined.

Sarah felt a little rush of urine between her legs.

'It was Joseph. He found me. After all these years of searching, it is he who has found me. He saw the newspaper - the one with his photograph in and my address. The big two page appeal. The one I paid for with his own diamonds. And he recognised himself and rang me and I've just been talking to him and…'

Janek was gabbling now, his face twitching grotesquely. Sarah struggled to slow his delivery down. She felt her own hysteria rising. She got a hold of herself. She had to. 'Ice cold streams, ice cold streams,' she whispered as a mantra. 'Are you sure that it was Joseph?' she gulped, only just able to say the name.

'Yes,' replied Janek, still twitching. 'It was him. He said things that he could not have known…unless he was the real Joseph.'

'Like what?' whispered Sarah.

'Like place names and…'

'And?' she repeated back.

'Yes and…' echoed Janek pathetically.

The door bell crashed again.

'We're closed. We're completely closed,' bellowed Sarah. Then she turned to Janek and hissed so close to his face that some of his blood actually flecked her cheeks, 'And?'

'..And he said that his head had been split open by a rifle butt during the war and that he had been clubbed downstairs and he described the woman who nursed him back to health afterwards,' sobbed out Janek in a terrible rush of admission. 'I know that he was telling the truth because it was me who did the clubbing and I know the woman too, and everything. I've never told a living soul what I did, so it must be him, do you see?'

'It was you who did that?' quavered Sarah, not moving an inch from Janek's face.

'Yes it was me. But he doesn't know that. He doesn't know that I am the same man. I went under a different name then and he did not recognise my voice. There is no reason why he should, it was years ago.' Janek started crying again, great wracking sobs, 'But he will know me, he will recognise me,' he wailed, 'He will. When he sees my face.'

Sarah was stunned; gulping in air like a landed fish. This was part of the truth she had been after for so long. It was painful, but also it was exciting, because it had been prompted by Joseph himself. The boy who was lost had been found…The boy who had been lost was found. Suddenly she grew strong and practical. 'None of that matters now,' she said. 'Can you contact him? Do you have his address and phone number? Do you know exactly where he is, Janek? Do you?'

Janek sniffed an affirmative.

'Where?' she demanded.

Janek slapped about his pockets. It was agony for her, watching him sift through each one. In the end, he turned up scrawled writing on the back of an old map. Sarah closed trembling fingers over it, but Janek held on to it and his eyes narrowed.

'Janek, give it to me. This is a horrible scrap of paper. I must write out a copy - for safety's sake,' she explained, with a calmness which she was far from feeling. He let it go and Sarah sprang for the pad on the hall table.

'34 Lorca Rise, Asuncion, Paraguay 73042 (00 895 21 676731),' she read out loud while penning, her voice quavering as she proceeded through the address. When she was done with her copy, she handed the original back. Janek snatched at it like a child and hugged it close to his chest.

Sarah was still standing; she was not curled up with a slip of paper. The difference between them gave her the strength to fortify her voice: 'When will you visit him?' she asked.

'Soon. I have said to him, soon. He thinks that I am acting on behalf of his dead father's estate. That is what I told him.'

'But his father was in no position to leave anything,' interrupted Sarah.

'I know,' replied Janek, too stunned by events to realise that she knew something that he had never told her. Sarah stayed absolutely silent, realising her little slip.

'But the second he sees me he will know me for the man I am, and the monster I was,' bawled Janek, 'And then what will I say, Sarah? What will I do?'

'I do not know what you will say then, or what he will do,' she answered candidly, looking at her palms. 'Or what I will do,' she whispered under her breath. Then Sarah took Janek's head in her hands once more and held it tight to her. 'Tell me, tell me about Joseph and what he just told you on the phone,' she demanded over the caress, and her eyes were tight shut to receive the information.

Janek was barely in a state to talk, but she got the information out of him, haltingly:

Joseph had recovered fully by the end of the war. It had been touch and go for a while, but the woman who nursed him back to health had done a diligent job. He left her in the summer of 1945. By then the victorious Soviets were very active in the area and were suspicious of young men without verifiable stories or papers, so Joseph was in a perilous position for he had lost everything. For a while he hid away, sometimes alone, sometimes with other dispossessed strays.

After a couple of months he was introduced to a blood-sucking, ruthless old crook who used him for dangerous errands like stealing food from the Red Army. The man could extort this price because he was a dab hand at forging documents. He guaranteed fresh papers and a new identity to anyone who stole for him for six months. Joseph slaved for his half year and, at the end of it, the man was as good as his word. Indeed, he had grown to like Joseph in his own rough way and to respect the boy's light-fingered abilities.

He advised him to change his surname, from Steinberg to something less obviously Jewish, on account of the suffering his people had experienced. He said that no one could be sure that the killings would not start up again and that it was better to be safe than to be sorry. He had heard that the Russians did not treat Jews well. In addition, he told Joseph that all the Cracow Jews had been killed by the Nazis, every last one of them. And Joseph had been filled with a terrible sadness, for that meant that he had lost his entire family and was left all alone in the world. Then the forger had felt sorry for him, as sorry as he had ever felt for anyone, so he prepared for the boy the best papers he possibly could, naming him Joseph

Wisniewski.

Travelling mainly by night, except when he could hide away in train trucks and lorries, Joseph got to Berlin and then on to the American zone. Once there, he bartered and stole and worked until he had saved enough passage money to get to Britain. His aunt had always said that if ever he found himself desperate and alone, he should try to get to London, England. She said that it was the poor Jew's haven. Once there, one could always work and save up the fare to America. Back when she was alive, she had always said that. So Joseph determined to do exactly what he'd been advised. But he was sold a bum ticket: not to London, but to Cardiff.

For two years he was employed by a tailor there and given board and lodging in the man's house. He was treated well, like a son in fact, and when the family decided to emigrate to South America, they offered him to go with them. Joseph did. It was a step closer to The United States and besides, he was in love with the tailor's daughter.

It was 1949 when they settled in Paraguay, part of a sizeable Welsh community there. He never got to America. Instead he married the tailor's daughter, Bronwen, and she wanted to remain close to her parents.

Most of the time Spanish and Welsh were spoken, but Joseph liked the English he had picked up during his two years of tailoring in Cardiff, so he searched out classes in Paraguay in order that he not lose the language through lack of use - for two years is a meagre apprenticeship in any tongue. Every year he found some little place or club where he could practise.

Then in about 1974 he found a group which met once a week above a dentist's in the capital city. It was the best club of its sort that he had ever attended. Everyone turned up regularly, they really stretched one another, and the dentist, a Hungarian, would get hold of old British *Times* and *Telegraph* newspapers so that they might expand their vocabularies together.

Then one day, Joseph arrived to find everyone gathered around a single newspaper: *The Times* of the *11th August 1976*. It was over a year out of date, but when he walked up to the other club members, they all started laughing and pointing and shaking a pair of the pages. Joseph Wisniewski could not imagine why old news should generate such interest. Then they had handed the paper to him. Immediately, he saw what they had seen: a photograph of himself, decades old, and next to it a startlingly accurate picture of the man he had aged into. He read Janek's name and address at the bottom of page fifteen. A few hours later he had rung the contact number listed.

When Janek finished telling Sarah all this, there was not a stroke of energy left in his body. He slumped down into her lap and lay there. Streaks of blood had dried around his mouth, his hair was pitifully mussed. Slowly, patiently, she tried to coax him into the living room and its comfortable sofa, but he just grunted and snuffled unintelligibly at her.

In the end she got out of him a reedy, 'I know, I know, I know,' followed by a single, 'Joseph,' - barely loud enough to be audible.

That was when Sarah gave up and decided to leave Janek where he was. She went herself to the living room, detached one of the sofa cushions and placed it under his head.

'At least I am leaving you comfortable,' she whispered. 'It is more than you deserve.'

Then she stared at her copy of Joseph's address and slipped up the stairs to her room.

CHAPTER 17

Terrible dreams woke Janek – of swinging rifle butts and blood and headlong falls and screaming girls and gunfire and copper tubs full of boiling water.

He jerked up. He was still in the hallway. The sun was streaming in through the glass of the front door and hitting him full in the face. He could still feel summer's potency in it, October though it was. And he could remember every detail of the previous day. He sprang to standing, very stiff, very excited, but also weepy with nerves.

'He will hate me,' he said to himself, 'He will hate me. He will despise me…' The taste of dry blood at the corner of his mouth stopped this one way conversation and he got up to wash.

Once clean and morning-pissed, Janek no longer wished to chunter away to himself, instead he wanted to talk to Sarah. He took a look at his watch: eight-thirty. That was an acceptable time to wake her; when there were such momentous issues to discuss. He wanted to be flying off to Paraguay by the end of the week - airlines willing.

He went straight up the stairs. No tea, no cheese on toast, no boiled egg. He was all a-quiver, far too much so to prepare Sarah a breakfast.

He knocked quietly.

No answer.

Then a little more loudly.

No answer.

He called.

No answer.

So he opened the door six inches and called again: 'Sarah? Can I come in?'

Still no answer.

Janek was starting to reconsider whether 8:30 was late enough to disturb her, when he perceived that the room was bright with morning sunlight. The curtains were fully drawn. Surely no one could remain asleep in that glare? Janek pushed the door open and stepped in.

'Sarah, it's me. I was wondering whether…'

The room was empty, the bed not slept in.

Janek spun round. He called out Sarah's name. He made sure of every corner. He checked the upstairs lavatory, then returned to the room and sat on her bed. It had been warmed by no body, only the sun's rays. Then he saw that Sarah's things were gone: her case, her writing pad, her alarm clock, her clothes. Her table and chairs were still there, but there was no cardigan thrown over them - as usual - or hand-written notes to herself on the desk to act as a prompt to memory. Janek found himself recalling half a dozen other little quirks of Sarah's, even ones he had no idea that he had ever observed. There was no evidence of any of them. He spun round the room again then sat heavily on the bed.

'What the fuck?'

The words were barely out of his mouth when he sprang up again.

'Letter,' he hissed to himself. It took Janek half an

hour to search the whole house. At first he fully expected to find an explanatory note on the mantelpiece, or the kitchen table, or sellotaped to the television screen, but as the searching wore on, he began to doubt more and more.

After failing to turn anything up in the other rooms, he stumped back to Sarah's. Inside was a nasty shock, something he had missed when he had been in there before. The giant photograph of Joseph was gone - the one Sarah had requested of him. The frame was there, but the image itself had been cut out, a millimetre from the mounting the whole way round.

'Bitch,' Janek spluttered and sank to the floor. He finally had his answer - there was no 'them' at all. This would teach him to shack up with mad women. She had run out on him, when he needed her most; at the emotional crisis-point of his life she was nowhere to be seen. Their agreement had been that she would look after the house and the business when he was off chasing leads. And now that the ultimate lead had come in, she had betrayed him. She had even grown rich off the back of him - to the tune of thousands - cash.

'There'll be no sign of that either,' he cursed bitterly.

The expletives gave him strength and he kicked out at the door, splintering a part of it. Another two kicks actually took a chunk of wood off.

The violence turned his thoughts in a different direction. He remembered telling Sarah about his brutish attack on Joseph. Had she been repulsed? Could she no longer stand to be in the same house as him? Was that what this was all about? He berated himself for telling her. Hadn't he kept his secrets from her for ages? Well hadn't he? And with relative ease? So why on earth had he spilt the beans? He could so easily have left for Paraguay, and Joseph, without divulging any dirty details.

Then Janek was ashamed, ashamed that he had cursed Sarah so fulsomely. She would probably ring to explain why it was that she had felt compelled to leave, or return in person to tell him. After all, what woman would want to live under the same roof as a skull-smashing monster? And she knew how important this trip to Paraguay was - important to both of them - so she was bound to come back and smooth things over; he was sure of it. She was just a flighty woman who had panicked. She had always been flighty and now this bloody revelation of his had tipped her over the edge. Janek emerged from her room certain of these things.

He was still shaky and upset upon sitting down in the kitchen for tea, but his ear fully expected to hear the phone ring at any moment, or there to be a knock at the door. The sofa cushion in the hall had further convinced him that Sarah would return, for if she were truly repulsed by him, if she really loathed him, then why would she have taken the time to fix him up a pillow? For Janek was positive that he hadn't carried it into the hall himself. The waiting was horrible though - particularly in conjunction with the amazing developments of the day before. It was extremely difficult for Janek to plan his trip to Paraguay or map routes, at the same time as having his domestic situation so disrupted. And when he tried to plan what he might say to Joseph, he would end up explaining himself to the absent Sarah instead. And his mental space was taken up in humdrum ways too:

Who would look after the cat now that Sarah was gone – or at least so seemingly unprepared to live in his house?

Would Phil house-watch again?

Was Phil even available?

As the first hour of staring fixedly at the phone passed, Janek's attitude flipped back once more and he started to resent the woman who had caused these crappy distractions - didn't she realise that he couldn't field all this shit and give Joseph the attention he deserved? For God's sake, he had just found the boy after three and a half decades! Also, he was scared to ring the airports and investigate flights in case Sarah picked the same moment to call him. In this way, it proved almost impossible for Janek to settle on one action, or even one thought, at a time. He would feel sorry for Joseph and what he had done to him in 1943 and then this would transmute into feeling sorry for himself.

At ten-thirty he actually slapped himself - hard around the face - for telling Sarah about cracking Joseph's head open. The next moment he was beset by his own guilty memories of the incident. The rollercoaster gave him no respite.

It was his door-knocker which shocked him out of this yo-yoing. Its rap-rap coincided exactly with the clock striking 11:00. He jumped up, quicker than a ten-year-old, ran nervous fingers through his hair, struggled manfully to control his breathing.

This was it!

Here she was.

No temper. He must not show any anger.

He told himself not to jerk the door open...

...He jerked the door open.

On the doorstep were three very different people: a suit, a pretty thirty-year-old woman, and a decayed-looking hippy. The morning rush had started. They had all read the Lord Lucan article and they all wanted to escape England too.

'Fuck off, fuck off,' Janek screamed. 'Lord Lucan is dead and you will be too if you ever knock on this door again!'

He slammed the door shut and sank down to the level of the floor mat. 'Sarah, Sarah,' he wailed. 'Why? Why?' He stayed stock-still for half an hour. No telephone call came. Then he got up from the floor mat. There was no point being pathetic, waiting by the door like an abandoned old dog. Besides, Sarah had her own key. Why the hell hadn't he remembered that?

Janek settled himself in the room which best overlooked the street. He thought that Sarah might return but not have the guts to come up the front path, or to face him. With this view, he would not miss her. However, all he saw were Disappearance Club hopefuls staring up at the house after their unheeded knocks. Also: postmen, locals, boys with footballs. The last was the only sighting that nearly had him up and moving, for he had seen Phil in among them. He would need to speak to the boy about house-minding and cat-sitting...

...But Janek did not get beyond a crouching start; he would only need Phil if Sarah did not come back and he simply could not believe that she would fail to return.

In the afternoon, conflicting emotions crippled his ability to do anything: practically he had to arrange his journey to Paraguay, but emotionally he needed to know why Sarah had chosen this moment to run out on him. To cap it all, he had caught sight of Renault woman slumped in her car seat. Her broken, bitter face had returned his gaze the moment he'd started peering in her direction. Janek was looking out for Sarah, but this other woman's tormented face was what he got. For the first time since she had started haunting him, some six years before, he fully empathised with her. To lose someone in a flash, when it was least expected, and then never to receive an answer to your whys and wherefores, was an acute pain indeed. Especially when it was someone you loved.

Janek couldn't stand seeing the woman any longer, nor the queue of escapee hopefuls that had formed outside. He stalked back to his kitchen and hazarded a few phone calls…

…There were no direct flights to Paraguay. One had to travel to Rio de Janeiro or Buenos Aires and then catch connecting flights and there weren't many of those: it seemed that Paraguay had managed to piss off all of its larger neighbours. Janek buried his head in his hands. This would have been a bugger to organise, even with Sarah around.

He tried to find out about road and rail services. Maybe there were land connections between the three countries? But this proved too much for him to nail down in his overwrought state. It is no small feat to obtain South American communications information, and timetable details, across telephone wires at a seven thousand mile remove. Janek slammed the phone down. Most perturbing of all, the process was taking too long and he was scared of missing Sarah's call, should it ever come.

At one point the phone did ring and his hand shot out for it like mercury running. 'Mr Lipsz?' the man at the other end said. 'It's *The Daily Telegraph* newspaper here…'

'No,' Janek replied curtly and crashed the receiver back down.

As night fell, he was back at the window, willing Sarah to turn the corner. The footballers were gone, the punters were gone, even Renault woman was gone. For hours Janek watched foxes skitter past and listened to their screams. The noise matched precisely his tattered nerves.

Some time after dawn, when the foxes were still hard at it, ripping open bin liners and worrying rabbit hutches, his eyes started to close. In spite of his dejection, sleep claimed Janek and for the second night in a row, he simply nodded off exactly where he slumped. Nature's sweet restorer didn't rest him much, though, for he twitched and groaned in fitful and disquieting sleep. In the gross night, images scrolled through his mind as if on an illuminated reel: helmeted soldiers banged up interminable flights of stairs, scores of young Josephs lay broken at the bottom of them, and copulating forms were left riddled with bullets. Janek suffered hours of these dreams; even in the rude light of morning he was still twitching and moaning.

It was the crash of his door knocker that woke him in the end. At first it served only to reinforce the stamp of the stormtroopers' boots up the stairs of his mind, blending in perfect synchronism with their heavy tread, but in the end, reality filtered through the suburbs of his brain and Janek's head jerked up with the force of a recoiling gun. He lurched for the door on legs gammy with awkward sleeping.

'Sarah?' he slurred while sliding bolts and turning locks.

The day's glare hurt his eyes.

'Hello, I've come about running away from it all,' beamed a beautiful young woman on the doorstep. Then Janek remembered why he had engaged so many bolts and locked so many locks. He slammed the door in her lovely face.

And so his day began again. There was no let up. Neighbours peered behind nets at the people knocking and massing outside number 33…Knocking and massing…Knocking and massing…Renault woman parked in her usual spot at her usual time…

Janek knew that he had to swap this waking nightmare for the streets of Asuncion, Paraguay, but he was at a loss how to do it. So he hid in a dark room at the rear of the house, where he could not be seen by anyone standing in the street - hid and rocked like a cornered animal. There he sat curled over his phone, willing Sarah to ring.

Once he almost contacted Joseph for travel information - the number was still in his pocket - but decided at the last minute that it was a step too far, too familiar. There was too much painful history there for him to be comfortable doing that, even if Joseph was as yet unaware of his true identity. Besides, he worked out that it could not have been much after dawn all the way across the Atlantic.

The hammerings on his door grew in number and

intensity. Janek felt besieged.

A little life-belt did float by though - in the form of an old friend ringing. At first Janek gnashed his teeth that it was not Sarah calling, but then he saw a light at the end of friendship's tunnel - 'Stefan,' he gasped, interrupting his old chum's pleasantries. 'I need your help...'

Janek outlined his situation and made it clear that he wanted Stefan to book him a flight which would land as close as possible to Paraguay's capital, Asuncion. And for as soon as possible.

Stefan was a retired tax officer: drama and desperation were not what he was comfortable with.

'Please,' begged Janek, 'And I'll pay you back, cash, twice as much as it costs.'

'It's not the money,' replied Stefan huffily.

'No, it's my sanity. Do it, Stef, please. It will mean the world to me,' croaked Janek.

In the end, Stefan agreed and Janek made him write down all the details of neighbouring countries and the possible connections which he might research. He could tell that his old friend wished that he had not bothered ringing at all, but that did not matter, just so long as Stefan came up with the goods.

Now Janek had two phone calls to wait for...

He did not wash.

He did not eat.

He did not clean his teeth.

He did not pick up his post from the floor...then he did...because he thought that there might be a letter from Sarah down among the bills and the offers. But when it was obvious that there was not, he just let slip all the envelopes and slunk back to his little lair beside the French window. He stared at the telephone receiver, willing and willing it to ring.

There in that corner, dejected, cramped and dirty, his mind started to needle him. It began innocently enough with him wondering what Joseph would actually look like. Maybe the artist's impression would turn out to be wrong: age might take a face in many directions, although the main one was invariably downward.

Then Janek's thoughts took a nasty turn and he gulped at them, his own though they were. He imagined Joseph shooting at him and running blades through him. He saw the boy he had spent over thirty years tracking down, now a man, standing over his old, inert body, spattered with gore. And in his own lifeless hand were the diamonds, still in their little bag, because Joseph had not given him the chance to hand them over before killing him.

'But that has always been the risk,' Janek shouted out loud, screwing up his eyes and trying desperately to shake away the bloody image, 'Always been the risk.'

And outside the new punters heard his frantic outburst and rushed to the door and hammered and hammered and hammered. So that Janek had to shut his ears as well as his eyes, as well as try to tame his thoughts.

When he reopened them, which might have been five minutes later, or an hour and five minutes later, something had given way inside him: a plank of stability, a rung of reason, maybe just a little synapse somewhere intricate. For when Janek looked at his cat trotting towards him for a stroke, it wasn't the usual Oskar he saw. This version had a decayed ear, all collapsed in on itself like corrugated gristle. Janek tried to remember when it had been burned or ripped in a fight. There had been no such injury as far as he could remember. Then he doubted his eyes and peered yet more closely and still the ear was ugly and prune-like. It was only when the animal landed on him and he could actually feel the ear, that he could tell it was quite normal.

'Oh God!' he groaned, stroking the cat intensively - more for his own therapy than for Oskar's comfort. Never in all the years of war and resistance and torture and tortured searching, had he ever before stooped so low. Seeing things! That was something that the deranged did! He stropped Oskar's ear to try to massage the image out of his mind's eye. Fifteen minutes later it was still flashing vividly there, although the physical cat looked as whole as ever.

Gin! That was the answer. Why the hell hadn't he thought of it sooner? Easing Oskar down, he light-footed it over to his drinks' cabinet, snatched a bottle up and returned to his little spot. The cat was still there, washing.

An hour, and an empty bottle, later it didn't seem quite so bad that neither Stefan nor Sarah had called...

...Janek would still have given his left bollock for one of them to, but not both of themz – his blollocks that wasz. It would be poshitively lovelyish if they both rang and saved his blollockssh, mind. He was lying flat out on the floor, but had to hold on. In his stomach the liquor breakfast felt alive. Oskar was purring in a deep rumble. Janek passed out and Oskar stretched out upon him.

The sun was just going down when Janek came round. His head felt like there was a blacksmith's forge inside it. Oskar was comfortable on a chair. Both the cat's ears looked normal in shape and proportion. For the third time in two days, Janek had fallen asleep on the floor, albeit for just a few hours this time. The only part of him which did not ache was his hair.

He saw the phone and then pulled at his greasy mop, right to the roots. If Sarah or Stefan had called and he had missed them, then he was just going to turn his face to the wall and give up. Then Janek noticed the answer machine lead – it was plugged in. And his relief was so intense that he sobbed.

Quiveringly, timidly, he hauled himself up and peered at the display. There was one message. Janek gasped in expectation and stabbed clumsily at the play button. He was almost too sore and too unsteady and too nervous to maintain a standing position. It was Stefan - and despite the gin, Janek could understand every word of his message.

'Hello old boy…sorry I was a bit off with you before. You know me: I'm a lad for sitting in front of the tele with a crossword, not international affairs. But I think I've nailed down what you want. I'll send everything first class…'

Janek listened as he had once listened for Nazi patrols. Not one other sound intruded.

He stopped the tape.

'Excellent. If he's posting the tickets, they'll be here in two days,' Janek said to himself.

He shook his head as if that might clear the gin out.

'Right.'

He took a positive step out into the hall then stopped - the hordes were still out there, he could tell by the shadows they cast through the glass of the front door.

'Shit!'

Janek scuttled back to his foxhole in the garden-room.

At least now he had something set in place. For such an armchair-loving accountant, Stefan had come up with a very good package: Janek was booked to fly out to Brazil in five days' time. After arriving in Rio he then had two and a half days to reach the River Paraguay (which actually had its source in Brazil) and there, board the paddle steamer *Precious Kinkajou*. Stefan had booked him a ticket for that too. This would set sail at twelve sharp on the third day and follow the river into Paraguay itself. After a day's steady steaming, the original water course would turn into the River Pilcomayo which flowed right into the Paraguayan capital, Asuncion.

That meant that Janek should be standing in front of Joseph's house in about ten days' time – not exactly fast out of the blocks, but well within the time scale Joseph might have expected. Janek had said to him that he would arrive 'soon' and anything less than a month, when one was travelling across the globe, had to be classed as 'soon'.

With everything else churning around inside it, there was not much room in Janek's head for gratitude, but he made a mental note to thank Stefan properly. One day.

In his pocket he still had the money he'd taken from his new clients on the day of Joseph's phone call.

He riffled through for the cash to pay Stefan back. That had to be sent, the first moment he left the house; there was no knowing when he might have to call upon his friend's assistance again, especially now that Sarah was gone.

Sarah! He began to feel angry with her again and much less inclined to excuse her actions. This was the end game, the last great chapter of what they had both been working towards and she had bailed out - and after doing more than anyone! What about the last newspaper article? That had been all her hard work! It beggared belief that she should run off now. And why? Just because he had admitted to walloping some kid round the head in the war - a kid who had survived anyway?! Hadn't she lived through the war herself? Didn't she know that during that awful time, everyone had lashed out first and asked questions later? They'd had to. She probably had herself!

'They'd had to…' Janek took that little thought of his and weighed it. The gin was wearing off now and he could assess things squarely once more. 'Was it true? Had there really been no other way? No other choice? Could he not have done things differently?' Alone though he was, Janek actually flushed, and not some feeble, half-arsed red flecking of the cheeks, but a full scarlet which extended down his throat. 'Of course you had a choice,' he snapped at himself, 'Why else would you have spent your life looking for the boy?'

Out the corner of his eye he could see his staircase. Half the cupboard under it was visible from the secure position he was occupying. The light from the sodium street lamps was early-evening-orange and coming in through the glass of the front door. It cast an eerie glow. The irradiated hall reminded Janek of a developing room for photographic plates. A tongue of the luminescence seemed to be flicking about the cupboard doorknob.

Janek's own blush-red glow receded, to be replaced by a shocking white. 'There were many other choices,' he whispered to the doorknob and to the spectral light bathing it.

Partly because he felt pulled, partly because the punters had started filtering away, and partly because he needed the diamonds anyway - now that Stefan had arranged his travel for him - Janek made for the understairs cupboard. He did not walk over, but shuffled on his buttocks; one leg pulling as the other pushed. It was an undignified form of locomotion, but Janek felt undignified. He cleared himself unencumbered access to his little safe: a broom handle shifted here, a hoover attachment shoved there. The device swung open as easily as it always did 'The only reliable and uncomplicated thing in my life,' he mused.

Janek was intimidated by the street light. Before the safe and its contents, he was always intimidated by light, whatever its source. He did not want any at all. He wanted every bulb, every star, every ray to hide their fires so that guilt could be detached from sight.

He pulled out the tray. There was the bag of diamonds and the chamois leather envelope. He pocketed both...then, cursing the light, drew out the chamois leather envelope once more. Its flap curled invitingly at him.

Willing his hands steady, he eased out the photograph.

The young girl was as beautiful as ever, in spite of the new creases and folds across her. Her eyes were gorgeous, deep Jewish eyes - as it seemed to Janek, dancing to the infatuated fluency of an allegro violinist. Her mouth was a rose bud out in rain.

He closed his hands together with the image between his palms, shutting out her loveliness.

'You had a chance, and you had a choice Janek,' he coughed out in angry, tearless sighs, 'Of course you had a choice.' In the agony of his guilt, his mind's eye saw the exquisite eyes and lips again and on his own lips, there teetered a single word: 'B'... 'B'... 'Ba'... After three attempts he said it out loud: 'Barbara.'

And then Janek put the photograph back inside his breast pocket. This time, he had no choice but to travel with her, for at last he had found Joseph, her brother. Barbara's brother, Joseph.

Janek passed another rough night, although in a bed this time.

He dreamt of his own trial, before judge, jury, witnesses - and Joseph. He moaned and twitched as every detail of his culpability was brought before the court. 'Choice...Choice...Choice,' thundered the prosecution lawyer and Janek bleated in his sleep at every shouted syllable. Only when he was falling at the end of a hangman's rope did he wake, sweating and screaming.

There was a knocking at the front door. It was loud and urgent. Janek had translated it into the gallows' trapdoor bolts snapping open, but now he heard the insistent sound for what it really was. He peeped out from behind his bedroom curtains.

It was a smart young man with a briefcase, no doubt full of his own amateur escapee's kit. Janek was careful not to make a sound. He had only a few more days to endure; only a few more days with these arseholes camped outside. He had to ignore them, had to think about his own kit - his packing for Paraguay. A bag of diamonds and a photograph would not suffice. It was going to be torture tip-toeing around his own home, collecting up all the necessaries, but he had prepared for this trip so many times in his head, that the items could probably be gathered up quite quickly.

Two fresh knocks came, as well as a bellow through the letter box.

After heaping together a number of things from his bedroom and bathroom, Janek snuck down the stairs and into the little garden-room spot where he was safe from the prying eyes of would-be disappearers. He took with him another half-bottle of gin and, though it was early, poured himself a measure. It was a rough old breakfast, but if the punters were going to start hollering up and down the road for him again and start waving their *Telegraphs* as they had the day before, then there was no way that he could fry up a full English - the kitchen window looked directly onto the street.

Janek was in two minds about the drink: there could be no more stupors. He needed to be compos mentis for the phone and for the rest of the packing, which would have to be done stealthily. He decided on doubles rather than triples.

It was a miserable way of passing time: drinking on an empty stomach and ducking low every time there was a fresh knock at the door. Janek reckoned that before the clock had even turned eleven, there were six people on his doorstep and about the same number round by the side of the house, trying to peer in. He sweated into his gin and drank it down.

Peering out from his little spot low down by the French windows, Janek engaged in some bird spotting; there was very little else a man in his position could do. In three hours he managed a first-rate monitoring job: two robins, eight green finches, four gold finches, a thrush, two blackbirds – a male and a female – a dozen starlings, innumerable sparrows and a greater spotted woodpecker. The woodpecker was a big red-bummed beauty which set about doing the peanut feeder a bit of genuine damage.

Suddenly, and to Janek's disappointment, the bird took fright at some kind of human movement down at the bottom of the garden and flew away. Quickly this disappointment turned to anger - a person's leg appeared over his fence. Some pushy bastard was actually climbing over! Then his anger turned to a feeling of excited deliverance: it was Phil. The boy was after his ball; obviously the last few days had taught him that it was pointless to knock, so he was taking matters into his own hands.

Disdaining the gathered crowds, Janek burst out of the French doors and ran towards his young friend. Phil was shocked, as much at Janek's appearance as his headlong gallop towards him. Janek took a hold of the boy's arm and steered him forcefully back to the garden room retreat. Cries and shouts came from a number of the waiting people.

Janek bawled out a hearty 'Fuck off', just to dissuade any of them from copying Phil's direct action then slammed the doors to. Once inside he sat the lad down, right next to his gin bottle, as if they were the two most important things in his life.

'You've got to help me,' he wheezed.

Phil could smell the gin on his breath. 'You been drinking, Mr Lipsz?'

'Of course I've been drinking. I've not been doing anything but drinking,' snapped Janek, 'Now listen…'

Phil took in the old man's emotional state; noticed his bagged eyes and ridiculously greasy hair, cow-licked into a dozen different shapes and directions. He decided to sit perfectly still.

'I need you to look after my cat for two or three weeks. Can you do that?'

'When from?' Phil asked gingerly.

'Five days' time. Will that be ok?'

Phil looked a bit troubled.

'Well come on, lad, out with it.'

'I'm not sure.'

Janek sagged.

'It's all these people, see. They're calling at your door all day long.'

'You think I don't know?' groaned Janek.

'And my mum, she don't like it. None of the grown ups do. We don't mind, us kids,' said Phil broad-mindedly, 'So long as they don't get in the way of our goal. My mum's had enough of it though, 'specially of the ones who knock on her door as well, asking for you, like.'

Janek gritted his teeth.

'What they all here for?' Phil questioned.

'Oh…an advertisement gone mad…don't worry about that now,' retorted Janek.

'It's just I don't see how I could get in past 'em all,' added Phil. 'And my mum would be bound to see me coming and going. She spends half the day lookin' out, she does! She wouldn't be 'appy about me coming over here.'

'You could nip over the fence the same way you just have. And in the dark. I could give you my back door key.'

Phil exhaled noisily, as if the volume were an aid to his thinking. 'She'd bloody kill me if she found out. She reckons you been up to no good…said that you was a gangster and that Lord Lucan is buried in your garden. I tell ya, she'd kill me if she knew I was just sat down here with you now.'

'There's got to be a way,' pleaded Janek…'Come on, I've fetched your ball out of my garden for years…'

Phil was considering.

'…When all the other folks down here kick up a stink if you kids so much as whack it against their fences.'

Phil inhaled as noisily as he had exhaled.

'I know…I've heard 'em,' continued Janek. He stopped talking to see whether he was getting anywhere with these emotional appeals.

'Is Lord Lucan buried in your back garden?' Phil asked quickly.

'No, of course not,' whined Janek Then he remembered the money in his pocket. 'Look, here! There's two hundred pounds,' he said with desperation, peeling off four fifties from the wad. Will that help to square things with your mum?'

Phil's eyes lit up: 'My mum would dig up Lord

Lucan for half that much,' he said jubilantly.

'Then give her a hundred and keep the other hundred for yourself, lad.'

Janek could tell from Phil's body language that he had decided to feed the cat, and for the first time in days, he felt just a little bit pleased with himself.

Phil nodded greedily. 'I'll do it,' he said, 'But Mr Lipsz, I want you to do me a favour...'

Janek looked at the boy, with his football under his arm, and his young, expressive face.

'Give me it all in twenties, then I can give my mum forty quid and keep a hundred and sixty for myself,' he explained slyly.

Janek laughed. In spite of the last few days, and Sarah, and Joseph, and everything, he laughed. 'And I'll give you an extra tenner too, to share with those other boys out there; they've been waiting for you a long time.'

Then Phil slipped out with the money, Janek's instructions, the back door key and his usual promise not to let anyone else in. But just before he ran back to the fence he turned to Janek, money still in hand, and asked in an 'I won't tell anyone else but...' voice, 'Aren't you a gangster at all, then, Mr Lipsz?'

'No, Phil, I am not. You have my word on it.'

The boy looked a trifle disappointed then nodded, as if deciding to accept this last statement as truth. Then he opened his mouth to articulate something else. Janek could see all the way to his young filling-free molars...He was uncomfortable with the time Phil was taking: the French doors were open, his head was hanging out of them and there were still plenty of punters outside, baying and knocking.

'I have found him - my Joseph,' said Janek, addressing the silence and his own disquiet. It probably wasn't the answer to the question Phil was about to ask, but he bounded off nonetheless and Janek snapped the garden room door shut.

Four days later he left for Heathrow, in his car and at night.

CHAPTER 18

If Janek had been less nervous he would have enjoyed the cruise down the River Paraguay. It was a beautiful, unpolluted waterway. Old Spanish colonial piles dotted the banks, raffishly decayed - there was charm in buckets for anyone less preoccupied.

As the vessel nosed into the interior, the buildings became fewer and farther between and were replaced by open, river-crossed woods and savannah. When he was able to access the mental space, Janek looked out for otters and fishing ocelots. Once he saw a snake cutting through the water alongside the boat. And always, there were herons and egrets sifting for food at the margins. Janek told himself that these beautiful sights were good omens, but deep down he knew that picture-postcard views had no bearings on the affairs of men.

Twice the paddle steamer stopped on its way down this river: at Puerto Cooper and at Rosario. Everyone got out, to stretch their legs and to spend some money. Janek did not talk to anyone, did not spend anything. Almost all of his striding about was in his own head, hashing and rehashing endlessly. He already had what he intended to say to Joseph off pat, but could not leave it alone.

'It's what I say first is most important,' the other

passengers heard him muttering to himself.

'If he will just let me get into my stride, then I'll be able to explain,' was another commonly overheard line.

Now and then he would cry out a pained, 'Barbara!' too, and the people closest to him would whisper to one another in shock.

Soon there was an appreciable space between him and the other passengers. Children would be escorted past him at speed and the adults would peer over, only to turn sharply away when they thought that Janek had caught them staring. He noticed them less often than they thought, for most of the time his pupils were not focusing anything on board: the rehearsal of his opening address to Joseph took up every ounce of his being.

Really, it was only ever the wildlife and the water margins that drew his vision, and even then, Janek had to make a definite decision to rest from his preparations in order to focus on them. For he feared overtaxing his mind and rendering it liable to seeing visions again, like he had with Oskar back home: he stared out at the water creatures to ensure that their ears were as Nature intended. He had to preserve his essential stability - what there was left of it - for his encounter with Joseph.

Occasionally he would finger the diamonds in his pocket; roll them over, one at a time, like worry beads. He had had no trouble getting them through customs. 'When should I give them to Joseph? Straight away, or after speaking?' he mused. He decided to offer them up after finishing what he had to say. That way it would not seem as though he were trying to buy forgiveness.

'What about the boy's expectations though?'

There he was, saying it again - the boy! Joseph wasn't a boy any more; he would be a mature man in his forties…maybe with a belly and a stoop.

But what about Joseph's expectations? He was anticipating someone with information about his dead father. An innocent someone!

'What kind of a shock is it going to be when I turn up with my great big broken nose…recognisable anywhere in the world…the man who cracked his skull open!…A bloody enormous shock, that's what,' he spluttered out loud as an American tourist tip-toed past with her young daughter.

Janek looked down at the deck; he was making a spectacle of himself. He strode off towards the on-board lavatories. There were mirrors in there.

A couple of his co-travellers were already using the facilities. They looked up at him with annoyance and distrust. When they exited, Janek heard one of them say to the other, 'The Victorians had their excursions at the asylum, these days, the asylum comes away with you!'

Janek looked up at his own reflection. He looked terrible. He could see why people might take against him, even without the intense one-way conversations he was having. He was six days unshaven, his skin was greyer than lead, the gaunt lines which had sprung up on his face a few months previously were now deep scars of stress and anxiety. The hair on his head was noticeably thinner. His lips were two sharp lines of drawn white.

He wanted a mirror to see how much of the old 1940s Janek was still discernible. Looking objectively at himself, he reasoned that it might very well be that Joseph would not recognise him. The nose and the general set of the face were still there, but other than that, he had changed and aged massively - even from the man he had been a year ago, let alone three decades ago!

'Will Joseph know it's you? Will he? Your new looks may just buy you time - enough to say sorry and get your story out. It might just turn out that way…It just might.'

Another man came in as Janek was declaring 'might'. The newcomer looked at him askance. Janek hurried passed him, back onto the main deck. He sat down, hissing himself advice, 'Talk to yourself if you have to, but don't answer yourself back.' - Janek was concerned that his fellow travellers might complain to the crew: he must not jeopardise his place on the boat.

He need not have worried. As he looked over the rail, he could see that the craft was turning with the current and preparing to join the Pilcomayo River: there was nowhere left at which he could be jettisoned. Asuncion, Paraguay's capital city, was the next, and last, port of call.

The banks started to be reclaimed by humanity. Residences sprang up once more, people waved at the paddle steamer, the bird-life became less conspicuous, the otters vanished. They were passing through the outskirts of Asuncion.

Suddenly and feverishly, Janek started pulling out pieces of paper and scribbling down what it was he was going to say to Joseph. In minutes he had covered a couple of sheets. Then with great sweeps of dismay he was crossing out swathes, or adding bits with furious flourishes of his pencil.

Unnoticed by him, marinas appeared on the steamer's starboard side and boys in little boats were throwing up fruit for coins that Janek's fellow travellers were dropping down to them. Soon Janek was the only passenger still seated. All the others were tight by the rail, even hanging over it, and making a great deal of noise. He heard none of this though. Tears had started streaming down his face as he tried and tried, desperately, to fashion his Joseph-speech to something acceptable: suddenly it all seemed too little, or too much, or plain wrong. He knew every single word of it off by heart, but somehow, at this eleventh hour, he had no idea which bit to start in with. He was panicking and his pencil hand shook like a November leaf.

A large bald man with a kindly face had stopped waving at the fruit sellers and was watching Janek. Like the rest of the passengers, he had seen him talking to himself, had even taken note of his utterances on occasion. Now he really observed the strange old man, tired beneath his tired skin, scratching holes in paper like a child dismayed at its own ham-fistedness. He walked over from the side rail and stood beside Janek, who was still so frantically and wretchedly about his revisions and rewritings that he did not heed the bald man's shadow one iota.

'May I advise you?' asked the man, close to Janek's ear.

Janek jumped measurable inches. His hands shot to his face, like a man's will when he is shocked from a deep sleep. His pencil fell to the floor. The bald man picked it up and as he handed it back, volunteered his advice to the open-mouthed and staring Janek: 'Do not worry so much, my friend. People - they forgive almost anything over time and if forgiveness is in their hearts, then it does not matter what you first say.'

It was pretty good English, but Janek easily picked out the German accent.

'I know that it is none of my business, so I hope you do not mind, but I could not help overhearing you on the way out here.'

'No. No, that is quite alright,' replied Janek, mulling over the man's words. He was still startled and wanted to be sure that he had caught them correctly. After an appreciable pause he answered: 'But what if there is no forgiveness in their hearts?' he said and his Polish accent asserted itself strongly, as if in competition with the Teutonic tones he had just heard.

'Then that is when your problems begin, my friend. But in that case, it will not matter what you say; first or last,' replied the German.

'Thank you, that is excellent advice,' said Janek, pocketing his scruffy notes and smiling, almost shyly. Through the diffidence he maintained his strong Polish twang, however.

Everyone was disembarking.

A tall blonde lady was waiting for the German man by the gangplank. He nodded a goodbye at Janek and went over to her. They walked off arm-in-arm, Janek watching.

It wasn't until they were almost out of sight and Janek all alone on deck, that he ran after them. 'One minute!' he shouted. 'One minute.'

The German couple heard him and turned. Soon Janek was level with them. 'Wait, please,' he said, rather unnecessarily as they had already stopped. 'Please, what is your name?' he asked of the man, this time with much less accent.

'Arndt Meissner,' the man replied simply.

'Arndt?' asked Janek, and here he paused, 'Were you ever in Poland, Arndt?'

Herr Meissner had been to Poland twice as a tourist, but instinctively he knew that those visits were not the kind Janek meant.

'No,' he said. 'I was on a U-boat in the Atlantic.'

'I see,' replied Janek. 'Thank you.'

'You are welcome. It is much better on top of the water than underneath, do you not think?' added the German, pointing back up the gangplank to the paddle steamer from which they were disembarking.

'Yes…No…I mean, I did not appreciate much of the trip and its sights. Maybe if I had spoken to you earlier,' said Janek with warmth.

'Good luck,' returned Arndt and extended his hand to Janek. They shook hands, perhaps for ten seconds, and then the German and his wife stepped on to Asuncion's soil.

Janek smiled after them. Maybe, just maybe, the meeting was a good omen. It had to have more pedigree than the ocelots and herons and pretty riverscapes that he had clutched at before.

The substantial ground of Asuncion felt good under Janek's feet. He hadn't really been aware of the shift and heave of the boat before, but immediately upon disembarking, he appreciated the solidity beneath him.

The main street was bordered by attractive nineteenth century buildings, none of them more than three storeys high. Half were open to the street as shop fronts; all manner of goods and food stuffs being presented there in coquettish fashion. The people themselves were vigorous and healthy looking. Under different circumstances, Janek would have liked to browse.

He took out the original piece of paper upon which he had noted Joseph's address. On his person there were eight separate copies, all in different pockets. He was taking no chances, even though the information was etched firmly in his memory: 34 Lorca Rise, Asuncion, 74042. The strong sunlight shot off the white paper and danced a hot number on his pupils. Janek remembered that Paraguay was smack on the Tropic of Capricorn and looked around for a bit of shade. He tried again under a butcher's awning. He knew the address in every particular, but it was an emotional necessity for him to look at the original anyway. He needed to feel supported.

Janek stared back at the paddle steamer, still at port. It, and the river down which he had come, had been the last physical entities separating him from his destiny. Although he had endured a rough time aboard the vessel, strangely, it now seemed a safe haven: on the dry land of Asuncion City, he was no longer at any kind of remove from Joseph…other then the distance he had to walk with his own two feet.

Janek breathed deeply, snapped his eyes from the boat and set off, firm of purpose. He needed to find somewhere where there would be maps and English speakers: a library or visitor information centre.

He found the latter very easily; there was one in the anteroom of the high street's pretty little Catholic church. It was staffed by two mature ladies and a raven-haired beauty of about twenty. One of the older ladies spoke English - Janek could hear her telling a man the way to the bullring. After a few minutes the enquirer left the centre, bound for his blood sports.

The way had become clear for Janek, but he was unable to take a step closer to the woman. When he swallowed, there was nothing in his mouth but an old strip of lino, curled up, taut. Never had his mouth been so dry. His skin was the opposite - saturated with the sweat of nerves. Janek quailed when the woman looked up at him, for suddenly the image of himself in the steamer-lavatory mirror flashed before his eyes. In addition, he registered how damp he had become; his profuse sweating could only have further degraded his appearance. But the Paraguayan lady was a professional - if she was shocked by the sight of her new customer, she did not show it. She asked if she might be of assistance, first in Spanish and then in English - when the first language seemed only to generate a greater cascade of perspiration from the man before her.

Janek's tongue caught and scraped at the hard edges of his mouth as he tried to articulate his destination. It was a simple little address but he stumbled terribly over each word. When at last the woman enunciated it back to him, perfectly clearly, he nodded his head in a wild affirmative, spraying sweat over half the office. Only then did he think of handing her one of his address slips. Stressed and wet from the 'dialogue' they had had, the tourist official took it, retired behind the safety of a desk, and then drew Janek a map. 'It's about two miles,' she said handing it to him, 'There are taxis up by the market.'

Then she remembered that the drivers often refused customers if they looked shifty or ill or deranged - 'Or you could walk,' she added quickly. 'It is a straightforward route.' The woman asked for the map back and sketched in a few landmarks, thereby hoping to persuade the strange man before her to trust to his legs rather than to the taxi drivers' benevolence. Janek thanked her and set off in the direction indicated. He did choose to walk - so that he might compose himself.

Two miles? What would that take?…About forty minutes? Not long to get a hold of oneself and stop impersonating a steamed vegetable.

It did not occur to Janek to tidy himself up or to scrub up at all; his head was far too full of the terrifying task at hand for anything as sensible as that. He just willed his pores shut and called to mind the words of the kindly German who had overheard him on the boat.

'I must have been chattering away like a mynah bird,' Janek observed…'A mynah bird in need of a padded cage.'…He laughed at his own joke, but the mirth was not genuine. It too was a function of will: Janek was trying to construct levity, endeavouring to keep his maelstrom of doubts and emotions in check - because in his mind's eye, for every forgiving Joseph he perceived, there were three pitchfork-wielding Josephs tilting at him in revenge.

If it hadn't been for such thoughts, and his quest, he might have enjoyed the stroll: the sun was neither too hot not too cold, the sky duck-egg blue, the trees' branches a-waving, many colourful birds doing their stuff up in them - frightful old clichés - but a dispassionate observer called to describe the scene, might very well have said that these wide Paraguayan streets were the very seat of the planet's soul.

Janek was far too preoccupied to notice details, but in a broad, general sense, he was heartened that Joseph had ended up in such a place. It was his due after...after...after…after meeting him one awful night in 1943.

Janek stopped. Tears…great, guilty, nervous tears. Why should Joseph have forgiven him? How could he? Or be ready to forgive him now? After what he had done? After what had happened?

Startlingly, Janek's right arm jerked out at the elbow, quite independent of his conscious control. His lower lip jerked in similar fashion. There in the beauty and warm loveliness of Paraguay, still a mile distant from his thirty-two-year goal, the pressure of events suddenly weighed so heavily upon Janek's consciousness and conscience, that both proved too flimsy to hold him. He fell through the net of stability into instability and started yelling. His audience was the trees and the passers-by and the quaint 1950s cars being driven around the corner on which he stood, gesticulating and shouting:

'Shut up, shut up, you fool. Shut up or you'll get us all killed...'

'For the last time…shut up…'

'Save him, bitch, save him…'

'Touch the old man and I'll shoot you dead…'

'If the boy dies I will find out…if he dies I will be back here for you...'

'You know me, I always carry out my threats…'

'I swear on my mother's soul, I'll kill you both if

he does not live...'

'Now hurry…'

The nervous laughter of two youths was what brought Janek back from his collapse; one a boy, the other a girl. They were taking no pleasure in his breakdown, merely reacting emotionally to an unsettling sight, as children will. They were locals, out for a stroll, and the deranged were not regulars in their lives.

When Janek heard them, their uneasy tones jolted him back from his desperate memories and on the instant, he stopped reliving them at volume, stopped reliving them at all. The two kids saw that something had clicked off inside him - or on - and were scared. So before the strange man clocked them fully, they started to run away, looking over their shoulders with every stride, to check that he was not coming after them.

It was then that Janek managed to focus them clearly; before he had been too dazed by his own mental frailty…Or rather, he thought that he could focus them - for their faces were not strange to him: the boy was Joseph, exactly as he had been in 1943 and the girl was his sister, Barbara, as beautiful and as vivacious and as alive as she had been that fatal night.

'Hey!' he shouted.

They did not stop.

'Hey!'

Janek gave chase. He had to see their faces up close.

Passion and desperation lend a man stamina. They even strip away years, but not whole decades, so although Janek could keep the two teenagers in sight, he could not catch them up. They were too lithe and young and the territory was their own. Also desperation was lending them legs, for they had no insight into their pursuer's motives.

After ten minutes Janek had lost them completely. He came to a stop where two roads bisected and there was open parkland to one side of him and a canal to the other. Janek was stumped - they might have gone in any direction. His heart was bucking like a trapped piglet.

'Uuuuhhh...Uuuuuhh,' he puked.

The vomit had barely hit his shoes when he looked straight up again and started: 'Two roads bisecting, a park on one side, a narrow canal on the other,'...that was what the woman had said, the one at the visitor centre! She had even written it down for him. He slapped about himself for the little map she'd drawn. He brought it out in a clawed fist.

'Two roads bisecting, a park on one side, a narrow canal on the other,' he read. There it was, in black and white. He had arrived. And he'd done the last mile at a sprint, chasing a teenage Joseph and Barbara. Even if they were just a Joseph and a Barbara of the mind, that had to be an omen - a good one - along with the big, bald German.

Ten yards farther on there was a sign on the canal towpath wall: *Lorca Rise*. After thirty-some years, he was finally standing in Joseph's street!

Janek was full of fear - his legs were bandy with it - and with the running. He took a dozen rubbery steps then stopped. He willed his limbs firmer and looked up: number 6 Lorca Rise. He was outside number 6.

Fourteen more houses to go.

Number 34 had a great wide door, red as a London pillar box. Also there were railings and plants and large sash windows. A man was sitting beneath one of them, reading. Janek stood in the middle of the pavement and stared at him. He sobbed with absolute abandon - for two minutes. Then he just shook out hard, internal tears, for fear that Joseph would hear his crying and notice him before he was ready.

It was Joseph. There was no room for doubt. He had lost his hair, but even at a distance and through a pane of glass, Janek could see the essential stamp of the boy he had once been.

'So Joseph will recognise me too then...Not necessarily...He hasn't been looking at a photograph of my face every day for thirty-two years.'

Janek argued with himself along these lines, sometimes coming down on one side, sometimes the other. At one point a woman's gown flashed past the window and Janek ducked down as if shot at. His emotions were rioting. There was terror, joy, relief, guilt, desperation, pride, disgust, warmth, coldness.

He took a step closer to the door, rehearsing as he did so:

'There's never been one day I haven't...'

Another step.

'I didn't mean to...'

Another.

'She has always been in my...'

Another.

'Good afternoon, my name's Janek Lipsz, but you will remember me as Roman Zaleski...'

Janek shook his head violently and stopped, 'No, no, no that's no good.'

He took another step.

'I can never atone for…'

He took another.

'Please accept…'

Another.

'For thirty-two years I have…'

Another

'That's it,' he said smoothing down his hair: 'For thirty-two years I have been searching for you…'

Another step…

…There wasn't another step. Janek was at the big red door. He stood nose to it, trying to get his hands dry. He couldn't.

He reached for the knocker. Blood and screams and soldiers and cracked heads flashed before his eyes and he dropped his hand. Janek tried once more. The incomparable Barbara hove into his mind's eye; he snatched the hand back. Again he tried. This time Herr Meissner's encouraging words tinkled in his ears, so he did knock.

Immediately Janek felt a flush of heat all over his body and suddenly it seemed impossible to take in enough oxygen. He was gulping and gulping air, but still there was a deficit. He leaned against the railings, then stood straight, then took a step back, then set a hand against the door, then snatched it away. No position seemed right. In his head, Janek was saying over and over again, 'For thirty-two years I have..,' 'For thirty-two years I have…'

On the eighth recitation the door opened.

The world did not slow down at all: there was no slow motion. That is a myth. In one second, Janek saw Joseph's cheeks broad with good-living, his forehead furrowed with age, his eyes the same as ever, his bald crown deeply scarred where it had been shattered with the stock of a gun.

Janek managed only one unrehearsed word: 'Forgive…'

'You!' screamed Joseph as he lashed out at Janek with vicious force, envenomed hatred turning his punches into mule kicks. His teeth were bared with animal fury, his chin thrust maniacally out. Every blow was accompanied by a wild cry of violent intensity. Two women from inside the house dashed out to the front path and started calling shrilly. Joseph did not hear them, for his own bellowing hatred was everything. No part of him was human, save his memories and suffering, which had to be avenged.

Janek was punched and kicked out into the street. There was no let up: Joseph was all over him. The two women were still hard by the house.

At first Janek shouted his explanations and rehearsed lines, but as his teeth loosened and his lips split, the job became harder and harder. Then he could feel things starting to spin and he knew that his message was garbling in the delivery. Not once did he fight back. He would not raise a finger to Joseph ever again, not though the passivity cost him his life.

And that might well have happened, if the reunion had been somewhere remote, but on the city street of Lorca Rise there were other people about and they dragged Joseph off. Not for quite some time, though, for his savagery was frightening. But once he had clubbed the older man to the floor and would not stop striking his prone form, then the people decided that they had to act, in order to keep some of the old man's blood inside him.

It is usually the case that if a young man thrashes an old one in full view of others, then the onlookers will side with the weaker party and restrain the younger male - if society has not been too weakened by the rights of the aggressor and the fear of litigation. Paraguay had not been so weakened and Joseph was bundled unceremoniously to the floor, screaming and swearing in a mixture of Spanish and Polish.

At first every word he said was lost in the pother of adrenaline and rage, and in the scuffle with Janek's rescuers, but then four words sounded clear over the commotion: 'He killed my sister…he killed my sister…he killed my sister.'

The phrase acted upon the semi-conscious Janek like a starting pistol - he was off running at speed. For the first few seconds he was everywhere; arms and legs flying in different directions on account of the beating he had received, but then he was sprinting solidly, back to the only place he knew: the town centre quay. He did not care if his heart gave out on the run - his life had been lived now - so no one could have out run him, except Joseph.

But Joseph could not run, for his knee had been injured when the bystanders jumped him. It was pinned under the weight of five of them and through he pain he was still shouting, 'He killed my sister…he killed my sister…he killed Barbara.'

The Precious Kinkajou was still at dock. Janek saw it through the one eye of his which had not been beaten quite shut. Through this chink of sight he could make out its preparations to leave: ropes were being uncoiled, baskets loaded, people were waving, engines were roaring, funnels were tooting. Everything was hustle and bustle.

It wasn't clear who saw Janek careering up first - maybe a member of the crew, maybe a snotty Yank. Whoever it was, he did a ten second job of letting everyone else on the vessel know. The loudest voices bayed that Janek not be allowed back on board.

'Goddam nut!' someone shouted.

'Mad as a plate of eyes,' someone else.

But it was obvious from Janek's determined and bruised face that it would take more than invective to keep him off board. He near-vaulted the gangplank and landed spreadeagled on deck. Four crewmen came briskly over to provide the necessary muscle to dump the nutter back on Asuncion's soil. They had been called to action by the most vociferous and least tolerant passengers. Each man laid forceful hands on Janek's prostrate form. He was face down, heaving and rattling with exertion. Suddenly a strong, authoritative voice rang out.

'Leave him. He is with me.'

It was the German, Arndt Meissner. Two crewmen let go of Janek, two did not.

'I said take your hands off him. He is my guest.'

'But has he paid the return fare?' asked a young uniform.

'If he hasn't, I will,' growled Meissner. 'Unhand him.'

The crew looked to the other passengers for support - the Americans and Brazilians and Spaniards. Nearly all of them were mumbling and shuffling and looking at their feet.

'Well if he wants to look after the nut,' said one.

'And vouch for him,' snapped another.

'I vouch for him,' barked Arndt, stabbing at his own barrel chest.

The passengers started filtering away. A few nodded their heads at the German, even smiled a little, but theirs was an academic acceptance - the vessel had left Asuncion's quay.

'There was not then forgiveness in his heart?' asked Meissner as the vessel hit deeper water. He was cradling Janek's head and his wife was passing him tissues to staunch the flow of blood from Janek's injuries. The German expected no answer and did not get one.

'A lifetime is not long enough for some people, which is not good. Not good for you and not good for them either, because we do not get another one.'

Janek was listening - he had to - because this man was the only reason he had not been left lying in his own gore on Asuncion's dock, but he was listening with only one percent of himself. The other ninety-nine was tangled up with something he had seen, something which had shaken every ounce of his being: one of the women who had come out to the front path of number 34 Lorca Rise was none other than his Sarah!

CHAPTER 19

The boat crossed into Brazil before Janek spoke.

'I am so stupid,' he mumbled through his split lips, 'I can see her now, in his face - now that he is in his forties. They are mother and son.'

Arndt Meissner nodded although he did not understand what his Polish acquaintance was talking about.

'It is all so clear now. With the photograph it was impossible to tell: there were too many years between them.'

Arndt and his wife smiled.

When they said goodbye in Aracatuba, Janek refused their offer of help in finding him medical attention, so the German couple wished him all the best, handed him their address in Munich, and then bade him a fond farewell.

Janek travelled and bummed around Brazil for five desultory weeks. There was no point hurrying back home - his life's work was done. Also, the *Telegraph* mobs would only be there waiting for him and he was quite done with the Disappearance Club. He was officially retired.

In a pub in Rio he took out the photograph of Joesph's sister, Barbara. He moved his pink gin lest some spill on her. Janek looked at the image without flinching, which he could almost never do. She had come in for a lot of punishment lately. As well as the creases, there were splodges of dried blood - his blood from when her avenging brother had attacked him.

'I am sorry my dear, what I did was unforgivable,' he said to her then slipped the photograph back in his pocket.

Janek did a lot of drinking in the backstreets of Rio, and eating and pottering and loafing and wondering - wondering what the hell he would do with the time that he had left. Now and then he would take a peek at himself; in hotel lobby mirrors, in bathrooms, in barbers' shops, and try to gauge how long that would be. Seven years? Five years?

He even asked a few people. He rather enjoyed putting them on the spot. It was because all meaning and focus in his life was gone. Before, when Joseph could not be found, the boy had always been the one massive constant: Janek had defined himself by his search. But now that Joseph, the man, was found, and Janek was certain that he was hated by him, that constant was gone.

It did give Janek some succour, though, to know that he had helped Sarah to her son. It was obvious now, that she had latched on to him and The Disappearance Club only as a means of finding her Joseph. He did not know why she had been so secretive about everything though and he could not account for her various stories. But those things didn't matter, not when measured against the enormity of them finding one another. Perhaps he had done a little bit of good after all?

All that was really left were the diamonds.

Occasionally they did still burn in his pocket: Janek felt that he must sell them and somehow get the money to Joseph's address. He even took a couple of days off from the pink gin to try and secure a good price at a few of the local jewellers' shops, but very quickly it became clear that they were all just out to cheat him, so he decided to leave that final job until he returned home.

Thus it was that he was in his personal bathroom at the Copacabana Palace Hotel completing his final South American task: stitching the bag of diamonds into the lining of his jacket. There were thousands of thieves and pickpockets in Brazil - if the stories were anything to go by - and it would not do to have the gems whipped before he got back to Hatton Garden.

He slipped the jacket over his shoulders. It was a perfect job; the diamonds didn't stick out any more than a folded handkerchief. Once that was checked, he looked up at his reflection in the mirror and immediately revised his life expectancy down by two years: the bags under his eyes were looking particularly fulsome…

…A few seconds later Janek collapsed. His head hit the side of the bath, hard. A spurt of blood strafed the lavatory porcelain. Janek was unconscious before he hit the floor.

It was the chambermaid who found him. There was a nasty cut above his right temple and the hotel manager did not like the look of Janek's face either, although most of the bruising was just slow healing stuff, courtesy of Joseph's fists. Accordingly, he had Janek taken to the local hospital where he was stitched, sedated and made comfortable in a private room. The hotel insurance covered customers for injuries sustained on the premises.

Janek came round later in the day.

Within two breaths of waking he lurched out of bed in a blind panic, crashing about everywhere, until he found his jacket and checked that the diamonds were still safe in its lining. The nurses had stowed his clothes in a compact wardrobe situated in the corner of the room. The little bulge was comfortingly present.

The noise of his clumsy clattering brought the nurses running and chastising in rapid Portuguese. Two of them led Janek back to his bed. He was biddable as a lamb, now that he was sure Joseph's birthright was safe. Later a doctor came to see him. He spoke excellent English and asked about the bruises on Janek's face. He also explained that the hospital lab was doing tests on his blood.

Janek could have told the man that the tests were unnecessary. He knew that it was all the crap that had tipped him over the edge: the paying of hotel bills, checking of receipts, ringing room service, ordering food and drink, trying to secure a good price for diamonds, sewing them into the lining of his jacket; when all the time his enormous failure was lurking, just awaiting the chance to jump him. And in that hotel bathroom, his vast reservoir of suppressed wretchedness had asserted itself. He had come thousands of miles and three decades for nothing! He had been able to say only one tiny word to Joseph. Just one feeble word! For weeks his inner self had been managed and constrained, and bribed with alcohol to accept this calamity, then finally, before that bathroom mirror, it had slipped its leash and walloped him - hard.

When the doctor left Janek got up again, turned the little key in the wardrobe door and checked on the diamonds once more. That done, he returned to bed, lay quite still and gave himself up to a deep lassitude. He was interested in nothing, certainly not his own recovery; there was nothing physically wrong with him, he knew that.

He was positioned on a first floor wing with views over an attractive stretch of land. No one ever seemed to walk across it and exotic birds and lizards had claimed it as their own. But Janek's old interests no longer animated him; he barely noted them. When he could be bothered to look out, the birds were just little feathered flashes to him. When the lizards tested the sills of his window, they might just as well have been wind-skittered twigs. Sleep was Janek's only friend. Waking hours were an ordeal, just to be endured until the merciful haze of slumber fell. Even then he was not fully secure, because sometimes the incomparable Barbara would appear to him in his dreams, or he would hear her marrow-freezing screams as accompaniment to his own snoring.

He would ask her forgiveness a thousand times and a thousand times she would refuse him. And then Janek would recreate in his dreaming mind those terrible events of 1943 and he would witness again and again, in graphic detail, why she could never forgive him - and why her brother had not forgiven him. And the vividness of the Joseph-Barbara memory would wake him, yelling and yelling out his distress. Always, then, a couple of nurses would come crashing through the door. Occasionally they sedated him and the ensuing peace was bliss. When he was not being administered sedatives, he begged them for drink, but his tumbler full of gin never arrived.

In the end, after tests and two weeks of Janek turning his face to the wall, the doctor explained that they could find nothing physically wrong with him. He was to be discharged. With a mind to his emotional state, however, the hospital management had decided to drive him to Rio de Janeiro airport in an ambulance. They had already checked his pockets upon admittance - to establish identity and nationality - and had found there a valid plane ticket. So, with due consideration given to the clauses in the hotel insurance policy, and therefore the cost, it was deemed that the mentally unstable of Britain should be sent back to Britain. Transporting him off and away would prevent any incidents on Brazilian soil for which they, as his carers, might be considered responsible.

Janek knew none of this. He wouldn't have cared if he had. A pointless existence can be carried on just as well at home as abroad. He had wind of something on the final day, though. There were forms to sign and an early lunch to eat and big breezy smiles from the nurses. With a massive effort of will, Janek cut a little path through his own apathy and summoned enough energy to sign the release forms. He remained sufficiently animated to slip on his diamond-jacket too - when the nurses popped out with the forms. Then Janek settled back into utter prostration.

That was how he was when they wheeled him to the ambulance and how he was on the journey to the airport and how he remained upon take-off. He barely noticed when the aircraft became fully airborne or when it hit turbulence just past Aracaju. He slept across the South Atlantic. Over the North Atlantic, however, he awoke, on account of harrowing nightmares:

'Barbara, Barbara, I couldn't do anything... Barbara...Keep quiet. Don't scream...You alone understand...You alone can forgive me,' he moaned.

Then an air stewardess, who had been paid a little something extra by the hospital, stuck a needle in Janek's shoulder and afterwards he said nothing more.

At Heathrow he was wheeled off the aeroplane last, still groggy. He was not completely knocked out though - his right hand lay across a lump in the lining of his jacket. There was little else in his world which he cared as much for. And when, as the last of the effects of the sedative wore off, he registered the familiar sounds of his England more and more fully, Janek considered it of no real consequence that he was back. He had given up.

The old Janek would have been planning a letter to Sarah, even a telephone call, but he had given up on her too. What else could he do? Of course she hated him...just like her son. Why shouldn't she? He had destroyed her family.

An official at the airport asked him what he used to do for a living - just for conversation's sake - while he checked the medical report that the Brazilian hospital had sent along. The man had obviously taken one look at Janek and assumed that he was no longer of working age; just twelve months before, people had always assumed the opposite.

'I wasted my time…I was a professional time waster,' Janek replied.

'Don't we all do that, guv'?'

'I suppose so.'

Janek's responses came from a tired little spot twenty thousand miles away and were sighed out with every ounce of his world-weariness. He handed over his passport with a perfectly indifferent arm.

'No, but come on, mate, what did you do? What did you really do?'

'I ran a disappearance club for people who were pissed off with their lives,' Janek croaked out mechanically.

'Wow. I read about that. Was that you, was it?'

'It was me, until I found out that I had been wasting my time.' Janek choked on a little of his own spittle and then became animated: 'You know I could just have gone over there to farm nutria like a lot of the post-war Germans did and probably bumped into Joseph on a shopping trip in Buenos Aires. Do you know that?'

The man didn't know that and looked nonplussed.

'But instead I came to this shit hole,' Janek continued.

'Well if you don't like it here you know what you can do, don't you?' flashed the official, suddenly angry. He stooped low to Janek's ear to deliver his message, 'Fuck off back to your own country and hustle your drinks from the gutter there.'

Obviously the hospital had noted his craving for strong drink in the report.

Janek did not reply at first. It didn't matter what people thought of him. He could be shunned by everyone for all he cared. 'Does that mean I've cleared passport control, then?' he replied at last.

The official's face contorted with rage, 'I give you three years mate, by the look of ya. Then you'll be six foot under and no mistake…'

Janek was impassive.

'Three years tops, arsehole!'

Mightily pissed off, the man charged with attending to him stormed off. Janek was left quite alone, in his wheelchair, suitcase unceremoniously dumped handle-side down. Feeling like the little furry fungus which sometimes grows on damp walls, Janek heaved himself up, levered his case to, and then rose. The stewardess-adminstered sedative no longer rode a single ounce of his system; he walked straight off. Anyone watching would have thought the wheelchair some form of fraudulent prop. Janek looked about him, tearing up, eyes red as infected gums. What next?

A few hundred weary, sorry steps to find his car...

It was still there, in the airport car park, cold and frosted over. Janek didn't bother scraping the windows down. He didn't even put the heater on for his own comfort. He had never before realised quite how boring life was, when one did not have a grand plan or aim. And he felt contempt for the wankers who trudged through life without one…Maybe that was why he did not bother clearing his view in order to see them - such losers were not worth the effort. More than that, he was disgusted with himself…'If only I had thought twice in that split 1943-second…'

On the drive back he considered crashing into the concrete hulk of a bridge support: just testing the speedometer as far as it would go, and then shutting his eyes with the seat belt off. But it was Oskar, his cat, kept him from actually doing it: Phil was a good lad, but he couldn't be expected to adopt a cat at his age.

So it was that Janek did arrive back at 33 Orchard Road, very late at night. As soon as he stepped into the hall, Oskar was all over him, as if the cat actually guessed what its owner had been contemplating.

Phil had collected the Disappearance Club post and stacked it on the kitchen table. It was inches thick. Janek could not help but look for something with Sarah's handwriting on. There was nothing. He left the pile of letters. As far as he was concerned, the table could fall to the floor before he would ever open them. Then, for the first time in months, Janek went to sleep under his own roof, just curled up on the sofa. Oskar leapt up and parasitized his warmth.

The first anyone down the street knew of Janek's return was when Phil came in to feed Oskar the next morning. It was about ten, but the gloom of the day made it seem much earlier.

'Oh hello,' he said after Oskar had miaowed his welcome from on top of Janek. 'I didn't know you was back.'

Nor did Janek - his dreams were all war-torn Poland and emotion-torn Paraguay.

'You wanna wake up Mr Lipsz, it's gone ten. Come on.'

Janek mouthed something.

'Come on. Up you get.'

Janek grimaced in his sleep.

'You look about as comfortable as a bollock on a razor blade.' Phil liked to be rude in the presence of adults; when he could get away with it. Janek being unconscious meant that he could get away with it.

But his words had percolated through the levels to Janek - not the sense of them, just the noise. The old man jackknifed up. Lunged. Oskar was catapulted across the room by the suddenness of the movement.

'Quiet you fool! You'll kill us all! Shut the fuck up! You'll kill us all!' he hissed. Janek had Phil by the neck and was forcing it round in a technique that he had learned in The Resistance. The vertebrae could be snapped quite easily, so long as one had the move just so...

Luckily, Janek was out of practice. He was staring down at his handiwork and wondering why Joseph's neck wouldn't snap. Then he was fully awake. Wide awake. He saw that there was no Joseph...saw that he had the peace-time Phil by his little peace-time neck - and quickly let go. He looked in horror at his own hangman's hands, hanging in the air, the fingers curled like talons. Phil was gasping for breath: 'Je...huh...s... huh...us...Chr...huh...ist.'

'I'm sorry Phil. I'm sorry. You must not disturb me in my sleep. You must not. I am sorry. I thought you were someone else and that it was a different time and a different place.'

Phil was rubbing at his throat, trying manfully not to cry. He succeeded by not saying anything.

'You alright?' asked Janek, concerned.

Phil nodded.

'Are you sure?'

Phil nodded again.

'I didn't know what I was doing.'

Phil nodded some more.

'You mustn't disturb me in my sleep.'

Phil shook his head.

'I thought you were someone else.'

'You ever do anything like that to the cat?' gasped Phil, trusting himself to speak at last.

'No,' Janek replied, 'He doesn't talk to me in my sleep.'

Phil smiled, a tiny, thin smile. 'This is something I'll definitely not be telling my mum.'

'Probably best,' replied Janek, swinging his legs off the sofa.

'Mr Lipsz, was it a successful trip?' asked Phil, finally lowering his hands from about his neck.

Janek shook his head.

'Oh,' said Phil, 'I figured it must have been.'

Janek shook his head again, 'Disastrous.'

'I thought…Well you know…What with you being away so long, that something must have come of it. You said you was only going for three weeks and it's been about two months now.'

Janek snatched at a stray newspaper in order to look at the date then let it fall through his fingers. 'Jeez! Was I gone that long?'

'I reckon you were, Mr Lipsz. Me and Oskar have been just fine, though.'

'What did you do for food for him?'

'I bought some more.'

Janek looked at the boy with a big smile of wonder and gratitude. It was like the very occasional ones that Sarah used to bestow upon him.

'Well…you did give me lots of money and I only gave me mum thirty quid in the end,' explained the boy.

Janek saw the livid bruises forming around Phil's neck. 'What you going to tell her about those?' he asked, pointing at them.

'Oh,' said Phil. 'Don't worry about that. There's some big boys at the park who push us around sometimes. I'll say it was them.'

'What about your dad, won't he want to go knock 'em about?'

Phil's eyes filled up. He wiped away the wetness. 'He left, Mr Lipsz…while you was away.'

Janek took in the boy, really considered him: his bruised neck and his loyalty and his selfless care over the months and now his loss…

…'Just a minute,' he said. Janek dashed upstairs. It was the first time he had dashed anywhere since Paraguay and his whole body complained to him in official pain. Two minutes later, and more slowly, he came back down with a metal box which he had just fished out from beneath a couple of bedroom floorboards.

Phil was stroking Oskar.

'Come here,' said Janek, sitting down heavily.

Phil was a little tentative.

'Come on,' Janek encouraged. 'I'm safe now.'

When they were both seated he flipped open the lid. Inside were rolled wad upon rolled wad of bank notes, all tightly circular within elastic bands. Janek started dividing them into two piles. In a couple of minutes there were nine little bundles in each: one pile at his own feet, one pile at Phil's.

'Pass me that bag,' he said, pointing to a green carrier that was trapped under the foot of a chair. Phil did. Janek put one of the piles into it.

'Right,' he said, 'There's enough money there to buy half a house. I'm giving it to you, for everything you've done for me.' He thought for a moment and then scooped the rest of the money in. 'A whole house,' he corrected…'But you promise me one thing: you open yourself a post office account and you pay it in and you keep it a secret from everyone. That doesn't mean if things get tough at home, you don't take a bit out now and then to help, but it means that you never let anyone see the book or tell 'em how much you've really got. And you pay the money in in dribs and drabs so no one at the post office gets suspicious. You got it?'

'I've got an account there already,' beamed Phil, beside himself with excitement.

'Anyone know you've got it?' asked Janek, his eyes narrowing.

Phil nodded.

'Then open a new one,' he snapped. 'The old one's no good to you. Do you understand?'

'I understand, Mr Lipsz.'

Janek looked the boy straight in the eye, checking that he did indeed understand.

'Wow. Thank you…thank you, Mr Lipsz. I really don't know what to say. I mean, nothing like this has ever happened to me before - ceptin' when you've given me bits of money like.'

'And probably no one will ever just hand you money again, Phil. Not that much, so don't waste it. When you're a grown man, that's when you'll really need it. Try to save it till then.'

Phil tried to say something, but the words would not form.

'Come on lad, out with it.'

Phil looked at the floor, then up again. 'But don't you have a son of your own, or daughter, or someone like that to give it to?' he asked at last, in a quavering voice.

'No,' replied Janek, softly, quietly.

'And what would your missis say if she found out?' Phil asked even more tremulously, 'I know she wasn't your real missis, but wouldn't she have something to say about it; about all this money?'

Janek was surprised at the question. 'This has nothing to do with her. She has no say in it,' he replied.

Again Phil looked up uncertainly. 'She left you, didn't she, Mr Lipsz? I saw her go one night with a case, one night out of my window. I stay up sometimes, even though everyone thinks I'm in bed.'

'Yes Phil, you are right, she left,' Janek replied sadly.

'And you didn't find your Joseph in the end, did you? When you went away?' Phil continued.

'No. I didn't. You're right.' Janek paused…'Look, I think you better run along now and find yourself a hiding place for that money.'

'Ok. And thanks again Mr Lipsz,' trilled Phil, diverted from any further questions by this direct reference to his unexpected bounty.

Janek showed Phil to the door, after the young lad had given Oskar a thorough stroke. He was just about to shut it behind the boy when he called his cat-sitter and chief inquisitor back. The sun was bright on both their faces when Janek spoke: 'We've never lied to each other Phil, you and I, so I'm not going to start now…I did find 'my Joseph' as you call him, but he didn't want to see me. He didn't want to see me at all. That's the truth.'

Phil looked up at the old man's face and saw there his age and his sadness and the deep hollows of his cheeks. 'I can't understand that, Mr Lipsz. I can't understand why anybody wouldn't want to know you, not once you'd shown an interest in them.'

'Thank you, Phil. Thank you. That's one of the nicest things anyone's ever said to me. And it makes what I'm about to say now even more painful.'

Phil looked worried.

'I don't think you'll be seeing much of me any more. I think I'm going to keep myself pretty much tucked away from now on…'

'Oh you don't need to worry about those funny people knocking on your door any more,' gushed Phil, 'They stopped coming about two weeks ago. Must've got the message.'

'That's good. That's very good. But I don't mean that, Phil. I'm still going to tuck myself away, whatever. I'm awfully tired Phil and not so very happy these days, so you will have to forgive me if I seem unfriendly or if I'm just not around anymore. You have my permission to climb over the fence and get your ball anytime.'

'Alright, Mr Lipsz. Thank you. But I do hope I'll see you sometimes.'

The old man smiled.

There was a tooth loose in his smile.

Janek was true to his word. He became a recluse. He did not answer the door. He did not walk out by day. He did not take on new Disappearance Club business. He did not bother with existing members either. He did not cash any cheques sent to him. He did not open post. He did not send post. He did not answer the telephone. He did not go to the doctor when he fell ill.

He did make and keep one appointment - at a solicitor's - in order to write his will. And he did intend to visit the shop in Hatton Garden where he had received such good service, and there sell Joseph's diamonds for him, but he never got round to going. The weeks just limped on.

He rarely drew the curtains, but he did sometimes take the sun in his garden and he did bury Oskar there too, when he found him dead one day at the foot of his bed.

Not once did he enter his garage-office, nor look upon the huge photograph in it. Janek ignored all knocking at his double gates. Most of the time he sat in the gloom of his living room; staring, cogitating, sleeping. The past was his companion now and his sorrows were the fruit of those times. Very little outside of his head impinged. He had done his living and now he just sat.

Thus it was, that one day, Janek did not realise that there was someone at his window, looking in through a gap in the curtain. He had heard a knock on the door, but had not moved even one of his atrophied muscles in response to it. Nor did he pick up on the conversation going on outside:

'Is he always like this, Phil?'

'Oh yes. I haven't seen him for months. He never comes out. Not even to his office - specially not to his office. We get our own ball now, every time. It's sad, cos it's actually the ball he got us.'

'How long's this been going on for?'

'Ever since he came back from South America.'

'Doesn't he speak to anyone?'

'No one. As far as I know.'

'And he never comes out?'

'I don't see him. Twice I see'd him put out his rubbish, that's all.'

The football bounced away; Phil had returned to his friends.

The visitor tried rapping on the glass. It was no good. Janek had ignored a hundred irate callers; now he could imitate a toad, impassive under a rock, better than any man alive.

The visitor tried calling: 'Janek…Janek…Janek Lipsz. I know you can hear me, Janek Lipsz.'

Janek Lipsz wasn't sure that he could.

'Janek, open the door or I'll just let myself in.'

Dim through the misty panes, Janek was trying to place the voice. He had heard it somewhere before: probably it belonged to one of those loyal relations of the disappeared who came with yearly money for ne'er-do-wells they could not quite break off from.

'Janek! For God's sake, get up!' shrilled the voice.

Maybe that bloody Renault woman. It was definitely a woman's voice…Then suddenly Janek jumped to his feet, like a beefeater caught loafing by the queen. He was all of a dither - he had recognised the voice. Without looking up at the rattling window he lurched for the door.

It was a small, weak little man who drew it open. The bones of his face seemed too large for its drawn skin and pinched mouth. More scalp than hair showed and his clothes hung about him with a pitiful vastness.

'Sarah?' he croaked.

'Yes Janek, it is me. May I come in?'

CHAPTER 20

Janek opened the door wide and shuffled himself to one side.

'You look terrible Janek.'

'I know.'

Sarah and the apparition walked to the living room. Janek slumped himself back in his sofa seat. Immediately he remembered himself: 'Would you like some tea?' he asked, trying painfully to raise himself. The dash for the door had drained him of energy.

'No thank you.'

'Just as well. There are no tea bags…Maybe I have coffee though,' he said, trying once more to persuade his lower back to work.

'No thank you,' Sarah repeated. Then her voice changed in tone and the very warmth seemed drawn out of the room. 'I want to know what happened Janek,' she said. 'I know that Barbara is dead, but Joseph says that you raped his sister…my Barbara…my little girl.'

'That's not true,' answered Janek, quickly and with spirit. 'That's not true. He wasn't there…not in the room. He didn't see what happened.'

'Then you must tell me Janek. You must tell me.'

A horrible wailing came from the seated figure, swathed in his loose cloth. It was a terrible animal sound, full of a lifetime's sadness and regret.

'I am her mother, I must know the truth Janek…The truth!' At this point Sarah took Janek's awful sobbing head in her palms. They spanned entirely his sunken face and even through her own pain and the suspense of the moment, she was appalled at his physical decline. Quickly the softness in her hardened: 'Janek,' she shouted, 'Joseph is not the only person who told me that you raped Barbara. There was also Roza Dymek, the inn keeper. She told me many years ago.'

Suddenly Janek was human again. He snatched away Sarah's hands. 'The Dymek bitch couldn't tell the truth if her own soul depended on it,' he sneered, forgetting misery for one indignant second.

'Then you tell me, Janek…Do you know I came here to kill you that first day down in your office? To stab you on account of what she told me.'

Janek nodded slowly, cogitating…'But then you saw your son's picture on my wall and found out that I was searching for him and so you spared me, and helped me; worked even harder than me, because you were working with a mother's passion. That's right isn't it?'

'Yes Janek, that's exactly right. Now tell me what happened to my daughter.'

'It is so clear now.'

'Tell me!' hissed Sarah.

Janek stared at a little point on Barbara's mother's forehead. 'Sit down,' he said, addressing it.

'I would rather stand to hear this.'

'You will need to sit down.'

Sarah did, on the sofa, but as far away from Janek

as possible.

'I was with Fryderyk Wysocki and Alfons Krupa hurrying at a run along a little road ten miles out of Cracow. They were my most trusted men. In The Resistance we had all types: the calm, the frightened, the emotionally unstable, the talented, the useless, and the dependable. They were very dependable.'

Sarah wrung her hands with impatience.

'No Sarah,' said Janek noticing, 'It is important that you know these things. You need to know that I owed these men much and they, me. We had saved one another's lives many times and that kind of thing forges a bond between men, stronger perhaps even than the bond between man and wife - at least, in times of war.'

Sarah breathed deeply.

'We had been laying dynamite under railway tracks…the ones that the Germans used most heavily and were keen to be clear away from the scene of our activities. Being caught in the vicinity would have meant summary execution. We were perhaps a mile from the tracks when we saw three figures running towards us, two in sprightly fashion, the third limping, clearly in pain. We cocked our guns and darted off the road to find bushes in which to hide. They advanced closer: two teenagers and a woman in her thirties. It was the woman who was moving with difficulty.'

'My sister, Miriam,' Sarah said to herself.

'Your sister?' Janek asked tentatively.

Sarah nodded - both an affirmative and a demand for him to continue.

'They were obviously running away - escaping. I could tell at once why: they were Jews. That much was obvious. In those days, one was conditioned to be able to tell. It was part of the culture of the time…'

Janek pulled at one of his grey, unshaven cheeks.

'…I jumped out from behind my bush. I wanted to know whether they were being directly followed, wanted to know whether we could expect German soldiers farther on our way. They didn't know much. Then your sister started asking things of me.'

Sarah's face formed a question mark.

'She was begging my assistance. The three of them were in terrible need of help. They had escaped from a convoy of cattle trucks and barely had clothes on enough to keep warm. The night would have done for them. Really, I did not want to help.'

Janek saw Sarah's eyes swell and an angry light fill them.

He carried on, 'Frankly we did not care much for Jews. Even in peace time the two communities were very separate. Maybe you remember?'

Sarah sat impassively.

'It was the way things were. When I was a boy I had no Jewish friends, although there were plenty of Jews around in the neighbourhood.'

'Please, please carry on,' urged Sarah.

'I was loath to help…even less inclined were Alfons and Fryderyk. So the threesome became frantic. They were scared that a patrol of soldiers would appear; up along the way they had come. The boy and girl were all for getting on as fast as possible…Joseph and Barbara…'…'Joseph and Barbara…' The words weighed upon Janek, leaden, guilt-heavy. He felt that he had sullied their names, just by forming them on his lips. He looked up at Sarah for an echoing response, but there was nothing reflected in her face, other than absorption in his story.

'...But your sister delayed, much to their annoyance. The two children had obviously concluded that we would offer them no help. Their aunt had not given up on us, however. Maybe she had worked out that with her bad leg, the three of them would not be able to get anywhere fast. She took me to one side, probably because I was the least hostile of the three men before her. Then she slipped a hand into her bosom. I thought that she was going to offer me sex in return for my help, but actually she whipped out a packet of diamonds. It was full to bursting. She offered me three quarters of the packet if I would let her and the children come along with me. I accepted half - about forty gems - but said that I would take only the children as it was clear that she could not keep up a good speed. We were evading capture ourselves I said. She agreed. There was much crying and hugging when she told Barbara and Joseph. Before we left her, Alfons and Fryderyk, who had seen something of our transaction, forced more of the diamonds out of her. I think she was left with only a few stones.'

'You mean you just left her there?'

'It was not a manly thing to do, but manly things often get men killed in war. Without the diamonds, we would certainly have left all three of them to their fate.'

'Do you know what happened to my sister?' Sarah craned forward. She had already got this part of the story from her son and was on the look out for lies and inconsistencies.

'Hasn't Joseph...?'

'Yes, but I want it from you,' interrupted Sarah.

Janek gulped, 'About ten minutes later we heard two shots ring out from the road - after we had turned off for the comparative safety of a rough track.'

Tears raced each other down Sarah's cheeks.

'Please understand; it would have been all of us, if we had advanced only at her pace. The soldiers would have shot us all…'

'Then what?' Sarah demanded savagely.

'We went to Roza Dymek's place. We thought that it would be safe there.'

Sarah's eyes were cold upon Janek.

'I knew her of old to be unscrupulous and driven by greed…'

Janek read Sarah's look. Her eyes were equating the two of them.

'…Even by the standards of the time,' he said flatly. 'She feared us too. And because of that, hers was a kind of safe house.'

Sarah's lips were drawn thin. The colour was leached from her cheeks.

'The Dymek woman was not happy to see us, not happy to see the two people we had brought along; she did not want to get into trouble for harbouring Jews. Stormtroopers had been at her place the day before, she said. They had carried off her goats and hens, she said. It was all more than a poor woman could be expected to stand, she said. We ignored her, lay down a few bank notes to pay our way and sat down at the main table of the inn. It was a rough old place, but just right for our needs. And when she said that the Germans had been through it already, we even started to relax, for we felt sure that they would not return within such a short space of time. Soon we were drinking far too much for men on the run, but that often happens in war - when a man thinks he has found a safe haven.'

Sarah's tongue was between her teeth. The account was taking too long, although she could tell that Janek was telling her the truth.

'Please,' said Janek, noticing her impatience once more, 'This is how I must tell it. If you want the whole truth, I must give you everything….or not be able to admit the half of it.'

Sarah inclined her head grimly.

'Soon we three men got to playing cards - poker - for money. Joseph and Barbara were sitting very quietly in a corner, probably thinking on the two gunshots they had heard. And at their age, they could be left to their own devices.'

'Easy profit for you, those diamonds!' spat Sarah, unable to control herself. Then appended, 'Sorry,' immediately afterwards. The apology was in no way heart-felt, but she wanted Janek to carry on, rather than defend himself.

'Well,' Janek continued hesitantly, 'we got more drunk and played more poker. The three of us were carelessly confident that no troops would visit Roza Dymek's again so soon…Anyway, it was not long before all my paper money was on the table. You see I had what I thought was a hell of a hand - a sure-fire winning hand. I went all in, cleaned my pockets right out. Fryderyk and Alfons still had plenty of money though, God knows where from. I had not betted sensibly: they both had turns before me and I was clean out of cash. And to make matters worse, they both thought that they had winning cards too. I looked to be out of the game, still holding a hand which I was sure was the monster at the table.'

Sarah twitched impatiently at the detail and the imagery.

'You have to understand that I thought it the killer of all hands,' urged Janek, then subsided as he realised his choice of words. In very quiet tones he continued, 'To stay in the game, they insisted that I ante up my diamonds. I refused.'

'So you lost?' said Sarah.

Janek said nothing for a moment. This was where the story really started to stink. 'No. Not the diamonds. I did not risk my diamonds.'

'What did you risk, Janek?' demanded Sarah.

'You have to realise that the war had robbed me of everything: land, home, family, job. The diamonds were the first bit of wealth to come my way in years, in all my life, actually,' he gabbled.

'What did you risk, Janek?' Sarah demanded, her voice hard with rage and suspicion and a faint quaver of tearful disbelief.

'Your daughter, Barbara. They wanted her...' His voice was tiny and pitiful…'You have to realise that I thought it the poker hand of all time. I didn't think there was any way I could lose - and it was their suggestion; Alfons's and Fryderyk's. Not mine. I would never even have thought of such a thing.'

Janek sprang closer to Sarah, tried to clutch her hand - it was so much better telling all this to her than to Joseph. She would understand; she had lived with him. She knew that he wasn't a monster.

'Get away, get away from me,' she screamed. 'You pig. You animal. How could you do that to my little girl? And after you had been paid a fortune to protect her. To think I have lived under the same roof as you.' Sarah sprang up from the sofa, at a loss what to do with her twitching limbs. She stood quivering by the mantelpiece, desperate to be as far away from Janek as possible. Suddenly her voice lowered and it was heavy with menace, 'Did they ask you to put up all the diamonds, Janek?'

Janek looked away, tears falling, decades of shame scalding his cheeks. He opened his mouth but nothing came out.

'The truth, you bastard,' screamed Sarah.

'Just two diamonds. They said that I had to put up two diamonds,' Janek wept.

Sarah insisted that he say it all again, for his broken sobbing had rendered half of the words unintelligible. When he had, she picked up a vase from the mantelpiece beside her and hurled it at him. It caught him high on the scalp and he bled immediately and profusely into his right eye.

Janek just sat there, thoroughly wretched, blinking at the flow, but not wiping at it in any way. He knew that he deserved much worse.

'You bet my little Barbara instead of just two stones? I should slash your throat open right now,' she yelled, 'From ear to ear.'

Still Janek sat there. Just sat there bleeding.

Slowly, bit by bit, his passivity allowed Sarah to master her rage. She breathed deeply, spoke calmly: 'Don't ever touch me again, Janek. If you touch me again I will kill you, even if we are only half way through my Barbara's fate I will kill you…What happened next, Janek? Tell me.'

'Won't you sit down again?'

'Fuck off. I am standing here. I cannot bear to sit near you. Now carry on.'

He did, in the lowest of tones. 'They wanted her. She was very beautiful, they had been drinking and…and…'

'And?' echoed Sarah…'And she was a Jew?'

'Yes. I think that was in there somewhere,' admitted Janek. 'Not particularly as a racial thing, I don't think, but because it meant that they could get away with it. It is my view, now, that they planned the whole thing from the start - cheated at cards just so they could have her.'

'And would you have risked her in a card game if she had been one of your own Polish, Christian girls?'

'Maybe not,' replied Janek with candour and Sarah suppressed the urge to rush to the kitchen and snatch up the longest, most vicious knife there, because after the brutal honesty of his answer, she was more than ever sure that he was telling the whole truth.

'I want every detail,' she said, gritting her teeth.

'I lost.'

'And?'

'And it happened.'

'I said every detail, damn you.'

'Immediately they jumped up and grabbed the girl.'

'Barbara.'

'Barbara,' returned Janek in an ash-grey voice.

'Neither she nor her brother knew what had been going on at the poker table, but they could see in Alfons's and Fryderyk's eyes what they wanted. Also it was clear from how they were touching her.'

Janek saw the tears rolling down Sarah's cheeks

and he turned away from her in the telling of his dirty past.

'Look at me, as you tell it, you bastard,' she screamed.

'Joseph tried to fight them off, but they were too strong for him and Fryderyk pulled a gun on him too - on them both - and hauled Barbara towards the stairs. He was twisting her arm and Alfons was yanking at her hair. Joseph was screaming and shouting. So was she.'

'What? What were they screaming for?' choked out Sarah.

'For them to leave her alone and…'

'And what else, Janek?'

'And for me to help.'

'Did you. Did you help at all?'

'I offered Alfons and Fryderyk the two diamonds if they would leave the girl alone.'

'Just the two?'

Janek nodded.

'The little Yid bitch wasn't worth any more than that on reflection?' spat Sarah.

'They wanted her, not the diamonds.'

'But you didn't bother offering, because to you, saving her wasn't worth more?'

'Yes, yes! That is true!' shouted Janek. 'I did not care enough. The girl was not important enough to me. Barbara was not important enough to me. In those few minutes she was not, I admit it.' He paused, 'That was me then, in war time; you know the two communities were never close. I am sorry.' His voice had fallen tens of decibels, it was quieter then the ticking of a clock.

'What happened next?'

'She was raped.'

'I know that.'

'By both of them. In an upstairs bedroom.'

'I want to know what happened'

'What, you want the details?'

'Yes.'

Janek dredged the words up from miles within the darkness of himself. They were terrible, fevered words: 'One held her down while the other did it. Then they switched round. The three of them were entirely naked and she was screaming for them to stop, over and over again.'

Sarah was hysterical now. 'How do you know, how do you know, if you weren't there sticking into her too?'

'Because I went up to plead with them to stop…when I heard her screaming and pleading…'

Janek howled out 'pleading' like a baby.

'Where was Joseph?' asked Sarah, trying desperately to master herself.

'I told him to stay downstairs. I thought that Fryderyk might shoot him if he appeared in the room. Joseph will tell you I was only gone a minute and always my clothes were on. He will tell you that. He must tell you that.'

Suddenly Janek became hysterical too - hysterical in his insistence that Joseph confirm these facts - and his eyes appeared to swivel independently of one another. Sarah saw that she had to calm the seething emotions between them, if she was ever to find out what else had happened to her daughter. With a massive effort she composed herself.

'I believe you Janek. I believe that you did not rape Barbara yourself.'

Her statement pulled Janek back from the brink of utter collapse.

'Now what about the landlady? What did she do?' asked Sarah.

'Oh she didn't care, she hated all Jews and she was scared of Fryderyk. Scared of the three of us. She just kept out of the way, out of sight.'

'Surely you could have done something more? Stopped your friends somehow?'

'They had got to the stage where men do not easily withdraw, particularly ones who are shot at most days. The threat of death makes many men rapists who would otherwise be gallant. They would not stop on my say-so. In fact they offered me to join them. They swore at me because I would not help them hold Barbara down.'

Janek tore at his jacket. The shame of what he had next to say boiled within him. It tumbled out in abject confession, ripped forth from nearly forty years of closely guarded secrecy. 'I had my gun...they were naked and vulnerable...I could have stopped it. Right there and then, I could have stopped it. I even raised the weapon. Your Barbara saw me and in her eyes, her lovely, sad eyes, there danced a silent cry for help. Silent, so that her attackers would not hear: she was helping me. But I turned away. I did nothing. I didn't shoot. I didn't threaten, swear, or lash out; nothing. And I have been damned for it ever since. Turning away from her was the worst thing I have ever done and I have done hundreds and hundreds of wicked things.'

'Why Janek? Why? Why could you not find it in yourself to do something - anything?' sobbed Sarah.

'I did not feel that I could,' wept Janek. 'Both Alfons and Fryderyk had saved my life on more than one occasion and I, theirs. I was just not prepared to attack them for the sake of one Jewish girl I did not know. That is the truth. And I would have had to attack them both. That is what it would have taken.' He let the admission out in a vast rush of heaved air, before collapsing backwards.

'Don't you dare,' shouted Sarah, 'I'll faint if anyone does…Then what happened? I understand that Barbara was raped, but how was it that my daughter didn't survive the night?' she continued.

Janek cleared his head and resolved to see the horrible tale through to the bitter end. If the girl's mother could take it, then so could he. 'Her screams became even louder when I turned away. They were all for my help, every single one. They were awful, tortured wails…so I do not know how it was that I heard the German patrol outside over them, but I did. They had come on account of the screams I suppose, maybe recognised my name in them too, for I was a wanted man in the area. The soldiers were not more than fifty yards from the house. I knew that it was bolted for the night, but that meant only two minutes space - at most. Immediately I rushed back to tell Fryderyk and Alfons - and to tell them that they had to shut Barbara up, or we would all be killed. But they could not, they could not even quieten her, she had become hysterical. Completely. Then I am afraid I decided to save only myself. I ran straight for the landing and the stairs. It was a narrow, rickety flight; so imagine my desperation when I found Joseph dashing up the other way.

The patrol was hammering and hammering on the door downstairs. Roza Dymek had no choice - she had to let them in. I shouted to Joseph, 'Go down. Go down. Down the stairs. Out the back.' But he was just screaming and bellowing at me, making no sense at all in his own despair and panic. I do not know whether he knew that there were German soldiers outside or whether he had just come up the stairs to try and save his sister.

Shut up I said, they will hear you. They will kill us all. Shut up. Shut up.

But Joseph would not, just like his sister, he would not. Then I heard Roza Dymek lifting the latch - and I hit your son. I had to. I had no other way of silencing him. Another time I might just have tapped him, but in my panic I cracked his skull open, right at the top of the stairs and he fell headlong down them. Next thing, the soldiers were all over the place so I dashed in past Fryderyk and Alfons and Barbara and out of the window in their room. They were naked and confused and shocked…

I heard the gunfire as I ran.

Barbara was killed in the bed alongside her two rapists that night. Joseph will not know those details because he was lying unconscious at the bottom of the stairs, with his skull fractured.'

The grief that Sarah had kept in so long exploded forth in wave after wave of wretched howls and Janek tried to shut his ears against them because he wanted to go to her, but knew that he was far too unclean to do so. Then he did watch and listen because he felt that he deserved to feel and see the awful pain. Sarah saw him staring and the shock of his hooded eyes, close on her, tamed her weeping enough to speak. 'What happened then?' she asked through her tears.

'The soldiers sent a few bullets after me, through the window, but I had sprinted a good way off and there were farm buildings dotted about which took most of the shots. So they ran back out of the house and pursued me. They did not find me though. I knew the woodland tracks, no one better. I covered about three miles and then I watched them from inside a hollow tree, watched them climb into a troop carrier and drive off. I had given them a hell of a run around and, as it happened, to a point so close to the main troop deployment, that they could not be bothered to return to the inn. I think that that was the case, anyway. Another time, and maybe not so late at night, they would have returned to arrest Roza and Joseph. Maybe it wasn't laziness though - perhaps they had given Joseph up for dead and decided that Roza was just a stupid peasant…That was not the case though, neither way round. Joseph was very badly hurt, but not dead, and Roza Dymek was never a fool. After the troop carrier had accelerated into the night, I returned to the inn.'

'Why? Why did you go back, Janek?'

'Because I did not know who was dead and who was not. At that point I had only heard gunshots, not seen their aftermath. Also, there was Joseph. In that tree hollow, I had no idea whether he was alive or not.'

'What about my little girl? Was she quite dead when you got back? What about Barbara?' coughed out Sarah.

Janek hung his head, 'She was dead. Shot.'

'I want to know everything.'

'Shot many times,' whispered Janek, avoiding Sarah's eyes and looking at a point on the wall behind her. He could see the shadow of her head going back and then rocking forward again with the force of silent sobs.

'But not Joseph,' Janek rushed out, addressing the bobbing shadow, 'He was still alive. Just. So I charged Roza Dymek with the task of saving him. After what I had done to the boy and after what I hadn't done for his sister, saving Joseph's life suddenly became like a debt of honour to me. But I could not nurse him myself for I was a wanted man.'

'Why her?' asked Sarah through tears, 'Why Roza Dymek? You said she was an untrustworthy bitch.'

'Yes. But I also said that she was greedy. I gave her two diamonds to save Joseph - two diamonds worth more than her entire inn - and I promised her three more if she saw to it that he survive the whole war. I said that she must make him well again and then hide him. In fact I promised that I would kill her if she did not. And I would have. Roza Dymek knew me well enough to know that I was not a man who threatened idly. Indeed, her father had pulled a gun on me upon my return to the inn and I had hurt him so badly, that both of the Dymeks were left in no doubt that they would die at my hands if the boy did not live. And Joseph did not die, because they cared for him like a son - out of fear. That is why he is alive today.'

'What about my Barbara, what became of her?' asked Sarah with infinite sadness.

'I carried her from the inn and buried her. I did that myself. In the forest, quite some distance from the inn. And I made sure that no part of her body was overlooked. I knew that it was the Jewish way.'

This detail proved too much for Sarah. She screamed out her anguish. Janek bawled in unison and his words were almost incomprehensible, 'I gave Roza Dymek the same two diamonds I would not risk in that fucking poker game…I am so, so sorry. So sorry.'

'Shut up!' Sarah hissed, getting a strong hold of herself. 'Shut up!'

Janek did, immediately.

'Do you remember where you buried her?' she rasped.

'Yes. Exactly where. To my dying day.'

'Then we are leaving for that place. I am going to see the spot where my daughter lies. And I am going to see her too, whatever there is left of her. I will see my darling Barbara once again. Do you understand? We are leaving today.'

'But…'

Sarah thrust determined fingers into her handbag…'I have two visas.'

Janek was summoned upright by the force of Sarah's resolution.

'That boy out there, the one you always liked, the short one…'

'Phil,' Janek replied giddily.

'That's the one. He will look after your cat while you are gone.'

'There is no Oskar, not anymore, I buried him three months ago.'

'Right…well now you are going to unbury my Barbara, because I must see her.'

Ninety minutes later the two of them were bags in

hand, closing the front door. Janek's car was parked right outside the house. Both front tyres were flat: vehicle and driver had decayed in unison. So they were walking to the station and from there, taking the train and tube to Heathrow. It was many hours till their flight to Poland. Even at a very slow shuffle, there would be time to spare.

Orchard Road was bustling: mothers pushing prams, men up ladders cleaning gutters, someone moving in, two cats fighting, half a dozen boys playing football. 'Hello Mr Lipsz,' said one of them.

'Hello Phil, how are you?' Janek replied.

'Fine.'

'What about that curling shot of yours?'

'It's getting there, Mr Lipsz...You going somewhere?'

'Yes. One last time.'

'What about the house Mr Lipsz? Do you want me to look after it, do you? And Oskar? I haven't seen him for ages.'

Janek decided not to tell Phil about Oskar.

'Not this time, Phil, thank you. That won't be necessary.'

'No?'

'No.'

Janek set off down the road, then turned back to the boy. 'It's good to see you again, Phil.'

'You too Mr Lipsz.'

'Bye Phil.'

'Goodbye Mr Lipsz.'

Sarah was a model of patience throughout the exchange, just stood a little way off and took in the sights of the street. Down at the bottom of it, near the council houses, was a blue Renault that she remembered.

Janek drew level with her. They walked together, but preserved a perfect metre's distance.

'Renault woman is down there,' said Sarah. It was the first thing she had said to Janek in over an hour.

He nodded, 'Like always.'

Sarah stared hard at him. 'You still haven't told her anything?'

Janek shook his head, 'Haven't spoken to anyone in months.'

'Don't you think it's about time?'

Janek looked down the road at the car.

'You do know where her husband is, don't you? You haven't forgotten?'

'No, I haven't forgotten.'

'Then make her decade, Janek - tell her.'

'I don't think she'll much like what I have to say.'

'But she'll be free of this road and free of you.'

It was fifty-one paces to the car: Janek watched and counted every one of them rather than catch Renault woman's eye early.

'…Forty-nine, fifty, fifty-one…'

He stopped beside her left wing-mirror, looked up, and caught the full force of the ragged woman's glare. She had a tooth missing - Sarah had punched it out - and she was far too lost in despondency and depression to bother with crowns or bridges. Janek made a winding motion with his right hand. Slowly the driver's side window edged down. The woman's face was hard as builders' rubble.

Janek breathed deeply, 'He's in Antanimora Prison. That's in Madagascar. He hit hard times, tried to smuggle drugs through their customs and got caught. He's not due for parole until 1984. As far as I know, the Madagascan authorities allow visitors. Give me a piece of paper and I will write the address down for you.'

Two trembling hands passed pen and paper up to Janek. 'Here,' he said a few seconds later, handing both back to the woman, 'Goodbye and good luck.'

CHAPTER 21

Within twenty-four hours Janek and Sarah had arrived in Poland. And in that time, Janek seemed to have grown in poise and physical strength. He was still thin, but no longer wasted-looking. It was as if Sarah's resolve had recharged his sinews. The old country affected the chemistry between the two of them as well: they were able to talk about Barbara and Joseph without the emotional explosions - their homeland seemed to have calmed them.

In contrast, the drive to the airport and the flight itself had been extremely uncomfortable. They had been pained in one another's company. There had been a great open wound between them and whenever either of them spoke, or even moved relative to the other, it gaped in pain and bled. But on the first Polish train they boarded, out to the south of the country, things between them changed. As the woodland and the farmsteads rattled past, they found that they could speak once more.

'How did you find me in the first place?' Janek asked.

'With great difficulty,' Sarah replied, 'After the war I spent five years in Poland, searching for Joseph and Barbara and my sister, Miriam. It was very hard going and I only ever gleaned tiny scraps of information.

They were almost always about Joseph. That made me think that he might have survived. Also, it made me pessimistic about my sister's and Barbara's chances.'

Janek listened with every particle of himself.

'In the end I arrived at the inn run by Roza Dymek. I wasn't really following a lead: I must have visited most of the inns in the southern half of the country, asking and querying. I look less obviously Jewish than the rest of my family and that helped. It was still an issue - Jewishness - in post-war Poland and my gentile appearance opened mouths. I arrived at the Dymek place on a very grey day. It was ramshackle and smelt of damp - certainly neither of my family diamonds had been lavished on it. The woman, Roza, was welcoming enough. So was her father. He walked with dreadful difficulty though, as if his legs had been terribly injured, or old age had crippled them.'

Janek blanched so much that Sarah noticed immediately the change in him.

'Wrap up,' she said, before continuing...'There was a big log fire going and I drew up to it with the stew and the strong drink I had ordered. No one else had stopped by, so the Dymeks chatted to me, particularly the old man. He took an instant shine to me - men often did in those days - and he came and sat down opposite me and ran his lustful eyes over my body, right from the very first mouthful of stew. It had been served to me by a very young woman, not Roza: she had bustled off to fix up my room. I took the girl to be the old guy's granddaughter. I could see his face in her. She laughed a little at his crudity. He didn't care, nor did I...I was after information. So I questioned him directly: described Barbara and Joseph, without

421

revealing that I was their mother, also told him their ages, where they had been last seen, and I dated their disappearance to Spring 1943.

The old man's attitude changed at once: his eyes looked upon my face, not my body. For the first time, he stopped licking his lecherous old chops at me. He became guarded. There was suspicion in his eyes, but something else too. I could not identify it. Not once, in all my years of searching and probing, had I seen a similar response. Then he hobbled off on those same gammy legs…'

Again Sarah was distracted for a moment by Janek's wheyish face.

'…It was the last I saw of him, but his daughter, Roza, shot down from upstairs, untying her apron as she came. It was obvious that the old man had limped off to inform her of my questions…Straight away she asked if I had been sent by Roman Zaleski. I did not know that such a person even existed at that point. The name meant nothing to me, but I could tell that it was important to her. So I moved my arms about in non-committal fashion, keen to get any information that I could. I lied - said that I knew Roman Zaleski - but denied that he had sent me. Immediately Roza Dymek launched into a wild story. She was almost hysterical in tone…

…Where is Roman Zaleski? she shouted, Where are the three extra diamonds he promised me? I saved his Jew. We kept him here all the war, hiding him in our barns whenever the patrols approached. All Zaleski ever did was take the dead girl. It was me left with all the blood to clear up, and a crippled father. And those two friends of his, I had to drop them out of the window myself. Heavier than bullocks they were – dead weight. But he's never been back with the three diamonds he promised…Oh no! And I nursed Joseph and tended to his wounds like he was my own son - and not a dirty, stinking Jew…

I knew then that I had finally arrived at the right place,' explained Sarah…'But why did you change your name Janek? And why didn't you give Rosa Dymek the three extra diamonds you promised her?'

'Had to change it. It wasn't safe being Roman Zaleski,' Janek replied hollowly. 'After the war, the Russians saw the old Resistance men and women as a threat, because we were an armed and organised force. So they began hunting us down one by one. It was quite systematic. So, like Joseph, I changed my name - in order to get out. My contacts helped me to a quality forger. I escaped before the Russians caught up with me. It was a close run thing; many were not so lucky…I arrived in Britain, settled, and started up my detective agency, always with a mind to finding Joseph and explaining things, also with a mind to handing over to him his family diamonds, the ones your sister had given me. I vowed never to ease my own life with them. It seemed to me immoral to live off the jewels, after what I had done. My promise to Rosa Dymek, whom I had never liked, seemed unimportant next to my desire to get the gemstones to Joseph; although I suppose, if I had not had to flee Poland quite so rapidly, I would have seen to it that she got her three extra diamonds.'

Sarah nodded. The Polish countryside slipped by. A portion of Janek's colour returned to him. Tentatively he enquired, 'Sarah? How was it that you tracked me down to Orchard Road? I mean, my new name tricked the Soviet authorities. So how did you see through Janek Lipsz to the Roman Zaleski beneath?'

'Luck. You may have tricked the Russians, Janek, but you did not trick the British. They checked on people coming out of the old Europe. They were after the war criminals and the mass murderers. They knew that villains would come over The Channel together with the genuine refugees. So they checked up on you, as well as countless others and found out that Roman Zaleski and Janek Lipsz were one and the same person. They deemed you a good man; a real refugee. That is why you were let in and allowed to stay. Both names are on your papers. I saw them.'

'You saw them?' coughed Janek, his voice going up an octave in surprise.

'Oh yes and a photograph of you. That was where luck played her hand. In 1976, the year after I arrived in Britain, the authorities relaxed their usual tight secrecy and permitted public access to the documents. I went to the archives looking for Roman Zaleski but found Janek Lipsz. From there it was easy to get hold of your address.'

'I see,' nodded Janek, 'So you only arrived in Britain in '75?'

'That's right. Before that, I spent many years searching the mainland for Joseph and for Roman Zaleski - to find and love my son and to kill Zaleski - to kill you. You see, Roza Dymek told me her version of that terrible night - what she thought she knew - which was that you had raped Barbara along with your two friends and that you had clubbed Joseph nine parts dead afterwards.'

Janek felt a wave of nausea.

'Even as she told me these things, though, it was clear that she was after my assistance. I never told her that the two teenagers of her story were my children. In fact she seemed to think that I was a lover of yours, or had been. So she asked me if I would help her to those extra diamonds you had promised. She wanted me to remind you of your debt to her, and for me to collect it as well, if I could. She had it in her head that I might find you in France or Switzerland. Also that Joseph had gone to one or other of those two places. I don't know why she thought that. Anyway, her hunches were all that I had to go on, so I searched both countries after Poland.'

'You could not have been much further from Britain and Paraguay.'

'And I fell ill too, which slowed me down. During the war I was forced to farm and dig ditches in northern Germany - I think I told you before. It was back-breaking work with little food and I succumbed to its effects a number of years after the actual ordeal. For a long time I was very weak. That kept me from crossing over to England sooner…'

Sarah paused.

'…My blonde hair saved me. I was taken for a Pole when my mother and father were identified as Jews. They pretended that I was their servant. That was why I got the work detail on the farms and they got…' Sarah's voice tailed off. Janek stared grimly ahead.

'Miriam got out with my children and father's diamonds, but the three of them were quickly caught. I heard from survivors that they had given their guards the slip…actually escaped the cattle trucks. In the end though, it was only really Joseph who escaped wasn't it?' Sarah's tone demanded an answer.

'Yes. He was the only one who really escaped,' Janek replied grimly.

'Once Roza Dymek had recounted everything, I knew that my daughter had been killed, that my son had been injured but nursed back to health, and that my sister was almost certainly dead - Joseph had told her about the gunshots back on the road, the ones he'd heard in his aunt's direction. Roza Dymek passed all this on to me.' Sarah let fall one enormous tear before continuing: 'And even if it was just out of fear and greed, she did a good job of caring for my boy so when I departed I left her ten times the price of my meal. Then I determined to find Joseph and you - in that order.'

'But it happened the other way round,' commented Janek, surprised at his own interrupting of Sarah.

'Yes…and not in France or Switzerland, but in England. When I discovered where you lived, your actual address, I sat and sharpened my knife for an entire day. I didn't do one other thing. Didn't eat, didn't drink. And you know, I almost sunk the blade into your neck a few seconds after we first met, down by the double doors to your office.'

'But when you saw the photograph of Joseph inside the office and found out that I was searching for him too, you knew that you had to spare me?'

'That's right. And work with you too - or most likely, never set eyes on my son again. That's why I came back the next day to offer you my services. You see, there was no government information on Joseph, unlike on you. He must have slipped through their net.' Sarah took two short breaths. 'Janek, how did you come by my Joseph's photograph? I just don't see how…'

'Barbara's clothes; things had spilled out of her pockets when…when...'

'Go on,' nodded Sarah.

'…when she was attacked. I picked them up afterwards. Obviously she had secreted away some family photographs. I kept only a couple. One was that image of Joseph which ended up on my wall. When I set up in England I had it enlarged and framed, but not before commissioning hundreds of copies. Every one of my escapees got one.'

Sarah nodded again.

Janek cleared his throat, 'Not once did you let on, not once did you give yourself away Sarah, even with your son's photograph staring down at us…It must have been very hard for you; living in such close proximity to me.'

'Yes it was. I remember once standing over your body while you slept and picking out the places I was going to plunge my knife blade in…but I didn't, and we found Joseph.'

'And that night, after Joseph rang out of the blue, you left with his address and went straight to him?' asked Janek.

'Yes. I knew that I could beat you to him if I left at once - and that my vanishing would delay you too.'

'It did. I was very upset.'

Sarah shrugged.

'What happened when you got to Joseph? What was the reunion like?' inquired Janek, shyly.

'That is none of your business. It is not part of your story,' snapped Sarah, angry for the first time since England.

'Helping the two of you back together is the only bit of good I have done. I should like to know if it was a happy occasion,' pleaded Janek.

'I will not discuss it with you; it is not your business.'

Janek shrank down into his seat. Quietly, almost inaudibly, he asked, 'I was a fool to go to Joseph wasn't I?'

'No. I think it was the bravest single thing you ever did in all this nasty, vicious business,' replied Sarah.

'Does he hate me?'

'Of course.'

'Have you told him nothing about me and my search? Will you tell me that?'

'Yes I have,' answered Sarah crisply, 'Rather often actually, and he was interested, but it made no difference to his hatred for you. Did you ever really believe that it would?'

'I spent so long rehearsing what to say,' Janek whispered.

'There is no amount of rehearsal could ever make your story clean, Janek. You once told me there wasn't a person alive old enough to hear it. You were right.'

'I could have done nothing else, then?'

'You might have written to him, I suppose, rather than just mumbling 'forgive' on his doorstep - with dried vomit on your face. Did you know that you had vomit on your face when you called?'

Janek shook his head.

'I will tell Joseph the things he does not know; the things he is unaware of because you battered him nearly dead while they were happening…He still suffers from terrible migraines to this day, you know.'

Janek shuffled his feet…'I don't…I don't suppose I can…can ever meet with J…'

'No. You will never see Joseph again. Absolutely never,' Sarah replied.

Once the train arrived at their destination the two of them secured a bus to take them farther out into the country. Afterwards it became necessary to hitch lifts, even to walk. On their fifth day of travelling they came to roads and pathways that Janek remembered from his Resistance days. Most of the time they talked as they had on the train, chipping away at the past and at how their pasts interlinked. Occasionally, mundane matters intruded such as food and lodging and transport - the two of them had nothing booked: no vehicles, no accommodation, no connections.

They were an odd couple, certainly an old pair to be thumbing rides on tankers and jumping on to antiquated buses and stopping at midnight inns, but their very strangeness interested people and opened doors which might otherwise have remained shut. Everyone wanted to know about them, especially after hearing the dilute twang of their Polish accents. They wanted to know where they had been and what they had done for their native brogue to have become so softened. Janek and Sarah revealed only snippets of their history.

In all it took them more than a week to get to the

narrow and twisting Cracow road that they wanted - the one upon which Janek had first met the fleeing Miriam and Barbara and Joseph. On one side of the road was a farm - a piggery - on the other, a series of drainage ditches. Their ride, a hay truck, crunched to a halt. One of the farm's boars flicked its ears at the vehicle. There was a vast wooden frame fitted to its neck and shoulders, roughly triangular in shape. The piggery fence had gaps all along it. The frame was obviously designed to keep the pig in as it was larger than each of the gaps: a cost-effective solution. Janek and Sarah climbed down from the cab of the truck. It was the fifth they had travelled in.

Sarah wanted to walk the rest of the way to the Dymek inn. She wanted to tread the same ground her children had trodden; she wanted her footsteps to follow her sister's fatal ones. She said nothing, but Janek read these things. 'It was up there,' he said, 'That's where the shots came from.'

A muscle twitched at the side of Sarah's mouth. 'My children,' she said hollowly, 'In which direction did you saviours take them?'

Janek followed a blackbird's dipping flight rather than return Sarah's stare. 'We passed up this way, beyond the ditches and then up between the hills and the trees…'

Janek was about to provide details…to explain why he had chosen the dipping and rising terrain…to say that the Resistance fighters had often used the cover of trees to mask their movements from those marching, or driving, along the road. He stopped short though: he could tell that Sarah's mood was changing. She had become tearful and snatched at curls of hair which obscured her vision…stray locks which had not bothered her before.

Watching her, Janek remembered his first ever words to Barbara, immediately after they had heard her aunt being shot: 'Hurry up you little fool.' He had rasped them out into the war time air, sharply and dismissively. Shame scalded him as he recalled the hot words.

'What did you say to my children as you dashed along?' Sarah sobbed.

'Not much. There wasn't the time. The gunshots had just rung out from down by the road.'

'Not much? But what?' pressed Sarah.

'I can't remember,' lied Janek. Then he stopped walking, stood still. 'That is not true. I do remember. I called your daughter a little fool because she paused at the sound of the gunfire. I made her hurry on. I was not sensitive. There was no time for sensitivity.'

'Anything else?' asked Sarah, her eyes pearly with trembling tears.

'Nothing else. My manner did not invite conversation.'

They walked on in silence then, and rapidly, as if copying the conditions of thirty-four years before. Janek knew where he was going. The way was full of familiar landmarks: old oaks he had sniped from behind, ditches in which he had hidden, burnt out houses he had torched as punishment for their occupants' collaboration, a tall old beech tree from which a German soldier, caught outside alone, had been hanged by one leg and beaten to death.

'We shall have to be careful when we arrive at the inn. It may still be owned by the Dymeks, but then again it may not. Perhaps it will no longer be an inn at all,' said Janek, in an attempt to chase away the scalding image of the dangling soldier.

Sarah nodded, clearly irritated that the silence had been broken. She had been imagining her children's footsteps and was trying to match them exactly.

'If it is still in the family,' continued Janek, 'you may have to go in on your own. And I will have to find somewhere else to pass the night. Somewhere out here. It should not be hard; I did it often enough during the war.'

Sarah snapped her head up. 'Why?' she flashed, suddenly suspicious, 'You are not backing out now.' And she actually advanced menacingly upon Janek. 'You will not run out on me.'

'No I will not, it is just…'

'Just what?' snarled Sarah, so close to Janek's face that he could actually see the pores of her nose contracting.

'Step back and I shall tell you,' said Janek, struggling to preserve a calm front.

Sarah stepped back, although still deeply perturbed at Janek's comment.

'You remember you said before that Roza Dymek's father hobbled about on painful legs and that you thought that he must have been crippled by an injury or old age?'

'Yes?' Sarah answered warily.

'It was not old age that crippled him. It was me.'

'You?'

'Yes. Me…When I returned to the inn after the soldiers had given up the chase, he and his daughter, Roza, were not happy to see me. They thought that I had made targets of them and that the Germans would be back and maybe cart them off. Also, one of the soldiers had punched Roza in the face. Nothing special by the standards of the time, but it was clear that the two Dymeks thought that it might well be a taste of worse to come - if they had anything more to do with Roman Zaleski. So they began screaming at me to leave the second I returned. I barely listened to them though, for I was too busy staring at Joseph - head smashed, one arm jutting out crazily - half lying in the main parlour and half on the bottom three steps, leading down to it. In his broken form I didn't just see what had happened to him, I saw what had happened to his sister upstairs too. And guilt leered horribly at me. I could focus on nothing else. The Dymeks were just background squawking to me…That is why I did not see the old man approach with his luger pistol.

I first noticed his eyes - when he interposed them between me and Joseph: cold, ready-to-kill eyes. They were what broke my guilty trance. I hit him, hard as I could, right in the throat. His age-dulled reactions were what saved me. As he gagged in agony, I got the gun away from him. Roza Dymek rushed me then, but I had their gun and I had my own too, and after having dropped my guard once, I wasn't about to drop it again. In a moment I had them both on the floor.'

'The old man's legs though?' asked Sarah.

Janek inclined his head a little. 'I realised that Joseph would die unless I could force these scared and angry people to nurse him back to health. There was no way I could treat him. I was a wanted man, living my life on the run. I felt the diamonds in my pocket and decided there and then that I would pay the

Dymeks to save him. But I knew that gems alone would not persuade them; I could tell that they needed the additional incentives of pain and terror...So I tied the old man up to a chair: his feet to the legs, his arms to its back, and then I kicked Roza time and time again, all over her body, until she agreed to fill an old copper bath full to the top with boiling water.'

Sarah leant back against a tree trunk, horrified at what she knew was coming.

'Yes,' Janek nodded. 'At gunpoint, I made her place that bath at her own father's feet and then I tipped the chair back and then down again so that his tied legs were in boiling water right up to the knees. And I held that chair in place till I could hear in both of their screams that they really would save the boy and hide him too - till the end of the war. And I promised them that I would be back to kill them both if he did not live, and because of what I had done to the old man, they knew that I meant it.'

Janek paused.

'Then I made doubly sure of them by plunging the old man's legs back in the water - so that there could be no mistaking my seriousness.'

Sarah's upper lip curled in disgust. Janek noticed every millimetre.

'Do you think that they would have saved a half-dead Jew-boy otherwise, Sarah? It would have taken just one hour of cold, night air to have killed him stone dead. Neither of them would have had to do anything more than to drag Joseph outside and leave him there.'

Sarah's lip relaxed.

'So you see, I might not be entirely welcome at the inn - if either old man Dymek, or his daughter are still there…I can't believe that the father would still be alive today, but she may well be. And that is the reason why I might not stay under the same roof as you tonight. Bear in mind, that old luger pistol could still be in residence too and I am taking no chances. It only needs one person with a good memory for faces to take a shot at me and then our whole trip will be at an end.'

'You did not keep the gun then?' asked Sarah, her voice shaky as she imagined the torture bath.

'Oh no. Not at all. I thought that the Dymeks might need it one day to defend Joseph. And I figured that they would not be likely to get their hands on another one - I knew what it took to get hold of such German guns.'

Sarah gave a little sideways movement of her head which betrayed that she did not know what it took to get hold of such German guns.

'You spent a long time farming those Boche fields, didn't you? You have no real idea how things worked back home,' said Janek without a whiff of condescension. He could tell that she was no longer suspicious of him and as talking to her was less painful than watching her peer into the leaf litter for phantom footsteps of her children, he determined to tell Sarah how the country peasants got their lugers.

'Generally, a young soldier would be lured out to the woods, usually by a pretty girl who valued revenge more then her chastity. Then when he was in that most vulnerable of positions, he would be killed - stabbed by the girl herself or garrotted from behind by her friends. It was a nasty business, because the only soldiers stupid enough to get caught that way were the ones who actually took 'no' for an answer from our Polish girls. The ones who just ravished any woman they wanted weren't so desperate. And...' Janek stopped dead - he was echoing Barbara's last moments far too closely.

'I don't want to talk anymore, Janek. I just want to get to the inn. How much further is it now?'

'We should be there in fifteen minutes,' Janek replied, angry with himself for sledge-hammering through so many raw nerves.

An unpleasant atmosphere curled thickly: Janek worrying about who might be in residence at the inn, Sarah walking grimly on, images of poor Barbara's violent end filling her head. The only positive was that a heavy twilight was deepening and Janek could not see the misery etched into his companion's face. To catch sight of it would have been to witness too directly the consequences of his immorality.

There were bats and owls about. The clouds were mackerel-blue. But it did not rain. Rain would have been a release.

It did not rain.

Janek stopped.

'What have you stopped for?' came a voice which was one tenth Sarah and nine tenths gin-trapped wolf.

'The last marker - a fork in the path.' Janek squinted into the bushes and the spaces between them...

'There,' he said at last. 'That is the way.'

They slithered and slipped in the gloom, down a secret track trodden only by badgers and foxes since the end of the war. Thorny branches whipped at them on their way and there was a trickle of water that they could hear, but not see, which added to the ooziness of the descent.

They toiled for more than the fifteen minutes Janek had estimated when suddenly he said, 'There is a building, barns too.' Quickly he grabbed at an exposed root to stop his descent. Sarah thudded into him, then scrambled clear, distressed that they had touched.

'That is the place,' Janek croaked. 'I am certain of it.'

Immediately Sarah fired questions at him. She wanted to know the time of their arrival in 1943...She wanted to know whether her children had been tired...She wanted to know whether her children had held on to one another on the way down...She wanted to know whether Barbara had ever mentioned her...She wanted to know why the world was such a God-forsaken hole...

'You must go first,' said Janek cutting through. 'You must find out if the place is still an inn, and if it is, you must find out whether the old Dymeks are still there. Only if they are not, can I follow you inside. Say that you stayed there in the 40s. Ask about the old timers; see if you can shake any of them out of the woodwork. Go. I will wait here.'

Janek expected an argument, but Sarah asked only for the route her daughter had taken. Janek pointed it out as best he could in the meagre light. She followed it.

It was strange watching the woman he had once hoped would be his, walking towards the scene of his greatest moral fall. How fate had had its laugh at him - he was the insect skewered on the pin, still revolving, alive...

Janek saw the door open to Sarah. Alone on the broad root he wept. Cold, bowed, dirty without and within, he sobbed.

He worked hard to be dry-eyed when Sarah burst back up the bank…

'Roza Dymek's youngest daughter is there now and the inn is still in business. Her mother and grandfather died years ago. She has rooms for the night and food too. I said that we had got separated in the woods, but that I would return with you. She seemed delighted that I was an old visitor; even more delighted at the dollars I showed her. Let us hurry.'

An angry, stinging wind sprinted up the bank and harassed Janek like canvas. It buffeted him this way and that. He rose, slipped, rose again…and a few seconds later there came shining for them an outside light from the inn: an electric lamp switched on, high in the eaves of the gable end. The old place looked exactly as it had in all Janek's tortured dreams. He ran the rest of the nightmare through his head: the screaming parboiled old man, his screaming daughter, the slumped Joseph, and the bullet ridden Barbara, dead beneath the dead meat of her two rapist-attackers.

Janek searched Sarah's eyes, probing for a softness which might answer his needs. 'Hold my hand,' he pleaded.

'What?'

'Or my arm, if you prefer.'

'What? I'll never…' spat Sarah.

Janek slowed to a halt, 'Then I cannot go down there. I cannot…This once, you must help me. Then tomorrow, when it is light, I will be strong enough to do whatever you want.'

Gingerly, coldly, Sarah took hold of Janek's arm, like it was a lump of rotten old meat she was scooping out of precious, clean water.

'Thank you,' he whispered.

The gable lamp framed the Dymek place, but the glass of the windows stared out at Janek like the cold, soulless eyes of landed fish. He jolted. 'I cannot have an upstairs room. I must have a ground-floor room - you must tell her,' he wailed, 'You must tell the woman.' And he clawed at Sarah in animal desperation. She took his hand then and stared at him. To Janek her eyes were indistinguishable from the fish eyes and try as he might, he could not see the woman beneath.

'Janek!' came a voice from the fishmonger's slab, 'Janek, you have always known this day would come - one way or another - with Joseph, without Joseph, or on your own. Always you have known.'

'Have I?' moaned Janek pathetically.

'Yes. It is only me you did not foresee.'

'Only you?' Janek repeated and the angry wind lashed him once more. It was cold and hard and he wished with a soul-hunger that Sarah's eyes were not the same. 'Sarah, do you forgive me?' gasped Janek, clutching at her face. 'I know Joseph cannot, but can you?'

'A ground floor room Janek...that is what you need,' she replied and her face was hard as basalt rock.

Janek looked crushed.

'Will you help me in there, Sarah? Please?'

'More than you helped my Barbara.'

Janek hung his head at her answer and the wind, like an executioner's axe, slashed at his exposed neck.

Strongly, urgently, Sarah yanked her burden along and a minute later the two of them were standing within the Dymek hall.

Janek could not look the young landlady in the face. He was scared that he would see her grandfather there, or that she would recognise in his own aged features the torturer of 1943: there was no knowing who else might have been in the house that terrible night or whether key holes had been looked through.

The angle of his vision took in the fire - still log-burning. Janek saw Barbara and Joseph huddled around it. There was also the same rough-hewn table occupying central position, the one around which he and Alfons and Fryderyk had played their cards. Then out the corner of his eye, Janek spied the curve of the stairs where Joseph had lain slumped and the joints in the floorboards where the boy's blood had pooled. He snapped his eyes shut and let out a strangled sob.

'My companion is exhausted,' explained Sarah. 'His legs are too weak to climb stairs; is there a ground floor room he can have for the night?'

It was an irregular request, but Roza Dymek's daughter remembered the fist-full of American dollars that had been flashed at her. 'Certainly, I can fix one up,' she replied, 'And would you like something to eat?'

'Just the room,' gasped Janek.

'My companion needs to lie down as soon as possible, but I will have something; something hot and meaty.'

Janek did not open his eyes once while the room was being prepared: the past was less intense with them shut. But in spite of this protective measure, his other senses did slip him down through the decades: sometimes he could hear himself - his young self - pacing the floorboards, shouting threats at the scalded Dymek grandfather. At other times there was the smell of cordite from the shootings and the rank, rank sweat of fear. When he touched the hard, dark wood of the furniture, his fingers almost curled to pick up the cards that Fryderyk had dealt him…

'Your room is ready, sir.'

Janek allowed himself a little upward glance. The inn-keeper had her mother's jaw, her grandfather's eyes. He recalled the last time he had locked with those eyes and looked abruptly away. 'Thank you,' he said, turning involuntarily to the stairwell. There he saw Joseph, crumpled - everywhere provided awful viewing.

'Come on,' said Sarah, going to him. She offered her arm. It took them twelve paces to cover the route along which Janek had hauled Barbara's dead body out of the inn. It was torture for him. Again he shut his eyes, this time to block out the trail of blood she had left. Then Sarah led him sharp right into an unfamiliar room. Quickly she slammed the door to, sensing that it was what Janek needed. Inside it smelled of fresh sheets and lavender, not blood or sweat or Nazi cordite. Janek inhaled, what seemed to him, his first clean breath since entering the building.

'I will bring you some food,' said Sarah.

'No. Not for me. I said that I did not want any,' replied Janek, shaking his head.

'You will have some food,' commanded Sarah, 'It is the price of my support. Tomorrow you must dig and that is not a task to be undertaken on an empty stomach.' She left him in his refuge and went to check on the progress of the lamb stew that she could smell cooking. Her intention was to spoon as much of the meat into Janek as possible. Then, hopefully, he would be physically fit to dig the next day. Come the morning she hoped to turn up a spade in one of the outbuildings.

The inn seemed very informal. Sarah had no idea whether it was ever thus, or whether her dollars had made it so. Whichever it was, she felt completely comfortable opening doors and peering into corners. She went into a number of back rooms. They were scruffy with pans and crockery and utensils. Next to a side door she found a solid-looking spade, well-riveted at the lug. Sarah glanced over her shoulder to check that she was not being watched then tucked it away. That was one job done - no need to search the outbuildings in the morning.

After she had fed Janek, who took a fair bellyful of meat at her insistence, she continued her search of the ground floor: there were certain other things required for the next day. And the fact that the young landlady had retired upstairs after cooking the lamb made Sarah's job that much easier. A sleepy dog did growl at her once, but immediately it read Sarah's determination and so did not move against her.

Upstairs in her own room, Miss Dymek stared in wonder at the $50 note that had been handed to her. She tried it against both ears and listened to the lovely rustle of freedom.

To her surprise, it took Sarah just one hour to find everything for the next day. She went back into Janek's room and wrapped the items in a spare blanket. Then she turned her attention to him. He was staring blankly at a coat peg. 'I need to know which room it was,' she said matter-of-factly.

Janek's coat peg leered at him.

'Where Barabara died,' she explained, although Janek needed no explanation.

'Why?' asked Janek pathetically.

'Because I have a choice of rooms - now that you are down here - and I want to sleep in my daughter's room.'

'Turn left at the top of the stairs. Then it is the first door on your right,' he mumbled quickly.

'No,' responded Sarah. 'You must show me. This building might have changed or been altered.'

'But…' replied Janek.

Sarah held up an imperative hand.

'But…' Janek tried again.

Sarah shook her head.

'But we have already told the girl that I cannot get up the stairs.'

'Then we must be quiet and hope that she stays in her room.'

Like the house dog, Janek read Sarah's inner steel and swung his legs onto the floor.

The corridor in reverse was just as harrowing as before - still full of blood.

'Can't you just climb the stairs and tell me what you see?' Janek pleaded.

'No.'

'I can't do it,' he whined at the bottom of them.

'If you could let my Barbara be dragged up by her hair, then you fucking well can do it,' Sarah snarled.

'Or must I drag you?'

The threat got Janek moving. He scuffed his feet one over the other and at the same time, the smells and the sights and the sounds of that fateful night came back to him full-flood. He could smell violent sex and he could see Joseph lying bloody on the floor. The gorge of what he had eaten rose within him.

Every step was agony, for he could see himself at the top of the flight, lashing out with the stock of his gun, and the splash of blood on it, streaked all the way down to the barrel…He dared not pass himself at the head of the stairs.

Janek stopped, his head just level with the banister rail. He peered fleetingly over it - registered that the old room was still there. The door was open and he saw once again where his friends and Barbara had died. He took in the patches on the wall where a number of the soldiers' bullets had missed their human targets. Someone had done a very amateur plastering job.

'It is the room,' Janek gasped.

'Is it the same bed?' hissed Sarah, now drawing level with him.

'Oh for God's sake…'

'You mean your sake,' she growled.

'Alright…my sake,' sobbed Janek uncontrollably. 'I do not know. I cannot remember beds. For pity's sake let me go back down.'

Janek looked decades older than his sixty-six years: his mouth hung open as he sucked in desperate air. Sarah stared at the pathetic old man and derived strength from his tears, simply because she was not weeping herself. 'Get down,' she scoffed. 'We set out at five tomorrow. Sleep if you can.' Then she passed

Janek roughly by, her spade and collection of finds scraping hard against him from within their blanket wrap. She had decided to sleep with them in her room - they were far too important to leave anywhere else.

'Won't you help me back to my room?' Janek pleaded.

'No. Tomorrow there is worse to come. You must learn to cope.' And with that 'cope', Sarah slipped into Barbara's room and shut the door. She ran her fingers along the bed covers, along the rough plaster of the back wall, through the brass patterns of the bedstead. Then she slipped to her knees and prayed. She whispered the prayer so that Janek should not hear. She would not have him be party to it.

It was an unnecessary precaution: Janek could hear nothing but gunshots and screams and shouts in German and his own heart rattling. The long walk back through the cacophony unmanned him totally. He was gibbering when he finally made it back to his ground floor room. He slammed the door shut on the deafening past.

Sarah was back at his bedside by four-fifty a.m. with the spade in her right hand and a flask in her left. 'We leave in ten minutes,' she said.

The sight of the spade made Janek's eyes start in their puffy bags. She was really going to go through with it then - digging up the body. The flask sickened him; his mind ran to picnics. It was as if Sarah intended to make a macabre jaunt out of the exhumation.

'The spade is for you,' she said, offering it to him.

He did not take it at once.

'This is where the Disappearance Club started didn't it? Wasn't my girl the first person you hid without trace?'

Janek looked everywhere but Sarah's eyes.

'Take the spade, Janek. The Club is being disbanded today.'

The walk back up the badger track was much easier in the early light. There was not much cloud cover and the sun was shining strongly. A young athletic wind was blowing, not yet troublesome, but threatening to firm up. It might have been the same one as the night before - or a fresh companion.

On the incline, oaks and chestnuts swept down low: massive trees with cross-sabre branches. Overhead, squirrels chittered and raced their endless arboreal trails. Off to the right the stream which the two of them had heard the night before, but not seen, was revealed. It was a fast-running brook which chattered sweetly, picking up a darker colour and a little warmth from the cow dung which steamed at intervals along its length.

'Where are we heading?' asked Sarah.

'The caves. The limestone caves.'

'How far are they?'

'A mile and a half.'

Sarah puckered her mouth, raised an eyebrow. Janek read her thoughts.

'I was fit and strong then, also the way was well trodden in 1943. And your daughter was light, even in death.' Janek was shocked at the detail coming out of him. 'I knew there were rocks there - to cover the grave with. The people hereabouts were starving, so most of their dogs had been turned out by 1943: no one could afford to feed an extra mouth. I had seen packs of them eating dead bodies by the roadsides. It was quite a way to go uphill with her, but I was determined that Barbara would not be eaten.'

Janek thought he saw a flicker of respect in Sarah's face.

They pushed on past the night before's trail. On all sides, trees closed ever more tightly in. The stream meandered too and flowed almost into their new path. The resultant mud clutched at their boots.

'These trees were all cut and broken back in the war: every month we ferried guns and dynamite up through the woods here and hid them in the caves. I should think that there are still boxes of both down in the deepest holes.'

Sarah was sweating with exertion: 'It is a hard slog, Janek. I can't imagine carrying someone up here. Why did you care so much?'

'I owed it to Barbara,' he replied simply, 'Because I did nothing for her in life. And if I had left her, the Dymeks would just have tossed her into the first ditch they came to.' He was crying now - his first tears of the day, but Sarah was dry as desert sand. 'She was the only person I bothered burying all war, maybe my efforts were for all of them,' he choked out.

They came to the top of a ridge and stood beside the stream's source: a little bubbling spring.

'May I have some?' asked Janek, pointing to Sarah's flask. He had overcome his negative feelings towards it. She nodded. He took a deep swig, assuming that it would be tea or coffee. He spat most of the mouthful out.

'Whisky?!' he spluttered.

'I packed it for me, the spade was for you,' said Sarah by way of explanation.

Janek felt the spirit burn all the way down. Maybe that was what was keeping her tears at bay? He drank from the spring instead - until he was quenched and the taste of the alcohol dissipated.

Straight ahead were more woods: close growing birch and pine trees. The land was flatter and drier. Nimble little rodent feet skittered under leaves. Their scurrying acted to form a question in Janek's mind. Next thing he knew he was saying it out loud: 'Has Joseph any children of his own?' he asked timidly, his voice mousy with fear - fear that Sarah would not grant him an answer.

'Yes, two, a boy and a girl,' she replied, surprising herself at the immediacy with which she supplied the information. 'You chased them through Asuncion's streets.'

'So those two kids weren't just creations of my mind. I saw them and they...'

'They were real. You terrified them,' interrupted their grandmother.

Janek stopped between two huge birches, 'Tell me about them. Have you said anything to them about me? Does the girl know of my part in your finding her? Please tell me.'

'Maybe later,' replied Sarah sharply.

Desperate questions and a hot desire for answers trembled Janek's lips. 'Couldn't you tell me just a little and then later on we...'

'Which is our way?' pressed Sarah, refusing to be drawn.

'Another half mile through these woods,' Janek answered absently, lost in weepy recollection of the girl's face and how perfectly like Barbara's it was.

They pushed on for fifteen minutes, until the trees began to thin and he began to master his tears. Then Janek came to a halt and pointed. 'There!' he said, 'Can you see the limestone outcrop? That is where the caves start. We must head for them. And we must search for an old holly tree. It always stood out from the birch and pine around it...I picked it for Barbara's headstone.'

Sarah grew scared: 'What if the tree has been chopped down?' For the first time in the morning her voice cracked a little and when Janek looked at her, he saw that her eyes were wet.

'I don't think so. In these parts they think it unlucky to fell holly and the wind wouldn't have brought it down. Holly roots for good. I remember that I had to dig ten paces away from the trunk, so thick were its roots '

Sarah swigged from her flask.

'Come on,' Janek said.

An hour later they found the tree. It had two colossal trunks, both perfectly straight. It was male: there wasn't a berry on it.

Fifty metres away there gaped three huge open shafts into caves. Sarah said nothing, but her heart warmed a little towards Janek, like the stream in among the steaming dung. It would have been so easy for a hard-pressed man on the run just to have dropped Barbara's body straight down one of the immense holes.

'How far down do they go?' she asked.

Janek was surprised at her question; it seemed so out of place. He was jittery and the big spade shook in his hands. 'The one on the left is deepest,' he replied quickly.

There was a cairn of rocks set about ten metres from the holly tree. Janek walked unsteadily over to it. Sarah blanched at it…and followed.

'Here,' he quavered. Then, as quickly as his trembling hands would allow, Janek dismantled the cairn.

Sarah swallowed down a mouthful of whisky.

Neither of them said anything.

A raven landed.

The sun shone fit to dazzle.

The bird jabbed at, and caught, a dragonfly.

Janek sunk the spade. It cut deeply. His tears flecked the handle.

Sarah drank and watched, her eyes resolutely dry once more.

Janek sunk the blade time and time again. After old holly leaves and pine needles and wormy topsoil, came limestone rubble. For every spadeful of earth there were two of unforgiving rock. It was in hefty brick-sized lumps and with each one, Janek had to find an edge and work away at it in order to lever the stone free. The going was slow - about a foot an hour.

The raven returned and with it came a harrying wind. Janek fixed his tear-blown eyes on the big hook-billed bird and screamed at it. How did they always know?

The wind blew even harder, snatching at his spade and whirling the soil and rock fragments. They were in his hair and mouth and he was sobbing - at his past and at his lack of success. He had dug down a metre, but where was the body? He had not buried the girl any farther down. He was sure of it.

He wheezed out his distress.

Then the raven called. Janek saw red, spun round, hurled a rock at it. The bird scattered in alarm. That was when he noticed Sarah staring at the hole. Her eyes were no longer dry. She was every inch the expectant mother, but there was only limestone for her to see. Limestone and wormy soil. They were not what she had come for.

'Ignore the bird,' she wept.

Janek could smell the whisky on her words. And before the fume had risen higher than the gravestone-holly, the raven had landed again, this time with two more of its kind.

'Ignore the birds,' Sarah repeated.

Janek shovelled out more limestone; lumps the size of melons now, some of them. There was clay as well, in among the rock which made their edges hard to prise up. Janek cried desperately, both feet in the hole, as he strained to lever the sticky slabs free.

Was it just a hole? Wasn't it a grave at all? Had his memory deceived him?

The same terrible thoughts were searing away within Sarah's head. Was there anything down there at all? But try as she might, she could no longer even see to the bottom of Janek's hole, because her hot tears and his straining legs were in the way.

Half a dozen ravens called.

Janek kept upright in the charging wind only because he was working at a metre's depth. Just his upper body showed. Sarah was seated on the mound of earth and limestone rubble that he had shovelled up. The wind and the anxious uncertainty were forces too strong for her to stand up against.

Janek had been digging for over three hours.

With every spadeful he was checking and rechecking the intricate little corrugations of his memory, to see if there was a detail of the burial he had missed. And with every stoop and bend he was aware of Sarah's awful suspense - just behind him.

He shut out the birds' cawing, as he had been told, and worked furiously, desperately. At his feet was a large limestone ball which was stuck fast with clay and old roots.

He pulled and pulled and levered with the lug of his spade. After ten minutes of this heaving, which left Janek sweating into scarlet eyes, a little gap appeared in the earth wall which provided some purchase for his shovel blade. And on the other side, deep down, he found also a hole in the stone for his fingers to work away at. The block came millimetre by millimetre, until with a sucking clabber it oozed free. Janek had to wipe his eyes before throwing the limestone ball aside: wipe them clear of tears from within, and sweat from without. Both had rendered him virtually blind. He sleeved his face part-dry. The wind took a last root edge off the lump of rock. He looked down.

It was a skull. The purchase his fingers had found was an eye socket.

The ravens cawed in unison, but this time Janek did not hear them. He let out a noise, quite inimitable. There was joy in it and sorrow and tiredness and decades of shame and a morning of hard labour and the triumph of human bone over limestone.

And Sarah recognised the sound at once. She threw her flask down and grabbed the skull. She cleaned it with feverish hands and sobbed out loving words to it.

Janek looked down at his feet and went straight back to work…not in a hole, but in a grave. In moments he had worked the remaining mud and limestone and roots clear. He had to find the rest of Barbara, immediately. Also, he did not want to sully Sarah's grief with his invasive eyes.

Other bones firmed up. There was a femur and a tibia and both clavicles, a lower jaw as well, to go with the skull he had raised, and across it lay a perfect hand with all the little bones in place. He left each precisely where it was. The wind died. Then Janek became acutely conscious of where he was standing. Suddenly he felt that his boots were profaning the grave of his victim. He jumped up from it.

The holly tree creaked somewhere up high. The ravens circled above his head and he stood before Sarah. She was looking down at the skull's eye sockets as if there were still answering pupils in them. Janek could not look away from mother and daughter; the pair of them held his sight. He felt his own wracking sobs breaking at the pity of it.

Then Sarah opened her lungs. She screamed and screamed and screamed out her loss. Even the ravens scattered at her sorrow and circled at a quieter, safer distance. She inhaled enormous chestfuls of air and expelled them in frenzied shrieking. Janek's sobbing was nothing to it. He had never felt lonelier in all his life. He stood quite motionless before this mother's grief for her murdered child.

Then, as the ravens resettled, Sarah looked up at him for the first time since holding her daughter's skull. She raised a quivering finger and snarled out, 'You!'

One terrible, accusatory word.

'You!' she repeated.

'Forgive me,' begged Janek.

'I do not forgive you,' she screamed.

'I buried her with respect.'

'I do not forgive you.'

'I saved Joseph.'

'I do not forgive you.'

'I gave up my life for the search.'

'I do not forgive you.'

'There has not been one day I haven't regretted…'

'I do not forgive you,' Sarah bawled.

'Not one diamond did I ever spend on myself,' Janek pleaded.

'I do not forgive you.'

And then Janek reached inside his coat pocket for the bag of diamonds, because he had nothing else left to say…and could think of nothing else to do, but to lay the gems on the earth beside Sarah's feet. As he reached in, though, Sarah did the same towards her own inmost pocket - she had found at the inn one special thing in addition to the spade and the flask and the whisky. And now she curled her hand around its snug firmness, at the same time that Janek felt the give of the diamonds beneath his fingers.

They took out their final comments together: Janek lay his down at Sarah's feet and Sarah shot away the top of his head.

The bullet took the scalp and bone clean off…for the last thing she had collected from the inn, off a ledge above the back door, was the old family luger, wrapped in a grubby oil cloth.

Janek lay spread-eagled across his own hummock of limestone and clay. Dead. The top-most inch of his skull was metres away, at the base of the holly tree. He bled oozily into the excavated mound, his head a crimson jug tipped past its pouring point.

'All the time, the ravens were calling for you, Janek,' Sarah said softly.

For two seconds she stared at the left-most cave shaft, the one Janek had told her was the deepest, then she grabbed hold of his right boot and hauled him with all the must-do strength she had and dropped his body…

…into her daughter's grave - right on top of Barbara's bones. Then lowered in the girl's skull; lovingly, tenderly. She retrieved the top of Janek's too and set it carefully in place above his lifeless eyes. Next Sarah shovelled back the clay and the limestone and the soil and the pine needles and the holly leaves. And with the strength of a mother's love and a revenger's necessity, she heaved the original rocks back into place, over the new joint grave. Next, she splashed the last of the whisky over the blood stains that her shovelling had missed.

At last she stood still over the barrow.

'I forgive you now,' Sarah said and then turned away from Janek and her daughter.

Back at the inn, Sarah returned the luger pistol to its little spot, the spade too. She apologised to Miss

Dymek for the depletion of her whisky and then strode off from the inn, back along the old Cracow road.

No one discovered that the gun had been given an airing, nor that it was one bullet short, but the envelope that Sarah had left taped to the main bedroom window was found within an hour of her leaving. Inside it was another $50 note and three of her father's best diamonds.

THE RUFUS CODE:

1,5/16,23,27,38,52,54/62,65,91,102,115/138,142,1065
/1066,1078/1082,1109,1120,1121,1126,1193/1200,
1220/the/

2,8,30,38,49/92,99,109,131,136,144,145,163/190,192,
226,242,277./391,400,401,408,409,410/416,419/470,
538/539,540,546/585,586,596/608,622/656,675/

28,29,30,32,88,97,102./104,111,116,118,125,131/159,
194,202/205/231,238,308,313,314,319,345/347,357/
431,432,443,525,537,549/551,560,1358,1359,1360,
1369,1370,1387/

29,46/53,69/84,97,131,133,180,188,197,198,204./223,
225,231,239,243/340,357,366,367/372,380/503,515,
517,526,527,528,529,532,543/553,557/

31,32,33/78,79,92,135,146,150,178,210/262,264/266,
267,283,288/294,295,296/297,316,357/407,414,434,
440,444/

6,100/103,179,224,225,258,278./283,291,297/326,349,
350,351,381,412,458,461,468,469,470,471,562,570/
592,593,681/699,765/

34,92,101,104,107,113/146,152/158/165,167,181,188/
196,202,207,208,243./255,298,324,335,342/345,365,
434,454/561,583,588/

1,4/12,16…27,28,51/70,72,81,85,96,114,225/236,251,
254/295,345,361,380,382/386,390,409/415,485,502/
511,520/527,533,534/

10,25,38,54,66/100,106,107,110/119,133,144,188,192,
193,194/216,222,236,238,244,246,262,274/281,289,
308,318,336,337,338,339./351,366,367/375,393,416,
426,432,433,455/

6,10,133,136,138,140,152,156/171,262/279,280,281/
289,297,666/829,865,876/882,894,896,952/1031,1036
/1323,1339,1384,1386,1387,1419,1428,1429,1433,
1503/

3,11,17,18/333,338,353/457,462,510,511/525,528,531,
548/555,557,566/572,635,638/645,724,730,741,747,
853,854,859,892/894,895/

12,30/66,67,408,409,411',415/438,445,491,498,506/
609,610,670,675,687,703,710,713,767/771,772,773,
774,775/785,850,853,881,882,918,921,964/966,967,
1143, 1162/PHILIPTHESECONDOFSPAIN.

Triangle, Rhombus, Hexagon, Octagon, Polygon.
Do not worry about regularity.

***

*He/she who solves the code…or believes he/she is detective
enough to have done so, please visit the website:*

www.thinkingplainly.com

.

ABOUT THE AUTHOR

I usually wear glasses; hence my staring myopically out at you from this photograph. Black-and-white they told me it had to be...but to my mind it makes me look even more bug-eyed than usual. Anyway, I am a London/Kent based writer, born and raised in the south-east. I would like to live in nowhere's middle, farming rare breeds and pottering around amidst bee hives. Instead, fate has landed me in the suburbs among the charity shops, 99p stores, and the big glass-front building societies - just turn left off the A20 down one of Life's bypasses to get to my place. My two big loves are the English countryside and old, real ale pubs. Indeed, if you ever bump into me, it will most likely be rambling in the former or quaffing within the latter. I'll buy you a pint.

Until then, tinkerty-tonk.

Of Fat Cats and Small Fry
Rufus Garlic

Collection Two
R.G Rankine

Three Minutes
R.G Rankine

15 Soon
R.G Rankine

The Warspite Series
Book Two: The Witch and the Dark Arts
Alfred Duff

Sari Sari Burning Bright
Rufus Garlic

Betting
Rufus Garlic

The Legacy
Rufus Garlic

The Skeleton in the Closet
Rufus Garlic

Sacked
Rufus Garlic

The Warspite Series
Book One: The Godling
Alfred Duff

Collection One
R.G Rankine

My Father Loves
R.G Rankine

The Silent Spaces
R.G Rankine

Thinking Plainly

19126120R00278

Printed in Great Britain
by Amazon